DECEIVED

BITTER HARVEST SERIES

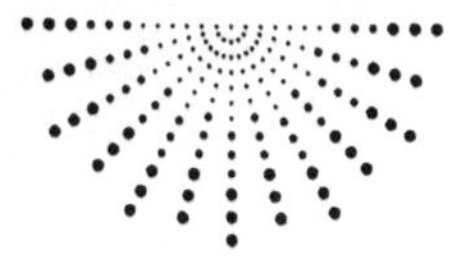

ANN GIMPEL

Edited by

KATE RICHARDS

CONTENTS

Deceived — v
Copyright Page — vii
Deceived: Book Description — ix
Cataclysm — xi

1. Hell Yeah, It's the Shifters' Fault — 1
2. We're Out of Here — 21
3. Sworn Enemies — 37
4. Mirror, Mirror Tell Me True — 51
5. Paradise Found—Or Not — 65
6. Renegade Mirror — 77
7. What Are Friends For? — 91
8. No Good Choices — 105
9. Strong Magic — 119
10. Sisterhood in Action — 131
11. Bloodbath — 145
12. Escape Made Good — 161
13. A Hard Sell — 175
14. Gathering of Unlikely Allies — 187
15. Prophecy — 199
16. Prophecy Be Damned — 211
17. Sucker for Lost Causes — 225
18. Battle Cry — 237
19. When Magic Isn't Enough — 249
20. Bold New World — 263
21. Into the Unknown — 273
   About the Author — 283
   Twisted: Book Description — 285
   Twisted, Chapter One: That's Impossible — 287

DECEIVED

BITTER HARVEST, BOOK ONE

Dystopian Urban Fantasy
By
Ann Gimpel

COPYRIGHT PAGE

DECEIVED: BOOK DESCRIPTION

A runaway spell is the most dangerous weapon of all.

Vampires aren't supposed to feel anything beyond hunger and bloodlust, but Viktor still feels a whole lot. He hates what he's become, but there's no escape. Not from the dying city smothering him, or from his maker, an arrogant tyrant who demands absolute loyalty.

Ketha's a shifter and a seer, for all the good it does her. Not enough magic is left to power much of anything. In a rare victory, an image forms in her glass, and she understands how magic broke the world—and how to fix it. The only antidote is an alliance with vampires, but she can't convince anyone to cooperate.

Desperate and trapped, she turns what's left of her magic on the Vampire assigned to lock her away. He's different, not quite as callous or aloof as his kin. It's a gamble, but she's out of options. Maybe magic can't bail them out, but love might be able to salvage what's left.

CATACLYSM

A splintered sign sits under faded wooden archways looking out on Ushuaia Harbor. On the rare clear day, you can still see *El Fin del Mundo*—the end of the world—inscribed on its bleached planks.

The ass end of South America has always been a lonely place, desolate and at the mercy of incessant winds howling through the Tiera del Fuego Mountains. But the sky used to be gray, and the ocean blue. Not anymore. Even the snow isn't white but a murky mixture of puke green and sickly violet. It covers everything year-round since the weather patterns changed too, yielding perpetual winter.

During those early months after the Cataclysm formed an impenetrable blockade around Ushuaia, everyone blamed everybody else. Shifters claimed it was the Vampires' fault. Vamps said Shifters spawned the destruction. Humans caught undercurrents of sketchy magical dealings between Vampires and Shifters, so enchanted trickery may have been the lynchpin that unraveled the world.

After about two years, the blame game played itself out. No

one cared anymore, and it didn't up the odds of survival as resources grew scarce.

People—magical and human alike—tried to leave Ushuaia after the Cataclysm. Malevolent tempests—the same ones that turned the sky gray black and the ocean red—attacked everyone who braved the barrier. No one ever returned.

Food and water have become huge problems. Rustic desalination pumps converted salt water until it became too poisonous to consume. Runoff from nearby mountains is suspect, but it's all that's left. Nothing lives in the ocean, and constant storms, coupled with bad water and scarce food, have killed off much of the local animal population.

Locating humans to drain has become close to impossible, so Vampires have grown far less picky, resorting to consuming blood any way they can get it. Soon, not even a rat will be left.

Shifters and humans formed an uneasy alliance in *Ciudad de Huesos*, City of Bones. Neither group trusts the other, but their shared hatred of Vampires has been a potent motivator. Humans barter vegetables for protection and a magical assist from the Shifters so they can keep producing food. Nothing grows without water, though. Sooner rather than later, there will be no more harvests.

City of Bones is an apt name for Ushuaia since its streets are choked with them. Vampires clawed their way to the top of the heap and remained there, their toehold unbreakable. Didn't cost them much. After the Cataclysm, they drained everyone who stood in their way, making new Vamps to swell their ranks and killing those who proved too much trouble. Shifters considered fighting back, but they were too few. As a hedge against unfavorable odds, they concealed themselves with magic and focused their energies on keeping as many humans alive as they could.

HELL YEAH, IT'S THE SHIFTERS' FAULT

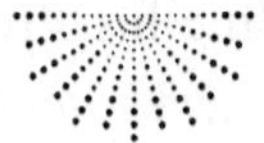

"GET OUT HERE." Raphael didn't raise his voice. No need. Vampires had exceptional hearing.

Viktor Gaelen hustled into the room where his sire sat at a scarred rolltop desk, checking things off on a list. Fuming at being reduced to little better than a servant, Viktor growled, "What?" Before he got any more words out, a knock boomed from the far end of the suite of rooms.

Viktor sprinted for the door to avoid the temptation to tell Raphael he could find himself another butler. Those conversations never ended well.

Two dark-haired Vampires sauntered inside, their mouths dotted with dried blood. One angled a foot and kicked the door shut. Both stood at attention. Beyond the dried-blood smell, the sour tang of fear oozed from them.

They'd apparently been summoned. No one showed up voluntarily looking as guilty and cowed as this pair.

Viktor nodded their way and headed back toward the bedroom where he'd been calculating one more plan to move himself and a ship he had in dry dock through the barrier holding Ushuaia prisoner. Pages of math equations covered a table where he worked, but he wasn't concerned about Raphael deciphering them. If the old Vampire had gone to school, it was before the birth of modern calculus in the 1600s.

"Where do you think you're going?" Raphael asked in the deadly quiet tone Viktor associated with danger.

"Back there." Viktor jerked his chin at the door leading to the apartment's inner rooms.

"No. You're not."

Viktor didn't reply. Telling his sire to fuck off wasn't on the menu. Those conversations never went well, either.

Raphael stalked to the two Vampires standing near the door, an iron saber trailing from one hand.

Viktor blinked and looked again, wondering if he was hallucinating, but the sword was still there. The blade lived in one of the inner rooms. Raphael must have moved it in anticipation of whatever was about to unfold.

"Where have you two been?" Raphael asked, the words silky smooth but threaded with the same compulsion Vamps used to lure their victims.

"Here and there," one of the Vampires answered.

"Could you narrow it down?" Raphael took a step nearer his minions.

Viktor balled his hands into fists. He knew what was coming, saw it in the eagerness spilling from his sire. He shouldn't watch, but unless he shut his eyes—a gesture sure to draw Raphael's attention—he didn't have a choice. In addition to being a blood-thirsty pig, Raphael liked an audience.

The other Vampires weren't stupid. In a lightning-fast move, one twisted and made a grab for the doorknob. Before he could turn it, Raphael hefted the blade, swinging it laterally. Its sharp edge cleaved through flesh, bone, and sinew with a sharp cracking sound, and the Vamp's head rolled from his shoulders. Blood sprayed from severed vessels, painting a macabre pattern on the walls and floor.

Viktor breathed shallowly to lessen the stench of blood, shit, and urine, but his stomach still twisted painfully. Bile burned the back of his throat.

The other Vampire fell to his knees, hands clasped in supplication and eyes so wide, white showed all around the irises.

"Where have you been?" Raphael repeated in a bland, conversational tone.

"Feeding from your prisoners. I'm sorry, sire. We were so hungry. It won't happen again. You have my word."

Viktor blanched. Christ. Talk about a capital crime. Why had the Vamps even shown up here? They'd have been better off running for the hills. At least until they hit the barrier.

"Your word isn't worth much." Raphael sounded almost cheerful as he swung the blade a second time.

Viktor stood, rooted in place. Would he be next? Raphael was arbitrary and capricious, and he loved killing.

"Fucking coward. Get moving." Raphael prodded Viktor with the business end of the blade. "Don't let all that blood go to waste. I made them. I can't feed from them, but you can."

Viktor shambled forward, blood hunger doing battle with nausea as he latched onto a geysering carotid. The queasiness would fade. It always did as soon as blood hit his stomach.

"Better." Raphael's voice cut through the haze that settled around Viktor's mind as he fed. "When you're done, clean up the mess." He dropped the sword next to Viktor and returned to his desk as if nothing had happened.

VIKTOR TOSSED the last bucket of bloody seawater out an open window. He'd had to hustle water up from the bay, two buckets at a time, cursing Raphael with every single step. Other Vamps had shown up and claimed the corpses, hauling them off to finish draining them elsewhere. Viktor had struck a deal with them.

Blood in exchange for transport. It simplified his cleaning chores.

Raphael hadn't moved from his desk. He dipped an old-fashioned quill pen into an inkwell filled with something murky and continued with whatever he was writing.

Viktor glanced at the ornate iron sword he'd balanced against one wall after cleaning blood off its blade. He wanted nothing more than to snatch it up and behead his sire. Wanting and doing were two different things, though. According to Vampire lore, hideous consequences would ensue if he had the balls to raise so much as his little finger against the one who'd made him.

Raphael set the pen down and stood. He paced from one side of the lavishly decorated room to the other, his silence more menacing than idle conversation would have been. In the years since Viktor had become Raphael's minion, he'd observed three basic modes: patronizing lectures, blood frenzy, and silence. The latter was the worst because it was hard to gauge what lay behind it.

Or what would come next.

Lightning blitzed across the corner of his vision, splitting a sky that had shaded to dark gray. Muted booms rocked the building. Was today when it would finally crumble, joining several of Ushuaia's other multistory structures in rubble choking the streets? He lived in this building, but in an ancient sub-basement that backed onto an equally ancient tunnel system. The main reason he'd chosen his damp, subterranean abode, putting up with a windowless room that was never truly warm, was because the intricate warren of passageways offered an escape route. At least he wouldn't wake some evening trapped beneath tons of concrete and twisted rebar.

His sire was in a foul mood, particularly considering his two kills, but the silent standoff was getting to Viktor. He took a chance and cleared his throat.

"What?" The other Vampire stood and spun to face his spawn.

It was easy to see where he'd gotten his name. Beautiful as any angel, Raphael's hair swirled around him to waist level in a silky, dark cloud. A high forehead and square jaw framed fangs that were extended, probably because he was hungry. Like everyone else in *Ciudad de Huesos*, Raphael sported a collection of skins and rags hanging off his lean frame. Vampires—at least the original variety like Raphael—didn't notice the cold as much as other races, but the ever-present chill sank into everyone's bones after a while.

His blue-gray eyes shot darts at Viktor. "What?" he repeated.

"How'd you find out about the two poachers? Did someone rat on them?"

Raphael snorted laughter. "I don't require informants. I know everything about each of my minions."

"Of course, Sire. Didn't mean to suggest otherwise." Viktor regarded his sire with as direct a gaze as he could muster. He'd gotten away with a whole lot, which meant Raphael was lying about knowing everything. He didn't. Not by a long shot. Not that Viktor had done anything quite as egregious as drinking from Raphael's private stock, but almost.

"You missed a spot." Raphael pointed at a spray of crimson decorating one wall near the floor.

Viktor shrugged. "You need a maid. I'll get it later. You called the Tribunal into session. They'll be waiting for you."

Raphael spat saliva mixed with blood onto the cold hearth. "Let the bastards wait. I'm Nosferatu."

Viktor clung to his neutral expression. He hadn't even known Vampires existed before Raphael captured him, and he'd turned a deaf ear to his sire's constant nattering about Nosferatu this and Nosferatu that. When he'd dug into Raphael's neglected but considerable library, he'd discovered Vampires actually emerged from an alliance between the devil and Sekhmet, Egyptian goddess of death and slaughter. He'd never bothered to mention that to Raphael. No reason to dispute the old fucker's delusions about his origins.

Viktor stood straighter. "There's the matter of the Shifter we captured—"

Raphael made a chopping motion. "Enough. I don't require reminding. All the Shifters have been a thorn in our sides for a long time. We have to kill them. If we'd done that before the Cataclysm, we wouldn't be in this unspeakable mess."

"But there weren't any Shifters here before the Cataclysm—" Viktor held up a hand. "Sorry. Didn't mean to contradict you."

Raphael stalked closer, dripping arrogance. "Of course, there were. You wouldn't have known about them—or us."

"True enough," Viktor muttered.

Raphael's nostrils flared, and he added, "We have to locate them. No more excuses. They'll make a substantial addition to our food stocks, and I tire of sustaining myself on animal blood."

Viktor opened his mouth to point out they'd been searching for the Shifters for years without so much as a clue, but Raphael knew that. Vampires might have supernatural strength and speed, but Shifters commanded a far greater array of magical ability.

"What are you thinking?" Raphael narrowed his eyes.

"Nothing. You were saying?"

Raphael snapped his fingers, clearly struck by a revelation.

Viktor waited to see what atrocity his sire was cooking up now. To mask his aversion to Raphael's ideas—not a minion-like reaction at all—he glanced around the room. Carved wainscoting circled the walls, and high cove ceilings held delicate paintings left from an earlier era, before the world shifted on its axis, trapping them in the few square miles around what had once been the southernmost seaport in the world.

"It would be perfect," his sire went on, oblivious to Viktor's inner conflict. "Definitely a win-win solution. With Shifters out of the way, their magic will fade. Absent their protective spells, we'd be able to locate the humans." He swiped his palms together.

"Problem solved. Between humans and Shifters, they'll feed us for a long time—provided we're careful and don't drain them to the point of death."

Viktor muttered something noncommittal.

"Don't you see?" Raphael swung to face him. "We'd develop a system so some would always be ready. Once they were up to snuff, we'd feed from them again. We did something similar back in the Middle Ages when life was cheap, and no one ever complained about a missing relative or two."

"What do you plan to feed them, Sire? So they don't die." Viktor should have kept his mouth shut, but it was an important question.

"They'll eat whatever's keeping them alive now," Raphael sputtered. "It's a perfect plan that will provide a perpetual food source for us." He narrowed his eyes to slits. "Whose side are you on?"

"Ours, Sire. Who else's?" Viktor ginned up an earnest expression and hoped Raph didn't question him further. Vampires were decent at sniffing out lies.

Sidestepping the specter of genocide for Shifters and humans, mostly because he figured they'd all be dead—Shifters, Vamps, humans, and anyone who'd remained in the shadows—before too many more months passed, Viktor said, "Perhaps we'd be better served harnessing Shifter power to address the poisoned water. They must be doing something, or the humans wouldn't still be growing crops to sustain themselves."

Raphael rounded on him, the noxious, rotten-egg stench of hungry Vampire thickening by the moment. "Intriguing idea about detoxifying the water. Those crops will keep the humans alive, so they'll last longer for us to feed on."

Viktor didn't bother pointing out that securing the Shifters' cooperation for anything was unlikely. He switched topics to move Raphael away from killing and death, his two favorite themes. "Do you suppose there's any life left beyond the storms that hold us captive here? I used to tap into radio broadcasts until electricity dwindled to almost nothing. The last few times I tried, though, I couldn't find any left on the air."

Raphael's eyes sharpened with sudden cunning, a harsh reminder how ancient and powerful he was. "Why would you ask about life beyond Ushuaia? Does it have something to do with that indecipherable chicken scratch back at your worktable?"

"Same reason you highlighted with your plans for the Shifters and humans. We're running out of food. That's what my calculations are about. Resource allocation." Viktor hoped to hell Raphael couldn't read his mind. He'd been fishing for information to see how viable his plan to breach the barrier with his ship would be.

Raphael didn't know about *Arkady*, and Viktor aimed to keep it that way.

Vampires weren't particularly blessed with magic. Not that they couldn't intuit the odd thought and light fires and do other sleight of hand parlor tricks, but magic had a price. Most Vamps were too depleted from not having fed properly for years to squander any energy on superfluous activities.

His sire resumed pacing, tension evident in his straight back and precise stride. "Yes, there's life outside Ushuaia. Of course, there is. There has to be."

Viktor held a neutral expression. Raphael had no idea. His answer was sheer bluff, or he'd have tossed out facts to back up his statements. Maybe it would be easier to rid himself of Raphael than he'd thought.

Who am I kidding? He may not know shit about what's beyond the barrier, but he knows a whole lot more about being a Vampire than I ever will. I'd do well not to underestimate that part.

Raphael altered his back-and-forth path and walked close enough to thump Viktor's chest with an extended index finger. "It's the Shifters' fault. All of this. They hold magic to see beyond the barrier."

"If that's accurate, maybe it's not in our best interest to kill them," Viktor ventured. If Shifters truly held information that could help them or the ability to make their water resources last longer, it was worth challenging Raphael.

A long, sibilant sound slithered from between Raphael's perfectly formed lips. "What good is knowledge if we can't breach the barrier? Look at that." He trotted to a grimy window and pointed outside at lightning flares striking the red-tinged ocean. Every place they hit, the ocean bubbled around them, as if it were claiming the energy, absorbing it to make certain its waters turned even more lethal. "I've been alive for a long time, and I've never seen its like, nor anything remotely close."

Viktor shrugged. There had to be a way to get around the barrier. Some complex escape hatch no one had discovered yet, but he kept his mouth shut. Raphael didn't appreciate vague concepts without facts to back them up. It was how Viktor had known his assertion about life outside Ushuaia was speculation.

"The Tribunal?" Viktor gestured toward the door.

"You're worse than a social secretary," Raphael grumbled and walked briskly out of the room.

Viktor snatched up a ratty jacket woven from llama skins and slid into it before following his sire. He had warm clothing aboard his ship, but explaining where it came from would be a problem. Every shop in Ushuaia had been looted years ago. Raphael would notice any deviation from "normal," and he'd ask questions until Viktor came up with a satisfactory answer. Better to dress in rags like everybody else.

Raphael had turned him a few months after the Cataclysm converted Ushuaia into a prison. He hadn't particularly wanted to be a Vampire. Raphael had forced his will onto him, much as he'd muscled his way through five hundred years of feeding and swelling the ranks of his Vampire tribe.

Back then—pre-Cataclysm—there'd been a whole lot more humans. Viktor had been a cruise ship captain on his way to the Falkland Islands when a tsunami drove his boat into the South

American coast, fetching it up on deadly rocks. He'd done his best to save his passengers and crew. In the end, he'd herded the fifty who were left out of nearly a hundred across brutal coastal mountains and into Ushuaia. Only to find it taken over by Vampires.

Vampires.

Who would've thought something like that was even real?

Worse, Vamps captured them immediately and transported them to a mountain cave system with primitive cells, probably built by some iteration of indigenous hunter-gatherers. Viktor had spent months there, long enough to curse his stupidity waltzing into Ushuaia unprotected. Long enough to discover Shifters also existed, and that Vamps hated them. Long enough to hear about the Cataclysm that shattered the world.

Long enough to stop caring what happened.

And more than long enough to be disappointed when another morning dawned and he wasn't dead yet. Turning into a Vampire hadn't changed a damned thing on that front. But it did make it much harder for him to die.

Viktor pelted down stairs falling into disrepair. Raphael was a long way ahead of him, and he didn't particularly want to attract his sire's attention.

Master Vampires were old and strong. According to Raphael, his particular type of Vampire stood at the top of the heap. Princes or kings or something. They took what they wanted and created a legion of Vampires to stand by their sides. Something about the draining and resurrection created loyalty to one's sire. It was supposed to, anyway.

Viktor swallowed back a bitter taste. He could feel the bond to Raphael like a tightly coiled spring deep in his belly, and he resented the hell out of it. Over the nine plus years since his making, he'd experimented with ways to break away from Raphael, but nothing ever worked.

It was why he cast longing glances at the iron saber. Maybe if he were quick enough, he could circumvent the bond.

He'd have to be goddamned fast, though. And successful. Punishment would be swift and certain if Raphael suspected his devotion wasn't absolute. He'd considered talking with some of Raphael's other minions to sow the seeds of a rebellion, but fear always stayed his tongue, and he hated himself for his cowardice.

Cold hit him like a wall as he left the building where they lived and hustled across a debris-choked walkway to their council chambers. Abandoned cars littered the streets. Ushuaia had no fossil fuels or refineries. All the gasoline had been trucked in. Once it ran out, cars became useless. Because he wasn't paying attention, he tripped over a pile of bones, the remains of some unlucky humans who hadn't survived either the Cataclysm or a Vamp feeding frenzy. Bones lay everywhere, bleached by incessant storms and stripped by animal predators desperate for a meal.

Dead people.

Dead cars.

Death extended on all sides of him. He shouldn't give a shit. Vampires didn't feel pain or sorrow or loss, but he still did. Setting his jaw in a hard, tight line, Viktor buried emotions that ran far too close to the surface.

Even though he didn't inhale deeply, the frigid air still bit deep, smelling a shred more poisonous than it had the day before. He stole a glance at the sky. Sunlight eroded Vampire abilities, but it wasn't a problem here. Though he was certain the sun still sat in judgment over the planet, its presence over Ushuaia was rare.

"You were the one in a hurry," Raphael scoffed from the shadows of carved double doors.

"So I was. Sorry." Viktor joined his sire, grateful when the doors clanked shut behind them, sealing out some of the cold.

Raphael sent a penetrating look his way before starting the trek to the tenth floor. Electricity was in short supply. What little they had came from wind farms, hastily expanded during the early years after the Cataclysm. Humans had overseen their growth and run them, but they'd abandoned the farms once they became a prime target for Vampire abductions. Without ongoing attention, the wind farms were falling to ruin like everything else. When juice flowed, Viktor used his tiny allocation to heat his quarters. Sometimes he envied the older, colder-blooded Vamps. They didn't require warmth in quite the same way he did.

More to divert his attention from the endless, winding stairs than anything else, he asked, "Any idea why you—" He stumbled over his words, and tried again. "Why I feel the cold more intensely than you?" It was an inane question, but Viktor was curious what his sire would say.

Raphael twisted his classic features into a sneer. "It's the Shifters' fault. Everything is. They perverted our power and used it to augment their own. Beyond that, you're not a pure blood straight from the old country."

"Does that mean if you'd found me before I left Germany and turned me there—?"

"Enough. Do not question me."

Viktor dropped behind his sire to avoid any possibility of eye contact. He'd eat his socks if Raphael knew any more about Vampires than he did. Probably a whole lot less, given his discovery about the unholy alliance between the devil and Sekhmet creating Vamps in the first place. All that Nosferatu crap was a smoke and mirrors act. Plus, there was no fucking way Shifters could have had shit to do with new Vamps being more susceptible to cold. Those changes had to be a corollary of the Cataclysm and its perversion of the energies that used to keep the world in balance.

One more flight and they'd be there. Viktor wasn't winded. Vamps were strong, but he needed to do more. Short rations and little exercise made him slower than he should've been.

Raphael trotted down a long, dark hallway, with Viktor at his heels and pushed into the space they used for the Tribunal. Ten Vamps shot to their feet, waiting for Raphael to stride to the front of the room. Once upon a time, this particular oval-shaped chamber had been a chapel on the top floor of a hospital. It still held a simple elegance with painted sconces and wooden benches arranged around a central nave. A bronze Christ figure hung from the far wall, his sightless eyes gazing disapprovingly on what had become of a once-sacred place.

Viktor quashed a temptation to genuflect before the icon and faded to one side, standing next to Juan Torres, the closest thing he had to a friend within Vampire ranks. They'd worked on the same ship before the Cataclysm. Even though they didn't spend much together, it was more because Vampires weren't into *social* than any other reason.

The coppery stench of blood rose from where Raphael bent over a large, squirming rat one of his minions had thoughtfully provided. Viktor's mouth flooded with saliva, and he swallowed fast before it dripped down his chin.

The rat squealed, vocalizing horror as life drained from its gray, furry body. Viktor gave himself a sharp mental slap. For some reason, the transition from human to monster hadn't been as effective in him because he still thought in human terms. Concepts like manners and compassion and sensitivity weren't anywhere in the Vampire lexicon.

Juan elbowed him surreptitiously and shot a pained glance his way. Before Viktor could mine for details, the chapel door slapped against its stops. Two more Vamps dragged an unconscious woman into the room. Iron manacles bound her wrists and ankles, so she had to be the Shifter they'd captured.

Viktor had never laid eyes on her before, and he fought to hide his reaction to her beauty. Long dark hair shot with red and gold dragged on the floor. Her eyes were closed, but sculpted cheekbones dusted with freckles showcased full, red lips. Tall and broad-shouldered, she moaned incoherently as the Vamps manhandled her to where Raphael stood.

Rat still in one hand, Raphael eyed the Shifter. Blood dripped down his chin and onto the floor. Not only was Raphael eating in front of them, he was squandering some of his meal. Viktor fought an inane desire to race to those fallen, crimson blobs and lick them up. Never mind he'd just fed.

Damn it!

He had to get a better grip on his emotions. Vamps, the ones where the turning worked, anyway, didn't experience much beyond hunger, desire, and anger. They'd moved past fear and caring and the rest of it. So what if Raphael was an insensitive boor? Vamps didn't view the world through that lens.

"Drop her there," Raphael ordered.

His voice broke into Viktor's churning thoughts.

The Shifter's body made a *splatting* sound when her two escorts did as ordered before withdrawing to where the other Vamps spread throughout the chapel. Viktor's nostrils twitched at an unusual scent. It took a moment to understand he was smelling the Shifter's blood. It reminded him of wildflowers and the stunted Antarctic beech trees that used to grow in the *Tiera del Fuego*. The scent drew him, soothed him, made him feel whole again, not splintered into a no-man's land where he no longer knew himself. Not exactly Vamp, but not human, either.

He clasped his hands behind his back, squeezing hard to avoid the temptation to kneel next to her and cradle her head in his arms, smoothing stray strands of bright hair away from her grime-streaked face. Most of all, he wanted to get her away from Raphael before the Master Vampire decided to try to turn her. If that didn't work, she'd end up a meal—or many meals, depending how long they could keep her alive.

The thought disgusted him. She was perfect. One of nature's creations. The magic seeping from her—despite her iron manacles—wrapped her in an iridescent shroud that felt pure, decent. He hadn't had much congress with Shifters, but none he'd run across felt anything like the woman sprawled on the floor. Granted, he'd only seen them from a distance, but still...

He clamped his hands together harder before one of his Vampire kin noticed the unrest that had to be streaming from him. To be on the safe side, he shuttered his thoughts, burying them deep.

Raphael nudged the woman with one booted foot. As decrepit as the rest of his clothing, his boots weren't much more than strips of dried-out leather secured by duct tape. The Shifter moaned, and Raphael hauled off and kicked her.

Viktor clamped his jaws together so hard he feared his teeth would crack. If he'd had any inkling the Shifter would kindle something inside him, an awareness he'd been certain died along with his humanity, he'd never have—

Never would have, what? His mental voice inquired caustically.

For some unexplained reason, he was one of Raphael's favorites, and the Master Vamp rarely went anywhere without Viktor by his side. Leaving was out of the question. He had to wait this out. Soon enough, he could retire to his grotto beneath the building across the street. Maybe fortune would smile on him, and it would collapse, trapping Raphael in rubble that might take years to dig out of.

Fat chance. That fucker is strong as sin—

A low groan drew Viktor's attention back to the Shifter. She'd rolled to a sitting position, and her eyes were open. A fine, clear golden color, they formed slits as she stared defiantly at Raphael.

"You've captured me, Vampire," she sneered, displaying very white, very even teeth. "Now what? Do I get to be everyone's dinner?" She swung her head from side to side, encompassing the room full of Vamps. "At least remove my shackles. If I'm going to die, I'd rather face you as a wolf."

Thick black robes, sashed in brilliant red, clung to her slender frame, but the fabric was whole, not patched. Could Shifters leverage magic to repair simple things like that? Viktor wished he knew. His only information about other magical beings came from hearsay and rumors—and Raphael's library. A long-standing

Vampire rule, though, was no interaction with Shifters under any circumstances.

No one had ever explained why, and he'd never cared enough to ask.

Until now.

He inhaled sharply, and then did it again. Maybe filling his lungs would spur his turbulent thoughts into something beyond chasing their own tails. Would Raphael follow through on his threat to kill the Shifter and the rest of her kind? Or would he glom onto Viktor's idea about using their magic to counteract the increasingly bad water?

"My name is Ketha." She flowed to her feet in a single, graceful motion and folded her arms beneath the swell of her breasts. "Rat got your tongue?" She jerked her chin at the dead rat still clutched in Raphael's hand and skinned her lips back from her teeth.

Before Raphael could answer, she went on. "If you're going to kill me, get on with it, but know this—" Her voice took on a mesmerizing quality, and magic rose in waves around her, turning the air shimmery with color. "You will never escape Ushuaia without us."

Raphael faced off against her. "What makes you think we want to escape, Shifter?"

Ketha shrugged, favoring the Vampire with the full force of her golden gaze. "You like it here? Soon there won't be anything left to eat or drink, and then all of us will die. Even Vampires. But if you're good with that"—another eloquent shrug—"I suppose there's nothing to talk about. Go on." She made shooing motions with one long-fingered hand. "Get on with it. I'm prepared to die. We don't have too many more months here at the ass end of the world before none of us will be left. Take a chance, Vampire. Face me as a wolf."

Viktor knew his sire well and recognized barely suppressed rage in the set of his shoulders and the cold, dead aspect to his expression.

"I'll pass. I suppose you have the answer to all our problems." Raphael quirked a well-formed dark brow.

A small, secretive smile played about Ketha's mouth. "Even if I did, I'd never tell you. Funny thing about being captured. It quiets the tongue."

"Show some respect. No one addresses me like that."

"It appears I just did." Ketha tossed her shoulders back, bringing her to a height with the Vampire, and a snarl rose from her throat. "You need us. Unfortunately, we need you as well, but what I had in mind was equal partners at a conference table, not being knocked over the head and dragged here."

A vein throbbed in Raphael's temple. Small cracking sounds rose from the rat as he crushed it in one hand, splattering blood and entrails across the white marble floor.

"Viktor." Raphael wasn't looking his way, but the summons was clear.

"Sire?" Viktor's gut twisted with apprehension. What would come next? Would he be assigned some grisly assassination? Worse, would he be ordered to feed from the creature staring down the room with her unnerving gaze?

If that happened, and he ended up guzzling her blood, he'd never be able to live with himself. It had been hard enough feeding on what was left after other Vamps had drained humans. Whoever he'd once been would be irretrievably lost if Raphael forced him to kill the Shifter or drink her blood.

What the fuck is wrong with me? Not a Vamp. Not human. Not anything at all but trapped in a place I once considered home—when I wasn't at sea.

"Get up here!" Raphael thundered.

Viktor trotted smartly to his side.

Whatever this was, he wanted it over with. Then he'd take the iron blade and do what he should've done long ago. Damn the consequences. His life wasn't worth shit. Why prolong it? And maybe, just maybe, he'd manage to do away with Raphael. At least then he could live out however many months he had left free from his sire's oppressive yoke.

Raphael drew a set of old-fashioned handcuffs from one of his many pockets. Moving faster than a human eye could follow, the Vamp snapped cuffs on Ketha right behind the wrist manacles. "Take her to the caves," he said and all but pushed her into Viktor's arms.

Viktor latched a hand firmly around Ketha's elbow. Her intoxicating scent filled his nose, but he ignored it. "What then?" he asked Raphael.

His sire sent an incredulous look his way. "Lock her up and return. I'll decide her fate once she's told us what she knows about escaping Ushuaia."

"I already explained how that would happen." Ketha's tone was pointed. "At a conference table as an equal. So long as you hold me captive, my wolf and I will die before we help you do anything."

Raphael slanted his gaze her way. "It appears we're at a stalemate. Perhaps some cell time will alter your perspective."

"Don't count on it."

Relief weakened Viktor's knees, but he did his damnedest to hide the excitement sluicing through him. He didn't have to kill Ketha. Didn't have to do a thing beyond delivering her to the prison caves. He'd leave her in the cell he'd occupied because it was farthest from the ravages of the poisoned ocean and more comfortable than the others.

An insidious thought intruded. Before he could stop himself, a treasonous path stretched dead ahead. He'd know where she was, which meant he could free her. In truth, he never had to lock her up at all. Too late, he felt the subtle edges of her magic probe his mind. He engaged wards, but a smile turned her face into something profanely beautiful.

"Lead out." She hip-butted him. "This room stinks of Vampires, and it's giving me a headache."

Raphael snarled and lunged for her. He grabbed her shoulders and shook her until her teeth rattled against each other. "Keep a civil tongue in your head, or I'll rethink my generosity. Never forget who runs things in Ushuaia. This is blood's dominion. *My* dominion."

Ketha stood her ground. "Funny, but I thought I and my Shifters were in charge. Besides, if you were going to kill me, I'd already be dead."

Viktor tamped down growing admiration for the woman. As soon as Raphael let go, he hustled her out of the room.

"Remain quiet." He kept his tone stern and herded her toward the stairwell. "Vampires have excellent hearing."

2

WE'RE OUT OF HERE

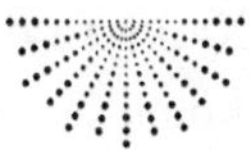

A FEW HOURS earlier

Ketha St. Ange crouched around a cooling hearth in the center of a group of twelve Shifters. The discussion had run much longer than she'd anticipated, so she added a shot of magic to keep the bricks warm. They'd run through most of the burnable fuel long ago, and this was the only way to stay comfortable absent a constant outflow of magic.

None of them had shifted in months. The shift mechanism blew through buckets of magic, and none of them had any to spare for anything nonessential. The concept—nonessential— mocked her. Talent sat in this room, ability that had close to zero application in their current circumstances. The women had worked in fields from anthropology to nuclear physics to medicine to chemical engineering to her own vocation of microbiology. If the University of Wyoming even still existed, it had long since severed her tenured faculty position.

That happened when you didn't show up for work.

"We still don't have a solid plan," Aura complained, narrowing her green eyes. Eyes reminiscent of the mountain lion she turned into.

"How could we when it requires cooperation from the Vampires?" Ketha looked askance at the other Shifter, whose blonde hair was piled atop her head. Like the rest of them, she was wrapped in warm black woolen robes.

"Are you certain of that? About having to work with the Vamps, I mean?" Rowana asked. Silver hair fell to her waist, and her dark eyes looked tired. Her other form was an eagle, and she'd overflown the city to help Ketha find a way out until scant food and questionable water curtailed her power along with everyone else's.

"Yeah. I'm sure."

"It feels like a total screw job," Rowana went on, "that you finally have a lead on how to defeat the magical shroud surrounding Ushuaia, and we need Vampire energy to kindle the spell."

Ketha rocked back on her heels. "It is a screw job, but there's not much we can do about it. Shifter power mingled with Vampire energy is what got us into this mess—"

"You can't know that," Aura interrupted. "Not for certain."

Ketha thinned her lips into a harsh line. "Yes, I do know it for certain. Weren't you listening?"

Breath steamed from the other Shifter, visible in the chilly air. "Oh I heard you right enough, when you said you'd scryed the past but you might not have gotten it right."

Ketha lunged to her feet and stomped in front of where Aura sat, effectively cutting her off from the hearth's meager warmth. "Of course I got it right. I'm a seer, or have you forgotten?"

"Then why'd it take you ten years to figure this out?" Aura shot back and stood, facing off against Ketha.

"Stop it, you two." Karin, an older wolf Shifter with snow-white hair, made her way across the room and laid a hand on each of their shoulders. "We have enough problems without fighting one another." Her once-plump face sagged into a web of fine lines, but her copper eyes radiated kindness. She was their doctor and hated conflict.

"It's a fair question"—Ketha kept her tone neutral—"except I explained how shocked I was when I was able to break through this time. Every other attempt, something blocked me, and I've tried hundreds of times. My guess is that whatever was powering the wards around the information ran its course. Some spells are time-linked. Like as not, this was one of them."

Aura looked at her feet. "It wasn't that I didn't hear you. I have a hard time believing it's not some kind of a trap."

"Set by whom?" Ketha asked.

"The Vampires. Who else? To lure us into some deadly snare where they turn us into dinner." Aura raised troubled eyes. "We can't afford to make any mistakes. Not even one. If we don't get something right soon, we'll all starve to death. Humans aren't growing enough, even with our magic assisting them, and we're becoming weaker each month."

"Which is exactly why we have to come up with a foolproof plan to get the Vamps to cooperate." Ketha licked at dry lips. "They can't be doing much better than we are. They need blood, and there's not much left besides rodents and that pack of jaguars north of town."

"There's us, and the humans who've figured out how to stymie them with our help," Aura said dourly.

"None of that." Karin shook a motherly finger her way. "Negative energy will come back to bite us in the ass."

Rowana got up slowly, as if her joints pained her. She usually shooed Karin away when the other Shifter offered healing potions, telling her to save her magic for someone who had real problems. "Let me be certain I've got this right." She kept her voice low.

"If you're going to recap what I said," Ketha broke in, "use telepathy. I don't sense anyone about, but it pays to be cautious."

"That was exactly what I was about to do," Rowana replied. "I want to make damn good and sure I understood you because it's a pretty fantastic tale."

"Telepathy," Ketha urged again.

The other Shifter nodded, and magic flickered around her. Guilt pricked Ketha. All magic cost something, and none of them had any to spare.

"*According to your vision,*" Rowana began, "*a small group of Shifters and Vampires met somewhere in northeastern Russia, right before the Cataclysm, to figure out how to blend their different types of magic—*"

"*That's where I got stuck,*" Aura cut in. "*Since when do Vamps want to change anything about their pathetic selves? We already consume blood in shifted form, so what the hell would we have gotten out of this trade?*"

Ketha turned her hands palms up. "Don't have the answers for that. All I know is what I saw in my glass. I agree it wasn't a complete picture. Maybe my next go will flesh things out better."

"*Anyway,*" Rowana went on, "*one of us had sex with one of them, and it broke the world.*"

"*It's more complicated,*" Ketha said. "*From what I gleaned, the Cataclysm resulted from a combination of the spell we hatched up to give Vamps the ability to shift and the forbidden mating. If it hadn't been for the sex, the spell would probably have run its course.*"

"*And there'd have been no Cataclysm?*" Rowana raised one eyebrow into a question mark.

"Precisely," Ketha replied.

"*Why would Vamps even want to be more like us?*" Aura spoke up. "*I thought they loved lording it over everyone and sucking them dry.*"

"Can't answer that, either." Ketha switched back to talking to conserve magic. "There are other enclaves like ours scattered throughout the world, though. I have no idea how many, but I've caught pulses of life outside Ushuaia. For the first couple years, we could communicate with them, but then the barrier grew stronger."

"Doesn't make sense to me," Aura muttered. "The deal with the Vamps. Not that I've spent much time around them, but it flies in the face of everything I thought I knew."

Ketha exhaled wearily. "I have no idea why they wanted to change themselves—or what we would have gotten out of the deal. I don't have to explain how magic works to you. It usually takes several passes at something complicated before the whole picture emerges."

She took another breath, collecting her thoughts. "I don't want to work with them, either. They make my skin crawl. About the only good thing we have going here in Ushuaia is total separation from those bastards, but"—she employed mind speech once again—*"we have to mirror the original sin to make things right. And then we'll be free from here. I hope."*

"Including sex?" Rowana drew her lips back in distaste.

"I didn't see that part. All I saw was the need to comingle our power with Vamp energy so the spell that started ten years ago can run to its conclusion."

"It can't be that simple." Rowana's nostrils flared.

"Like as not, it won't be," Ketha agreed. "But at least it gives us a place to start. Before my last vision, we didn't even have that."

"I miss our men," Aura said. "Just a stroke of bad luck we ended up here without them."

"We've been over that ground." Karin shook hair back over her shoulders. "And more than once."

Ketha scrubbed the heels of her hands down her face, hoping for patience and energy. Indeed, they had covered that ground. Their small group had traveled to Ushuaia to intercept an eclipse that would focus huge amounts of psychic energy at a point in the Beagle Channel right outside Ushuaia Harbor. The plan had been to harvest the power and carry the bounty back to their Shifter packs in Wyoming.

Nothing wrong with their strategy, except the Cataclysm struck before the eclipse was due, stranding them at the southern tip of South America with an equally unlucky bunch of humans and Vampires.

The expected eclipse never happened, probably because of the Cataclysm.

Ketha squeezed Aura's shoulder. "I miss our menfolk too. And the rest of our pack. Maybe, if we're successful, we'll be reunited with them someday."

"Seems like too much to hope for," Rowana countered. "The men were never as sharp without us there. It's possible the Cataclysm killed them."

Ketha straightened her spine. "Stop right there. Christ! It's only been ten years. We have no idea about any of that. They're in Wyoming for chrissakes. A place where there's lots of food, dozens of other Shifter females. Maybe the Cataclysm requires saltwater to feed itself. Maybe nothing's changed back home." She stopped long enough to take a ragged breath. "Hope is all we have. When we let it slip away, we're finished."

She shook herself from head to foot to dispel the disquieting image of everyone she'd known and loved, dead. "I'm going to take a walk. I'm exhausted. Maybe there's some shred of Earth energy left for me to tap into. My poor wolf hasn't asked to run in months."

"Be careful," Karin admonished.

"I will. I'll ward myself. Maybe one of you could scrounge something up for supper?"

"We will," Karin assured her. "I'll stop by the human farm dome nearest us and collect payment for our protection and our magic."

"Good plan. We haven't been there in a while, and fresh greens would be welcome." Ketha turned to leave.

She plodded to the stairs leading to the outside world and made her way to a well-hidden doorway, letting herself out into a frigid day. They hadn't always lived in this basement, but it was far easier to heat their underground space than it would've been to keep a normal house warm. She wrapped power around herself, both to hide her presence and to keep from shivering. None of them had adequate clothing, and the temperatures just kept dropping.

When they'd flown into Ushuaia, no one planned to remain longer than a week. They'd brought a collection of robes for the ceremony to capture the eclipse's psychic energy. Good thing, since the robes were woven with magic, and their fabric was self-repairing. All their other clothing had long since moldered into rags. Good for bedding material, but not much else. At least they all had stout winter boots.

A shiver tracked down her body as she made her way along what had once been the outskirts of the city. Mostly because the Vamps took over the center of Ushuaia, Shifters had planted themselves in a small area north of town, not too far from the swirling, roiling mess that held them captive.

As if her thoughts about the barrier summoned chaos, lightning bolts—dirty yellow tinged with red-gold fire—surged from the skies, striking scant feet from her path. Ketha made a face and moved over, skirting energy that made her hair stand on end. Back when they were stronger, she and the other Shifters had tried every spell in their collective knowledge to defeat the magical obstruction that imprisoned them.

Nothing worked.

The shielding seemed to feed on the energy they sent to defeat it, so they'd stopped squandering power years ago. Even though they weren't providing raw material, the storms raging around their slender slice of land had grown progressively more powerful.

Ketha turned south, burying her hands deep in her robe's pockets and thinking about Vampires. If ever a creature was entrenched in who they were, it was Vampires. Aura had brought that up, and the same inconsistency had troubled Ketha during her trance when she'd "seen" the past unfold like a Grade B movie.

Maybe the small group of Shifters and Vamps in northeastern Russia had acted independently and didn't represent anyone beyond themselves.

The more she thought about it, the surer she was it had to be true. For one thing, she hadn't heard zip squat about some plan to add Shifter ability to Vampirism. News like that would've traveled like wildfire. Also, their chosen meeting site, huddled in a cave in a remote Siberian location, suggested they wanted to maintain absolute secrecy. Something about the northern latitudes made it easier to hide magical activity, and insofar as she knew, there weren't any Shifters native to Siberia.

A wry laugh bubbled past Ketha's lips. They were smarter than to lock themselves into Nature's icebox. Unless they had no choice in the matter.

As if to mock her, a large icicle cracked off a nearby dead tree. Ketha pivoted to avoid being hit as it augured into the ground. She kicked the slab of ice, but it didn't move much. Good thing it hadn't landed on her head.

Dragging herself back to the problem at hand, she pondered what it would take to bring Vampires to the table. Would the possibility of escape be a potent enough incentive?

Why would they believe us?

When the answer came, its simplicity shocked her.

Because we've avoided them like the plague until now. We'd never seek them out if it weren't a matter of life and death.

"Yeah, but just because I see the world like that is no reason they do," she muttered.

She walked past the perimeter of one of the human enclaves. Half a dozen lay scattered around Ushuaia, mostly in spots where they could take advantage of runoff from acid rain and the tainted water running down from the Tiera Del Fuego. Grow lights suspended over hydroponic beds ran off a combination of magic and wind power. Ketha shook her head, fighting off hopelessness.

Eventually, the poisons in the air and water would kill them—if starvation didn't do it first.

The only reason humans were still able to grow anything was because of Shifter power. They'd died in droves right after the Cataclysm, mostly because Vampires had either turned them into new Vamps or used them for food. By the time they'd wised up and barricaded themselves into more-or-less Vamp-proof enclaves, only a few hundred remained. As far as she knew, they weren't producing children, but she'd never been invited inside any of the communities to see what they were up to.

Ketha and her Shifters had kept to themselves. They could breed with humans. At least they'd been able to pre-Cataclysm, but she hadn't seen the point in bringing children into the world only to see them suffer.

"Think," she admonished to rein in her wandering attention. "What would lure the Vamps? What would induce them to parlay with us?"

"They have to want out of here as bad as we do," her wolf spoke up.

Ketha grinned for the first time in a long while, surprised she still remembered how. "Bondmate! I've missed you." She sent loving thoughts inward.

"The feeling is mutual, but it's hard for me to do anything except sleep."

"Do not give up." Ketha swallowed hard. "You're part of me. I need your strength."

"I'll do my best."

"I know you will."

A low, whuffly growl rose. If she'd had any magic to spare, she'd have slipped behind one of the falling-down buildings, stripped, and let the shift magic take her. Her wolf hadn't spoken in weeks. Its appearance heartened her but didn't yield any clues about how to address her problem. The dark clouds moved aside, and, for the briefest of moments, a sunbeam arrowed through. She took it as an omen—a good one.

Removing her hands from her pockets, she flexed her fingers. Perhaps she could scry an answer to her dilemma. Looking backward was easier than seeking information about events that had yet to occur, but that wasn't a reason not to try. Her magic stores were adequate for something like that.

The Cataclysm hadn't attacked their power directly. Which probably meant the Vampires hadn't been affected, either. Their magic had never been anything close to Shifter ability, but they could cast simple spells. Most of their power was physical. They were faster than anything on two legs had a right to be and utterly without anything resembling a conscience. Some of the oldest could fly, swooping down on unsuspecting prey like a goddamned bat.

Stop right there. This will be hard enough without getting lost in how much I hate those fuckers.

Ketha glanced around, hunting for a spot she could settle in and spin a spell. She could return to the other Shifters, but things like this went down easier without distractions. Even if she closeted herself in the alcove she called home, Shifter energy swirling through their shared quarters might prove to be a distraction.

She made her way to a pile of boulders and wormed her way between two of them, sheltering beneath an overhang. The granite should shield her presence from all but the very strong-minded, and it was the best she could do on short notice. Settling on her haunches, she drew her glass from an inner pocket, blew on it to cloud its surface, and began a low, determined chant. Focusing power was rather like easing a shredded bit of thread through a narrow needle. Doable, but requiring intense concentration.

It took far longer than it should have before images began to form on her glass.

Hurry. Give me what I need to know.

An image formed but then slipped away before she could interpret it. Ketha poured power into her working, the glass unstable in her sweat-slick fingers. She was close. So close she could almost taste it.

A sound that shouldn't be there nagged. She blocked it out. Absolute attentiveness would kindle her spell. Nothing could interrupt her. Their survival depended on her success. She had to "see" which path would entice the Vamps to work with them. For her gambit to work, she might need to play out several scenarios, but she had the time—and the magic—to experiment a bit.

"Run!" the wolf shrieked into her mind.

Before she could react, blinding pain flashed as something hard and heavy crashed down on the back of her head. Her glass slithered from between her hands, and she slumped to the ground, fighting blackness. Just before it claimed her, the stench of Vampire invaded her nostrils, and she cursed herself for being a fool.

KETHA WOKE in the middle of a dozen Vamps. Iron burned her skin where manacles circled her ankles and wrists. If she'd thought the smell was bad before, it was an absolute reeking horror now. Vampires smelled of blood and death and rot. How could any Shifters worth their vows align themselves with these bastards? Taking care to be stealthy, she glanced about an oval room, inlaid with wood. It had a church-ish feel that was clinched when she spied a Christ figure attached to one wall.

Close to a dozen Vamps crowded into the space. All of them held an eerie beauty, but Ketha wasn't fooled. Their striking good looks ran less than skin-deep. Skilled, ruthless killers, they counted on blood to survive. Living blood. Blood tapped from dead things ran a poor second.

The back of her head throbbed painfully, and she shut her eyes to buy herself time to think. Maybe no one had noticed she wasn't unconscious. The Vamp standing nearest kicked her, right before he ordered her to wake up.

She flinched away from her attacker. Eyes flickering open, she regarded the one who'd struck her. Long, dark hair fell around his perfect face, and he augered fog-colored eyes her way. Ketha edged beyond easy reach of his booted feet into a sit, awkward because of her bound limbs. She didn't waste words telling him she was already awake, or that no one could rest easy in their midst. She stared at a newly dead rat clutched in his hand and beat back a knowing smile. If they were using rats for blood, the Vampires were in as desperate a predicament as she'd assumed.

"You've captured me," she sneered, opting for defiance. "Now what? Do I get to be everyone's dinner?" She swung her head from side to side, encompassing the room full of Vamps. "At least remove my shackles. If I'm going to die, I'd rather face you as a wolf."

The rat-wielding Vamp didn't answer.

"I'm Ketha." She held onto her slender advantage and flowed to her feet. Once she got her balance, she folded her arms as best she could beneath the swell of her breasts. "Rat got your tongue?" She jerked her chin at the rodent still clutched in the Vamp's hand.

Before he could answer, she kept right on rolling, taunting him. "If you're going to kill me, get on with it, but know this—" She summoned what magic she could, given the iron circling her wrists and ankles. The air about her shimmered with the blues and golds unique to her castings. "You will never escape Ushuaia without us."

The Vamp faced off against her. "What makes you think we want to escape, Shifter?"

Ketha shrugged, favoring him with the full force of her gaze. "You like it here? Soon there won't be anything left to eat or drink, and then all of us will die. Even Vamps. But if you're good with that"—another shrug she hoped spoke for itself—"I suppose there's nothing to talk about. Go on." She made shooing motions with her bound hands. "Get on with it. I'm prepared to die. We don't have too many more months here at the ass end of the world before none of us will be left. Take a chance, Vampire. Face my wolf."

The Vamp smiled coldly. "I'll pass. I suppose you have the answer to all our problems."

"I do." Ketha let a small, secretive smile play about her mouth. "But I'll never tell you. Funny thing about being captured. It quiets the tongue."

The Vampire's chilly expression didn't change. "Show some respect. No one addresses me that way."

"It appears I just did." Ketha tossed her shoulders back. She'd be damned if she'd let the blood-sucking bastard intimidate her. "You need us. Unfortunately, we need you as well, but what I had in mind was equal partners at a conference table, not being knocked over the head and dragged here."

Satisfaction warmed her when a vein throbbed in the Vamp's temple before he crushed the rat to bits of bone and tissue, splattering her with blood. Apparently, she'd gotten to him. What that meant remained to be seen. He summoned one of the others, a Vamp named Viktor. Ketha watched with interest when the other Vampire—clearly some minion—didn't race to comply, but took his sweet time making his way to where they stood.

Another gorgeous man. This one had copper-colored hair that fell to his shoulders. A high forehead, square jaw, and emerald eyes made him movie-star dazzling. Ketha bit down on her lower lip to force her thoughts away from his allure. Like the other Vampires, he was dressed in a motley collection of rags. Either they couldn't sew—or they had no idea how to create garments that resisted decay.

As Viktor drew near, she assessed him with magic and shielded her surprise. He didn't feel anything like the one with bloody rat remains on his hands, and the characteristic rot smell was absent. Moving with the unholy speed characteristic of his breed, Rat-Vamp slapped cuffs atop her manacles and snapped, "Take her to the caves," all but shoving her into Viktor's arms.

Viktor latched a hand firmly around Ketha's elbow, focused his attention on the other Vampire, and asked, "What then?"

Rat-Vamp sent a sharp look his way. "Lock her up and return. I'll decide her fate once she tells us whatever she knows about escaping Ushuaia."

"I already explained how that would happen." Ketha made her tone pointed. No reason to be subtle around these fuckers; they didn't deal in nuance. "At a conference table as an equal. So long as you hold me captive, my wolf and I will die before we help you do anything."

Rat-Vamp shifted his gaze her way. "It appears we're at a stalemate. Perhaps some cell time will alter your perspective."

"Don't count on it."

She turned her magic toward Viktor, wanting to know what was in his mind. The answer shocked and thrilled her. This one was different, malleable. It wasn't her imagination that he'd dragged his heels reacting to Rat-Vamp's command. Viktor might be her ticket to freedom. He might actually let her go—if she played her cards right.

"Lead out." She hip-butted him to spur him into action. "This room stinks of Vampires, and it's giving me a headache."

Rat-Vamp snarled and lunged for her, wrapping his hands around her shoulders and shaking her until her teeth rattled. "Keep a civil tongue in your head, or I'll rethink my generosity. Never forget who runs things in Ushuaia. This is blood's dominion. *My* dominion."

Ketha stood her ground. "Funny, but I thought I and my Shifters were in charge. Besides, if you were going to kill me, I'd already be dead." Ketha could've said more. Could have voiced her suspicion that he was intrigued by what she'd said, but she opted to keep her mouth shut. The sooner the weak one left with her, the sooner she'd be free.

Hopefully.

Rat-Vamp drew back his lips and extended his fangs, bloody from his earlier skirmish with the rat, but he didn't say anything further before Viktor herded her from the room.

"Remain quiet," Viktor said sternly and shepherded her toward a stairwell. "Vampires have excellent hearing."

Ketha took a chance. Easy enough since she had nothing to lose. Could he hear telepathy? Now was as good a time as any to find out. *I'm sure they do, and you don't want them to know what's in your mind. Lucky for you, Vamp magic can't hold a candle to mine, even bound as I am by iron.*

They'd started down stairs dimly illuminated by long-unwashed windows. A startled look flashed across his face, and it gave her hope. *Son of a bitch. You heard me.*

3

SWORN ENEMIES

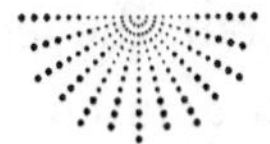

"So what if I heard you?" Viktor aimed for harsh and hoped to hell it came across. He had one objective, and it was to get the Shifter out of the building and well on her way to the caves—without any other Vamps coming along for the ride. If that happened, it would force his hand. And he hadn't yet decided quite what to do with the woman shambling along next to him, iron links clanking with every step. Defying Raphael when there were no witnesses was one thing. Open insubordination, quite another.

"Sorry. Doesn't matter," she replied, her voice rich, deep, lyrical.

The edges of her magic settled around him, soothing, calming, as they trudged down interminable flights of stairs. Her energy pushed him into a place he'd all but forgotten, and he craved it while recognizing how dangerous it was. Anything that happened regarding the Shifter had to be cautiously choreographed, or Raphael would separate his head from his body without a second thought.

He might be Raphael's favorite at the moment, but Viktor had seen his sire's favorites change many times. Small things set the

Master Vamp off, and losing the manacled Shifter by his side would be far from inconsequential. He'd have to have a convincing excuse and an airtight explanation for how it happened.

Ketha cast a speculative glance his way, and he did his damnedest to shutter his mind against her.

Would it work? Could she still burrow her way in?

She held her silence, but the corners of her full mouth twitched in what looked like amusement as they reached the door leading outside. Viktor pulled it open and shoved her through. Wind howled down the street, moving small rocks and debris with it.

Hunching against the gale, he tightened his grip on her arm and said, "This won't be pleasant, but we have to walk to the far side of the harbor and up into the hills."

"I can't make very good time with my ankles lashed together." Her words were totally without inflection.

"You don't have to make good time." Viktor swept an arm beneath her knees and lifted her easily. Once she was secure against his chest, he took off at a lope. Finally, a use for his strength. It was the only plus he'd found since being turned, but he'd had little enough opportunity to take advantage of it.

"Who was the one with the rat?" Ketha's words were muffled against his body.

"Raphael. He's my sire, and the sire of most of the Vamps here."

"Only most?" Her voice held mild amusement. "Why not all of them?"

"Some were here before he got here. Beyond that, it doesn't work anymore. Not well, anyway."

"What doesn't?" She moved her head away from him long enough to meet his gaze.

"Making new Vampires. The draining and restoration that creates more of us."

"Not at all?"

"It works occasionally because two or three have joined us this past year. Humans Raphael caught wandering outside their compounds."

"Fascinating. You're kind of like us, then. Your magic is weaker, but not gone entirely."

Her golden eyes were hypnotic, and he wanted to lose himself in their depths. They reminded him of his days at sea, of his life before Raphael got hold of him. He jerked his chin upward. "Stop it."

"Stop what? Asking questions?"

"Trying to snare me with your magic."

She laid her head back against his chest. "Ah, but I already have."

It was at least partially true, but he wasn't about to admit it. Footsteps pounded from a long way behind him, moving with speed only another Vamp could muster. Viktor kept going. Let whoever it was work to catch up.

"Don't worry." Ketha used her mind voice again, the one that had totally unnerved him in the stairwell. *"It's not Raphael."*

Viktor didn't mean to respond, but words slipped out anyway. "How do you know?"

"Because I read energy. Try saying the same thing, but not out loud. I'll hear you."

The specter of secret communication with the Shifter was enticing, but Viktor shook his head. As deeply as she fascinated him, he recognized danger in dropping his barriers to let her see any more than she already could. If he freed her—or, more likely, set things up so she could free herself—it had to be because he saw the advantages, not because she'd ensorcelled him.

When he didn't respond, she didn't ask again. The option he'd glommed onto back in the city where freeing her had burned like a beacon, grew murky. He had to be absolutely certain before he threw down the gauntlet and defied Raphael's will.

The old Vamp was canny. No matter what fabrication Viktor

came up with, odds were Raphael would claw it to shreds, uncovering the truth. It was how he'd established—and held onto—his position as top dog.

Viktor focused power, working to push into her mind, but she rebuffed his attempts, regardless of how hard he tried. At least she didn't mock him. Surely, she felt his blundering as he sought to break past her secrets, discover her true intent. They passed the far end of Ushuaia Harbor, and he headed for the overgrown path leading to the caves.

"You had to have heard me. Why didn't you stop?" Juan called from not far behind him.

Viktor turned, waiting for the other Vamp.

Not even mildly winded, Juan trotted to where Viktor stood with Ketha in his arms. "Why are you carrying her?"

"To make decent time. Wind's a real bear today, or didn't you notice?"

Juan shrugged. Blond hair was dragged into a sloppy queue secured with a length of leather. His hazel eyes always looked like he was on the verge of laughing at something no one else knew about. A week's growth of whiskers dotted his gaunt cheeks. "Guess I don't pay it any mind anymore. The wind or much of anything else."

Viktor headed uphill. "Why'd you follow me?"

"The question should be whether Raphael sent me."

"Did he?" Viktor glanced over a shoulder.

Juan shook his head. "He dismissed us right after you left. I didn't particularly want him to know what I was about, so I engaged in a few diversionary tactics before I started after you."

Ketha lifted her head and peered at Juan, walking behind them. "I'm guessing this Raphael fellow isn't well-liked."

"Vamps don't think in those terms." Viktor kept his tone curt and hoped to hell Juan would have the intelligence to shut up.

"A well-liked Vamp is a dead one," Juan cut in, his demeanor much too cheerful for his words.

"Sounds hideous." Magic streamed from Ketha, headed right for Juan.

"Watch it!" Viktor snapped. "She's been working on controlling me ever since we left the meeting room."

"I've had worse propositions aimed my way. Juan, and I'm at your service, *senorita*." He mock bowed and laughed softly. A native of Argentina, he'd been Viktor's navigator back when they worked for Dynamic Oceans. "The reason I followed you is I want to know if the Shifter's assertions are true."

"So you can report back to Raphael?" Viktor asked.

"No. For myself." Truth pinged cleanly off his words.

They rounded a sharp corner and came to an iron door recessed into the steep hillside. Iron muted everyone's magic, but Vamps weren't all that susceptible to it—unless it was part of a blade that beheaded them.

"I'll get it. Your hands are full." Juan pushed in front of Viktor and activated the combination of keypad strokes that would spring the latch. The device was mechanical, but surprisingly sophisticated.

"I can walk from here," Ketha spoke up.

Viktor set her on her feet. The warm place where her body had lain against his felt hollow, empty, and he fought a desire to scoop her against him again. She turned a knowing, golden gaze his way, tilting her head to make better eye contact. Before she could say anything, he clamped a hand around her arm and pushed her through the door Juan had already walked through.

A long, low, rounded tunnel led into the cave system someone had turned into a prison. Water ran down the walls, and the place held a perpetually dank smell. A small, dim globe of violet light formed next to Ketha, illuminating the walkway.

"It would be brighter," she said, "but it's a bitch to force much magic through all this iron."

"Vamps can see in the dark," Viktor informed her, surprised she wouldn't know that fact. As he thought about it, though, it made sense. He knew less than nothing about Shifters. Why should they know anything about Vampires?

"Where do you want to put her?" Juan's voice echoed, amplified by the tunnel's odd acoustics.

"Same place I was," Viktor answered.

"Now, there's a story I'd like to hear," Ketha murmured. "How long since Rat-Vamp turned you?"

They emerged from the tunnel, and Viktor stretched his back upright. He hated this place and wondered if she'd picked up on his antipathy. Still gripping her arm, he marched her toward the tail end of a series of cells formed out of rock and dirt. Juan already had the door of his old abode open.

Shoulders square, Ketha shuffled inside, mage light still suspended next to her. She turned toward him and held out her arms but didn't say anything. She didn't have to.

Viktor exchanged glances with Juan. The other Vamp nodded once, sharply, and said, "We can take them off. No way can she work her way out of here."

Viktor wasn't certain about that. The caves had held him and Juan and many other humans. They'd never stood the test of Shifter magic, not that he knew of, anyway.

Ketha shook her arms, and the handcuffs rattled against the other manacles. "Please." The single word—entreaty laced with magic—was impossible to resist.

Before Viktor could react, Juan dragged a small key from his pocket and sprang the cuffs. Viktor's eyes widened. Juan must've used sleight of hand to steal the key from Raphael.

"Do not say one word." Juan bit off the sentence and stared hard at Viktor. "You and I will talk later." He pocketed both cuffs and key.

Viktor reached for one of the links holding Ketha's wrist manacles together. The metal snapped beneath his fingers as if it were plastic, and the length of chain clattered to the ground.

Similar pressure made short work of the iron bands circling her wrists. Her mage light brightened immediately.

She rubbed her wrists. "Thank you. Metal burns my skin." She held her hands close to her light, revealing raw spots that validated her words.

"I can bring salve—" he began.

"No. What I need both of you to do is listen. I can heal myself with magic."

Juan drew close. "Listen to what, Shifter? Was what you said back in the city true? Is there a way out of this hellhole?"

Ketha nodded slowly, looking from one to the other of them. "An unholy alliance between us began this disaster. Another will set things right."

"How can you possibly know that?" Viktor demanded.

Ketha snorted. "Funny, but my Shifters asked the same thing. I'm a seer. I can scry the past—and the future." She inhaled deeply, blew it out, and did it again. "I've tried to figure out why we became trapped here ever since it happened. It was only a couple of days ago, though, that my efforts paid off."

"Explain," Juan broke in.

Ketha turned her hands palms up. "Not sure I can. Some spells are time-linked. Perhaps the one hiding the origins of the Cataclysm was linked to a ten-year mark. What I discovered was if we joined our power and focused it on the shielding holding us prisoner, we could defeat it. What we'd actually be doing is opening a sort of conduit to let the casting that began ten years ago run its course to a natural conclusion."

"Sounds too simple to be true," Juan muttered.

Viktor agreed, but he couldn't figure out why the Shifter might lie about something that would place her and her kin in a vulnerable position. So far, they'd avoided virtually all contact with his ilk. The few Shifters he'd seen had been from a distance.

"Why do you think there'd be a better outcome this time than there was ten years ago?" he demanded.

"Because the last spell was sabotaged."

"How?" Juan asked.

"By whom?" Victor chimed in.

"Sex derailed it." She set her mouth in a thin, tight line. "I have no idea who initiated it and threw a clod in the churn, but sex has always been forbidden between Vampires and Shifters."

"You've referred to your Shifters more than once. How many are you?" Viktor asked.

"An even dozen including me. All women. We came to Ushuaia to harvest power from an eclipse—except the Cataclysm occurred first."

"What happened to your men?" Juan asked.

"We left them back in Wyoming."

"Do you know if they're still alive?" Viktor asked.

"How could I? I can't see very clearly or very much beyond the barrier. At first, I could, but these past two or three years, it's turned all but opaque. There's life out there, but I have no idea where or whom. Look." Her voice softened, and all traces of magic fled. "This isn't about what we left behind. I don't know much about what Vampires can do. I figure you're not familiar with Shifter ability, either. Can you at least determine if someone is telling the truth?"

"Sometimes," Viktor answered carefully.

"We can pick up outright lies," Juan added, "but if a person is adept at weaving truth and falsehood, it might feel true to us."

Viktor made a chopping motion with one hand. "Don't give her information she can use against us."

Conflict soured his stomach. The Shifter kindled a spark of hope within him, but he didn't trust her. Desire sparred with wariness, creating a lethal combination. She sent a speculative look skittering across the air between them, and it made things much worse. She could read his mind far too easily, yet, when he probed hers, he'd found nothing but a blank wall.

"It's hard," she said and hobbled to a stone bench set into one wall.

"What are you talking about?" Viktor asked.

"Figuring out if you can trust me."

Her words were innocent enough, but they proved she'd been inside his head.

She extended her legs and lifted her robes an inch or two to reveal the manacles. "These too, please. Before the metal finishes burning down to my bones and kills my wolf."

Viktor wanted to ask about her bond animal, but the last thing he needed was for Ketha to kindle his compassion any more than she already had. He repeated his actions with the wrist manacles, shocked to see bone already showing through on one ankle.

Ketha bent forward, rubbing the reddened lesions circling both legs. "Thank you. I won't forget your kindness. Neither will my wolf."

"Vampires are never *kind*," Juan informed her. "Tell us more about how working together will free us. How many of us have to do this? If it's only a handful—and we can fly beneath the radar—it might be manageable."

"Before you answer him," Viktor cut in, "what about the other Shifters in Ushuaia? The ones who were here before you and your group arrived."

Surprise bloomed on her face so quickly it had to be genuine. "There weren't any others like us here. The nearest Shifter pack is fifteen hundred miles north in Buenos Aires."

Viktor filed the information away. It was one more thing Raphael had claimed to know where he'd been mistaken. Who knew? Maybe he'd killed a few and assumed there had to be more nearby.

"The number of Shifters isn't relevant. How many Vampires will you need for your scheme to work?" Juan repeated after casting a pointed look Viktor's way.

"I don't know. When your goons nabbed me, I was working on

scrying the future to clarify details like that." She scrabbled through pockets and closed her teeth over her lower lip. "Damn it. I've lost my glass. It must be back where those Vamps found me."

"Will it work in here?" Viktor asked. "You're deep within a hillside."

Ketha's mouth curved into a smile. "Shifters derive their power from the Earth. It's purer down here than I've felt in quite some time." She drew her brows into a thin line. "If I wasn't always hungry, I'd probably have thought of this strategy myself. Although, since I didn't know there were any caves in the region, likely I'd not have been successful locating one."

"You're saying you're stronger in here?" Juan clarified.

Ketha nodded. "And my power will continue to expand. At least for a while. There's a tunnel system beneath Ushuaia, but its energy isn't as clean as what I feel here. It's been one of the only places my wolf perks up."

"Yes, I know about the underground network." Viktor strode from one side of the cell to the other, the motion disturbingly reminiscent of the months he'd spent penned up in this space. "What do you need?" he asked.

"Food. My glass, if you can find it. It's an oblong two-sided mirror, about eight inches around." She tilted her head toward the sound of running water. "Is that fresh water or salt?"

"Fresh," Viktor replied, not bothering to elaborate it was the reason he'd chosen to sequester her here and not in one of the other cells.

"If we get you those things, will you find out more details about how we can escape the barrier?" Juan asked.

She clacked her teeth together. "I don't want to give you false hope. But I did scry a very small group of us who'd banded together to blend their magic. The Cataclysm that broke the world originated from their efforts."

"How can you be sure?" Viktor asked, feeling skeptical. "I never met a Vamp who was looking to mingle—or share—his power with anything."

"I'm sure because of the question I asked when I set my spell. For years, I asked the same question and came up with nothing."

"Might be a trap," Viktor muttered.

"Set by whom?" she countered. "The more I find out about you, the more certain I am Vampires don't have enough power to pull something like that off."

"Maybe not Vampires like Juan and me," Viktor countered, "but Raphael and the old ones are powerful."

Ketha shook her head. "Not in the right way. That type of inducement requires subtlety, refinement. I've yet to unearth any evidence Vampire power holds those elements."

"She's got that right." Juan made a derisive, grunting sound. "We have all the subtlety of a sledgehammer."

Viktor bit back a harsh laugh. "You seem to know a lot, Shifter. Why are your kind and mine sworn enemies?"

She sent an incredulous look bouncing between him and Juan. "You don't know that?"

"If he did, he wouldn't have asked. We know less than nothing about Shifters," Juan said. "Our law forbids contact with you, and neither Viktor nor I knew a magical world even existed pre-Cataclysm."

"Of course. Sorry." Ketha tucked her knees under her and arranged her robes around her body. "Sparing unnecessary details about the longstanding animosity between us, Shifters are linked to Earth magics through our animal bonds. We protect living creatures and respect nature. Gaia, mother of the world, watches over Shifters and guides our hand."

"While Vampires were spawned from darkness," Viktor muttered. "Living in shadows on blood—"

"With no respect for anything beyond our next feed," Juan cut in sounding far more bitter than Viktor had ever heard him.

"You can see the divide," Ketha said. "We protect. You kill. It's as if we're opposite sides of the same coin. But know this too," she hurried on. "Everything needs its opposite to exist. It's why Shifters never made any effort to eradicate Vampires. Our magic might have faded if you'd disappeared from the world. Or worse, another opposing magic would have cropped up to fill the void."

"Better the devil you know?" Juan met her eyes, but not for long.

"About the size of it," Ketha replied.

Viktor was fairly certain Vampires had no idea killing off Shifters would impact them in any way at all, but he kept his mouth shut. Perhaps Raphael and the other old ones held such knowledge, choosing not to reveal it.

"Something's happened to Vamps since the Cataclysm," Viktor began, not certain if sharing anything with the Shifter was wise, but she wasn't holding back, so perhaps he shouldn't, either.

"Yes?" She leaned forward. "I asked you about that earlier, and you said turning wasn't as predictable. Is there more?"

"Juan and I and the others who were turned post Cataclysm aren't exactly like Raphael," Viktor said.

"Mainly, we can't turn anyone. Never could," Juan cut in. "Even Raphael and the other old ones are having problems. Only a handful of those they try to turn become Vampires these days."

"What happens to the others?" Ketha asked.

"They die," Viktor said. "The ritual includes draining the potential Vamp. They return to life once they drink from us. Except it's not happening that way. Raph drains them, but about half never revive enough to drink his blood and live again."

Ketha scrunched her forehead in thought. "Any other differences?"

Viktor considered her question. "Not really. Nothing important."

"You don't have to answer this, but do you still keep human slaves to feed from?" Ketha took a ragged breath. "I was certain all the remaining humans were safe from you—unless they were stupid enough to leave their compounds."

"No slaves. Not anymore," Juan said and elbowed Viktor, urging him to continue.

"Before you helped them build those enclaves…" Viktor began, struggling how to word what was deplorable and indefensible. "Some of us raped humans. When they gave birth to our offspring —babies who cried for blood rather than milk—they left them where we'd be certain to find them."

Ketha made come-along motions with one hand. "What'd you do with them?"

"Turned them into food." Viktor's voice held a cold, dead undernote that told him how repulsed he'd been. "Vampires haven't the first clue how to raise an infant. We've always been able to have sex, but new Vamps came from turning an adult."

"Are there no women in your ranks?" Sadness streamed from the Shifter in dark-gray waves.

"Yes, but all of us have been living on short rations for years. The last thing anyone wanted was to share their hard-to-come-by blood with a baby. After half a dozen of those infants, Raphael made it clear he'd personally behead anyone who bedded a human," Juan said, adding, "After he followed through, that was the end of the baby problem."

"Why would he care?" Ketha asked.

Viktor shrugged. He'd asked himself the same thing. "Hard to say. If he has any soft spots, I've never found them."

Juan nodded in agreement. "It's past time to leave. I'm going to look for your glass. And I'll try to come up with some food." He plodded out the cell door.

"Appreciated," Ketha called after him, and then turned her unsettling, golden eyes on Viktor. She waited until Juan's footsteps faded before saying, "You were going to free me. Why'd you change your mind?"

"Why do you think?" he countered.

"Because Rat-Vamp would kill you."

"Smart Shifter." Viktor drew her to her feet and stood close. "I want to believe what you've said. And I want out of Ushuaia more than I can articulate, but it would be hard to explain why you're not in this cell if Raphael comes to talk with you. And he will. You piqued his curiosity with your hints about escaping the barrier."

"Better to play along?" She winked and wrapped her arms around him.

Her heady scent—wildflowers and Antarctic beech trees—held Viktor in thrall, and he stopped thinking. He crushed her against him and gave in to the temptation to close his mouth over hers. Memories of being human, of making love with women, spilled through him. She opened her mouth to him, tasting of summers and promise and bliss. He slid his tongue inside her mouth, and she moaned low in her throat, all heat and fire and need pressed as close as she could get.

Before he did something he'd regret and hiked up her robes to lift her over the thickness throbbing between his legs, he ripped his mouth from hers and ran out of the cell, slamming its door behind him.

He thought he heard a wolf howl, but he must have been mistaken.

4

MIRROR, MIRROR TELL ME TRUE

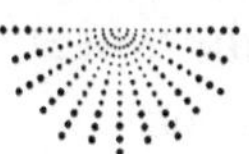

KETHA CAUGHT HER BREATH, every nerve, every cell, alight with wanting the Vampire who'd run from her as if the dogs of Hell nipped at his heels. Why had she kissed him? What was wrong with her? She hadn't meant to do anything of the kind, but her arms and lips and body had developed a will of their own.

Maybe because it's been years since I've made love.

She smiled wryly, knowing that wasn't it. Viktor might be her sworn enemy, but somehow turning hadn't touched his soul. He was a new breed Vamp, but he didn't hold their coldness, their lack of conscience. Despite his efforts to keep her out, she'd seen every thought, every nuance in his mind. Followed his inner struggle whether to trust her, and how much.

He was a decent man, more man than Vamp, despite the passage of time. Could she turn him back?

Why would I want to?

The question rocked her to her moorings. If they were successful, and the barrier fell, would the magical working rooted ten years in the past play itself out and transform all the world's Vamps into Shifters?

Shit! If that happens, how will it alter Shifter magic? What about the old Vamps like Raphael? The ones who are pure evil. What kind of animals would they bond with?

The implication of animals as wicked as their Vampire bondmates wreaking havoc was disturbing enough Ketha buried it deep. If what she suspected were true, the spell that broke the world and created the Cataclysm was the work of a small, secret group. She'd bet her last nickel—or peso—that most Vamps and Shifters had no idea why the world had turned upside down. If anyone else had figured it out, there wouldn't still be a barrier keeping them sequestered from the rest of the world.

Maybe.

"What do you think?" she asked her wolf, not expecting a reply.

"Both those Vampires are decent men," the wolf replied.

She sat up straighter. That had been her impression too.

"We must trust someone," the wolf went on. *"I'm no longer strong enough to help you much."*

She reached inward, heart aching for the animal who'd chosen her when her moon blood first began to flow. "How can I help?"

"You can't. All the bond animals will perish if nothing changes. Poisoned air. Bad water. Not enough food." The wolf quieted, and she heard it panting.

"Take your time, heart of mine."

"Nothing else to say. I love you. If there's a battle to be fought, I will do everything I can to aid you."

Ketha blinked back tears and got to her feet. She trotted from one side of her cell to the other, glad to be free of the manacles. After she tripped over a pile of metal links twice, she kicked all the debris that had bound her beneath the stone bench that served as both chair and bed.

She made her way to where water cascaded down a back wall and through a hole in the floor to somewhere far below she couldn't see. Cupping her hands, she sluiced the icy liquid over her face and then drank her fill. It didn't seem quite as contaminated as the water she scooped outside, but that made sense since this stream was cleansed as it traversed miles of underground earthen riverbed.

Returning to the bench, she sat cross-legged on it. Surely, the Shifters involved in that Siberian meeting had been privy to hidden knowledge, or they'd never have agreed to parlay with Vampires—not if it signed their own magical death warrant and loosed a horde of evil on the world.

Damn it! I'd give a whole lot to know more.

Ketha longed for her library back in Wyoming. Or older, wiser Shifters to confer with. She'd become the leader of their small band here by dint of being strongest magically. Over time, they'd looked to her for answers, but she had no one to advise her. Before, it hadn't mattered so much, but Ketha had a premonition she'd only get one chance to escape Ushuaia. Persuading the Vamps to cooperate would be a dicey proposition at best. If they agreed by some miracle she couldn't quite see, and she muffed the spell, they'd all die, surrounded by menacing, gray-black skies and the red-tinged ocean.

The sound of boots pounding over earth snapped her head up. Ketha wrapped her arms around herself and sent power zinging outward to see who approached. Breath whooshed out of her.

Juan. It's only Juan.

She'd been frightened it was Raphael. She didn't feel up to sparring with him. Not yet, anyway. She'd be on firmer ground once she'd taken a peek into the future and come up with better answers.

"That was fast." She got to her feet, waiting for him to unlock her cell door. There seemed to be some kind of touchpad next to the door, but it couldn't be electronic unless it ran off a long-acting storage battery, which was possible.

He opened the door and let himself inside, holding out her glass and a cloth sack. "We can move quickly when we want to.

Finding your mirror was easy. It was right where you dropped it. Sorry the rations are so skimpy, but—"

She held up a hand. "Don't apologize. I'm grateful for anything."

Juan walked past her and put the items on the bench. When he turned to face her, his face was set in resolute lines. "Don't fuck with Viktor," he said without preamble. "He's one of the good ones."

Ketha looked at him, wondering where that had come from. She didn't bother denying her original idea to manipulate Viktor into freeing her, but there was no way the other Vamp could know that. Instead, she tried a different tactic.

"You're his friend."

"Vampires don't have friends, but he and I were close when we were human. I worked with him, and men don't come finer or more honorable than Viktor Gaelen."

"I sense his inner strength," she said, picking her words carefully. "The best I can offer is I'll be honest with him."

"If that's the best, it'll have to be good enough, but know this, Shifter"—Juan turned the undiluted force of his hazel gaze on her —"if you use him or hang him out to dry, I'll make you sorry you were ever born. Viktor may have some of his humanity left, but I don't."

"You're wrong about that," she called after his retreating back, but Juan didn't even turn around.

Ketha made her way to where her glass lay. No time like the present to return to what she'd been doing when she was captured. The more she had in the way of facts, the better the chance she could convince the Vamps to help.

She hunkered in a corner, feet anchored on a patch of dirt and her back against dirt and stones. The more contact she had with the earth, the stronger her magic would be. Ketha blew on the glass to cloud its surface and gazed into it, chanting softly. She needed a vision of the future, perhaps more than one. It required more magic and a different incantation to look forward rather than back. Calling up the past was simple. A matter of recreating what had already occurred.

The past was cast in stone, whereas the future glimmered with untapped possibility. No one knew exactly which future would come to pass until it happened. If she could tack down the options, though, she could exert some influence over them.

Maybe.

The glass cleared, images forming before her. Ushuaia lay tucked into the Tierra del Fuego range as if she viewed it from an aerial perch. Energy surged around the town, lending the sky its black-tinted aspect. Powerful magic coursed around the city, swirling in deadly jewel tones. Any hopes she'd had about the humans who'd fled early on surviving evaporated. The power held a hungry aspect. If she looked from a certain angle, it formed hundreds of mouths edged with razor-sharp teeth.

Ketha let earth magic flow through her, welcoming its soothing calm. Along with the magic came a clear sense of her wolf, and its presence heartened her. At least so far, her vision lacked people. She altered her focus, narrowing it to pick up something other than the magical barrier. It was strong. So powerful its magic overshadowed everything else.

Rags fluttering in the wind drew her attention to a group of Vamps marching along the remains of Ushuaia Harbor, Raphael in the lead. They made their way to the water's edge and threw something into the blood-red tide.

Ketha bit back a scream and tamped down hard on her emotions. Strong reactions would bring her casting to a halt. The *something* that had been tossed into the ocean like so much garbage was a Shifter. Judging from the silver hair drifting in the water, it was probably Rowana.

"I sure as hell don't want this to happen," Ketha muttered and withdrew her casting enough to alter which bit of the future showed itself to her.

Things were unfolding faster, maybe because her magic was warming up, or because the future was anxious to show itself—in hopes someone could shape it into something better.

The glass clouded before clearing again, offering her a new aspect. She altered the tone and timbre of her incantation. This time, when images formed, she saw a group that included all her Shifters and a dozen Vamps. Ketha counted twice to make certain Rowana was still among the living, and she breathed easier once she'd reassured herself. Raphael was there. So were Viktor and Juan and others she'd seen earlier today.

"Your show, Shifter." Raphael pointed a long-nailed index finger at the trance image of her.

"Not exactly," Ketha corrected him. "It's all our shows. Not only mine."

The Vamp looked down his nose at her. "Get on with it before I change my mind."

Ketha smiled before withdrawing her energy enough to see what materialized next in her glass. At least one future held what she needed, but she couldn't stop there. The more she knew, the better prepared she'd be to guide them toward the future she wanted. They had to do something. Remaining in Ushuaia, *Ciudad de Huesos,* was a death sentence for them all. Spreading the fingers of her right hand, she struck the mirror gently and instructed it to form a timeline. Once the wavery blue line stopped pulsing, she moved an angstrom closer to the present and tapped the glass.

"Here," she muttered. "Show me what's right here."

Mist swirled in the glass, mingling blues and greens and violets. When it cleared, the same harbor view formed. This time it was all the Shifters—Ketha counted them again to be certain—and a group of Vamps, led as usual by Raphael. She reined in her antipathy for the Vampire. He was everything she hated about his race.

Arrogant, cold, remote, callous.

Worse, she couldn't imagine him as a Shifter. He'd encourage his bond animal to destroy the world. What the fuck had those Shifters in Siberia been up to? Anything that would strengthen Vampires was madness.

In her glass, Raphael halted abruptly and spun to face her. "I've thought about this, and it's half-baked, ill-conceived. You're as likely to blow the lot of us to Hell as you are to fix anything."

Ketha squared her spine. "What part about all of us dying didn't sink in, Vampire?"

He shrugged. "We can live on a lot less than you can."

"I don't think so." The Ketha in her glass spread her arms wide. "Look at yourselves. Whatever you're feeding from has been drinking the water. It's toxic. I sense your energies fading. You won't die off tomorrow, but by this time next year, none of us will be here."

"Your opinion. Not mine. I'm done here." Raphael snapped his fingers and took off at speeds only Vampires could manage, with his brood right behind him.

"What now?" Aura met Ketha's gaze.

"I have no idea."

Ketha struck the glass again, resurrecting the timeline. Maybe one more slice of the future would give her something to work with. Imminent decay had dogged the Vamps in all her visions, so she moved slightly farther into the future, hoping for a point between the last image and the one where they'd been more agreeable. She needed grist for the mill, facts she could argue to move Raphael from no to yes.

Mist formed a vortex, drawing her into it. Ketha immersed herself in the calming blues, greens, and lavenders, but the colors didn't yield images.

"Come on," she urged. Had she blown through so much power she couldn't support another summoning? Ketha didn't think so. Magic thrummed hotly, filling her cells with nascent ability.

A thread of black arrowed through her glass, followed by a phalanx of them until the mirror's surface grew opaque.

"That's what Shifters do, I suppose." A mocking voice intruded into her trance. "Practice worthless magic."

Ketha started and dropped the mirror, relieved it didn't shatter on a stone. Power fled, leaving her empty and shaking. When it came to spells, abrupt closure never boded well for the user. She blinked hard to bring the world back into focus and pushed to her feet. As an afterthought, she nudged the glass into the corner she'd just vacated.

Raphael's energy settled over her in a choking miasma. She finally heard his heavy tread, and he came into view, striding toward her cell. He smelled of rot and dead things. Of blood. Of endings.

"Didn't lose any time settling in, I see." His mouth parted in the falsest of smiles.

"Should I have?" Ketha straightened her spine, still fuzzy-headed from all the magic that had coursed through her.

Raphael turned his hands palms up. "I'd have liked it better if you'd been pacing or crying or clawing the walls. I'd also have preferred your manacles were still in place. I expected better from Viktor."

A snort blew past her lips, and she sobered up fast. "You like your victims hysterical, huh? Not to mention shackled. Means they'll do whatever you want."

He was inside the cell so fast, she never saw him hit the touchpad or move the door. One moment he was outside the bars, the next he was right next to her, the smile nowhere in sight. "It's not wise to bait me."

She angled her head to one side, standing her ground even though she wanted to cringe and back away. "You said something like that before. If you wanted to kill me, I'd already be on your day's menu. You're half-starved exactly like the rest of your Vampire horde. And I'm a rich source of food."

"I'm here," the wolf breathed into her mind. *"Clean water helped."*

Ketha sent thanks winging inward and kept a watchful eye on the Vampire. If he'd heard her wolf, he didn't give any indication.

Raphael pushed past her and leaned against the wall catty-corner to the bench. He folded powerful arms over his broad chest and skewered her with his blue-gray gaze. "What did you mean about Vampires and Shifters working together to free ourselves?"

Ketha cleared her mind of anything that might yield clues if he chose to delve into it. She was fairly certain Vamps could read thoughts, though it probably cost them. "Simple enough," she retorted. "Vamps and Shifters casting a joint spell created the Cataclysm. Makes sense the same thing would reverse it."

He drew his brows into a disbelieving line. "Shifters and Vampires do not *work together*. On anything."

"Generally, I'd agree with you." Ketha nodded, adopting what she hoped was an affable expression. "This was a secret group with a secret agenda, meeting in a remote Siberian location."

Raphael sent a condescending glance her way. "Whatever have you been smoking? Or did you Shifters manage to hang onto some liquor after all these years?"

"Fine. Don't believe me. I saw it in a vision." Ketha moved her shoulders back, adopting an even straighter stance. "You walked in on me casting magic. I'm a seer. I can see both the past and the future, although the past is clearer because it's already occurred."

"And the future?" Raphael quirked a dark brow.

"I see different iterations." Ketha capped it there. No point in explaining how she planned to manipulate those variations to achieve the result she wanted.

"Excuse me if I'm having a hard time believing you." He slouched against the wall, still eying her much like a large, lethal predator would have.

"About what?"

"Mostly about Shifters and Vampires working together. We never have, and we never will."

Ketha crossed her arms beneath her breasts, mirroring his posture, minus the slouch. "It surprised me too, but, as I said, my visions regarding the past have never been wrong, so this one isn't, either."

"Maybe the magical shielding keeping us imprisoned here has affected your *seer* powers," he suggested, emphasizing the word seer until it sounded dirty.

She considered it and cursed her predisposition toward fairness. Better to tell him he was full of shit and be done with it. Damn the consequences. Instead, she muttered, "Possibly, but the magic felt pure to me when I cast it." Ketha chewed on her lower lip. "The barrier has a perverse aspect. Its aberrant energy fills me whenever I'm outside and worsens the closer I get to it. I'd have noticed if it distorted my spell."

"I don't sense that about the barrier at all."

"That's because your power comes from evil." Ketha kicked herself. No reason to antagonize him. "What I meant to say was—"

He held up a hand. "You said exactly what you meant to, my dear. No matter how wicked you believe me to be, I appreciate honesty. And I recognize it when it rears its Goody Two-shoes head."

"Look." Ketha tried a different tack. "Our magic is different."

"What you meant to say," he cut in smoothly, "is Shifters wield magic, whereas Vampires deal in superhuman strength and speed. Because we're at the top of the food chain, we don't require your level of skill mucking around in arcane pursuits."

She chewed on her lip some more. No point in confirming his comment with an assent. Besides, the first part was right. "The reason you came to see me was to find out what I know about escape from our mutual predicament, right?"

The corners of his mouth twitched into a grimace. "That, and I wanted to get a better feel for who you are."

She looked askance at him. "What'd you discover?"

"You're weak, like all your kind. Your spells are nothing but sleight of hand tricks."

"Malign me all you want. Will you take a chance on working with me and my Shifters so we can all escape this hellhole?"

Raphael's perfect features dissolved into uncontrolled laughter. When he'd stopped laughing, he asked, "What kind of fool do you take me for? I wasn't born yesterday. Or the century before, for that fact. You expect me to put myself and my minions within spitting distance of one of your spells. How the hell do I know this isn't some sort of trap, and you'll harvest our magic to craft your own escape route, leaving us here to rot?"

She smiled sweetly. "If all I have at my command is *sleight of hand tricks*, you don't have much to worry about."

Raphael skinned his lips back from his teeth and spat guttural words in an Eastern European language.

Ketha dropped her hands to her sides, balling them into fists. She longed to blast one right through his supercilious face, but she didn't stand a chance in hand-to-hand combat against a Vampire. His superior strength and speed would flatten her.

I have to find something that works. Some argument that will get through to him.

She adopted a neutral tone with mild compulsion laced into her words. Nothing too dramatic, or he'd notice. "We really haven't talked much. Perhaps we could continue this conversation tomorrow. Once you've had a chance to mull over the possibilities."

"I've already done all the mulling I'm likely to do."

Ketha took a step toward him, facing him squarely. "We'll all die here. It won't take too many more months before the water fails entirely. Once that happens, you'll wither too. You're already drinking blood from creatures half-dead from bad water, and it will affect you sooner or later."

A crafty look crossed his face, but it was gone before she was certain what she'd seen. "Vampires never die, merely enter stasis.

If you were in a generous mood, you could alter the water," he suggested smoothly. "Same way you're modifying it for yourselves and the humans."

"You overestimate Shifter magic. Perhaps if there were more of us…"

She hurried on before he could accuse her of lying—or demand Shifters turn their power toward distilling clean water. While that might work over the short term, it would fail eventually.

"Back to escaping from here. Is my plan foolproof? Of course not. But Vamps and Shifters combining our power is the only route for any of us to leave. I'm certain of it. Check my words for truth. We'll only need to work together for a scant handful of hours to perfect the spell. Once it's over and done with, you'll never have to lay eyes on me or any of my Shifters again."

Ketha stopped shy of telling him she'd welcome a world where she never had to share the same air with him, either.

His lips curled into a sneer, and Raphael pushed away from the wall. "You'd like me to believe that, wouldn't you? You think I'm stupid, but I feel your magic trying to worm its way through my warding."

"I'd never make the mistake of underestimating you," she murmured and turned her hands palms up.

"Words," he growled. "Empty words." In a flash of movement, he was gone, the cell door clanking behind him.

Ketha inhaled deeply, spit out the breath, and did it a few more times. She was trembling from the aftereffects of her magic and Raphael's unexpected visit. She hadn't exactly been ready for him, and things hadn't gone well.

She didn't need her glass to see into this future. He'd play a macabre cat-and-mouse game with her until he wearied of the sport. Then she'd be history.

Ketha tottered to the bench and sat. She had to get out of this cell and Ushuaia before that happened. All she needed were a few

Vamps. Maybe she could manage without Raphael ever knowing —until it was too late and the spell was too far gone to sabotage. Once they were free, he'd flee. She would too, sidestepping his ire.

But I saw him acquiesce in that one future vision.

Was there a future she hadn't seen where she and her Shifters proceeded without Raphael? What happened in that one? Did they need Raphael to succeed? Or could they do this without him?

Ketha squeezed her eyes shut and rubbed them with one hand. She needed more information, which meant another vision state, but she was too frazzled to call that much power or to focus her concentration.

Food and sleep would help.

"So would not being a prisoner," she muttered, feeling sorry for herself before she recognized it as useless indulgence.

Ketha reached for the cloth bag and opened its string closure. Her eyes widened as she pulled out a carrot, two potatoes, and a dead rat. Juan must've raided some kind of secret greenhouse for the vegetables. Or maybe he knew where one or more of the human enclaves were—and wasn't telling his sire. Rats were easy enough to come by, and this one was conveniently drained of blood. Ketha dragged a knife from its sheath beneath her robe and made short work of skinning the rat.

The Vampires hadn't bothered to search her. Or maybe they had and had laughed at her four-inch blade, not viewing it as any kind of threat.

A pit at the far end of the cell held rocks and charcoal bits. She walked to it and focused a thin beam of magic to heat the rocks. Once they were ready, she placed the meat and potatoes on them. She munched down the carrot while she waited.

The scents of cooking food soothed her. She didn't see how, but maybe things would turn out better than she expected. Once she'd eaten and rested, she'd look into her glass again, trolling for more clues about the future.

A muted squeak drew her attention to a pair of fat, curious

rats, drawn by the smells of her dinner. Magic sizzled, and she stunned them both. An idea blasted her, and she ran with it. Letting her robe pool around her, she unlaced her boots kicking them off. Naked and shivering, she summoned shift magic. It might be an extravagant use of power, but tonight they'd have two meals, by God.

Hers and her wolf's.

Her black-and-gray timber wolf roared into being and scooped up both rodents, crunching hungrily. Ketha welcomed her animal nature with a vengeance. Its presence made her whole, and she savored the hot tang of blood sliding down her gullet. When those rats were gone, she broke a cardinal Shifter rule and used magic to lure half a dozen more.

Not only did the wolf not censure her, it added its power to hers until a cavalcade of rodents marched through the cell, ripe for the plucking.

5

PARADISE FOUND—OR NOT

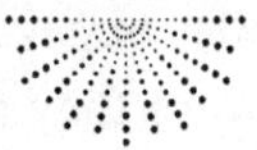

VVIKTOR RACED AWAY from his old cell with speed most Vamps couldn't have matched. His groin throbbed with need, and Ketha's scent filled his nostrils, making him long for the impossible. A life where he was still human. Frustration pounded through him, and he punched a boulder as he flashed past it. Pain didn't make a dent in the arousal turning his blood molten.

The feel of her in his arms defied credibility. He craved her with an intensity that shocked him. Even though being turned hadn't quashed all his human emotions, he hadn't felt this strongly about anything since Raphael drained him and offered his wrist, flowing with dark-red blood. If Viktor hadn't been dying, he might have had the strength to resist, but the desire to live overwhelmed his capacity to reason. It wasn't that he hadn't known what would happen before he glommed onto Raphael's wrist, but he hadn't counted on the strength of his desire to keep living—regardless how it happened or the cost.

He'd had long years to castigate himself for that day. Years he'd contemplated ways to do away with himself. Vamps healed so fast, though, that anything shy of cutting off his own head wouldn't have done the trick.

Viktor glanced up from his headlong dash away from the cave containing the cells. He'd gone farther up the mountainside, not down to what was left of the city and harbor. The track wound ahead of him. Covered with brambles and brush, it was clearly not used often—or at all. Curious where it led, he continued upward. Snow patches dotted the trail, but they didn't slow him down.

A condor flew past, its huge wingspan inspiring. They appeared to be surviving. Were they still nesting, raising chicks? And then he wondered how it was possible since decaying fish had been the seabirds' primary food source. As he climbed higher, rock fall joined more frequent snow, and he slowed to work his way around obstacles.

Raphael had ordered him to return immediately, but he shrugged it off. Juan said the Master Vamp had dismissed the group, which meant he'd likely retired to his quarters across the street. Viktor didn't delude himself that his sire was pacing the floor worrying what happened to his minion. No. If Raph were fixated on anything, it would be figuring out how to maximize having captured Ketha, his latest prize.

Viktor wasn't certain he could take part in that conversation without giving something away. Even though feelings didn't slow Raphael down, the canny Vamp was quick to pick up on them in others. He'd be sure to ridicule Viktor—right before he made double damn sure to spirit Ketha somewhere Viktor couldn't reach her.

An enormous thicket studded with inch-long, thorny spines blocked the path. Crawling over it was out of the question. His wounds would heal fast, but he wasn't interested in becoming a pincushion. He glanced up, then down, searching for a way around the obstacle. The second time he scanned above him, he could've sworn the faintest of paths wound through the steep, rock-strewn slope. He closed his eyes and sniffed. Vampires had exceptional hearing and eyesight, and a sense of smell that could detect years-old human presence. He inhaled again, concentrating. Faint traces of human blood tickled the edges of his brain.

It was good enough.

Viktor started up the all-but-invisible zigzag track, dislodging rocks as he climbed. Following the trail was time-consuming; he kept losing it and finally changed strategies, heading straight uphill. Because this route was more direct than the original one had been, he gained altitude fast. Angling for a low point in the ridgeline, he crested it and stopped dead.

Rather than what he'd expected to find—the other side of this mountain trailing downward—a flat butte extended before him, surrounded by steep cliffs on two sides. Divots suggesting long-ago human habitation dotted a flat area about the size of a soccer field. Two condors winged past him, landing on the far side of the mesa. They squawked defiantly as if to announce he was trespassing on their turf. Without waiting to see if their raucous chiding had any effect, they shuffled into an opening in the cliffs, fluffing their feathers around them.

Viktor stared after them. Had he stumbled onto a condor nesting ground? Two pools lay in scrub grass near the base of the cliff where the birds had disappeared. Did underground springs flow from the mountainside? He loped to the first pool and knelt, expecting the characteristic odor of tainted water but not finding it.

He dipped two fingers into the pool and brought his hand to his mouth, tasting with all his senses deployed. And then did it again. Once he was certain, he dropped to his belly and drank. The water was cold, crystal clear, and tasted like it was supposed to, the taint of metal and wicked magic conspicuously absent.

Once he'd filled his belly, he rinsed his hands and face, glorying in the feel against his skin. Viktor rocked back on his heels and looked around him. How had this tiny spot escaped contamination? It shared the same air that was eroding the rest of *Ciudad de Huesos*. A quick study of the cliffs revealed multiple openings. He shot upright and headed for the nearest one, hoping to hell he wouldn't disturb a nest of young condors.

Viktor listened intently at the opening. While the sounds of birds nesting and feeding reached him, they weren't coming from this particular cave. What were the birds eating? All the fish were long gone.

Or were they?

If all the water wasn't poisoned, perhaps some fish—at least the freshwater varieties—still remained. It was also possible the condors had discovered a way to fly beneath the magical barrier and bring food back to their nesting ground.

He pushed into the cave, stooping to duck past its low entrance. Once inside, he dilated his pupils to make use of every scrap of available light. A medium-sized enclosure spread before him. Drawings on the walls suggested early humans had once occupied this space, and probably the other grottos scattered around the mesa as well. The hard-to-access location would have provided a defensible position from both predators and neighboring tribes.

Sure enough, the remains of a fire pit rested against the far wall, complete with bits of blackened bone and charcoal-coated rocks. He knelt next to it, thinking. It was an almost-sure bet the Vamps didn't know about this place. If they did, they'd have set traps for the condors. Blood was blood, and condors were considerably larger than rats.

"Ketha!"

He clapped a hand over his mouth, but her name—part entreaty, part prayer—had already escaped. This would be a perfect place to hide her. Unless Raph grew suspicious and ordered a twenty-four-hour watch on Viktor.

Even if he did, there's water up here. And shelter. Maybe even food. I wouldn't ever have to come here once I either led her to this place or sent her up the mountain on her own.

Determined to find out as much as he could, he let himself out of the cave and began a systematic examination of the other ones. Condors flew at him from a few, but he employed a light version of the Vamp immobilization spell. The one they used to hypnotize their prey. He was careful not to injure the birds, merely stunning them long enough to trudge through bird shit and examine each grotto.

He found what he sought in one cave on each side of the mesa. Underground rivers thick with breeding fish were tucked deep into the mountainside. Either it was spawning season, or the Cataclysm's foul magic had forced changes in the trout life cycle. Rather than riding the current out of their subterranean pools, the fish congregated in small groups, almost as if they knew leaving the protected area would sign their death warrants far faster than condors eating them would.

Viktor reached into the water and grabbed two fish, devouring them raw. The succulent, transparent flesh tasted sweet and cold going down, like everything used to before the Cataclysm's magic snared the city. He smiled, as close to relaxed as he'd been since being turned. Life would have been so much worse if he were limited to blood to sustain himself.

Still chewing, he made his way outside into rapidly fading light. The day had gotten away from him, and it was long past time to hurry back and present himself front and center before his sire. Raphael would demand an explanation, and Viktor needed to come up with a credible excuse for being gone so long.

He tossed the fish bones aside and hustled down the mountain to the place he'd left the track. He needed to obliterate traces of his passage from this point on. Not easy if Vamps were looking for him with their augmented senses. He melted snow patches that held his boot prints as he worked his way down and pulled the worst of broken foliage aside, hurling it down the mountain. All the while, he pumped out energy to confuse his scent. Satisfied he'd done the best he could, he broke into a sprint, skirting the edges of the harbor and heading into the center of town.

He breathed deep, missing the sharp, salt tang of the sea. Something about it turning red had altered its smell until it made his stomach churn with disgust. Recalling the Garden of Eden he'd unearthed—with its clean, living odors—he pushed all traces of it deep. Hopefully, where no one would ever find out about it, even if they probed. He didn't see anyone at all on his way to the building where he lived. Dropping through a manhole cover, he entered the warren of underground tunnels spreading beneath Ushuaia like a demented spider's web. It was his usual method of accessing his room, and he aimed for normal.

Raphael wasn't waiting for him. Nor had he left anything as prosaic as a note. Viktor scanned the small room, seeking clues, but the other Vamp hadn't been here recently. Thank God. Viktor snorted at the archaic expression. If there were a God, He'd long since deserted Ushuaia. And Vampires. No god in his right mind would ever include Vamps among his flock.

On that cheery note, he said a quick prayer he hadn't burned up his meager allotment of electricity and cranked the dial on his ancient space heater. It sputtered, and the coils glowed red. Sighing with pleasure, he extended his hands toward the warmth, bending so more of him could take advantage of it.

One advantage of the windowless space he occupied was its size. Just large enough to hold a bed, a chair, a bookcase, and a useless floor lamp, it grew warm fast. Viktor retreated to the chair, an over-stuffed affair that had long since lost its cushioning, and sank into it. He kept his llama-skin jacket on, not ready to abandon it quite yet.

Books were an extravagance, but the library was one part of Ushuaia that had mostly avoided looting and destruction. Viktor plucked a volume of Dante's writing off one of the chair's arms and opened it to where he'd left off with the *Inferno*. It had seemed a fitting counterpoint to the Milton's *Paradise Lost*, which lay on the floor. As he read, he longed for a bottle of decent red wine, but spirits didn't mesh well with his Vampire physiology. He'd found out the hard way how ill he felt after imbibing, with the effects lingering for days.

Energy canted crazily, making the air come alive with small black darts. One poked into his leg, and Viktor drew wards around himself since he wasn't interested in repeating the experience. The space heater sputtered to a stop. Only one person held that level of power, and Viktor had been expecting him sooner or later.

The door burst open without so much as a knock.

"Good thing you weren't hard to find," Raphael growled and kicked the door shut behind him. "Damn my eyes, it's bloody hot in here. How can you stand it?"

Not surprised by his sire's ill-temper, Viktor shrugged and moved out of the chair, motioning for Raphael to sit.

The Master Vamp shook his head. "This feels like the backside of Hell. Join me in my quarters. Immediately."

The air shimmered, and Raphael was gone.

Viktor knew better than to make him wait. He bolted out the door and took the stairs three at a time. The door to Raphael's suite of rooms stood open. Viktor walked through, shutting it behind him.

"What happened?" he asked his sire.

"What didn't?" Raphael shot back from where he perched atop his rolltop desk.

Viktor moved to the wall farthest from the window because it was the warmest place in the room. He stilled his mind, burying his secrets deep. Raphael would get around to talking in his own time. The old bastard craved a sympathetic audience, loved being fawned over. Viktor could provide that. He'd done so many times before. Listened as Raphael spewed vitriol over the latest Vamp who'd had the temerity to cross him.

Raphael lived to plot revenge, and Viktor hated the part of himself that caved and played the lackey—every single time.

"Why aren't you asking questions?" Raphael demanded. Jumping down from the desk, he swung to face Viktor.

"I did, Sire. You didn't answer me."

"So you did." Raphael drew his lips back, fangs elongating. "I went to visit our captive."

Viktor maintained a neutral expression, but it cost him. "The Shifter?" he asked, playing dumb and hoping to hell Ketha was still alive. The mood Raphael was in, anything could have happened.

"Of course, the fucking Shifter. Who else?"

"I'm sure I wouldn't know, Sire. We have other captives. Or we did. Perhaps you've ended them by now." He trained guileless eyes on the other Vampire, silently urging him to say more.

Raphael's nostrils flared. "They're still alive. Barely. Except for the ones those minions killed. They're old news. I don't wish to discuss them."

"Of course, Sire." Viktor's face would shatter if he had to maintain his pleasant expression much longer. "What would you prefer to talk about?"

"The Shifter. Who else? Have you been taking stupid pills? Or has that overheated chamber of yours addled whatever you have left for brains?"

"I'm sure I couldn't say," Viktor gritted out and unclenched his jaw.

Triumph flashed from Raphael. He relished the bully role and had a love-hate relationship with his victims. Viktor had tried fighting back at first, standing up for himself. All it bought him was time in the same concrete bunker on a quay in the harbor where Raphael stashed all his Vamp enemies. Something about water muted Vampire power and made escape impossible.

Of course, it muted Raphael's ability as well, which was why he moved his victims to grill them. A special double-reinforced steel building a few blocks from the bunker proved perfect for his needs.

Raphael came to a halt in front of Viktor. "What do you think of her?"

The question came out of nowhere. "I'm sure I don't know what you mean," Viktor stammered.

"Of course, you do. What do you think about the Shifter? Is she telling the truth about escape from here?"

"How would I know?" Viktor replied flatly. "I scarcely have the seer power she lays claim to." He hesitated long enough to draw breath. The whiff of fear he caught from his sire shocked him. "I'm not even certain what it is seers do," he went on. "You're the one who's been a magical creature for centuries."

"Back in my court, eh?" Raphael shot a rare smile his way. "Nicely done."

Viktor shrugged slightly in a self-deprecating gesture. "You've been a most excellent teacher."

Raphael preened under the compliment, apparently not reading the nuanced sarcasm that rode beneath it.

"Beyond that," Viktor went on, "I might be more help if I knew why you were so upset."

"I am not *upset*. Vampires are immune to emotion." Raphael drew his brows into a single, dark foreboding line."

Oops.

"Of course, Sire. Apologies. I misspoke." Viktor waited, holding eye contact. Either it would work, or Raphael would erupt into an angry tirade and order him back to his room.

Breath whistled through the other Vamp's teeth, but his fangs retracted. Viktor took that as a positive sign.

"I stopped by the Shifter's cell," Raphael began. "And caught her casting magic."

Viktor barely blinked. "What's so odd about that? Shifters cast spells. Was she trying to escape? Had she shifted to her animal form?"

"Hardly." Raphael barked out the single word. "She was scrying the future. Tried to convince me it was Shifters and Vamps working together who'd created the Cataclysm." He shook his head, and dark hair danced around his face and shoulders.

"Doesn't seem very plausible, Sire," Viktor murmured because he intuited it was what Raphael wanted to hear.

The other Vamp crossed his arms over his chest. "No," he replied. "It certainly doesn't, but when I questioned her, asked if she might be wrong, she clung to her story. Even added to it."

"How so?" Viktor had become skilled at feeding his sire questions. If he wasn't overly curious or pushy, Raphael generally answered them.

"She claimed Shifters and Vamps working in tandem had created the Cataclysm, so only the same energy could undo it."

Viktor made a noncommittal sound, waiting. Raphael didn't disappoint him.

"The whole concept is ridiculous," the Master Vamp went on. "We do not work with Shifters. Period. She claimed it was a very small, secret group in Siberia, but I don't believe her."

"Why would she lie?" Viktor took a chance and played devil's advocate.

Raphael shrugged. "Who knows? That bothered me the whole way back here. She's shrewd, that one. She has something up her sleeve. I just haven't figured out yet what it is."

"There's always tomorrow," Viktor suggested. "You could feed. Things always look better with blood on board."

Raphael cocked his head to one side, assessing Viktor. Like as not wondering if his minion was mocking him. Viktor stared back, projecting a spirit of innocence and desire to go the extra mile to help his sire.

"Perhaps you'll come with me?" Raphael infused compulsion into his tone. The same compulsion that urged his victims to give up without a struggle.

Viktor suppressed a gag. The absolute last thing he wanted was to hunt with his sire. The Master Vamp was merciless, glorying in bloodbaths. Yet he couldn't refuse. If he did, he'd arouse Raphael's suspicions.

"Well?" Raphael prodded. "It's an honor when your sire invites you to hunt."

Viktor bowed slightly. "Of course, it is. I'm flattered to be chosen. What pleases you, pleases me. What would you like to hunt tonight?"

Raphael rubbed his hands together and bent toward Viktor. "Jaguars. One of them would make a most exceptional meal." He paused a beat. "I'll even see you get a portion of the meat"—Raphael indulged in an eloquent eye roll—"and the skin since you're perpetually cold."

What am I supposed to do? Jump up and down? Kiss his hand?

"Thank you, Sire. Appreciate your thoughtfulness. Shall we?" Viktor motioned toward the door. They should leave before Raphael picked up on his ambivalence. Once they were out hunting, the other Vamp's attention wouldn't be focused on him but on hot, fresh blood.

Besides, the sooner Viktor returned, the sooner he could sneak away to Ketha's cell and lead her to the haven he'd found. She'd survived today's skirmish with Raphael. She might not be so lucky next time the Master Vamp paid her a visit.

"One last thing." Raphael skewered Viktor with his direct gaze.

"What might that be?" Viktor maintained a calm, deferential aspect that went against the grain. He'd been biding his time for years, waiting for an opportunity to break free.

Soon, he promised himself. The endgame was in sight. He felt it in his bones and welcomed it—no matter what the outcome.

His sire moved within inches of his face. "You removed her manacles. And her handcuffs. Why?"

"She can't escape. Hell, I was in that same cell for months hunting for a way out. Never did find one. I saw no reason to leave her in irons, so I broke the chains and iron circlets." Viktor inhaled sharply, grateful Raphael hadn't said squat about the handcuff key. "I suppose you bound her again."

Raphael shook his head. "I want her to be free to use that scrying tool of hers. Maybe next time I show up, she'll have created a more credible story. One I can believe."

"Surely, there's nothing to her fantastic tale of us colluding with Shifters." Viktor followed his sire out the door.

"Probably not." Raphael glanced over a shoulder. "But I'd be a fool to leave any stones unturned. Not if they mean escape from Ushuaia." He rubbed his hands together. "Let's hunt and forget about that pesky Shifter for a few hours."

Yes, let's.

"Good enough for me." Viktor clattered down the stairs. At least Raphael would be by his side for the next span of time. Which meant he wouldn't be tormenting Ketha. That the Shifter had told Raph the same story she laid out for him and Juan added to her credibility—at least in his book.

Hope spilled through him like a hot tide. He squashed it to nothing before Raphael, who was suspicious to begin with, noticed anything amiss.

6

RENEGADE MIRROR

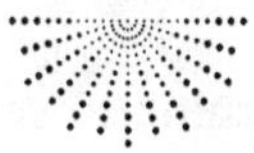

AFTER EATING, Ketha shifted back to her human form. Her wolf's spirits had improved after it fed, and they'd chatted of this and that, almost like the old days before the Cataclysm. The sheer normalcy of it heartened her, but she remained vigilant. The Vampire bastard could return at any time. He'd been furious when he stormed out of her cell, and it wouldn't take much for him to direct that ire—and his fangs—her way.

She kindled a spell to keep herself warm and stretched out on the stone bench. Her magic-imbued robes yielded some comfort, but stone was a real heat sink. At first, sleep was elusive. The more she replayed Raphael's visit, the more it bothered her. Beyond his cold calculation lay an instability bordering on madness. Predicting his next move would be damn near impossible, and that made sparring with him dangerous.

She couldn't give up, though. Not if he held the key to a spell that would free all of them from Ushuaia.

"I don't know exactly how disturbed he is. Not really," she said out loud to steady her frayed nerves. Ketha fingered the glass she'd retrieved and stashed in a pocket of her robe. Using it was

77

tempting, but she was so trashed, she'd likely fail. Any efforts tonight would burn through her limited magic for nothing.

Closing her eyes, she urged sleep to claim her, and then chided herself for being naïve. It didn't work like that. She could cast a calming spell but couldn't will herself to sleep. Now, if one of the other Shifters had been here, they could've ensured she slept. They weren't. She was on her own in the chill, dank cell that smelled of the poisoned sea.

Ketha quested for something to settle her tumbling mind. An image of Viktor—with his striking copper hair and eyes like glittering gemstones— formed behind her closed lids. Memory of the feel of his mouth on hers made her long for more. She sought tracings of his essence in her cell—both from when he'd been imprisoned here and from earlier today. Gathering them, she wove a mantle and draped it around herself, inhaling his scent shamelessly. He didn't smell of death and rot like most Vamps. Instead, he smelled of the ocean—before it turned red and ugly. Of the forest on a rainy day. Of storms at sea. He had strength, that one. And a staunch inner core that kept him going. Juan hadn't been lying when he'd called Viktor fine and honorable and one of the good ones.

Her tightly coiled muscles relaxed; so did her death grip on her glass. Surrounded by a sense of Viktor cradling her in his arms, she drifted into unconsciousness, lulled by the bits and pieces of his energy she'd collected.

KETHA HAD no idea what jolted her awake. Was it morning yet? It was too dark to tell. Grateful she'd managed at least some uninterrupted rest, she walked to the waterfall, sluiced cold water over her face, and drank her fill. It was past time to get down to business, and business meant using her glass to sort the future into something that made better sense. She'd try to establish détente with Raphael if she had to, but if she could locate a future where they defeated the barrier without him, she was all for that.

Ketha wasn't under any illusions. The old Vamp was as likely to kill her as listen to her, and with her gone, her Shifters would be in grave danger. Far worse peril than they faced now since they'd lack any inkling what the future held for them. Knowledge was power, and she was their seer.

She dug her glass from her robes. After a cursory stretch to get the kinks out of her muscles from sleeping on a stone slab, she took up the same position that had worked for her the previous day. Ketha inhaled deeply a few times to center herself and flush all thoughts of Raphael from her mind. He'd only get in the way, impact her concentration.

When she felt ready, she breathed on the glass and urged its cloudy surface to yield information. Rather than her previous approach of using a rough timeline, she asked for a strategy to defeat the curse that had formed the Cataclysm.

Ketha waited. And waited. Her glass remained stubbornly cloudy. Had she asked too much of it? Or was her power too diminished to cast such complex magic on her own? Shifting the previous evening had been pure indulgence. Would it undercut her efforts today?

This was a time to be surrounded by the other Shifters. They loaned their power to her efforts—if she asked for help. Their bond animals might be fading, but their subtle presence helped too.

As if thinking about her sisters summoned them, Rowana, Karin, and Aura formed dead center in the mist still covering her glass, their animals hovering behind them.

"Thank the goddess you're safe." Rowana focused dark, worried eyes right at Ketha.

"We've been hunting for you ever since you didn't return," Karin cut in.

"Where are you?" Aura demanded.

"Never mind that." Rowana shook her head, making her silver hair shimmer. "Get back here. Vamps are on the move, and we have to evade their gunsights."

"What are they doing?" Worry shot through Ketha, but she pushed it aside, not wanting anything to interfere with her tenuous magical connection to the other Shifters.

"Hunting for our lair, and they're getting closer." Aura scrunched her face in disgust. "We'd have moved already, but we were worried about you. You never did say where you are."

"Imprisoned by Vampires." Ketha snapped off the words.

"Where?" Karin squared her shoulders. "We'll get you out of there." Her wolf tossed its muzzle back and howled.

Ketha's wolf howled back, but she shushed it. This magically driven conversation would bring Raphael on the run—if he discovered it. "Don't risk yourselves. I have this figured out." Ketha was lying, but the others wouldn't be able to test her words through the enchanted link. "Get yourselves to somewhere safe. I'll join you as soon as I can."

"Later today?" Rowana pushed more magic into the connection, likely suspecting Ketha's assertion about having everything under control.

"If I can. I have to go. I was scrying clues when you found me."

"Be safe," Karin implored.

"Always." Ketha cut the connection before she dissolved into tears. The twelve of them had grown close, become more than sisters, and she'd hated not being totally honest. The specter of the others putting themselves at risk waiting for her was untenable, though. She had no idea if she could escape. Viktor had seemed like a sure bet, but he'd taken off after kissing her and hadn't returned. Perhaps he'd concluded helping her was a bigger risk than he was willing to take. The thought made her sad. She wanted to see him again but recognized it as folly. Vamps and Shifters were mortal enemies. Why was she even entertaining something that felt like a bad replay of *Romeo and Juliet*?

Because I like him.

He's not like the rest of them.

Bullshit! I have no way of knowing that.

Ketha squeezed her hands into fists to redirect her thoughts. Jamming her feelings into a hole, she fastened a bulletproof gate over them. No room for anything that intruded on her concentration. Not when Raphael could storm her cell at any moment.

Thinking about the old Vampire killed her casting. Or maybe longing for Viktor had done it. Regardless, the clouds dissipated from the glass. Ketha shut her third eye; her cell came back into focus. She took a few cleansing breaths, but the single-mindedness she sought eluded her. The glass stared back, its surface perfectly clear again. It took her third eye to turn it into a magical tool. To her earth eyes, it was nothing but a mirror.

To shake herself out of her inertia, she got her feet under her and paced from one side of the cell to the other, stopping by the waterfall to stick her face under its flow. While the cold revived her, she couldn't shake the image of Raphael hovering behind a psychic curtain.

What the fuck?

Why does that bastard have such a hold on me?

Ketha bit hard enough on her lower lip to draw blood. Once drops welled, she dipped an index finger in the cut, splattered drops into the air, and barked a few words in Gaelic, the Shifters' spell language. At least this casting worked, and the lines of the world—ley lines invisible to mortals—wavered before her.

Grim laughter bubbled. Raphael's fell power was embedded in several key locations exactly as she'd suspected. Drawing strength from the earth beneath her feet, she went to work on the first spot, neutralizing it. Now that she could see them, the Vamp's marks were a series of black darts. Ketha took care not to touch them as she worked—in case they tripped some enchantment that would alert Raphael she was undoing his work. Damn! He was worse than a dog that had pissed in every corner.

Lupine laughter riffled through her mind. Apparently, the analogy amused her wolf.

Finished, she tromped back to the bench, digging through her memory for everything she knew about Vampires. Raphael was one of the old ones, which meant he could do more than Juan—or Viktor.

A whole lot more.

Did he command enough magic to know she'd obliterated his markers?

"I have no idea," she muttered. "And I can't worry about it. If what I did means he shows up sooner rather than later, I'll live with it."

Motion from the mirror still clutched in one hand drew her attention. She hadn't asked it anything. Had it finally fallen prey to the Cataclysm's macabre influence? She set it on the stone bench and shook her finger at it.

"None of that." She tried for stern, but didn't quite make it. The glass was sensitive to emotion, so maybe it was reacting to her anxiety.

She engaged her third eye and crossed her fingers this would be a true sending.

Clouds formed on the mirror's surface. She knelt before it, waiting for whatever this was to play itself out. Her glass had only acted independently once since she'd inherited it from the last Shifter who'd been seer for her pack. Right before the Cataclysm, the glass had played host to jagged lightning that hurt her eyes to look at for long. After an eerie light show, the mirror's surface had turned flat, opaque black, refusing to be coaxed back to its mirror form for a week, third eye or no.

Ketha cleared her mind of anything that might influence the glass and fed magic into it. The clouds cleared, and a mixed group of Shifters and Vamps formed. All twelve Shifters and half that number of Vamps. Ketha peered intently at the Vamps and identified Viktor, Juan, and the two who'd dumped her into their midst in the chapel. The other two had their backs to her and their heads covered by cloaks.

While she waited, hoping to hell they'd turn around, she looked beyond them, expecting to see the ocean. Instead, a rock-studded, grassy plain with cliffs on both sides extended as far as she could see. Condors flew lazily, drifting on their extended wings. Pools of water glistened, reflecting bits of a gray-black sky.

Ketha turned to face the others in her vision and raised her arms above her head. Energy crackled around her, turning the air blue with her power. "Let's do this and defeat the Cataclysm," she barked, her voice harsh with barely contained energy. She hadn't asked a question, and no one answered, but the last two Vamps turned toward her.

Relief hit her in the gut. Neither was Raphael.

Her vision, the one she hadn't asked for, flickered, and she made a grab for it, but the image crumpled from the edges inward, disintegrating before her eyes.

"Goddamn it!"

Ketha punched a fist into the floor and yelped. After all the years she'd called visions, she was furious she didn't have better control over her emotions. Strong feelings always killed trance states, and she was far from a novice.

She knew better, but apparently it didn't matter.

Rocking back on her heels, she stood and forced slow, deep breaths before placing the glass back in a pocket. Two things were certain. She didn't need Raphael, and she had to escape her prison. But how? Would anything in this place yield to magic? A long, deliberate circuit of the cell yielded less than nothing. The stout, barred door was set into rock. No other exit route existed.

She made her way back to the door and craned her neck to look at the touchpad controlling it. If it was a mechanical latch system, she might have a chance. Anything electrical worked on a frequency her magic couldn't modify because magic predated electricity by a good, big bunch.

Ketha tilted her head and poured power into listening intently. If the lock was electric—which wasn't likely—she should hear something. Some small motor sitting on standby, waiting for a command.

Silence.

So far, so good. Not electric also meant the door wouldn't trip an alarm somewhere at Vampire Central—if it opened. Ketha gazed around the cell. Everything she owned was on her back. If she got lucky, she could sprint down the tunnel the moment the door opened and confront the second locked gate.

The narrow trail leading back to Ushuaia mocked her. She'd need to be fortunate indeed to both escape her cell and make it to where she could blend in with the city's alleyways and backstreets while she located the rest of the Shifters.

"We could shift," the wolf suggested.

Ketha mulled it over, but not for long. "We could," she agreed, not wanting to hurt her wolf's feelings, "but then I wouldn't have any clothes when we returned to the city. Besides, this is only the first of two locked barriers."

"I understand." The wolf's tone was formal. *"I will be here if you have need of my form."*

Emotion sluiced through her, and she blinked back the hot prick of tears. "Thank you, heart of mine."

"We're bondmates. No need for thanks." The wolf subsided into whuffly growls.

Driven by a sense of increasing urgency, Ketha sent a finely tuned jolt of magic right at the touchpad. Something hummed and then quieted.

Hope flared, so sharp it hurt. This was like picking a lock. If she played the damn thing right, the door would open. Ketha thought about what she'd just done and mixed a small amount of air with earth magic, trying again. This time, nothing whirred.

She flexed her fingers and called fire to mingle with her native earth power. Humming reached her sensitive ears, along with the sound of tumblers churning. The door shuddered, but the latch didn't give. Resisting a desire to curl her fingers around the bars and shake the door into submission, Ketha forced her racing heart to slow down. Crappy control over her emotions had already fucked up one thing today.

Time for success. Not failure.

She was shooting in the dark, but she summoned water. It flowed obligingly across her cell, eager to do her bidding. Her hands wove an ancient pattern in the air as she blended water, fire, and earth. Once she had them in balance, she focused them right at the touchpad and held her breath, urging the incantation to work.

With so little fanfare—no humming, no whirring—it shocked her, the door sprang open. Ketha wasted precious moments staring at it with her mouth ajar.

"Get going." The wolf's harsh command jolted her into action. She leapt through the opening and raced down the tunnel toward freedom.

I did it. I did it!

Save the champagne for later, a different inner voice shot back in far more sober tones.

One down. One to go.

Ketha reached the overgrown entrance to the prison cells. She ground to a halt at the barred gate while she peered outside, her magical senses on high alert for Vamp energy. She didn't sense anything, but she scanned once more to double-check.

Could the fuckers cloak themselves? She didn't think so. Vampires had been at the top of the food chain so long, they probably never bothered to conceal themselves—from anyone.

One more lock stood between her and freedom. Her heart thudded against her ribs; she gulped air. Water was farther away, harder to access, but she summoned it just the same, blending it with fire and earth to replicate what had worked on the inner lock. Chanting, she repeated the same incantation.

Nothing.

She curved her hands around the bars. Shaking them provided an outlet for her frustration and her fear.

"Try harder," her wolf urged. *"I'll help."*

She felt it weave its magic with hers, strengthening the animal side of her nature. It had been a long time since they'd joined their power this way with her in human form. She yearned to stop and savor the heady sensation, but time was a luxury. Raphael could return at any moment. Once he did and discovered she'd broken the inner lock, he'd bind her with iron, and she'd never, never leave these cells.

Ketha called her spell once more, taking time to build it from the ground up, one magical thread at a time. She made certain the elements were well seated before she focused a beam of compulsion at the touchpad next to the gate. This time when she uttered the Gaelic command to ignite her working, the door creaked open.

Gratitude and disbelief swelled through her. "Thank you," she told the wolf. "Thank you, my heart, my life."

"Move," it exhorted. *"We are far from safe."*

Shaky and light-headed, she stepped outside into a chill, gray dawn and ran down the path toward Ushuaia. She had one chance. That chance was now. As she pelted downward, the phrase, *he who hesitates is lost,* repeated in rhythm with her steps.

The city spread beneath her. Victory was close, but it didn't mean she could let her guard down. Breath steamed from her mouth; she did the best she could to muffle her presence with spells. Vamps ranged day and night. If any found her, she was done for.

She was panting, sour-smelling sweat dripping down her sides, when her booted feet landed on asphalt. She edged along the mountainside's border, keeping to back streets and skirting piles of bones—human and animal. Because these roads weren't used much, no one bothered to create trails through the rubble.

Soon, the webbing of debris-clogged streets would give way to a place she could duck into, the underground warren of byways cutting beneath the city. Once there, she'd risk stopping long enough to raise her sisters telepathically.

The characteristic scent of rot and death that meant Vamps sent her heart into triple time. Where were they? She was almost safe, goddamn it.

"Not fair," the wolf piped up. *"Shift, bondmate. We'll fight our way to freedom."*

Ketha shushed it fast. Life wasn't fair. So what? She increased the warding around her and ducked behind the remains of a concrete-block building. It damn near killed her not to run, but she forced herself to stand stock-still.

Vamps had a well-developed prey drive; running would trip it. Her best chance was them not noticing her. Brief jolts of shielded power told her three of them—Raphael and two others whose energy she didn't recognize—were headed right for the path to the prison cells, but on the main street. She felt certain they intended to interrogate her. Predicated on the outcome, she'd have ended up their next meal.

If she'd been there.

She suppressed the shudder threatening to make her teeth chatter and give her away. Waiting was hard, and she didn't have much time. Vamps moved fast. It wouldn't take long before they discovered her gone. Ketha wasn't under any illusions about what would happen once they found the empty cell. Raphael would explode, his fury driving him to hunt her with single-minded intensity.

The moment the Vamps were on the trail, she raced down the alley, running for all she was worth. Her chest burned, but she forced her legs to pump faster. Having the Vamps throw her back into a cell—or murder her on the spot—provided more than enough motivation. Familiar landmarks flashed by until she reached the first manhole cover on the edges of the more developed part of what had once been Ushuaia.

Ketha blasted the concrete round out of the way with magic and clambered down the ladder like a monkey, instructing the cover to reseat itself to conceal her escape route. She didn't need as much warding down here because she could borrow earth magic to hide herself. Not having to bleed off power for shielding would free up more energy to run. It also meant her mage light would do a better job illuminating her way. Fear of discovery imposed limits on how much light she could deploy, but the tunnels were the remains of a sewer system, and their surface was far from even. Navigating them, while moving fast, required concentration. And light.

She'd barely escaped, the margin narrow enough to turn her blood to ice. If her last casting—the one where she'd summoned water to join earth and fire—hadn't worked straight away, she would've been on the path and met the Vamps head-on.

Or I'd still have been in my cell.

She shivered from far more than cold permeating the warren of tunnels beneath the city. Was she close enough to her sisters to risk telepathy? Ketha had no idea, mostly because she didn't know where the other Shifters were. She needed a destination, a place she could stop and catch her breath and clear her racing thoughts.

Catch my breath, maybe, but I can't stop. Not for long, anyway. I'll never be safe anywhere near Ushuaia. Not after today.

Truth in her thoughts rocked her to her foundations. Maybe contacting her sisters was a bad idea. They'd be as vulnerable as she was if she reconnected with them. Ketha reconstructed her last vision. The one that had risen from her glass. She had to locate that mesa. It was the key to everything. Only problem was, she'd never seen any place like that anywhere around the city.

"Just because I haven't seen it doesn't mean it doesn't exist." The sound of her voice steadied her. Having a goal helped too. If her vision that included the mesa was truly the key to defeating the barrier—and escaping *Ciudad de Huesos* and Raphael—it meant her sisters were part of the solution.

They'd been in her vision. All of them. She'd have to come up with Vamps too, but she could only face one problem at a time.

Hoping she'd interpreted the signs about the mesa correctly, Ketha ran until she was very close to the place she and the Shifters had taken refuge. When little more than a wooden doorway stood between her and stairs leading to the women's underground grotto, she stopped and called for Rowana with her mind.

The other Shifter didn't answer, so Ketha tried again. Over the next span of time, she cycled through everyone's name, but no one responded.

Fear clutched at Ketha, turning her stomach into a roiling, burning mass of tension.

Crap! Did the Vamps kill everybody?

She didn't see how since Aura, Rowana, and Karin had appeared an hour or two before in her glass. Beyond that, Vampires preferred their victims alive.

Ketha's power was dwindling. She marshaled what she could and warded herself before creeping through the wooden door and up the stairs leading to her room, ready to bolt at the first indication of Vamp energy.

The wards on her room remained intact. She stopped long enough to inhale its familiar smells and test the hall leading to their common room. If Vamps had been here, they'd covered their tracks well. Ketha couldn't see them being that careful, and she began to breathe easier.

"You're correct," the wolf corroborated. *"No Vampires here. Not for a long time."*

Knowing her bondmate was within and vigilant drove her forward. She'd felt it withdraw from everything months back. *"I've missed you,"* she murmured, but it didn't reply.

A transit of the rest of their home convinced her that her sisters had escaped. Most of their slender possessions were gone, along with all their food stores, which suggested the women had time to pack. Ketha scanned with magic to convince herself she hadn't missed anything.

Something glimmered under the force of her spell, and she trotted to the long table they'd once sat around. A series of numbers flickered once, twice, and went out in a burst of Rowana's characteristic magic. Ketha smiled grimly as she committed the coordinates to memory.

She plodded back to the room she'd occupied for years. Exhaustion dragged at her, but she couldn't tarry. If things were bad enough her sisters had fled, she needed to at least make her way back to the tunnels. She rustled through a cracked dresser, taking what she wanted and stuffing things into an ancient backpack.

With the pack nearly full, Ketha looked longingly at her spell book. It had been with her since her moon blood began to flow, and she came into her own as a Shifter, bonding with her wolf. Because she couldn't bear to leave it, she dropped it atop assorted clothing, herbs, and other magical assists.

She shouldered the pack, staggering slightly beneath its weight. If she had to run like she had earlier, she'd abandon it, but she was too tired to plan that far ahead. Intent on rest, she scooped her threadbare quilt and lumpy pillow off the bed and tottered down the stairs and out the door, sprinkling power to mask ever having been there as she went.

Her mage light was dim, reflective of her waning magic, when she stumbled into a stairwell a quarter mile from where she'd lived. Partway up, she stopped on a landing and dropped her pile of bedding and backpack onto it.

The wolf was back. Maybe it would watch over her and warn her of danger. The ward she created to keep her invisible was sloppy, but she fell asleep before she could craft anything more elegant.

7

WHAT ARE FRIENDS FOR?

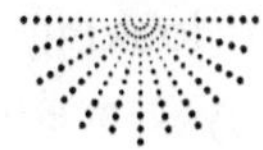

VIKTOR SPENT the last few hours of the night cutting the jaguar meat into strips. Eventually, he'd dry it for longer storage, but there wasn't any rush. Cold would keep the meat from rotting over the short term, and he planned to package up a lot of it for Ketha. Hunting with Raphael hadn't been any worse than usual. At least the Master Vamp had drained the big cat quickly and cleanly, tossing the carcass to Viktor in clear dismissal.

For once, Raphael hadn't kept any of the meat for himself. Maybe he was sated on blood, but surely he had to understand he'd be hungry again before the next moonrise. Granted, Raphael preferred blood over everything else, but his uncharacteristic generosity set Viktor's nerves on edge.

His sire was up to something; the question was what.

Puzzling through possibilities, Victor returned with the jaguar, tapping Juan to help finish the task. Bellies full for the first time in weeks, they went in search of Raphael to receive their next set of orders.

Their sire wasn't in his quarters, though. A cursory search of the building and Raph's usual haunts turned up nothing. He and

Juan combed the docks. Maybe Raph was torturing one of the poor unfortunate sods he kept locked in the bunker.

Viktor caught a glimpse of Glenn, another Vampire, and cupped a hand around his mouth. "Seen Raphael, lately?"

"Yep. Sure have. He passed by here an hour ago on his way to interrogate the Shifter." White-blond dreads trailed down Glenn's back, and his green eyes held calculation.

"Thanks. Saves me time looking for him." Spinning in his tracks, Viktor sauntered away. Once he was out of Glenn's sight, he took off like greased lightning with Juan right behind him.

Viktor ran so fast, his legs were a blur, but speed couldn't quiet his racing thoughts.

Juan caught up, grabbed him by the shoulder, and spun him around. "Bad idea, *amigo*."

"You don't get it." Viktor tried to break free, but Juan's grip was like being shackled to a boulder.

"Of course, I get it." Juan moved his mouth close to Viktor's ear. "Raph went to the cells, and you're frantic about what he'll do."

Viktor's vision hazed with fury. "She fascinates him, but he hates her because of it."

Juan dropped his other hand on Viktor's upper arm. "There is nothing you can do," he said, inserting a pause between each word. "What? Are you planning to charge in there like the cavalry? He's your sire, for chrissakes. Mine too. You know what'll happen if he catches even a whiff you might cross him."

Viktor's shoulders sagged, and he quit struggling. He had to remain alive, head attached to his shoulders. If Raph killed him, and he was more than capable of that, there'd be no one to shepherd Ketha to the protected mesa.

Juan let go and jerked his chin back the way they'd come.

"I can't leave her there," Viktor protested, fighting a welter of frantic feelings that made him long for the iron blade to end Raphael.

"You have no choice." Juan's hazel eyes bored into Viktor. "If Raph kills you, you won't be any help to anyone."

"Yeah. The same thought crossed my mind. So I just hope for the best, eh?" Viktor choked back bitter laughter.

"That's exactly what you do." Juan kept his voice low. "We return to town and pretend we could give a shit less what Raph is up to. Later today, after he's occupied with something else, that's the time for us to make sure the Shifter is all right."

Viktor glanced up the mountain toward where the cells were, battling conflicting priorities. When Juan tugged on his arm, he followed him muttering, "If that bastard harms Ketha in any way, I won't rest until he's dead."

"He won't damage her. Not yet anyway." Juan sounded certain.

"Why not?"

"She's a novelty." Juan shrugged. "They're few and far between these days. Once he kills her, game's over."

Viktor turned it over in his mind. Perhaps his friend was right. Viktor had been reacting, so taken by Ketha, his primary focus was spiriting her to the mesa where she'd be safe.

Safe, so long as he was very careful how he orchestrated things.

The specter of Raphael in the cell with her, doing God only knew what, had pushed him to an ugly place, one where protecting her overshadowed everything, and he'd gone a little nuts.

He cast a sheepish look Juan's way. "Thanks."

"*De nada.* What are friends for?"

"I have no idea. You're the only one I have left."

Sadness flickered across Juan's face, but it left fast, and the other Vamp quickened his steps.

Viktor's nostrils flared with disgust. He'd caved under Juan's arguments, but he wasn't any happier about it now than he'd been when he reluctantly turned around. A rock sat square in his path, and he kicked it out of the way, wishing it were his sire's head.

The air near him blurred, and Raphael took shape, dripping menace. "Nice, you finally detached yourself from the jaguar meat. That is where you were, right?"

Magic blasted into Viktor's head, sharp with the unpolished clumsiness of a Vampire truth spell. He stole a sidelong glance at his sire. What the hell had happened? Raphael's eyes were gray storm clouds, all traces of blue long gone.

Viktor rubbed his temples and tried for an injured look. "Why'd you do that? I was dressing out the jaguar, just like you said."

"What about you?" Raphael grabbed Juan's arm and spun him around.

"I've been with Viktor. Once we finished with the jaguar, we went looking for you like we do every morning." Juan trained candid eyes on their sire.

Determination to find out what happened burned a path through Viktor, but he knew better than to appear too eager. Raphael was deranged enough, he'd blurt something out sooner or later.

"Now that we've located you," Viktor said evenly, "what are today's priorities?"

Raphael sputtered, seemingly beyond forming words. He gestured with both hands before dropping them to his sides. "We have a problem. Fixing it is today's priority." His voice—once he located it—held the deadly quiet quality Viktor had come to dread. "Find the Shifter."

"What Shifter?" Juan asked, and Viktor could've high-fived him.

Raphael's perfect skin turned an unattractive shade of red. "The one from up there." He stabbed an index finger toward the mountain and shimmered into nothingness.

Two other Vamps ran onto the quay moments after Raphael disappeared. "Fuck!" Mario spat out the word. Dark hair streamed behind him, and fury flashed from his dark eyes.

"Fuck, indeed," Gene seconded. "Christ! Raph was out of there before we could figure out what happened. I hate it that he can move like a goddamned wraith when we have to run the old-fashioned way." As fair as the other Vamp was dark, Gene's blond hair was hacked off to uneven lengths. Both Vamps wore a mish-mash of rags held together with tape.

Viktor tamped down elation racing through him. Apparently, Ketha had engineered her own escape. "What happened?" he asked, seeking corroboration for his suspicions. "I've rarely seen our sire in such a temper."

Mario tossed his hands skyward. "We were going to ask the Shifter a few questions. Raph wanted details about the Vamp-Shifter coalition she claimed started the Cataclysm."

"Yeah," Gene chimed in, blue eyes glittering with glee. "We were going to hurt her a little. Make her squeal."

"Except she wasn't there," Mario said. "Poked a hell of a hole in our sport for the day."

"Any idea how long ago she escaped?" Juan asked. "Or which way she went?"

Mario made an unattractive snorting sound. "Raph left way too fast for any detective work."

"We were all about catching him." Gene screwed his face into a frown.

"No problem." Juan made shooing motions with one hand. "Why don't the two of you see if you can calm Raphael down? Viktor and I will check the cell for clues."

"Hey! That'd be great." Mario clapped Juan on the shoulder. "We'll take our time before we approach Raphael, though. Maybe he'll regain some perspective if we give him an hour or three."

"Good plan. If we show up now, he'll probably have us wash the floor with our tongues. After he's pissed on it." Gene dissolved into guffaws over his own joke and set off for the center of town, still laughing. Mario followed him.

Viktor didn't say a word. Vampires had excellent hearing, and he didn't want to give anything away. Not his elation. Nor his relief. This latest development meant he had to find Ketha to ensure her safety, but that felt simple enough. Particularly compared with his previous plan that had included springing her from her cell.

No need to do that anymore.

He turned and ran along the quay toward the track to the cells. Juan loped by his side. Viktor's head still hurt from Raphael's blundering truth spell. They were halfway up the dirt track to the cells when Juan ventured, "Seems to have worked out all right."

Viktor angled his head, speaking low. "Raph won't rest until she's dead."

"I know. Not many places to hide, either, on this side of the barrier. No one can cross it and live. Make no mistake, Raph will set every Vamp in *Ciudad de Huesos* after her, probably with some delectable prize for whoever captures her."

Viktor didn't reply. What could he say? That his next move after ensuring Ketha's safety would be to kill his sire? The less Juan knew, the better. He didn't want his friend compromised. They reached the opening to the tunnel leading to the cells. The barred gate stood wide open, and Viktor inhaled, sorting scents.

"Yeah," Juan muttered. "I tried that. Most of what I smell is Raphael's fury. Eau de carrion raised to the nth power."

Viktor tamped back a wry grin. The stench of the Master Vamp's anger was overpowering, but beneath it, Viktor caught the wildflower and beech tree scents unique to Ketha. He ached for her but didn't understand why. Vampirism should have moved him beyond caring about anyone.

"Don't fight it," Juan murmured.

"I have no idea what you're talking about." Viktor ducked through the tunnel and walked briskly to his old cell.

"You care about her. It's a gift that you can still feel anything for anyone," Juan continued.

Viktor didn't reply, mostly because the topic made him uncomfortable. He stared at the open cell door and tried to shut it, but the locking mechanism was broken. When he touched the pad to reset it, nothing happened. He whistled long and low. "Jesus! She broke it with magic."

"It appears so. Maybe you didn't notice, but she did the same thing to the main gate." Juan strode into the cell, glancing around. "She didn't leave anything." He picked up a cloth sack from the dirt floor. "And she ate what I left for her."

"Maybe food gave her the energy she needed to escape." Viktor breathed deep, letting her scent fill his lungs.

"Do you suppose she returned to the Shifters' enclave?" Juan walked to the waterfall cascading down the back wall and drank, slurping noisily.

"I doubt it. She's smart enough to know it's the first place we'd hunt for her—assuming we could find it. One Shifter is easier to hide than twelve." Viktor creased his forehead, thinking. "Bet wherever they lived is empty. Hopefully, Ketha told them she'd been captured, and they were smart enough to go to ground. I wouldn't put it beyond Raph to send a posse to smoke out the women."

Juan grimaced. "Think what he could do with the bunch of them. Watching someone near and dear to you tortured does tend to loosen the tongue."

Viktor balled his hands into fists. "It only works like that if they know anything useful. Maybe Ketha didn't tell the rest of them where she is. Jesus! How the fuck did we end up like this? Enslaved to that soulless monster."

"You don't really want me to answer that. We had a choice. That choice was life, so we grabbed it."

"And turned into monsters ourselves."

"It's not the same, and you know it. We're Vampires, yeah, but I see differences in some of us."

"Eh, maybe we haven't been Vamps long enough for evil to percolate all the way into our souls. Come on, Juan. We can talk while we're tracking."

Viktor sprinted out of the cell and through the tunnel. He thought about Juan's words as he raced down the winding trail. Once he was back on asphalt, he stopped long enough to ascertain Ketha had worked her way around the base of the mountain. She'd kept to back-streets clogged with piles of desiccated bones.

"The thing is"—Juan drew alongside him—"who we were before shaped who we are as Vampires. I'm pretty sure that wasn't true before the Cataclysm. Any Vamps created back then were all badasses. Rotten clean through."

Viktor cast an appraising glance his way. "Do you spend much time thinking about stuff like that?"

Color stained Juan's stubble-covered cheeks. "Not a lot, but some." He inhaled audibly. "I spend more time missing being at sea."

"The Southern Ocean, it gets into your blood," Viktor agreed. "We still have a ship in dry dock here. I visit her occasionally."

Juan's eyes widened, and he grinned. "I thought I was the only one who snuck in to check on *Arkady*."

"I'm there often enough, I'm surprised we haven't run into each other. It's the only place Raph's never followed me. Vamps hate ships, probably because water mutes their ability, but I've been careful to keep *Arkady's* presence a secret."

"Me too," Juan muttered. "It's been a relief to have somewhere to retreat to when I wanted to be invisible for a while."

Viktor exhaled sharply. "If it weren't for the barrier, I'd have sailed out of here long since. Taken my chances with the wind and tides."

"If you ever decide to do that"—Juan's tone turned deadly serious—"take me with you."

"Deal." Viktor shifted course, following Ketha's scent behind a concrete-block building. Her presence was stronger here, indicating she'd paused her headlong flight.

"Wonder why she stopped here," Juan murmured.

"I bet she sensed Raph and the other two. They were probably only a few streets over, following the main boulevard." Pain for Ketha jabbed him. She must have steel balls to have remained immobile with Vamps only a few hundred yards away.

"She went this way from here." Juan pointed and set off at a lope.

Viktor caught up. If it was this easy for them to track her, how the fuck could he hope to hide her from Raphael's wrath? He wished he understood how Shifter magic worked. She had ways of warding herself, but that particular magic didn't mask traces of her presence once she'd left a place.

Juan circled a manhole cover, shaking his head. "I don't get it. Her trail went cold. I thought maybe I could pick it up if I checked a full three hundred sixty degrees, but it's gone."

Viktor bent and dragged the heavy manhole cover aside. "Mystery solved." He angled a thumb through the hole. "She went that way."

Juan jumped through the opening, laughing. "No wonder you like her. You two think the same. You use these underground walkways too, as I recall."

"Ssht. Never know who might hear you." Viktor clung to the ladder and jimmied the cover back over the hole. He dialed in his Vamp vision to see in the suddenly black-as-night space and climbed down to where Juan waited.

The warren of tunnels was familiar, and Viktor led the way down branching side paths until they stood next to a wooden door painted with runic markings. He'd been through this portion of the tunnel system before and chalked the runes up to some pre-Cataclysm magic-wielder.

Juan, who'd been silent since Viktor shushed him, pointed at the door and raised his eyebrows. Viktor shrugged, not at all certain they could enter the Shifters' lair. For all he knew, it was spelled to destroy anyone who tried to get in.

He closed his eyes and listened intently. Other than the chittering of bats, rats, and mice, the old sewer system lay silent. If this had been where the Shifters lived, they'd left. And not all that long ago since many Shifter scents mingled with Ketha's.

"It's odd." He kept his voice very low.

"What's odd?" Juan whispered back.

"I've been through this section of tunnels hundreds of times and never caught a whiff of Shifter."

"Which proves they're not here," Juan replied.

Viktor agreed. If they were, their magic would have masked their presence. He placed tentative fingers on the latch, fully expecting it to burn him or freeze him or explode. Nothing happened. When he twisted the knob, it turned easily, opening to a metal staircase. Viktor started up it. No point in masking his presence. If he was wrong, and Shifters remained above, they'd sense him with their superior magic.

One more door and he stood in a small chamber. A bed and dresser took up virtually all the floor space, and Ketha's scent was overpowering. He resisted an urge to lie on her bed and breathe her in, but his cock thickened with wanting her.

Juan walked past him, opening a door on the far side of the room. Viktor followed him through. It led to a long hallway dotted with closed doors, which in turn led to what must've been the women's common area. A table reached from one end to the other. As he'd suspected, the grotto was deserted. The absence of items suggested the Shifters had abandoned it for good.

"Where do you suppose they went?" Juan asked.

"No idea, but I bet Ketha knows," Viktor replied, adding, "They communicate telepathically. We should keep moving."

"Which way?"

It was a reasonable question. Viktor walked to yet another

door he figured led up and out and inhaled, hunting for fresh traces of Ketha's scent. He smelled her here, but he smelled her everywhere in the Shifters' home. Her energy folded around him like a homing beacon, comforting and arousing by turns. The erection that had formed in her bedroom throbbed hotly between his legs.

He shifted his focus, putting himself in her place. She'd taken to the tunnels as soon as she could move about unnoticed. That likely meant she'd continue to use them. "Let's go back down," Viktor said, and retraced his steps.

"It's as good a plan as any," Juan agreed. "If she stayed in the tunnel, we'll catch her scent past where we detoured in here."

Viktor stepped into her bedroom and pulled dresser drawers open. Clothing remained, but the dresser was half-empty. Either she hadn't had much to begin with, or she'd taken things with her. Juan walked past him and clattered down steel risers to the tunnel system below. Viktor felt like a fool, but he couldn't stop himself from closing a hand over a threadbare flannel shirt and burying his face in it.

Ketha blasted into his brain. He could see her, feel her, taste her, and his cock jerked in his trousers, on the verge of release. He'd ignored the sexual side of himself since being turned, but it refused to take a back seat anymore. Some of the Vampires amused themselves by fucking, but he'd always shunned their invitations.

"Hurry," Juan called in a stage whisper. "She went this way."

Telling his overheated libido to take a hike, Viktor hurried down the stairs, shutting the door behind him.

"What were you doing?" Juan asked.

"Nothing important." Viktor ran through the tunnel, tracking traces of wildflowers and Antarctic beech. He was moving so fast, he almost missed where she'd turned hard left and passed beneath one of many archways lining the underground passageway.

"I smelled her out there"—Juan jerked his chin behind them —"but not right now. What happened?"

Viktor placed a finger over his mouth. If he was right about how Ketha's warding worked, she might be very close. Muted rustling from above them drew his attention, and he raced up one flight of stairs.

Ketha—her mouth stretched into a horrified moue—was half in and half out of a welter of quilts, dragging a backpack into place.

"Excellent!" Juan said softly. "We found you."

"Don't," she moaned, flinching away from both of them. "Kill me, but don't deliver me to that monster."

"We're not going to hurt you." Viktor reached for her, desperate to draw her against him, comfort her, erase the wounded-deer look from her face.

Ketha didn't fall into his arms like he hoped. Instead, she let go of her pack and flattened herself into a corner, fear streaming off her. The human part of him, the part that still felt, withered under her reaction. How could she believe he meant her harm? Or worse, that he'd hand her over to Raphael?

Ketha straightened her spine and looked from him to Juan. "Does that mean you'll let me leave? And not tell Raphael you found me? If not"—she skinned her lips back from her teeth—"my wolf stands ready, and we won't give up without a fight." The air around her shimmered with power, and a low, ominous growl rose from her throat.

"What it means," Viktor said reining in his churning emotions, "is we need to talk. If you still want to leave after that, neither of us will try to stop you."

He stared at the charged air, electric with promise. If he looked from a certain angle, the outline of a snarling wolf flashed in and out of view. An irrational urge to coax the wolf into the open and bury his hands in its fur rocked him to his core. He wanted the woman standing proud before him, wanted all of her with a single-mindedness that consumed him.

Viktor dragged a lungful of air deep, following it with two more to center himself and quell longing that would only get in the way. "We need to talk," he repeated, gratified she hadn't shut him out or told him to forget he'd ever met her.

8

NO GOOD CHOICES

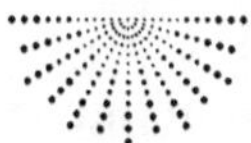

Voices dragged Ketha from sleep right before her Vampire alarm went off, shooting her heart into triple-time rhythm. Somewhere in the mix, her wolf shouted a warning.

Goddamn it.

She shouldn't have stopped to sleep, but she'd burned through so much magic escaping and warding herself, she hadn't had a choice. Power levied a price. If she didn't respect it, she would've fallen on her face without enough magic left to light a candle, much less create an invisibility illusion.

Viktor raced up the stairs and reached for her with Juan right behind him. Fear overshadowed need, and Ketha shrank away from his touch. Backed against the wall, she shuffled through options, desperate for clues that would ensure her survival.

"I'm here," the wolf spoke up. *"Ready to shift."*

"It's all right," she reassured her bondmate. *"Maybe, but not yet."*

At least it was Viktor and Juan who'd found her. Not Raphael and the two goons he'd had with him earlier. She sucked in air to steady herself and clear her mind, still fuzzy from sleep. It couldn't be a good thing the Vamps were here. Surely their presence was far more than coincidence.

"You must have been hunting for me." Ketha set a truth spell, wanting to make certain they didn't mislead her.

Viktor nodded. "Raphael hates to be outfoxed. Juan and I volunteered to look for you."

"Where are the others?" Juan asked.

Ketha narrowed her eyes. He couldn't be asking about Vampires. "If you're referring to my sisters, why should I tell you?"

"Because your options aren't great right now," Viktor replied. "Neither are theirs. We need to plan our next steps, but it's too open here."

"Well it sure as hell isn't safe in my old home. You went there first, right? You tracked me, so you must have."

"We did." Juan trained his gaze on Viktor. "You know these tunnels better than me. Where can we take her and not run the risk of discovery?"

The corners of Viktor's mouth twisted downward. "*Arkady* is our best bet."

"Who's that?" Ketha's suspicions flared. "The fewer who know you found me, the better."

"*Arkady* isn't a person. It's my ship. The one that wasn't wrecked during the Cataclysm. It's sitting in dry dock adjacent to the harbor."

Juan scrunched his forehead in thought and finally shrugged. "I don't have much in the way of bearings down here. How far is it?"

"Maybe half a mile."

"Can we stay in the tunnels?" Ketha asked, still not sure she could trust the two Vamps.

"We can," Viktor assured her.

Ketha closed her teeth over her lower lip, considering the ramifications of Viktor's ship. "Why is *Arkady* safe, and what are the odds of running into other Vampires down here?"

"It's safe because no one knows about it. Beyond that, Vamps hate water," Juan answered. "It reduces their speed and other abilities. Even though *Arkady* isn't exactly in the water, it's close enough to discourage them."

"Does that apply to the old ones?" Ketha asked.

"It's worse for them than us," Viktor said. "To address your second question, I've never run into anyone down here before, but I bet Raphael's sicced his entire force on you by now."

"How many Vampires are there?" Ketha inhaled shakily, not sure she really wanted to know.

"Something over a hundred. We've never run a census, so I don't have an exact figure," Juan replied.

"What happens if I say no?" Ketha edged toward her pack and slipped it over her shoulders. Leaving the bedding was a bad idea since it smelled like her, so she pushed everything down the stairs and barked a few words in Gaelic. The worn comforter and pillow burst into flames. She added to her spell, instructing it to burn fast and obliterate any trace of her remaining in the ashes.

Viktor hadn't approached her since he'd held out his arms when he and Juan first found her. Ketha craved the comfort he offered, but anything that sidetracked her from staying alive wasn't wise. He was a beautiful man. Too bad she hadn't met him when he was still human.

"This ship," she said. "The one Vamps don't know about. How big is it?"

"It'll hold sixty-plus passengers and twenty-five crew," Viktor rattled off without stopping to think about it.

Breath whooshed from her. "Must be huge."

"I'm guessing you've never been at sea. As ocean-going vessels go, *Arkady* is on the smaller side." Viktor motioned her back down the stairs and took off at a fast clip in the general direction of the docks.

"I did plenty of sailing as a girl, but it was on lakes. That's likely not the same thing."

"The Southern Ocean is rough," Juan cut in. "Viktor owned

two converted Russian research vessels with ice-strengthened hulls. Before the Cataclysm, laws governed which types of ships could sail in this region."

"Why'd you want to know how big the ship was?" Viktor asked.

Ketha aimed for nonchalance and muttered, "No particular reason." In truth, she'd thought it might make a perfect hideout for the Shifters, but she'd be damned if she'd reveal their location until she was positive they weren't walking into a trap. For all she knew, Viktor could be employing Vampire charm and coercion to lull her into a false sense of security.

"Of course you had a reason. You don't trust me, and I don't blame you. If our situations were reversed, I'd have a healthy dose of skepticism too." Viktor placed a hand beneath her elbow and turned her down a side corridor. "Not much farther."

Juan came to a halt a few feet ahead. Without turning, he slashed a hand downward, behind his back.

Ketha draped an invisibility spell around herself, blending into one of many stairwells dotting the passageway. So long as she didn't move, she should be safe from discovery. Thank the goddess, Vamp magic was so primitive.

Viktor chugged around her and joined Juan. The two chatted about the jaguar they'd dressed out the previous night.

"Awesome! More hands, eyes, and fangs. You must be hunting that Houdini Shifter too. Have you found anything?" An unfamiliar voice rang from the corridor ahead.

"Nope," Viktor called back. "You?"

"If you ask me, this ain't nothing but a fucking wild goose chase," another voice cut in.

"Don't complain, dude," the first voice muttered. "At least it got us away from Raphael for a while."

"Shit," Juan said. "Hasn't that old fucker settled down yet?"

"No." Voice Two sounded weary—and annoyed. Ketha resisted

the temptation to peek into his head. She needed to keep all of herself, magic included, safe within her spell.

"How many of us are hunting?" Viktor's tone was casual, but he was definitely trolling for information that might help them.

"Everyone who's not asleep," the first voice answered.

"Speaking of which, we'd best get back at it." Voice Two made an audible sniffing noise. "I do smell Shifters down here."

"That's because we stumbled on their lair down thataway." Juan made a grunting sound. "Looks like they left in a hell of a hurry. Didn't leave much but a pile of smoking ashes."

"Food?" Voice One asked hopefully.

"We didn't stick around long enough to check, but help your-selves," Viktor replied.

"Who else is down here?" Juan asked.

"We thought it was just us," the second voice said. "Most of the others don't much like these old sewers. They still smell like crap."

"We wouldn't be here," Voice One chimed in, "but Raph was insistent. Leave no stone unturned and all that happy horseshit."

"Well you can join the hunt topside once you've checked out the Shifters' place," Viktor suggested, a smidge of Vampire compulsion hiding beneath his words. "We were pretty thorough, and we're damn near done here."

"Hey! Great news!" Laughter was followed by, "Topside, eh? Once a sailor, always a sailor." Ketha heard hands slapping together and the heavy tread of two sets of boots racing past where she'd hidden herself. Vamps might not be stealthy, but damn they were fast.

She waited through a count of fifty before she crept out of her alcove, but she didn't drop her invisibility illusion. *I know you can hear me this way.* She spoke telepathically into Viktor's mind. *You won't see me or sense me, but I'll be right behind you.*

After a hesitation, garbled words slapped into her head.

"Slow down," she instructed. *"Visualize the words as if they were written on a blackboard, and then push them my way."*

His next effort was much better. *"How will I know if you get into trouble?"*

"Because I'll squeal like a stuck pig. Hurry."

The next span of time blurred past. Maintaining her spell and running as fast as she could to keep up with the Vamps took everything she had. The heavy pack didn't help, but she couldn't very well ask one of the men to carry it. Her spell book reeked of Shifter magic. Maybe she could find a safe spot on the ship to leave her things.

Her suspicions about Viktor's motives receded, but only a little. He'd lied to protect her back there. And done what he could to gain information that would help them. Did he have some ulterior motive? If so, what was it?

Her mental process stuttered to a halt. Were she and the two Vamps becoming a *them* in her mind? Ketha instructed herself to keep her guard firmly in place. She'd had a definite fall from grace when she threw herself into Viktor's arms in her cell. She'd have to exercise care it didn't happen again.

Not until I know a whole lot more.

Maybe not even then.

Juan and Viktor took a sharp right and started up a ladder. Must mean they were at least close to this ship of his. An inconsistency rattled around in her mind, finally taking form. Viktor had said his ship was in dry dock, which meant it might not be anywhere near the ocean. Juan's explanation about why Vamps avoided it had been lame. How could they not know about something that big? A sinking feeling tightened her gut into an uncomfortable lump.

Was he leading her into a trap?

Maybe she'd do well to fade back into the corridor and do the best she could on her own. Ketha stopped climbing and gripped the ladder's rungs, undecided.

"Where are you?" formed in her mind. *"We're here, but I can't see*

you." Viktor's mind voice sounded worried, but maybe that was part of his game to snare her somewhere escape wasn't possible. Then they'd drain her and pick her bones clean...

Ketha shook her head hard to dislodge the disquieting image. Fear left a metallic taste in the back of her mouth as she battled a desire to run as far and as fast as she could from Viktor and Juan. What she'd do after that wasn't clear, but safety wasn't measured in days right now. She'd take all the minutes she could collect and spin them into hours. Days would follow—if she were very fortunate.

"It's all right," the wolf spoke slowly, *"if they were bad men, I'd know."*

Ketha wanted to believe her bondmate, but apprehension kept her rooted in place.

"Damn it." Viktor's voice was low. "How could we have lost her?"

"Maybe we moved too fast," Juan replied. "Let's go back and make sure she didn't miss that last turn to climb into the dry dock building."

"Crap. We're safe for now. We need to be aboard *Arkady*, not out here talking, but we can't leave her out there. Not with a hundred Vamps breathing down her ass. She has to sleep sometime, and then they'll find her. Exactly like we did."

Truth pinged off his words. He hadn't said he wouldn't hurt her, but she was vulnerable by herself—for exactly the reason he'd stated. The Shifters had posted sentries for years. One woman and her bond animal watched over her sisters, ready to alert them if a threat presented itself.

But that had been when the threat level was manageable. Ketha didn't feel right foisting her current peril off onto anyone. Hell, it wasn't right to compromise Viktor or Juan, but they'd involved themselves.

Yeah, and they did it for me.

The revelation broke through her ambivalence, and she dragged herself up the last twenty rungs, coming out into an enormous warehouse. Juan and Viktor were heading right for her at a trot, so she let go of her illusion.

"There you are." Viktor feinted sideways so he wouldn't run into her. Relief thrummed beneath his words, and it reassured her she'd made the right choice—at least for now.

"I'll close things up." Juan kicked a heavy metal round over the opening she'd climbed through.

Ketha gazed around the interior of a staunch concrete and metal structure, kindling her mage light to see better. Viktor blinked, looking away from her light, and she recalled Vampires' supernatural sensory abilities. He could see fine without extra illumination. The sound of waves crashing against walls meant the structure was partially underwater.

"See?" Her wolf was back. *"This will be fine. You should trust me."*

Ketha sent warm, wordless thoughts inward. Maybe what Viktor and Juan had said about why Vamps avoided this ship wasn't as spurious as it had sounded.

Dead center in a ramp-like affair sat a ship, rising so far above them, she couldn't see the top. A long, low whistle escaped her. "However did you get it in here?"

"Ships float into dry dock," Juan replied. "A set of pumps pushes water back into the ocean and exposes the hull for repairs."

She strode closer to the ship, examining a hull that extended well above her head. "The pumps can't still be functional. There's so little electricity. Why isn't this platform flooded with seawater?"

"The building is watertight and was well constructed. The pumps were converted to run on wind power before the Cataclysm," Viktor explained. "Normally, *Arkady* would've been in Germany when the Cataclysm hit, but a hole in its hull had to be repaired before it was seaworthy enough to cross the Atlantic.

That's the only reason it ended up here. Come this way." He beckoned and walked toward the rear of the ship where a rope ladder led upward.

"Germany, huh? Is that where you're from? You have a bare hint of an accent."

He nodded and tugged on her pack. "Indeed it is, but I haven't been back for more than a handful of days at a time in years. Obviously, not at all since the Cataclysm. Let me have your backpack."

Ketha unbuckled the pack's waist belt, handing it over. Light flashed from the pack once Viktor slung it across a shoulder.

"What the hell was that?" Juan demanded.

Ketha snorted. "My spell book is in there. It doesn't care much for Vampires, or any magic-wielders other than me."

"A book made that light?" Juan raised his eyebrows into question marks.

"Yup." Ketha patted the rucksack. She had no idea what the ancient tome would do next and reached for the pack, ready to take it back.

"Apparently, it's sentient." Viktor sounded amused and gestured for Ketha to start up the ladder leading into his ship. "Maybe if the book senses it's following you, it won't turn me into a rock."

Ketha grasped the ropes trailing down the ship's side and began to climb. She wasn't certain her spell book had the ability to do much of anything without her guiding its efforts, but anything was possible. She clambered over a slotted railing and onto a green-painted concrete deck, waiting until Viktor and Juan joined her. Without pausing, the men ran across the deck and through a door at its far end.

She followed them into the ship and up several flights of steep, narrow stairs into a well-appointed cabin on the top deck. Inlaid with dark, polished wood, the space held a bed, shelves, a desk, and a welter of electronics that might have been navigational equipment. Everything in the cabin shone. The absence of dust said Viktor visited here often.

"This was yours." Ketha trained her gaze on him.

He nodded, looking pleased. "It was. Juan was my chief navigator and radioman. His cabin is across the hall."

"It's lovely and well-kept," she said, selecting her words with care, "but surely you gave up returning to the sea after the Cataclysm. Did the hull ever get repaired?"

"Yeah, all the patchwork was done months before the Cataclysm, but we were in the Arctic with *Gavrill*, our other ship. In terms of leaving, Viktor would float this baby out of here if he thought he could split the barrier," Juan replied.

"That's a huge if," Viktor said. "As things stand, the magic would twist *Arkady* around and spit her out, like it did with *Gavrill*. I still have no idea how we made it across the mountains and into Ushuaia. It's almost as if the barrier was still establishing itself those first few days. If it was anything like it is now, we'd all have died—"

"The magic was in flux for at least the first two weeks after the Cataclysm formed," Ketha cut in. "We saw it happening and guessed wrong."

"What do you mean?" Juan asked.

"We—the other Shifters and I—assumed it would dissipate, and we'd be able to rent a car and drive north out of here. Or get on a plane. Instead, it grew steadily worse until nothing could penetrate it." She took a measured breath. "I could communicate beyond Ushuaia for several years after we were trapped here. I stole what I needed from an electronic shop and fashioned a ham radio setup."

"I did much the same, but with *Arkady's* radio equipment," Viktor said.

"So you found out that the Cataclysm did pretty much the same thing all over the globe." She eyed him.

He nodded. "I never actually talked with anyone, but I picked up radio broadcasts."

"They were petering out about the same time my primitive setup failed." She rolled her shoulders to relieve an iron bar of tension sitting between them.

"Petering out because?" Juan raised one eyebrow.

"I suspect the Cataclysm doesn't want us to join forces with anyone. It's sentient, which means it's able to modify itself."

Viktor removed her pack from his shoulder and set it down. "That's a chilling thought."

He turned to Juan, directing his next words at the other Vamp. "What I'm about to tell her will implicate you if Raph grills you."

"So?" Juan inclined his head.

"So, I'm giving you a choice. You can leave the cabin. I'm certain Ketha can ward it so you can't hear what we say. It's probably safest for you."

"Nope. I'm already in so deep, I can't see where one more thing will make much difference. Besides, the main thing Raphael will want to know is if we found her."

"Maybe so." Viktor turned both of the room's chairs toward the bed and perched on its edge. "Settle in. This won't take long."

Ketha took one of the indicated chairs. Juan stood behind his.

"When I left your cell—" Viktor cleared his throat and started again, but color stained his cheeks. "I wasn't thinking straight. Instead of heading down the mountain toward the city, I followed the track up."

"Wasn't aware it even went that way," Juan mumbled.

"Yeah, neither was I," Viktor said. "Anyway, it's obviously not traveled at all, and hasn't been for a good long time. I followed it until an enormous bramble bush blocked the path. It wasn't something I could've climbed over—not easily, anyway—so I looked for alternatives."

Ketha leaned forward, magic senses ignited. Her seer gift was activated, but she had no idea why since she hadn't summoned it, nor gazed into her glass.

"I'm betting you found something." She focused on his eyes that had darkened to a mossy shade of green.

He raked his hands through his hair, shoving it away from his face. "You'd be right. A faint trail led upward. I followed it more by feel than sight and eventually crawled over the top of a ridgeline. I expected to see the other side of the mountain, but, instead, this large, protected plateau spread out before me, complete with a few condors—"

"Did it have cliffs on two sides? Rock-studded dirt and pools of clear water?" Excitement thrummed through her, and she got the same tingling sensation she always did when two halves of something magical found each other.

Viktor had been staring at the floor, and he raised his gaze to stare at her. "Yes, but how could you possibly know that?"

"Because I saw it in a vision."

Juan plopped into his chair. "Come on, you two. This just edged into *Twilight Zone* territory."

Viktor faced his friend, his expression drawn into world-weary lines. For the first time, he looked like the Vampire he was, and it both attracted and repelled her. "We've turned into *Twilight Zone* creatures," he said, his words edged with sorrow. "Why is it so hard to believe I found the same place she saw in one of her trance states?"

"Maybe because Vamps don't have that kind of magic." Juan looked away, hazel gaze averted to his hands clasped in front of him. "And maybe because I never gave up hoping someone somewhere could turn back the clock and undo whatever transformation made me into a Vampire."

His words struck a chord deep in Ketha. The group in Siberia had been aiming for a blending of magical lines. Loosed to finally complete itself, the spell would alter Vampirism permanently.

"If we can defeat the Cataclysm," she said slowly and deliberately, "Vampires will change, but I'm not certain quite what that will look like."

She kept quiet about her fears that Shifter magic mixed with Vampire abilities would lure bond animals that made hellhounds pale by comparison.

9

STRONG MAGIC

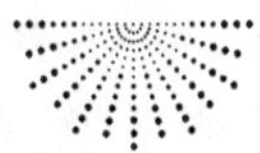

VIKTOR SWALLOWED HARD. Juan had the guts to admit he hated being a Vampire. Though the words were there, crowding behind his throat, Viktor couldn't force them out. To do so would mean he couldn't keep smiling nicely at Raphael. To do so meant he'd have to stop pretending and launch a full-scale rebellion against his sire.

Was he ready to take that step?

"Vik? Was there more?" Juan reached over and tapped his knee.

Viktor pulled himself out of his funk fast. It wasn't difficult. Acting as if all was well had become second nature. "Yeah. I checked all the caves off the mesa, and there are over a dozen of them. Judging from drawings on the walls, early humans lived there, but that's not the important part." He inhaled sharply, blew it out, and did it again. "The water up there is good, not tainted."

"How is that possible?" Ketha asked.

"I have no idea," he admitted. "Probably because of that, though, it's a condor nesting colony."

"I'm confused," Juan broke in. "Clean water only goes so far. What do they eat?"

"Pools in the caves are brimming with fish. The birds have apparently adapted to eating live prey." Viktor shifted his gaze from one shocked face to the other before adding, "I didn't believe it, either, until I grabbed a couple from one of the pools and ate them."

"Holy godhead." Ketha got to her feet and walked to where Viktor had dropped her pack in a corner of his cabin. Kneeling, she opened it and withdrew a thick, black book bound in creased leather. She paged through it, clearly hunting for something.

"What is that book, and what are you looking for?" Viktor asked.

"It's a spell book. This seems like a rehash of the creation story. I want to know if any other precedent exists for it, but it's not as if this tome is indexed. Either it shows you what you want—or it doesn't. Right now, it's not cooperating."

"Fascinating, but a sideline to our discussion. My plan," Viktor went on, "was to come to your cell and move you to the mesa. You'd have food and water and shelter in the caves. And a respite because none of the Vamps know the place exists."

She rocked back on her heels and looked at him. Her eyes were cloudy and distant, as if she'd moved to the realm she visited in her glass. "I have to get my sisters. We're all supposed to be there."

She looked so vulnerable and so raw, he moved to her side and drew her to her feet, book and all. Once she was standing, he wrapped his arms around her and held her with the book sandwiched between them. The Shifter tome sent jolts of uncomfortable heat into his chest, but he ignored them.

"Tell us what you saw in your vision," he urged. "Not that I'm opposed to helping spirit all of you up there, but it increases the chance of discovery tenfold."

Ketha nodded slowly. Extricating herself from his embrace, she retreated to her chair and sat on the edge of it. "I truly believe I have a way to defeat the Cataclysm, so the barrier will fall and nature can return to normal—at least in this part of the world. I'm less certain whether we'd be able to leave here. The Cataclysm is a widespread phenomenon. Crippling it in Ushuaia may not impact it elsewhere."

"What? So you think it's like a hydra that will cut its losses?" Juan asked.

"What did you actually see?" Viktor prodded without waiting for her to answer Juan.

She sent half a smile their way. "I don't know the answer to your question about the Cataclysm. Maybe a better place to start is how seer magic works when it comes to future events. Viewing the past is as simple as dialing up a movie. I don't always hit the exact spot I'm aiming for, but so long as a competing spell isn't occluding my efforts, I can 'see' the past accurately."

"What's different about the future?" Juan asked. "Other than it obviously hasn't happened yet."

"That would be exactly why it's different." Ketha narrowed her eyes to thoughtful slits. "There are many possible futures. No one knows with any degree of certainty which one will happen until it does. I have several methods I employ to gauge future events. One uses a timeline where I view snapshots, moving up and down it until I find a likely candidate."

"If you find one you like, can you influence it?" Viktor asked.

"Sometimes." She hesitated, maybe collecting her thoughts. "It was only very recently I saw the event that I believe precipitated the Cataclysm. My best guess is whatever spell blocked my efforts was locked into a ten-year timeline. In any event, Vamps and Shifters combining their disparate power—and then having sex—formed the Cataclysm. It's a calculated guess on my part, but I believe if we can recreate that combination of energies, minus the sex that sent the spell south, we can kick the Cataclysm's ass. The original spell can roll on through to its conclusion, which will withdraw whatever energy it's been feeding into the Cataclysm."

"Why do you believe sex was the problem?" Viktor asked.

She shrugged. "Because congress with Vampires has always been forbidden."

"If your *calculated guess* works out, what happens to Vampires and Shifters afterward?" Juan asked. He sounded so hopeful, it made Viktor's heart hurt for his friend. He'd had no idea how much Juan hated his Vampire status.

Ketha closed her teeth over her lower lip. "In truth, I have no idea. The original casting sought to create a permanent blend between Vampire abilities and our own. At the end of it, you would have been able to shift. I suspect if we can complete the magic, get it back on track, the spell will play itself out. Or maybe it will unwind completely. These things are impossible to predict."

"If it unwinds completely, we'll still be Vampires. How would the original spell have impacted Shifters? You told me once we were opposites who needed each other to exist." Viktor sent a penetrating glance her way. He had a feeling she was hiding something, but he had no idea what it might be.

A crooked smile lit her features, turning her into something unearthly and lovely. "I guess I did tell you that. None of this makes a whole lot of sense to me. Not yet, anyway. Making Vampires stronger via an infusion of Shifter magic could create a demon-spawned race no one could stand against. Why any group of Shifters would take part in something like that is baffling."

"Did they have a hidden agenda?" Viktor played possibilities through his mind.

She studied her hands. "That's exactly what I've been hoping, but I'll never pick up that level of subtlety through scrying." When she looked up, her expression was solemn. "Forcing the spell through to its conclusion is a gamble. It will probably defeat the barrier trapping us here. How it will impact Vampires or Shifters is far from clear, but we don't have much choice. If we do nothing, we'll all die."

"How does the mesa play into things?" Juan got to his feet and jammed his hands into his pockets.

Ketha aimed her next words at him. "So far, I've seen four visions of possible futures. Three included Raphael. In one, he tossed a dead Shifter into the ocean. In another, he was a reluctant recruit, but he was at least helping with the spell to defeat the Cataclysm. In the third, he flipped me off and marched away."

"And the fourth? The one without Raph?" Viktor stared down at her.

"That was the one on the mesa. I didn't summon that one. It formed spontaneously in my glass. All the Shifters were there and six Vamps. You and Juan. The two who dropped me in front of Raphael the other day, and two more I didn't recognize."

"How do you decide which version to give credence to?" Viktor asked.

"I pick the one that seems to hold the best chance of success. I'm not certain how to explain it, but when you were talking earlier, describing your trek up the mountainside…" She stopped to suck in a breath. "Before you'd even reached the mesa part, I got a magical hit. Kind of like a mild electric shock, and I knew what you were about to say would reveal something critical."

"So that's the one we go with," Juan said.

"It gets my vote." Ketha nodded slowly. "The only piece I was missing was where the plateau was. I'd never seen anyplace like that around Ushuaia, and now I know why. Once I woke up from where you found me in that stairwell, I was planning to look for it. Since I'd seen condors, I thought maybe if I followed some of them, they might lead me to it."

"Do you honestly believe you could have spent that much time outdoors and not had a Vampire net settle squarely over your head?" Viktor demanded. Fear for her ran deep, and a savage protectiveness rocked him to his bones. Because of that, his words were harsher than he'd planned.

"I hadn't gotten that far." Ketha sounded defensive. "I was afraid to put my sisters in any worse danger, so I was going to try to locate it on my own."

"Sorry. Didn't mean to be critical." Viktor looked away. "We probably need to check in with Raphael."

"I was thinking the same thing," Juan said. "We don't want to arouse his suspicions. Not any worse than they already are."

"How about if you show up first? Tell him I'm finishing my transit of the underground tunnel system, and I'll be along presently."

"Will do," Juan agreed. "Any idea what happens next?"

"I need to talk with the other Shifters," Ketha said, "but I can do that from here via telepathy. Once I describe how to get to the mesa, they can stagger who goes when, so only two of them are exposed at any given time."

"Why two?" Viktor asked.

"More than that are hard to conceal, but we do better when we combine power. It boosts each of our abilities. Plus, that means only six trips before all of us are safe. Maybe seven if I don't pair up with someone."

"I'm out of here," Juan announced and focused his next words at Ketha. "Hopefully the next time I see you will be on the mesa."

"If the goddess grants us grace, it will be," Ketha called after his retreating form.

"That was an old-fashioned, almost religious, thing to say," Viktor murmured, aware he and Ketha were alone, her scent heady and compelling. What would she do if he drew her against him again and held her close?

"Shifters are spiritual beings," she replied, and cast an appraising glance his way, almost as if she'd read his mind.

Who knew? Perhaps she had.

Viktor crossed the room and sat next to her on the bed he'd slept thousands of nights in. "I'd like to know more about you." He wanted to touch her, lay a hand over hers, but he didn't.

A complex array of emotions rippled across her expressive features before she caught his gaze with her golden eyes. "I want to know more about you too, but right now that's not a good idea." Before he could protest, she hurried on. "The most important thing is defeating the Cataclysm while we still can. Too many more months, and we'll all be too depleted to weave the magic to trounce it. For all I know, we may have passed that point already."

She licked her lips but didn't break eye contact. "You may have found food and decent water, but even though it's enough to keep a flight of birds from extinction, twelve Shifters and a hundred Vamps will decimate it in a matter of weeks. Maybe less."

"That's accurate, and I should remain true to the bigger picture, but…" Words failed him. How to articulate what he felt?

Ketha saved him the trouble. "I know." She laid the spell book aside and reached for his hand, cradling it in hers. "I feel the attraction too. I'd love to lose myself in your arms and feel your mouth on mine again. Once we defeat the Cataclysm—if it ever happens—there should be time to see if we're even still the same people. You may not want me once your Vampire energies change."

Viktor shook his head. "I don't believe that. You brought something alive in me that's been dead or dormant since Raphael turned me. You sing to the humanity left in me. That's only going to grow stronger if the Cataclysm crumbles."

Because he couldn't stand not to touch her, he cradled her head with his other hand, the one not clutched in hers, and threaded his fingers into her silky multihued hair.

Her gaze warmed, eyes becoming liquid with desire, and she murmured, "You make me weak, destroy my resolve," just before she tilted her head and touched her mouth to his, barely brushing her lips over his.

She tasted of love and longing and the life he'd left behind when his ship, *Gavrill*, pitched aground on rocks guarding the South American coastline. He traced the outline of her firm, full lips with his tongue. Little biting kisses followed, and he angled her head to bring his mouth down hard on hers, tongue probing for entrance.

She groaned softly before opening her mouth to him and tangling her tongue with his. Somehow, her arms had wrapped around his body, holding him with an urgency twin to his own. Her fingers splayed across his back, nails digging into his flesh. His cock hadn't exactly retreated since swelling to fullness in her bedroom back at the Shifters' grotto. It pressed against the front of his pants, uncomfortably close to the release he'd denied himself since being turned. Even though Vampires welcomed opportunities for sex, he'd chosen to maintain a separation from whom he'd been before. Sex had been part of that. Doing without hadn't felt like much of a sacrifice. Forcing himself on an unwilling human wasn't a place he'd ever have gone, and the female Vampires didn't appeal to him on any level.

Ketha tore her mouth from his, breathing in little panting gasps. A slow smile split her mouth. "You saved yourself for me. I like that. My motives weren't nearly as noble since we were stranded here without any male Shifters, but I'm one of those 'new virgins' too."

He smiled back. "You were inside my thoughts."

She shrugged. "Of course. How else will I find out what makes you tick?"

"You could ask."

"My way is faster." She moved an arm from behind him and cradled the side of his face in her hand before stroking down his neck to his shoulder. "You should get moving. We don't want to make Raphael any more suspicious than he already is."

He bent his mouth to hers again, needing the taste of her lips and delighting in what they wakened in him. His cock throbbed, but he pushed the sensation aside. Ketha was ever so much more than a vessel to slake his lust. He wanted to keep her by his side forever. If she was in his mind, so much the better. It saved the time and awkwardness of telling her how much she meant to him.

She pulled away a second time, her face splotched a lovely rose color with wanting more than kisses. The peaks of her breasts raised small hillocks under her robes as she rose to her feet and placed her hands on his shoulders.

"We are linked, you and I, in ways I don't fully understand. I felt it when I first laid eyes on you but didn't trust my instincts."

"Do you now?" He couldn't keep raw desire from his voice.

She nodded and licked her lower lip, swollen from their kisses. "You do need to go. And I need to connect with my sisters."

"I know." He blew out a breath, loathe to leave her side. If he didn't go, though, it would be like throwing down the gauntlet and challenging Raphael's hold on him.

"Not the time for that." Ketha had obviously been in his head again. "We want him as trusting as possible until this train is so far down the track, he can't derail it."

"That will be a neat trick. He's astute, that one. Perhaps between Juan and I, we can pull it off, though." Viktor thinned his lips, thinking. "Maybe we can plan a raid on a couple of the human compounds. That always gets Raphael excited. He'd much rather drink human blood than animal."

Ketha laughed, but it held grim edges. "I've gone above and beyond to keep the humans from dying out. Using them for bait wouldn't be my first choice." She slitted her eyes thoughtfully. "You hold my scent. Remain still, and I'll neutralize it. You might argue you'd picked it up in my cell or in my bedroom at the grotto—"

"He'd never believe that," Viktor cut in. "This is a Master Vampire we're talking about. He has the nose of a bloodhound, raised to the nth degree. He's always reminding me of his Nosferatu origins."

"Nosferatu, huh?" Ketha rolled her eyes.

"You've heard of them?" Surprise filled him. Deep down, he'd thought Raphael had made up the whole Nosferatu mystique to make himself look like a worse badass than he already was.

"Oh, yeah. From what I was taught, they're the original strain of Vampire. The one that came from that pact between the devil and Sekhmet. Stand up."

When he did, she walked around him, her hands weaving patterns in the air as she chanted. "What language is that?" he asked. "It's the same one you used when your comforter caught fire and burned."

"An old form of Gaelic. It's the language of spells for Shifters. Hush. I'm not quite done."

He stood still as she circled him, waiting until she nodded once, sharply, and said, "There. You're good to go."

He reached for her, but she shook her head. "Not that I don't want more kisses, but you'll undo all my good work if you touch me again."

He blew an air-kiss her way. Even if he couldn't touch her, the reality of her a few paces away filled him with peace and joy and longing. As if all the puzzle pieces in the world had clicked together, making him whole.

"Uh-uh." She shook a finger his way. "You can't do that, either."

"Do what?"

"Wanting me is spilling from you in waves. You'll have to get a handle on that part and jettison it."

"No shit," he muttered. "Shouldn't be a problem. Once I walk out of here, that is. Speaking of which"—he frowned—"where will I find you next?"

"Probably not here. Don't worry. I'll obliterate all traces of myself before I leave *Arkady*."

"I can see you get to the mesa safely."

Lines formed in the corners of her eyes. Sadness or resignation or maybe both. "Better if I get there on my own. I know how to find it now."

He wanted to protest, scoop her up, and run like the wind until he deposited her in the Garden of Eden he'd found. He opened his mouth, but she held up a hand.

"It's a lovely thought, but it's safer this way. We need to make preparations before we loose the spell to break the Cataclysm. For that, we need time."

"So my job is to keep Raphael fat, dumb, and happy as long as possible."

Ketha laughed softly. "Haven't heard that expression since before the Cataclysm, but yeah. That's exactly it."

"How long do you need?"

Ketha glanced upward as she considered his question. "Two days. By then, all the Shifters will be on the mesa. We should have the spell mapped out, and we'll be waiting for you and five other Vampires to launch it."

"Got it. Probably better not to reveal *Arkady's* whereabouts to your Shifter kin."

"I wasn't planning to. I'll see them when we're all gathered on the mesa."

He headed for the cabin door. Jesus, it was hard to walk away from her. He turned in the doorway and said, "You can reach me telepathically. If you get into trouble, don't worry about consequences. Call me."

She set her mouth into a grim line. "If I get into trouble, you'll find out quick enough. You won't need to hear it from me. Now, go, or all our planning will be for naught."

One of the hardest things he'd ever done was walk out the door, leaving the woman he was falling in love with alone to face certain death if Raphael got wind of any of this.

I have to make certain that doesn't happen.

He loped down stairwells and the rope ladder until he stood outside *Arkady*, facing his ship. It felt foolish, but he asked the vessel to watch over Ketha so long as she remained within its walls.

Icy resolve filled him as he left the dry dock building and ran hard for the city. The best way to keep Raphael from interfering was to kill him.

It was long past time, and the iron blade was waiting.

10

SISTERHOOD IN ACTION

KETHA MOVED from one side of Viktor's cabin to the other, the feel of his arms fresh in her mind—and her heart. She hadn't wanted him to leave, but encouraging him to stay would have been foolhardy. She yearned for him, desired him with a single-mindedness bordering on insanity, but if he'd remained, his absence would have been akin to waving a red flag in front of Raphael. She wasn't entirely certain she could eradicate the scent of full-on lovemaking, either. Viktor had been celibate since the Cataclysm. If he suddenly showed up with any hint of sex clinging to him, the gig would certainly be up.

She'd done the right thing, sending him away, but she missed him terribly, wanted him to fold her in his arms and kiss her until both of them were crazy with need and couldn't keep their clothes on.

Ketha fisted both hands until her nails dug into her palms. She needed to focus, goddamn it, not lust after Viktor like a bitch in heat. Once her breathing slowed, she shut her eyes and sent a shielded message to Rowana.

Two words for starters. *"You there?"*

131

The other Shifter's reply was immediate. *"Yes. Why aren't you here? We left you instructions."*

"I got them. Listen carefully."

In as few words as possible, she outlined her vision and how it matched up with Viktor's discovery. A rapid intake of breath through the telepathic link provided proof Rowana agreed the two events weren't mere synchronicity.

"We'll get to the place you described as soon as we can." Rowana's determination rang through their link.

"Too fucking bad we couldn't coax the sun to come out for a few hours," Aura broke in, followed by, *"Yeah, I was listening."*

"You might be onto something," Ketha said. Excitement shot through her, making her toes and fingers tingle.

"How so?" Aura inquired sourly. *"The Cataclysm totally screwed with the weather."*

"Some of us were weather workers once upon a time," Rowana replied, sounding thoughtful. *"None of us here, but my aunt was quite skilled in that regard."*

"Do you recall any of her incantations?" Ketha asked, barely breathing as she hoped to hell the answer would be yes.

"Better than that." Rowana chuckled. *"I have her spell book. Brought it because I was afraid we'd have to deal with a hurricane during the eclipse ten years ago, and I didn't want anything to get in the way of us harvesting that energy."*

"Find that book, and let's get cracking!" Aura exclaimed. Anticipation rippled through their connection, and Ketha could imagine Aura prodding the other Shifter in the shoulder hard enough to get the older woman moving.

"I'm on it," Rowana said, her steadiness shining through as it always did. *"The others will pitch in with their energy. My eagle is chomping at the bit to help too. I'm certain we can coax a few hours of sun out of the cloud cover tomorrow. It's getting late for that today, and we want to maximize our magic."*

"Let me know how it's going," Ketha said.

"Will do," Rowana replied. "It won't stop the Vamps, but it might slow them down a wee bit."

"Where are you?" Aura asked. "You should be with us, helping."

"It's a sound suggestion," Rowana said. "That way if this works, we'll all know right away, and we can get moving."

Ketha thought about where her sisters were holed up several miles away. "I'll come if I can," she said. "Raphael has me in his gunsights. Worse, every Vamp under him is hunting me. I'm in a safe place at the moment. With night approaching, my best bet is to remain here."

"Do what you need to." Rowana's matter-of-factness warmed Ketha. "I'll keep you apprised of my progress."

Ketha severed the link. Hope engulfed her, painful in its intensity. Sunlight might keep Raphael and the other Vampires inside. Or not. Depended how spun out he still was. Direct sun didn't incapacitate them totally, but any assistance was welcome. She wondered if the sun's appearance might add fuel to Raphael's suspicious nature, but then decided it probably wouldn't. It wasn't that the sun never shone in Ushuaia, but its appearances were few and far between.

Her inner clock said it was closing on six, which meant the day had ceded to darkness. What would she do between now and tomorrow morning? Would it be foolhardy to wait a few hours and then hightail it for the mesa while it was still dark?

She could retrace her steps through the underground warren of tunnels to the spot she'd entered them earlier in the day. From there, it shouldn't take more than forty minutes to make a run for the spot Viktor had described where the bramble bush blocked the track.

That was forty minutes she'd be exposed and vulnerable. If Vamps entered the path, moving either up or down, she'd have nowhere to hide. Vegetation grew so thickly, concealing herself within it would be damned difficult.

Next, she considered making her way to where the other

Shifters had hidden themselves; it was well off anyone's beaten track. The possibility of discovery was far less. Only problem was that their location was the wrong way. The Shifters' hideout placed her several miles farther from her objective.

Ketha chewed her lower lip, unsure of the best path to take. Because she couldn't make up her mind, she picked up the spell book and settled at Viktor's desk. If she was going to lead the incantation to break the Cataclysm, first she had to locate the spell, and then she needed to practice it until she knew it cold—her parts, plus those of the other Shifters and Vamps. They'd have to get it perfect the first time. Even a flawed version would loose magic strong enough to alert any Vamp within a fifty-mile radius. They'd storm the mesa, intent on destroying all the Shifters now that their location was obvious.

Ketha stopped paging through the book and thought about everything, the whole picture. Magic had been part and parcel of the world since its making. Even if overpowering the Cataclysm altered magic as she'd known it, some other form of power would worm its way in.

"Why would Shifters parlay with Vampires? What was in it for us?" She posed the questions out loud and opened a drawer, withdrawing both pen and paper. Her training in the hard sciences took over, and she crafted two lists, ginning up benefits and risks.

"You're making this too hard," her wolf observed.

Ketha stared at what she'd written. "What do you mean?" she countered.

"The Shifters lied," the wolf said flatly.

"Come on, sweetie. You have to say more than that." Ketha turned her attention inward.

"Don't you see? This was part of a plan to rid the world of Vampires once and for all. Shifters lured them with promises of power to augment their own, but what this spell truly would have done is turn Vampires into Shifters, pure and simple."

Her wolf's words held the ring of truth, but Ketha dug deeper. "How do you know this?"

The wolf hesitated. Ketha clamped her jaws together, determined not to ruin things. She wanted to shake the information out of her bond animal, but she knew better than to push. What passed between the animals in the place they walked without their bondmates was private. That the wolf was even considering sharing anything meant it fully appreciated how precarious their position had grown.

"The bond animals caught wind of the plot right before the Cataclysm," the wolf began. *"We talk among ourselves, but you already know that. The scheme was so bizarre I chalked it up to idle rumor. Given what's happened since, it's the only explanation that makes sense."*

The wolf growled softly before going on. *"There were two scenarios. The first would have defanged the Vampires, severing their link to the devil and Sekhmet so they'd revert to the humans they'd been. If that didn't work—and none of us thought it would—the fallback position was changing out a few elements so they turned into Shifters. Once that happened, they'd either welcome a bond animal—or not."*

"What would have happened to the ones who wanted to remain Vampires? Or who couldn't attract a bond animal?"

"It's kind of the same thing," the wolf responded after a considerable pause. *"If the spell worked the way the Shifters hoped, there'd be no place in this world for Vampire energy to flourish, so eventually they'd all die out. And far earlier than their artificially extended lifespans."*

"Why didn't you say something sooner?"

"At first, I held silence because all the bond animals understood if the Vampires caught wind of the trap, they wouldn't cooperate. They've never had any understanding of how magic works, so none of them recognized they'd been offered the impossible. Vampirism can't coexist with Shifter magic in the same vessel. After the Cataclysm, the damage was already done. I only started thinking about this again after that vision we shared where we saw that group in the cold, snowy place."

"Was it really forbidden congress between a Shifter and a Vampire that perverted the spell?"

"Yes, at least according to the bond animals present."

"Thank you for trusting me."

"We're bondmates." The wolf's simple answer warmed her.

Ketha shut her eyes, recalling the gathering in Siberia. She'd noticed sexual heat flare between a Vampire and a cat Shifter. If the two had been in love, it explained why they'd been so eager they hadn't waited for the spell to run its course.

Or maybe, as lovers often did, the Shifter had spilled the beans, and the Vampire, frantic to save his people from assimilation, interrupted the casting with sex and formed the Cataclysm. She opened her eyes and furrowed her forehead in thought. She'd never really know. Not everything.

Ketha returned her attention to the book. Understanding more about how the Cataclysm came to be might help get rid of it. Splaying her hands across parchment pages, she sent images of what she needed. The magical tome quivered and warmed beneath her touch, feeling more alive than it ever had.

Makes sense. I've never needed it more than I do right now.

She upped the ante on her spell, urging the proper incantation to show itself. Her fingers moved of their own accord, no doubt driven by the book's energy. Pages flipped past until heat jabbed her chest dead center, and the ley lines of the world surrounded her, pregnant with power.

Ketha stared at the spot the book meant for her to study. The Cataclysm hadn't existed when this book was penned with spells and blood and magic, but that didn't matter since the pages shaped and formed themselves to meet the user's requirements.

"Here?" She tapped the page with an index finger.

The same heat jabbed her in the chest again; the ley lines pulsed. Ketha took it as a yes. She picked up her abandoned pen and settled a fresh sheet of paper where she could take notes as she read. Ready for damn near anything, she dissected the spell that would either save them all or kill them a few months before it would have happened anyway.

Ketha wasn't under any illusions about the power she'd have to leverage to conquer the Cataclysm. The magic would be consuming enough, she might not have enough juice to keep living after the spell was shaped, formed, and sent out to do its task.

She shook her head hard and focused on the pages in front of her. What happened to her wasn't important. Not if it meant defeating the Cataclysm and allowing nature to regain ascendency over the land and oceans. This was far bigger than Shifters and Vamps and their long-standing enmity. This was about whether Earth would continue to exist and support any life at all.

Ketha skimmed the spell, which spanned several pages of closely spaced, handwritten Gaelic. Once she'd done that, she broke it into its component parts, using her pen and paper to draw out each element, including who'd be doing what.

Her hand cramped from gripping the pen. When she glanced down at multiple sheets of paper filled with her flowing script, she understood why. Hours had passed. She pushed to her feet and rotated her shoulder blades to get the kinks out of her upper body.

Sensing their job was done, the ley lines wavered and disappeared.

After a few deep breaths, she strode to the far side of the cabin and back again before grinding to an abrupt halt. She hadn't bothered to eradicate signs of her presence in the building or on this ship. Panic drove a fist into her midsection, and she hurried outside the cabin, sprinkling obfuscation spells as she went.

How could I have been so stupid?

She grimaced. She knew damn good and well how. She'd been focused on Viktor more than her own safety. Not a mistake she was likely to make again anytime soon. She stood on the bulkhead and spread shadow magic all the way to the door into the dry dock building and down the stairwell. By the time she was done, no one would know she'd ever been anywhere near *Arkady.*

Ketha breathed easier when she trotted back across the deck toward Viktor's cabin. She'd been sloppy and gotten away with it. This time. The slap of waves against the building followed her inside. Vamps' antipathy toward the restless sea had probably kept her safe.

Maybe Viktor's attachment to the sea was why he'd remained more human than Vampire. The more she thought about it, the surer she was she'd stumbled onto how he'd held himself relatively immune from Raphael's considerable powers of suggestion. Might be what had helped Juan as well.

She let her senses roam wide, and her eyes widened. Midnight. She'd lost six hours working on the spell. Not an unreasonable amount of time for such a major undertaking, but the passage of so much time still surprised her. Midnight meant half a dozen hours until dawn reached *Ciudad de Huesos.*

Now that the spell was taking shape in her heart and mind, she wanted to lay eyes on the mesa to gauge how its particular earth energies would impact the incantation. She'd have to alter some aspects, but wouldn't know which ones until she got there. Ketha closed her teeth over her lower lip. Some places muted magic; others amplified it. What if the mesa had a deadening effect? If it did, the spell probably wouldn't work.

"I can't think that way," she muttered. "I saw it in my vision. Viktor ended up there because the goddess led him to it."

Her words brought a smile. Viktor would never couch his journey to the mesa in those terms, but Ketha knew the truth. He'd been running from his attraction to her after their kiss, not paying attention. During his headlong flight uphill, his mind had been engaged in making sense of how he could feel anything at all for a Shifter.

Recognizing opportunity, Gaia, mother of the world, had

guided his steps. Likely, once he was where she wanted him, she'd retreated, allowing Viktor's natural curiosity to rise to the fore.

"Ketha," echoed in her mind.

"Yes," she answered Rowana. *"I'm here."*

"We have the weather well in hand. Look for sunrise around six thirty."

"Excellent news," she answered the other Shifter. *"I found the spell we'll need for the..."* Her words trailed off since Ketha wasn't at all sure it was wise to broadcast their intention, even in shielded telepathy, in case the Cataclysm was paying attention. She'd been sloppy about masking her presence on the ship, and she was damned if she'd make a similar mistake twice in a row.

"For the what, dear?" Rowana asked.

"To do the work we need to once we reach our destination."

"You're worried someone—or something—might overhear us?"

Ketha smiled grimly. *"You always had a psychic edge, sweetie."*

"No psychic edge needed to figure that out. We were going to alert the humans they'd have a few hours of sunlight tomorrow for their crops, but they can figure it out on their own," Rowana lied smoothly, and Ketha could have hugged her.

"Signing off for now. See you soon."

"If the goddess is good to us," Rowana replied.

The age-old Shifter blessing filled Ketha with gratitude, and she focused heart-energy on the eleven other Shifters hiding in an abandoned warehouse in foothills north of the city.

Ketha sat back in the chair fronting the desk and read through her notes, comparing them with the book's detailed instructions to make certain she hadn't missed anything. She jotted additional comments in several places, and then repeated her actions.

I'm being obsessive.

No. I'm giving this the care it requires. That's different.

The next time she straightened her back and rubbed grit from eyes that felt hot and sandpapery, it was past three in the morning. If she was going to make a run for the mesa, it was now or wait until the sun rose. Which would yield the best chance of success? She'd already seen all twelve Shifters on the mesa. Did that mean it didn't matter when—or how—they traveled?

Ketha knew better. Just because she'd seen an idealized vision in a trance state didn't mean she and the other women could throw caution to the winds. Nor did it necessarily mean all of them would make their target, regardless of how much care they took.

She reached into a pocket, fingering her glass. She could scry her options, but that would blow through magic—and take time. Instead, she shut the spell book and placed her palms on its creased leather binding. The book's power might offer her something, so she opened her mind and asked for guidance.

A Gaelic prayer soothed her frayed nerves, and Ketha shut her eyes, waiting. The book warmed beneath her touch, and an image of her on the mesa formed behind her closed lids.

"Aye," she murmured. Still speaking Gaelic, she asked how she'd gotten there. And when.

A small jolt of power jolted her chin, forcing her to glance upward at a night sky, cloudy with very few stars peeking through. Ketha snorted, feeling like a prime fool. The information had been there all along—if she'd had the presence of mind to collect it from the image in her mind. Her eyes flashed open, and she was on her feet before the last vestiges of power soaked back into the spell book.

She smoothed her copious notes into a neat pile and folded them into the book. Once everything was packaged up, she dropped it inside her backpack and latched it shut. Ketha hated to leave the cabin, but she slipped the straps around her body, anyway. Viktor's presence was stamped into everything, and his clean scent—oceans tinged with evergreen—cradled her, rich with promise.

She stood quiet for long moments, letting herself hope they might find a future together, before she buried her longing deep.

It would only get in the way. From now until the spell was cast, she'd need every shred of energy and concentration for only one thing: obliterating the Cataclysm.

Setting her jaw in a resolute line, she hurried out of the cabin, shut the door behind her, and made her way off the ship to the concrete round covering her exit route. Ketha stopped and sent a thin beam of exploratory magic through the concrete and into the tunnel beyond the ladder.

Nothing pinged off her magic beyond the rats, mice, and bats that lived in the subterranean system.

So far. So good.

She tugged on the manhole cover but couldn't budge it without a magical assist. Careful to prod it back into place once she clung to the ladder, Ketha cleared her mind of everything beyond making it to the mesa in one piece. Speed would be her friend, along with stealth. Cloaking herself in invisibility, she clambered down steel ladder rungs to the dirt walkway below and set out at a brisk trot, magic deployed on all sides. Light was essential, but she kept her mage light dialed to dim.

A quick assessment yielded disquieting information. Her magical well wasn't quite deep enough to both keep herself shielded and constantly check for Vampires. She could do it for a little while, but not for the time it would take to navigate the tunnels and sprint up the track to her objective. Her compromise was to borrow from earth energy to keep her invisibility illusion firmly in place and hope to hell she'd notice Vampires in time to go to ground. It had worked before when the two Vamps had shown up in the tunnels. Of course, having Juan and Viktor to talk with them helped, but even absent that, she felt confident her hiding place would've kept her safe.

"Keep watch," she told her wolf.

"I will."

Moving fast, she retraced her steps from earlier in the day, resisting an urge to stop one last time in the place she and her sisters had lived for years. The doorway stank of Vampires. None were there now, but if they'd vandalized her home, she didn't want to bear witness to the destruction. It would only make her angry—and sad.

Vamps marched to a different tune. One she'd grown used to but would never understand or respect.

Familiar landmarks flashed past. She was close to where she'd have to exit the underground tunnel system, which meant she'd be far more exposed. She'd known she'd have to leave the safety of earth energy surrounding her, but her heart still beat faster, and sweat dripped down her sides. She didn't want to waste energy on a calming spell, so she borrowed shamelessly from the anxiety that drove her forward.

The wolf prowled within her, wary and vigilant.

"Careful!" It breathed the word into her mind.

She was within sight of the exit point. Vamp stench hit her in the gut, almost doubling her over. Christ! Where were they? She flattened herself against a clammy wall and tightened the invisibility spell around herself, cringing as water soaked through the thick fabric of her robe. No convenient stairwells or ladder wells to hide in. Not this time. The nearest one was fifty yards back. Until she determined which way the Vamps were coming from, she didn't plan on moving.

"I fucking hate it down here," one Vamp growled.

"Why? Dark places mirror our black, black souls," another replied cheerily.

"Not this dark place," the first voice said. "It gives me a good case of the creeps."

"Stop whining," a third voice, thick with command, cut in. "Raphael sent us to hunt the Shifter, and we'll turn these fucking tunnels inside out. If we go back and say she ain't here, I want to be goddamned sure it's accurate."

Booted feet clattered down the ladder she'd planned to use for her exit. Ketha shuttered her life force deep within herself, barely breathing. Would they lope by her like she hoped? No reason for them not to. Only problem was at some point, they'd pick up her trail. She could only shield where she was and the near parts of her passage. The farther she got from the path she'd taken, the more likely the Vamps would be to catch her scent.

Please let them leave the manhole cover off, she prayed.

If they didn't, the noise of her moving it would alert their preternaturally sharp hearing. She'd have one chance after they walked by her. She had to be out of these tunnels and up that mountain trail fast. By the time they figured out she'd not only been here, but had fled, she had to be beyond their reach.

Not very likely, considering how quickly they could move. She shut down that train of thought fast. The Vamps ran past, never reacting to her presence, even though one's hand brushed her as he passed by.

She counted to thirty nice and slow before she bolted toward the ladder at the end of the tunnel. Gratitude spilled from her as she scuttled up the ladder and through the still-open manhole cover. Ketha froze for the moments it took to hunt for more Vampires.

The coast was clear, for now. It was the best she could hope for, and she took off at a dead run. The heavy pack was an impediment, but she needed its contents and couldn't take the time to sort things out of it. Plus, there was nowhere to leave items that wouldn't be a dead giveaway. If she were going to do lighten her load, the place would have been back on *Arkady.*

Her lungs burned and her throat constricted from thirst, but she didn't slow. Rounding the steep mountainside, she located the track and hurtled up it. She was almost at the turnoff to the cells when she smelled Vampires again. Heard them talking from the passageway leading to the cells. Frantic, feeling like a deer trapped by headlights, she dove into a copse of sticker bushes on the uphill side of the trail. Long spines cut into her flesh, and she muffled cries of pain. Her heart pounded hard enough to escape her chest.

Ketha pushed everything aside. Her discomfort didn't matter. What did was blood leaking from long gashes. She had to take care of it, but first she had to hide.

Her pack proved a major hindrance, so she unbuckled it and stuffed it beneath a bush, crawling in after it, flat on her belly. Blood dripped from multiple places the thorns had ripped into her. She poured magic into her invisibility illusion, while battling despair. Blood was where Vampires lived. Would her magic be enough to neutralize the scent? Panic filled her, and she alternated between healing her wounds and locating places her blood had dripped onto the vegetation, obliterating each spot as she found it.

She was blowing through wads of magic, probably running her stores down to bedrock, but she had no choice.

The barred door to the passageway leading to the cell clanged noisily, and the mutter of harsh voices—two of them—grew clearer.

"Fuck. No clues there."

"Nah. Told Raphael this was a wild goose chase. What do you say we hit that jaguar reserve of his? He's still stewing in his own juice." Rough laughter followed the words.

"Crap, man. You don't think he'll notice one of those cats got drained?"

"So what if he does? What's he gonna do, kill us? Besides, we'll take the whole fucking thing. Their meat's good. He's so spun out about losing that bitch Shifter, it's all he can think about."

"Bitch Shifter," the other Vamp hooted. "You're funny."

The Vamps flew past where she hunkered, surrounded by inch-long thorns. Hopefully, they'd be so focused on their victim, an unsuspecting jaguar she hoped would rip their eyes out, they'd miss her scent until they left the overgrown track.

Ketha drew a shaky breath, followed by another. She had to be careful leaving the thicket—because she didn't have either the time or the magic to erase any more traces of her blood.

11

BLOODBATH

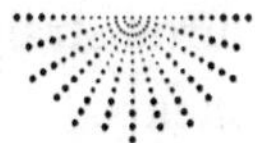

VIKTOR POUNDED down the streets of *Ciudad de Huesos*, dodging piles of bones. The afternoon was all but dead, and he hoped Raphael had moved past his unnatural obsession with Ketha. A return to rational thought would make it easier for Viktor to catch his sire unaware.

Ha! Wishful thinking.

He exhaled sharply, watching his breath form white clouds in the air only to have them snatched away by the ever-present wind. Raphael had a deeply unbalanced side. His absolute hold over the city and its inhabitants fed his narcissism and kept the power-mad parts in check. Ketha's escape from under his nose was a slap in the face. One Raphael wouldn't recover from until the Shifter was bleeding out of every vessel.

Viktor reached the building where they lived and pushed the door open so hard it banged against its stops; glass panes rattling alarmingly. Mounting the stairs two and three at a whack, he stopped on Raphael's floor. The sound of raised voices reached him from the far end of the hall, and Viktor girded himself for his sire's wrath.

Once Raphael became obsessed with something, no one was

145

immune from his attacks. Viktor covered the remaining distance and walked inside. He'd be damned if he'd alter his normal protocol and knock.

"It's about fucking time," Raphael snarled from where he stood, slouched against the wall that abutted the cold hearth, with his fists jammed into his pockets.

Juan raised a tired hand in greeting. Compared with their sire's posture, Juan stood ramrod straight, and he looked like he'd all but choked on faux agreements.

Viktor turned his hands palms upward. "I finished searching the tunnels, Sire. Didn't find anything."

Raphael opened his mouth and roared his fury. Fangs extended, he yanked his hands from his pockets. "Why can't a hundred Vampires, creatures I trained myself, find one puny Shifter?"

"I'm sure I have no idea." Viktor buried any traces of Ketha ten feet under in his mind. "So all of us are hunting?"

Raphael ground his jaws together. "What difference should numbers make? She's one Shifter. She smells like a Shifter. Why the fuck can't any of you locate her?"

"I'm sure I have no idea," Viktor repeated, not bothering to remind Raphael that they'd been trying to find the Shifters for ten years without success.

"You already said that." Raphael had edged so close, spittle sprayed Viktor's face. He took a chance and wiped it away.

"Look." Viktor squared his shoulders. "I spent years commanding men at sea. People do your bidding out of a sense of loyalty, not obligation."

Raphael narrowed his eyes to slits, retreating to the menacing calm that presaged a killing spree. "Your point, minion?"

"Just that."

"Just what?" Raphael's tone was quiet—and deadly.

Out of the corner of his eye, Viktor saw Juan shake his head in warning. His friend was probably right. Now wasn't the time to make Raphael suspicious of him, not if he wanted to take him by surprise and gain the upper hand.

"Nothing." Viktor glanced at his feet. "I misspoke. I didn't have a point."

"Better. I appreciate followers who respect command structure."

"Yes, Sire. Of course, Sire. Where would you like us to search next?" Viktor asked, his gaze still focused on the floor.

"Nowhere. You and Juan will remain with me and assist in strategizing as the men and women return with information."

"Excellent," Juan said. "Would Sire mind if I retrieved some of the jaguar meat?"

Raphael crinkled his nose in distaste. "I fail to appreciate your attraction to dead food, but go." He waved both hands and shot a meaningful look at Viktor. "I suppose you want him to bring enough for you too."

"That would be appreciated, but I figured I'd go with him."

"Figure again." Madness played about the edges of Raphael's aura, changing its black tint to one shot with reds and sickly yellows.

"You have an immediate need for my presence, Sire?" Viktor raised an eyebrow and forced himself to hold the other Vamp's gaze.

"No. But I'm not certain I can trust either of you." Before Viktor could lodge a protest, Raphael went on, "Or any of the rest, either. For all I know, you've been fucking the Shifters for years, and they've ensorcelled the lot of you."

Juan sidled out the door, mumbling, "Back soon."

Viktor exhaled wearily and spread his hands in front of him. "Use your truth ability," he suggested. "I haven't had sex—with anyone, including myself—since before the Cataclysm."

The blundering fumbles of Raphael's spell seared him, and Viktor waited for what his sire would come up with next. He didn't have to wait long.

Raphael shrugged. "So you haven't actually had sex. It doesn't mean you're not doing something else you shouldn't be."

"Like what?" Viktor asked, keeping his tone mild.

Raphael pounded a fist into the wall, reddening his knuckles. "Who the hell knows? I'm not a mind reader." He bent closer. "Not when someone wants to keep something hidden."

Thank Christ for that.

Viktor eyed chairs dotting the room. "Permission to sit, Sire. As you know, I don't have your strength. Even though you're disappointed by my lack of results, I have been hunting the Shifter since the crack of dawn this morning." He sent a sidelong glance skittering across the room. Would Raphael buy his story about being weak and tired?

"Go ahead. Sit." Raphael drew his lips back from his fangs. "You nailed it. You second-string Vamps are a huge disappointment. On every front."

"Sorry, Sire." Viktor dropped into the chair farthest from the open window to maximize comfort in the ice-cold room. Why had Raphael opened the window, anyway? Dank, chill air formed ice crystals on the glass and adjacent walls.

"You are such a wimp." Raphael stomped across the room and slammed the window shut so hard one of the panes cracked. "Spare me further apologies."

Viktor folded his hands in his lap. Holding silence would be easy since remaining cordial curdled his stomach into a burning mass of knots.

Juan trotted back into the room and dropped several strips of raw, semi-frozen meat into Viktor's lap. That done, he dragged a second chair close, but before he could sit, Raphael closed a hand over his arm.

Juan twisted in Raphael's grip before he remembered himself and quit struggling.

Raphael bared his fangs. "I did not give you permission to sit."

Juan's fair skin flushed with anger, and he choked out, "Sorry, Sire. I forgot myself. May I sit?"

"No. You can eat standing."

Viktor seethed with fury. He should've ended his sire long since. Raphael had no redeeming qualities. None. He was arrogant. Narcissistic. Petty. Spoiled. Conceited. Viktor recoiled but kept the emotion inside himself and his features bland. He'd described almost all Vampires. Certainly the old ones, but the majority of new ones as well.

Being annoyed and disgusted with Raphael for being what he was made as much sense as calling out a scorpion for its proclivity to kill things. The only problem with hating Vampires was he happened to be one.

Footsteps sounded right before a heavy fist fell on the outer door.

"Come," Raphael called, making no move to open the door.

Four Vamps filtered in. Glenn, Mario, and the two who'd dragged Ketha in front of Raphael a couple of days back. Like the rest of their kind, a motley collection of leather and rags hung off their muscled bodies. Viktor hunted for names for the ones who'd delivered Ketha and came up with Daide and Recco. Both men had short dark hair and dark eyes. Their Native heritage was apparent in high cheekbones, square chins, and high foreheads. According to Ketha, they'd be part of the incantation to dismantle the Cataclysm. Viktor didn't know them from Adam. Convincing them to come to the mesa might prove to be a neat trick.

Maybe I won't have to. Perhaps the magic powering this has its own way of ensuring all the participants end up in the right place at the right time.

He hoped to hell he was right and shifted his focus to the conversation playing itself out. Raphael was done rebuking the men for their failure, and they were wise enough not to contradict him or offer excuses.

"What are you waiting for?" Raphael prodded in his quiet

voice, the one that promised destruction was about to rain down on everyone's head.

"Sire?" Glenn looked mystified.

"Get back out there. No one is done until you find that Shifter."

"But Juan and Viktor are—" Daide began.

Viktor bit off a chunk of the jaguar, knowing what would come next.

"You dare oppose my orders?" Raphael's voice edged up a decibel or two.

"No. Of course not." Daide turned and fled out the still open door with the other three hard on his heels.

Viktor chewed and swallowed. He had to find a way out of this room, but he needed strength, so he polished off the meat before breaking the silence that had fallen among them.

"We could hunt for her," he suggested smoothly. "All of us. It might be better than simmering in our own adrenaline." Before Raphael could react, he continued, "If you want something done right, sometimes the best thing is to take care of it yourself." Viktor spread his hands, bloody from the jaguar meat, in front of him. "You've told us over and over how inadequate we are. Why not give us a field lesson in how things should be done?"

The corners of Juan's mouth twitched, but the other Vamp clamped down on his expression before anything could leak out. He recognized Viktor's strategy. The question was if Raphael would. Viktor kept breathing, nice and even, to make certain not to give anything away. If he could get his sire outside this room, he'd have a chance to take him by surprise and end him.

Breath hissed through Raphael's clamped teeth. His fangs lent an odd, acoustical resonance to the sound. "I thought I could do more good coordinating the hunt from here, but the four who left are the only ones who've reported in—except for you two." He shook his head until long, dusky hair cascaded down his shoulders, but at least he sounded more desolate than angry. Finally. His next sentence clinched Viktor's impressions. "I don't get it. I told everyone I wanted to hear from them at least every few hours."

"They probably didn't want to face you unless they had good news," Juan cut in smoothly.

"It's not as if any of us are trained in military operations," Viktor added. Since Raphael didn't contradict him, he kept talking. "Look at the disparity in who we were before the Cataclysm trapped us here. Everyone from businessmen to tramps and thieves. Heavy on the latter." Viktor stopped shy of mentioning that Raphael's uncanny fascination with the world's lowlifes was responsible for how their ranks were skewed toward con artists and sketchy vagabonds.

Raphael chuckled coldly. "You may be onto something, Gaelen." He pushed away from the wall. "What the hell? We may as well join the hunt. I'm not doing shit here."

Viktor tamped down elation spilling through him. He may have accomplished the initial step, but it was a long way from here to where Raphael's head left his shoulders. He unclenched hands that had formed fists of their own accord and got to his feet, ready to put part two of his plan into action.

"Good call, Sire."

Raphael shot an unreadable look his way. "You can quit laying it on so thick. This was your idea. If it doesn't pan out, I'll hold you personally responsible."

Nice to know.

"The reason I was late getting here..." Viktor hesitated and ginned up what he hoped was a combination of embarrassment and determination. He also prayed to every saint in the universe Raphael hadn't spent much time absorbing information from the books in his collection.

"What? Spit it out. What were you doing that I wouldn't have approved of?"

Vampire magic burned like liquid fire as Raphael probed his mind without much care what he destroyed on his way through.

Viktor rubbed his temples. "Stop that. It hurts. I looked through your assortment of books and scrolls to see if I could figure out something to use for Shifter bait."

Raphael drew his perfect brows together in a cross between confusion and thought. "You mean all those shelves in that area in the basement where I lived before the Cataclysm?"

Viktor nodded. "You haven't visited there much lately. The dust was thick, and I disturbed generations of spiders."

"Skip the lecture on my slipshod housekeeping. Did you find anything? I quit reading hundreds of years ago, but even when I did research, I was never interested in Shifters." Raphael strode to Viktor's side and gripped his upper arm hard enough to hurt.

Viktor cut to the heart of his scheme. "We should take the iron saber with us."

"Why? It's a weapon that can be turned against us." Suspicion rode beneath Raphael's question.

"Because iron is the only tool that can separate a Shifter from her magic. Otherwise, their power lingers even after we kill them. They can join that disembodied magic with living Shifters and make them infinitely strong. Iron will prevent that from happening—if we behead them." Viktor continued to breathe nice and slow to conceal his true motives. If Raphael chose to test his words, Viktor would end up splattered against the nearest wall with his guts hanging out.

"What else did you find?" Juan walked closer. "I had no idea our sire kept a magical library. You'll have to show me where it is."

"Oh, shut up." Raphael bared his fangs in Juan's direction. "What? The two of you have suddenly turned into Rhodes scholars?"

"When you've spent as much time on ships as we have," Viktor replied, "you want to know how things work—and how to fix them when they don't. Those answers are generally found by reading."

Something about his answer seemed to appease Raphael. He moved into the inner room that held the saber so fast, his body blurred. When he returned, the sword was secured in a scabbard belted around his waist.

"There," he announced. "We have the damned thing. Let's go." He crossed the room and trotted through the door no one had bothered to close. Viktor and Juan followed him.

"Where to first?" Viktor asked conversationally. His throat was dry, but at least his voice came out somewhere close to normal. The saber was coming with them. He'd have to figure out how to take possession of it, but one problem at a time. He'd managed to tell a bold-faced lie to his sire and not get caught.

"First stop is the jaguar pride," Raphael called over one shoulder. "I think better when I'm freshly fed."

"Do we get the meat?" Juan asked.

"Possibly," Raphael replied. "So long as you do exactly as you're told."

Anger flared, and Viktor reached for Raphael's neck, pulling his hands back before the Vamp could notice anything amiss. Squeezing the life out of Raphael before finishing him off with the saber would be one of the most satisfying things he'd ever done. Watching the fucker squirm and suffer would make up for a lot, but revenge wasn't all it was cracked up to be. Even if Raphael were dead, Viktor would still be stuck in a lifeless town with toxic water, a dwindling food supply, and a beached ship. Never mind a phalanx of untrustworthy Vampires. God only knew what they'd do once Raphael wasn't around to control them.

He loped after his sire with Juan pounding along next to him. He itched to strategize with Juan, but it wasn't possible. The two men had worked together long enough, they'd have to wing whatever happened. They left the building and cold enveloped Viktor, hurting his lungs with every breath. He drew his coat tighter around himself, but it didn't help much. Wind howled and chittered, driving chilly air through every chink in his clothing.

Raphael led the way to where the jaguars roamed in what was left of a national park north of town. Running at Vampire speed, they were there in under a quarter hour. Viktor scented the air to locate the jaguar pride and found other Vampires.

He smothered a grin. Raphael wouldn't appreciate anyone poaching in territory he'd announced belonged to him.

Juan poked Viktor in the side. When Viktor looked his way, he circled one fist around the other, clearly expecting some kind of shit to hit the fan. Viktor flashed a thumbs-up sign. Chaos might provide precisely the opportunity he'd been waiting for.

Raphael skidded to a stop and drew himself up tall. "Show yourselves," he bellowed in a voice ripe with command and compulsion.

Two Vamps melted out of deep shadows cast by trees and shrubbery. Blood smeared their lips and dripped down their chins. No denying what they'd been up to. One fell to his knees in front of Raphael, his face shrouded by long, dark hair. "I'm sorry, Sire. We were hungry."

"Yes," the other Vamp seconded. "So hungry. There's half the cat's blood left still. It's yours."

"What you don't get"—Raphael's voice was cold, disinterested —"is they're all mine."

The saber left its scabbard so fast, Viktor couldn't follow its trajectory. The second Vamp, the one still standing, crumpled to the ground minus his head. Blood geysered everywhere. Saliva flooded Viktor's mouth as the hot, rich, coppery stench invaded his nostrils.

"Go ahead." Raphael motioned to Juan and Viktor. "I can't drink it since I made him, but don't waste it."

Driven by hunger and not wanting Raphael to suspect how deeply Vampirism disgusted him, Viktor sank to his knees, closed his mouth over a streaming carotid, and drank deep. Juan knelt over the other side of the corpse. Meantime, the Vamp on his knees breathed in noisy, choking sobs, begging Raphael to spare him.

Ignoring the tableau, Raphael disappeared into thick timber, probably in search of the half-drained jaguar while its blood was still warm.

Juan raised his mouth from the corpse and jerked his chin at the iron saber discarded in the dirt.

Drunk and disoriented from gorging on Vampire blood, Viktor urged himself to get up, hoist the saber, and go after Raphael. Interrupting him while he pigged out on jaguar blood would make this a slam-dunk. Maybe. Viktor got as far as ripping his mouth from the still-pulsing vessel. His reactions were slow and sluggish. He couldn't shake the lethargy that came from feeding on overly rich blood. Animal blood was far easier to absorb. Human blood somewhere in between.

The Vamp who'd been on his knees, shaking and crying, lurched upright, grabbing the saber in one fluid motion. For a moment, Viktor feared the man might use it on him and Juan, but he leaned close to them and whispered, "I got this." Hatred flared from his fog-colored eyes. Before his words registered, he'd shrouded himself in stealth and bolted after Raphael.

Juan got to his feet and pulled Viktor upright, hissing, "Come on. He needs our help."

When Viktor was slow to respond, Juan slapped him hard across the face. Pain brought him around. "Thanks."

"De nada, mi amigo. Andale."

Stealth wasn't needed. Not now. They ran hard, following the scent track left by Raph and the Vamp with the saber. A clearing opened before them, rife with jaguar stench, but the remainder of the pride was nowhere around. Raphael knelt in the center of the clearing, intent on his meal. A big cat was draped over his lap, his mouth glued to its carotid. His eyes snapped open at their approach, but he closed them once he saw who was there.

The Vamp with the sword closed from behind Raphael. He'd obviously circled around, cloaking himself in Vampire stealth and speed. Viktor maintained a neutral expression, a minion waiting on his sire to finish feeding. Juan adopted an even more deferential pose.

The other Vamp timed it well. Raphael wasn't aware of the saber until even his supernatural speed couldn't save him. The other Vamp uttered a wild whoop of triumph and sliced through bone, flesh, and sinew. Raphael's head rolled off his shoulders and came to a stop near Viktor's feet.

Defying every natural law, his blue-gray gaze landed right on Viktor's face. "You knew," Raphael said right before his mouth went slack.

"Damn straight I did," Viktor growled. He hauled a foot back and booted Raphael's head as hard as he could kick. Spewing blood, it flew high and disappeared from sight.

The Vampire with the saber continued to whoop and holler, dancing a jig as he buried his face in what was left of Raphael's neck.

Juan hooked an arm beneath Viktor's elbow and yanked hard. Viktor followed him away from the grisly specter of Raphael's killer feeding from him.

Juan, who'd been muttering in Spanish, switched to English. "Hurry, man," he implored.

"Why?" Viktor asked. "That Vamp will be busy for at least an hour."

Juan stopped his headlong flight long enough to face Viktor. "Yeah, but once he's fed, he'll *be* Raphael. You can't feed from your sire without becoming him."

A sick, sinking feeling engulfed Viktor. "Crap. So we'll be bound to him the same way we were bound to Raphael? You know this how?"

"Because I paid attention to that initial set of lessons Raphael pounded into me after I was turned. You were too deep in denial about everything to care about the finer points of our new affiliation."

"Probably true." Viktor snorted. "Affiliation is one word for it. The one I'd have chosen is curse. Goddamn it all to hell. Trading one Raphael for another wasn't quite what I had in mind."

"Look at the bright side." Juan took off running again. "This gives us the window we need to get to the mesa."

Viktor caught up easily and ran by Juan's side. "We have to stop at *Arkady* and make certain Ketha and the other Shifters know what's happened."

The harsh planes of Juan's face softened, and he looked more like the man he'd been than a beautiful monster. "You really do care about her."

"More than that. I'm falling in love with her."

"Vampires can't love anything beyond blood, but I'm happy for you, *amigo*."

"Maybe it's a good thing I didn't pay better attention during our indoctrination." Viktor shrugged.

"Yeah. If I'd known ignorance would slow the transformation, I'd have tuned the propaganda out too."

"You're impossible." Viktor grinned and mock-slugged his friend in the shoulder.

Juan feinted left and punched back before taking off at Mach 10. "First stop. *Arkady*."

"Thanks. If we get lucky, Ketha's already well on her way to safety." Viktor hoped he was right. He exhorted every deity he'd ever prayed to, to keep her safe until he could take over that job.

By the time they entered the dry dock by its main door, he'd tried to reach her multiple times telepathically, but she hadn't answered. He stopped inside the building and gazed at *Arkady*, looming above them in the middle of the windowless structure.

"Ketha's not here," he told Juan. "We don't have to waste time climbing aboard the ship."

"How do you know she's not using magic to shield herself?" Juan sent a sidelong glance his way.

Viktor pressed his lips together. "I know her energy signature. It's here, but it's not fresh. She left at least an hour ago. Maybe two. And she sprinkled a whole lot of magic about to conceal she'd been here at all."

"If that's true, how can you feel her energy?" Juan's nostrils flared. "If I didn't know she'd been here, I'd have missed her scent."

Viktor shrugged. "It's a fair question, but not one I can answer."

Worry filled him, and his gut twisted uncomfortably. With all the Vampires Raphael had unleashed, Ketha's odds of reaching the mesa weren't great. Travel above ground would be more direct, but he raced for the manhole cover.

"Faster if we stick to the streets." Juan mirrored Viktor's thoughts.

"Yeah. I know, but Ketha went this way. I'm sure of it. She'd want to hide herself as long as she could within the tunnels. If something unspeakable happens, maybe we'll get there in time to interrupt it."

Juan barreled down the ladder after him. "No one's going to hurt her," he said. "No one would risk it."

Viktor wasn't so certain. Raphael's instructions had been to deliver Ketha to him, but Vampire loyalty was far from a sure thing. Tonight proved many of their ilk hated their sire. He sheathed his fears and bolted down corridors, relieved when her scent drew him onward. An array of smells collided near the exit point. Three Vamps and Ketha.

"Crap! This might not be good. Even I can smell her here." Juan gave voice to Viktor's fears, his nostrils twitching as he sought further clues.

Not wanting to take time to answer, Viktor hurtled up the

ladder. When he located traces of Ketha in the bone-littered alley-way, he was so relieved, breath left him in great, gulping gasps.

Juan skidded to a halt next to him. "She made it this far, *mi amigo*."

"Indeed she did." Viktor laid on the afterburners, intent on finding Ketha before anyone else did.

12

ESCAPE MADE GOOD

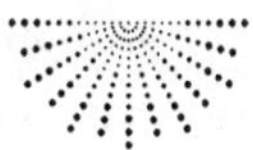

KETHA WAS BREATHING HARD by the time she extricated her pack from the bramble thicket. It took far longer than she would've liked, but at least she'd managed not to open any new wounds on her hands or body. Places that would leave telltale blood. Back on the path, she shouldered her pack and trudged uphill. Dawn was breaking, and she prayed it would scatter sunlight over Ushuaia.

The book had suggested she'd make the mesa before daylight hit, and she would have if it hadn't been for the last batch of Vamps.

She had zero magic left. Remaining hidden, healing her cuts, and wiping out all traces of her blood had sapped her. Nothing she could do about it but keep moving uphill. What it meant, though, was she'd be helpless if she ran into another pack of Vampires intent on turning her over to Raphael.

Don't think about it.

I can rest and recharge once I get to the mesa.

Light brightened around her, leaving her naked and exposed. She bit hard on her lower lip, relying on pain to pull her tattered emotions together. Vamp vision was actually sharper at night, so

161

even if she didn't feel safer without darkness to shield her, she was. Fatigue dragged at her, but she plodded upward.

One step at a time.

Where the hell was the sticker bush that had blocked Viktor's progress? When he'd described it, it sounded like a hop, skip, and a jump away from the cells.

"That's because he moves way faster than me," she mumbled.

Warmth flooded her back, and she turned, squinting against the globe of the sun cresting the horizon. Ketha held out her hands, flexing half-frozen fingers. She hadn't seen the sun in weeks. Its presence revived her, and she started uphill again. After two more switchbacks, the bramble copse that had stymied Viktor rose before her.

Ketha whistled long and low. Shifters appreciated nature, but she'd never seen a sticker bush of any kind anywhere near as substantial as this one. It extended at least twenty feet across the trail, completely blocking progress. Climbing around it looked impossible since it extended both up and down the steep mountainside as far as she could see.

The scent of water tickled her nostrils, and she understood what sustained the bush's growth. A stream, no doubt from the mesa, trickled down the mountain, feeding the luxuriant shrub. With thirst driving her, she wasted precious moments hunting for a break in the thorns where she could punch a hand through to cup water. There wasn't one. Wherever water flowed, the spine-coated bush flourished. Absent a stout pair of leather gloves, smashing through the branches would have opened fresh wounds. Something she couldn't risk.

Viktor had said to go up. She craned her neck, searching for a path on the rocky slope stretching above her. Nothing jumped out looking through her human eyes, and she had no power to scratch beneath the surface. No power to shift, either. No help for it. She'd have to pick her way and hope for the best. The slope was impossibly steep, but it was the last obstacle between her and the mesa.

She couldn't stop here, and going down would be suicide. Vampires would find her.

She'd confront plenty of problems between now and facing off against the Cataclysm's foul magic, but none of those would matter if she couldn't scale the near-vertical slope in front of her. Her thoughts strayed to the other Shifters. Most of them weren't strong enough to tackle this climb without magic. Hell, Ketha wasn't at all certain she was up to it.

She did her damnedest to marshal her flagging resources to tell Rowana and the others to bring a rope, but the other Shifter didn't answer. Probably because Ketha's telepathic voice was too weak to punch through.

Enough procrastination. Defeat wasn't in her vocabulary, particularly not so close to a critical goal.

Apparently, the wolf agreed because it growled, *"Move. Now."*

She set a foot on the mountainside above her, hoping the faint trail Viktor had alluded to would show itself. She looked up, but the top was so far away even thinking about it made no sense. Ketha narrowed her focus to finding footing that wouldn't send her plummeting down the mountain in a welter of rock fall that might cut her to shreds.

Blood would be her undoing. She had to keep all of it inside her body.

The sun's warmth that had felt welcome when it first hit her, made her sweat beneath her heavy robe. The garment, still damp from her escape from the underground tunnels, grew clammy and stuck to her back and breasts. Thirst dogged her, but she didn't have any water. The heavy pack altered her center of gravity, and she learned fast which moves worked and which threatened to unbalance her as she worked her way uphill.

Magic would have helped, but she may as well wish for a fairy godmother. She halted, panting, after a car-sized rock that had looked secure—and felt secure when she tested it with a foot—careened downhill, almost taking her with it.

Ketha leaned into the mountain, panting. The slope was growing steeper, and she was a long way from its crest. Viktor's Vampire coordination, strength, and speed had served him well.

Yeah. Too bad I don't have any of those things.

She started upward again, afraid if she remained still too long, fear would immobilize her. She was stuck. Going down would be as hard as continuing up. And far more dangerous. Since it was too steep to go straight up like she had been, she searched for patterns in the hillside that would allow her to mimic the switchbacks on the trail below.

She sucked in a startled breath when she picked out a route. Maybe it had been there all along, and she was just now seeing it because she'd asked the right questions. Shrugging slightly, she angled right and found somewhat easier going. Magic was like that. You had to ask the proper questions to get the answers you needed. Since Shifter magic had its roots in nature, maybe this mountainside was structured a lot like her power.

A soft laugh bubbled past her lips. She was really losing it, comparing this rough, rocky terrain to magic. "Whatever works," she muttered and turned hard left onto a path she could suddenly make out. At least she was going somewhat faster than when she'd started up the steep grade.

The sun had been up for a while by the time she reached the top, breathing as if she'd run a marathon. The last part hadn't been all that hard, but time-consuming. Ketha pulled herself over the ridgeline. The mesa from her vision spread before her, and tears filled her eyes, tracking down her face. Half a dozen condors flew lazily, stretching their wings in bright sunlight. The mesa looked like paradise with sun glinting off pools at its far end.

Pools meant water. Viktor had said it wasn't tainted. Her dry-as-dust throat spasmed. Ketha stumbled down a gentle incline and crossed to a pool. Shrugging her pack off her shoulders, she lay on her belly and dropped her face into the water, drinking. The liquid laved her parched throat, tasting clean and pure. She drank until the dryness left her mouth, and then she drank some more. How the hell could the water up here have escaped contamination from below? She'd always assumed the toxic air and water were by-products of the Cataclysm. If that were so, all the air and all the water should be the same.

Don't kick a gift horse in the mouth.

Ketha choked on a mouthful of water, laughing at her practical inner maven's advice.

She'd rolled into a sit, water dripping down her chin, when Viktor's scent reached her. Ketha bolted to her feet, shielding her eyes from sunlight with one hand. Juan and Viktor appeared in the same low spot on the ridge she'd picked to finish her climb. She stared at them as they loped through bright sunlight. While she'd known the sun wouldn't immobilize Vampires, she'd assumed it would have some effect.

It didn't. Not much, anyway.

Fear for her sister Shifters twisted around her heart like a fist. She had to contact them. Warn them.

Viktor reached her, his green eyes liquid with worry and caring. She opened her mouth to tell him how glad she was to see him, but he swept her into an embrace and crushed her against his chest, cradling her head in one big hand. Ketha wound her arms around him, reveling in the feel of him against her. Her throat thickened with a welter of conflicting emotions until words felt quite beyond her.

She wanted him to hold her forever, but he was a Vampire. No matter how kind he was to her, or how attracted she was to him, their magnetism still held a Romeo and Juliet forbidden aspect, and she'd do well to steer clear of entanglements. Especially now with the fate of the world hanging in the balance. She told herself to let go, to move out of the protective circle his body formed around hers. Instead, she clung tighter.

"I am so relieved you're safe." Viktor's deep voice rumbled against her hair. "When we returned to *Arkady* and you weren't there, I had more than a few anxious moments. You went to ground at the level of the cells, didn't you?"

Ketha nodded. "Vamps were in the cells, but they ran right by me."

"Thank Christ for that. I'd lay waste to the world if it meant keeping you safe." Viktor's arms were taut with tension where they circled her body, but his hands remained gentle, smoothing hair away from her face.

"I've been taking care of myself for a long time," she protested, her words muffled against his chest.

"Doesn't matter. That was then. Now you have me."

He sounded so possessive, and so unutterably male, she smothered a smile.

"Are any other Shifters here yet?" Juan's voice intruded, snapping Ketha back to reality.

She wriggled out of Viktor's embrace. "No. And that climb was horrible. At least it was for me. My magic's depleted, and…" She shook her head, smiling sheepishly. "Sorry. I'm babbling."

"Why didn't you shift?" Juan asked.

"It requires a boatload of power. I'm tapped out."

"Can you reach your sisters telepathically?" Viktor asked, sounding worried.

"I don't know if I have enough power to light a candle, but I'll try." Ketha's instincts, the ones that had nothing to do with her magic, sparked with dread. "What happened that they need to know about?"

"Raphael's dead—" Juan began.

"That's wonderful news," Ketha cut in.

"Yeah, it would be if another Vamp hadn't killed him and then feasted on his blood," Viktor said sourly.

"Huh?" Ketha squared her tired shoulders. "What am I missing here?"

"If a Vampire kills his sire, and then drinks his blood, the sire—in this case Raphael—gets a free ride back from death in a different body."

Understanding rocked Ketha backward on the balls of her feet. "Holy crap. That's hideous. Did the Vampire know what he was doing?"

"I'm sure he did." Viktor frowned, looking sheepish. "I'm probably the only one who didn't pay attention after Raphael turned us and gave us chapter and verse about the things we could and couldn't do as Vampires."

"Any idea why?" Ketha persisted.

"Why I didn't pay attention? It was because I never wanted to be a Vampire." Viktor shrugged uncomfortably. "I was weak, too enamored with staying alive, to refuse his wrist when he offered it."

"Not what I meant," Ketha said. "Whoever killed Raphael must have hated him. Why would they offer him a hall pass to live again?"

"Jorge is probably under the illusion he can harness Raphael's power, add it to his own," Viktor replied.

A snorting grunt emerged from Juan. "Yup. I'm sure Jorge believes he can control the old bastard. By the time Raphael is done, whatever's left of Jorge will be cut into ribbons and buried six feet under."

Ketha closed her teeth over her lower lip. "You're going to have to help me here. Vamps can insert their spirit or their essence or whatever you want to call it into another body and permanently eradicate the body's original owner?"

"So long as you're talking about two Vampires, yes," Juan replied.

"Something about being turned alters your soul's hold on your body," Viktor added. The corners of his mouth twisted downward. "I always figured no soul worth its salt wanted to share real estate with Vampire energy, so they're ready to flee at a moment's notice."

"So the part that was…Jorge"—Ketha stuttered, hunting for his name—"has been looking for an excuse to exit stage left ever since Jorge was turned."

"Probably," Viktor agreed. "Having Raphael barge his way in almost guarantees whatever was left of Jorge isn't there anymore, leaving the path clear for Raphael to take charge."

"It's too bad," Juan said. "At one point, Jorge was a decent enough sort. He sold boat repair materials here in Ushuaia, and Viktor and I did quite a bit of business with him."

"Ketha!" flared bright in her mind.

She looked from one Vampire to the other and held up a hand. "It's one of my sisters. Hang on. I can hear her, which means I can probably talk as well."

"Rowana?" Ketha projected her mind voice, hoping it would get through.

"Yes. Where are you?"

"The mesa."

Rowana paused long enough, Ketha was afraid she'd run her lean supply of magic dry—again.

"You still there?" she sent, and crossed her fingers a lack of power on her side wasn't the problem.

"Not only me. Six of us. How in the goddess's name did you get up this mountainside? We're at the bramble thicket, but even with magic, I fear it won't be possible."

"I'm on my way. It's not quite as impossible as it looks." A thought struck her. *"Can any of you shift?"*

Rowana hesitated. *"We haven't shifted for months. Now's not the time to test it—unless we have to. It would run what magic we have left down to bedrock, and if it didn't work, we'd be stuck."*

"Hang on. I'll be there as fast as I can." Ketha started for the far side of the mesa, intent on descending to help her sisters. Weariness dogged her, but at least she wasn't thirsty anymore.

Viktor caught her up easily. "What? Where are you going?"

"The other Shifters, six of us anyway, can't make the climb. They need me."

"Let us help them." Juan loped to her other side. "It's easy for us, and you look trashed."

Ketha grinned. "Never tell a woman she looks like shit."

"You're beautiful," Viktor broke in. "But Juan's right about you looking tired. Please. Do whatever you need to so the other Shifters will accept us, and we'll escort them up here."

Ketha sucked in a ragged breath, recognizing wisdom when she heard it. Question was whether her sisters would accept Vampire assistance.

No time like the present to find out.

"Rowana."

"Yes? We're waiting for you, but don't take too long."

"Two Vampires are with me. Vamps who helped me after I escaped from my cell. I trust them, and they volunteered to guide you up here. They're also part of the vision I had. The one that showed me this place. They're far stronger than I am. Please let them help you." Ketha stopped talking and waited.

"I don't give a jolly fuck if they're the devil incarnate," Aura's voice cut in. *"Tell them to get moving. I feel hella exposed here."*

"Did you hear that?" Ketha glanced at Viktor and Juan.

"I kind of did. Does that mean it's a go?" Viktor raised a questioning brow. At Ketha's nod, he and Juan vaulted over the top of the ridge and disappeared. Moving forward until she could see, she watched them scramble down the steep, unstable slope until its angle hid them from view.

Ketha tamped back a wry grin. Finally, a useful Vampire trait. She wouldn't have long to appreciate it, though. If her plan worked, they might turn into Shifters.

What would Viktor and Juan think about that? Should she tell them ahead of time? She made her way back to where she'd left her pack, considering how to proceed. The safest course—since she wasn't certain how they'd react—was to do nothing. Not until after her spell was done and the Cataclysm well on its way out.

If everything worked. The whirlwind that had shanghaied nature would put up a hell of a fight to hang onto its power.

She breathed deep, and then repeated it, filling her lungs with clean, pure air. Something about the mesa felt right to her in a way nothing had since the Cataclysm. Nature felt the way it ought to, not straining against unnatural bonds. It would take a while for the women to scale the mountain. The best use of her time would be resurrecting her magic as best she could.

Sleep was out of the question, but food would help. Condors clustered around two of the caves set into cliffs on opposing sides of the mesa. She felt certain the fish Viktor had mentioned could be found within. Striding purposefully toward the nearest cave, she reached for the birds' minds and reassured them she didn't pose a threat to any young that might be nesting within. They swooped and cawed, brushing her face with their feathers.

Wonder filled her that this tiny corner of the natural world was still intact. No matter how unlikely the remote paradise was, she'd take her miracles as they materialized, without too many questions. Ketha ducked into the cave. At first, she tried to avoid stepping in bird dung, but it was impossible, so she slogged through piles of it, heading for the distinctive tang of water.

Birds moved aside, and she knelt next to a pool teeming with trout. Scooping one up with her hands was simple. Once she had three, she made her way back into waning sunlight. It wasn't much past eleven, but the ever-present clouds were blowing in, driven by mounting wind. The Shifters' weather spell was fading. Maybe it had kept a few Vampires inside. Just because they weren't immobilized by sunlight didn't mean they liked it.

She pulled a knife from the sheath that hung inside her robes and gutted the fish. Once that was done, she focused a thin beam of magic on a large flat stone to heat it. Soon, her fish were sizzling merrily. The scent of them cooking flooded her mouth with saliva, and her stomach cramped from hunger.

Unable to wait, she plucked a trout from the stones, pulled the bones out in a single piece, and ate hungrily. She inhaled a second before her frantic attack on the food receded. She eyed the third trout and decided to save it for the other Shifters. She'd had enough for now.

Speaking of her sisters. Where were they? She'd figured it would take them a while, but they should be here. Rowana hadn't been kidding when she'd said their power was too depleted to shift. Ketha got to her feet and ran lightly to the side of the mesa leading back to the trail. She climbed to the top of the ridgeline and looked down.

Aura, Rowana, Karin, and the rest were strung out single file, moving slowly, their faces blotchy from exertion. Aura glanced up and saw her. Worry twisted the woman's blonde beauty into something harsh.

"What happened?" Ketha sent.

"What didn't?" the other Shifter retorted. *"All of us are safe, but more Vamps showed up. Viktor and Juan are at the bottom, fighting them."*

Breath curdled in Ketha's chest. *"Why didn't you stay to help them?"*

"Five of us did," Aura clarified, sounding bitter. *"The five young ones."*

"We tried to argue that they needed us," Rowana jumped in. *"They sent us packing. Said we were too out of shape to be more than a liability."*

"They didn't appreciate the value of mature magic." Aura curled her lips into a sneer.

"Ha!" Rowana countered. *"They knew we had little enough to spare."*

Five more minutes brought the three Shifters, along with

Becca, Moira, and Zoe to the crest. They tumbled over it and sat, panting, on the rocky ground.

Moira's nostrils quivered. "Is that fish I smell?"

"It is," Ketha answered absently, her mind on fire with worry for Viktor. If he got himself killed defending her, she'd never forgive herself. Aside from that, he, Juan, and four other Vampires were necessary for her spell to have even a faint chance of success.

She sank to the ground next to the other Shifters. "Tell me," she demanded. "What happened? How many Vamps attacked?"

"Well, now, 'tisn't as if they don't all know one another," Zoe said in her soft, Irish brogue. Red hair fell to her waist in tangles, and her brown eyes were pinched with weariness. "Four of those bastards showed up, and all of them got into a shouting match. I'm guessin' Raphael's dead, but he's been born again or some such crap."

"Anyway." Rowana took over. "Your Vamps made it abundantly clear they weren't turning us over to the four. Round about that time, the rest of us chugged up the trail and wove an immobility spell. Problem was it trapped all six of the Vampires, so it took a wee bit of doing to extricate the good ones. Once they were free, they shooed us on our way."

"Said they'd take care of the others and would be along presently." Aura tottered upright. "I'm getting water and, if there's enough fish, I say we cook a passel of them. We'll need a full complement of power before this day is over. For that, we must be fed."

Ketha got to her feet and returned to the ridgeline, casting worried glances down the empty mountainside. She focused telepathy and called each of the five Shifters presumably with Viktor and Juan.

No one answered.

It didn't soothe her worried places. She turned to Rowana. "I'm going down there to see if I can help."

"You'll do no such thing." Rowana pushed heavily to her feet and wrapped a hand around Ketha's arm. For one thing, your Vampire most specifically said you were to remain here."

"He's scarcely *my Vampire*," Ketha protested.

Rowana sent a meaningful glance Ketha's way. "Oh, but I believe he is. There's something about him when he thinks of you, and when you think about him—"

"Enough." Ketha made a shooing motion with both hands. "I'll give them half an hour. If they don't show up, I'm going down there to help. My magic's somewhat recharged."

"Have it your way." Rowana smiled sweetly. "Meantime, you can lead us to where you found fish. It's been years since they disappeared from the ocean, and they'll be a rare treat."

Ketha stalked across the mesa, aware of other Shifters both in front of and behind her. Why had she become defensive about Viktor? When the answer came, it was so obvious, heat rose to her face. She was falling hard for him, and there wasn't a damned thing she could do about it.

Please, she prayed to no one in particular. *Keep him safe. And keep me on track so I can lead the confrontation against the Cataclysm. If I make it through that, I'll sort through my feelings for him.*

Time dripped past. She paced while her sisters ate and drank and visited. They stopped trying to engage her in conversation early on, probably because they sensed her attention lay elsewhere. With each five-minute increment, her fear and discomfort expanded by a factor of ten. At the twenty-five-minute mark, she couldn't stand it any longer and ran headlong for the ridge, intent on summoning magic to cushion her descent.

13

A HARD SELL

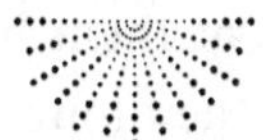

VIKTOR DREW his fist back and punched Daide square in the face to get his attention. Every other attempt at reasoning had brought less than zero success. Viktor didn't have high hopes for this one, but he was frustrated and running out of time. He held onto the other Vampire with his free hand to keep him from turning tail and catapulting down the mountainside.

Daide winced as his nose shattered, sounding like a gunshot. Blood mixed with snot ran down his face, but the damage began to correct itself instantly. He focused bleary, dark eyes on Viktor. "Let us leave, man. Raph's dead, and yeah, I know Jorge might turn into him, but it hasn't happened yet. Not completely, anyway."

"You don't get it," Viktor snapped. "You're part of what happens next. You and Recco need to follow those Shifters." He jerked his chin toward the steep hillside.

Fate might play a hand, supplying the Vampires Ketha needed for her spell, but two of them were right here. Viktor had no intention of doing anything but delivering them to the mesa, no matter what draconian measures were needed to accomplish it.

Juan moved to his side, keeping Recco's upper arm in a death grip. "What do you want me to do about him?" he asked Viktor. "Minute I let go, he'll haul ass down the trail."

"You damn betcha." Recco drew his lips back, displaying elongated fangs. "I didn't like it much when Raphael ordered us nine ways from hell. Not in a hurry to trade him for you."

Viktor inhaled noisily. He'd sent the last five Shifters after the first batch once it became apparent the Vamps had zero interest in chasing them down. None of them had known about Raphael's untimely exit. The second they found out, the four who'd been with Daide and Recco laid on the afterburners and ran off, whooping and hollering like a bunch of kids who'd been told school was canceled—permanently.

He curled his hand tighter around Daide's bicep. "What were you before the Cataclysm?"

"Huh?" The other Vampire rolled his eyes. "Who the fuck cares? That life is long gone."

"Whatever it was, whoever you were," Juan said, "you can be that person again. The Shifters have a way to defeat the Cataclysm. Once it's gone, Vampirism might disappear."

Viktor closed his jaws with a *clack*. He wouldn't have put it out there in quite that way. For all he knew, Daide and Recco valued their Vampire status and would fight claw and fang to hold onto it.

"What do you mean *defeat the Cataclysm?*" Recco drew his dark brows into a thick line.

Viktor tossed his shoulders back. The cat was out of the bag now. No reason not to answer. "The event that broke the world, creating the Cataclysm, was a small group of Vamps and Shifters holding a secret spell-casting session somewhere in the far northern reaches of Siberia. They were trying to add Shifter ability to Vampirism—"

Daide burst out laughing. Loud guffaws rolled from him until tears joined the blood and snot dripping down his face. "That's rich," he scoffed when he could talk again. "You're so full of shit, you're drowning in it. Why the hell would Vamps ever want to sully themselves with Shifter magic?"

He twisted in Viktor's grip and met his gaze straight on. "You were Raphael's special pet for a long time. All the old Vamps are exactly like him. Arrogant dickwads who eat, live, and breath being Vampires."

"It's the same thing I thought." Viktor shrugged. "Even Ketha said it surprised her, but she's some kind of Shifter seer, and she saw the whole thing unfold in a mirror she uses to scry things."

"Anyway," Juan cut it, "Ketha believes if we recreate the blending of Vamp and Shifter energy, we can finish what that group began ten years ago. It should end the Cataclysm. Hard to say what it will do to us—or them."

"Handy for the Shifters if we become more like them," Recco said smugly.

"Not really," Viktor replied. "Beyond ridding ourselves of the barrier holding us prisoner—and the odds of success aren't in our favor—the rest is a crapshoot. No one knows what will actually happen to Vampires or Shifters after we're done."

"Speaking of done, is Raphael really gone?" Daide asked. "Or is that some cock-and-bull tale you cooked up to convince us to throw our lot in with you?"

"Good question," Recco chimed in. "If Raph's not dead and he finds out about this, he'll hang all of us by our nuts with thumbscrews."

"Yeah. He's really dead," Juan said. "Go ahead. Test my words. All of us can sense truth so long as it's straightforward."

"Test mine." Viktor shook hair back from his face. "Raphael's body is gone, but Jorge drank his blood."

"Which means, Raphael will live again in him," Daide said, grinding his fangs against his lower teeth. "Might be an improvement—if Jorge can keep the upper hand at least some of the time."

"Ha!" Recco snorted. "Not as strong as Raphael was." He scrubbed a hand through his shorn locks. "If there's a chance we can alter our fate, I'm up for giving it a shot. Daide never answered you, but he and I were veterinarians, the only ones in Ushuaia. We mostly treated stock and ranch animals, but we worked for the national park service too. Seabirds. Seals. Penguins. You name it. If it got sick, we tried to save it."

Color rose to Daide's face. "You had to go and out us."

"No shame in what we did." Recco faced his erstwhile partner. "It was a hell of a transition from saving things to draining their blood. And drinking it."

The sound of someone moving downhill fast snapped Viktor's attention upward. Rocks cascaded in the wake of a hasty descent. He scanned the slope with his hyper-tuned vision and acute sense of smell.

Ketha.

What the hell? He'd specifically told the other Shifters to make sure she stayed put. He dodged a basketball-sized boulder that passed inches from his head.

"Stop!" He used mind speech rather than yelling. She was making such an unholy racket, she'd never hear him, no matter how loud he yelled.

"I'm coming to help you."

"We're good, Ketha. Stop before you kill Juan or me with one the boulders you're kicking loose."

The slope above them quieted. A flame of satisfaction flickered deep within him. She was worried. About him. Worried enough she'd laid her exhaustion and her fear of the steep mountain aside.

"Stay where you are," he told her. *"We're headed up."*

Viktor let go of Daide and motioned for Juan to do the same with Recco. "It could be a whole new world out there," he told them. "Let's do everything in our power to make certain the Shifters have what they need from us."

"Fancy words." Daide shook his head. "I stopped dreaming about ever being free a long while back. Figured the water and air and lack of food would do all of us in eventually, and I wasn't mourning our passing."

"Yeah. Me, either," Recco muttered. "Let's do this. Whatever it is." He smiled crookedly. "I want to see if it's going to work."

Viktor motioned them toward the steep grade, bringing up the rear. Thanks to Vamp speed, strength, and agility, they defeated the elevation with little wasted motion or visible effort. Ketha leaned against a scrubby oak at about the halfway point. He reached for her, but she shook her head and started after Juan, Daide, and Recco. Viktor followed, wanting to be as close to her as he could manage.

"You found two of the Vamps from my vision," she said.

"They found me," he corrected. "I was hoping fate would deliver who we needed to the right place, but when Daide and Recco showed up, I decided to nudge it along."

"What'd you say to convince them?"

Maybe because she'd conquered the mountainside once, she moved with authority, threading her way between rocks, stunted trees, and sparse bushes.

"I told them the truth," Viktor replied. "Actually, Juan did. Once it was out in the open, I ran with it."

"Interesting that it worked." Ketha stopped and turned to face him, breathing hard. It cost her far more than it cost him to climb so steeply. "Maybe I underestimated how enamored you all are with being Vamps."

He shook his head. "No. You didn't. Not for the pre-Cataclysm variety."

"Any idea how many besides Raphael are in *Ciudad de Huesos*?"

"Yeah, maybe half our number were here before the Cataclysm."

"Any other Masters like Raphael? Or goddess forbid, Nosferatus?"

"Uh-uh. Best I understand it, Raphael ended up in Ushuaia

around 1900. He'd been in Buenos Aires prior to that and got into a turf war with other Master Vamps there."

The corners of Ketha's expressive mouth twitched, making him want to crush his lips down on hers. "I'm guessing he lost."

"That was always my guess too. He never talked about any of it. Once he got here, he set about making new Vamps who'd be loyal to him. If anyone else ever had a hankering to create their own line, Raphael drummed it out of them fast."

"Killed them?"

"If his actions after the Cataclysm reflect how he was before, it's a likely guess. There's the odd rogue Vamp here who doesn't belong to Raphael, but they never made the mistake of starting a stable of their own."

Viktor closed the short distance between them and cradled her face between his hands. "I don't want to talk about him."

She leaned into his hands, and her expression softened. "I was so worried about you, I couldn't sit still. When Rowana told me you and Juan were fighting down below, it tore me up."

He brushed a thumb over her lips. "Thanks for looking after me."

"You're making fun of me."

"Not really. It's been a long time since anyone's cared what happened to me. It makes me feel like a man again." In truth, it made him feel a whole lot of things, like humble and grateful and amazed anyone could hold anything but disgust toward the Vampire he'd turned into. He tried to articulate some of it, but his tongue tangled over the words.

Ketha kissed the thumb he'd been tracing her lips with. She trained golden eyes liquid with caring on him. "You bring out parts of me I was certain were dead too, but this isn't the time— for any of that. We need to get to the mesa and finalize our plans. I spent hours with my spell book aboard your ship, plotting strategy."

He kissed the tip of her nose and let go of her while he still could. Much more time that close and he wasn't certain he'd be able to resist kissing her, running his hands under her robe to explore the tempting curves beneath it.

Ketha grinned wantonly. "Hold onto those thoughts, tiger."

His groin tightened with unslaked need, and a fierce protectiveness surged, running hot. "What I want from you runs deeper than thoughts. It will take the rest of our lives."

The longing in her gaze deepened, sharpened, but she turned and strode uphill purposefully. The faint path didn't offer space for him to walk by her side. Her scent kindled desire and filled him with optimism they'd find a way to be together once their task was done. For now, she was right to refocus them on what lay ahead.

"Are you going to tell me anything about it?" He followed her upward.

"You mean my strategy?"

"Yes. Before you start, though, describe the other two Vampires in your vision. I'm sure I know them, and maybe they'll be as straightforward to convince as Daide and Recco were."

"I can do that, but my visions aren't always exact replicas of how things play out. Remember I told you I see many iterations of future events?"

"I remember, but that particular vision had six of us and twelve of you. You're all present and accounted for. Doesn't that mean we're short two Vampires?"

"Possibly. The other two were mirror opposites. One was very fair. Shoulder-length white-blond hair, blue eyes. The other looked a lot like Raphael with his long, dark hair and intense, blue-gray eyes."

Viktor shuffled through possibilities. The dark-haired Vamp sounded a lot like Jorge, which wasn't necessarily good.

Ketha slowed near the ridgeline. "I can almost hear gears meshing in your head." She turned to face him. "I could help myself to your thoughts, but how about if you just tell me."

"It's possible the dark-haired one is the Vamp who killed Raphael."

Ketha slitted her eyes, nodding reluctantly. "I'm not thrilled by the idea, but it makes sense from a cosmic balance point of view."

"Say more."

"Raphael was in three of my attempts to scry the future. In one, he had hold of a dead Shifter. I didn't see him kill her, but it looked as if he probably did. In the others, he was wretchedly ambivalent about helping launch the Cataclysm spell."

Viktor considered the information. "Even though Raphael wasn't in the vision you chose to go with, Jorge may have been."

"About the size of it," she said, and set her mouth in a resolute line. "Some things are destined, preordained. Raphael—or his energy—appears to be linked to whatever will unfold once we set the spell in motion."

"How long will it take?"

"I'm not certain. It has multiple layers, each dependent on successful completion of the previous one. I sketched out one possible deployment to accomplish all of the necessary elements."

"Give me some idea," he persisted. "Minutes? Hours? Days?"

"If everything goes well, maybe an hour or two. If something doesn't work the way I expect it will, and we have to make last minute adjustments, it could take longer." Ketha hesitated, wrapping her arms around herself.

He folded her against him, surprised at the shudders racking her. "What?"

"If it takes too long, the Shifters will run their magical wells out of juice."

"So? We'll start over."

She shook her head against his shoulder. "Doesn't work like that. We have one shot at this. The Cataclysm is sentient, alive. It will fight back once it figures out we have a way to dismantle it. If it can, it'll tighten its noose around Ushuaia and kill us all."

Viktor drew back so he could look at her. "I don't understand how magic could be so powerful."

"Neither did I until I spent time with my book. Magical books are notorious for only giving you what you need when you actually need it. I've searched it before for information about the Cataclysm and how to defeat it, and come up empty-handed."

Viktor turned her in his arms and prodded her up a few more feet to a sandy ledge tucked beneath the ridgeline, where they could sit. The sun was long since gone, and a cold wind blew. The ledge would offer some protection and give them a few minutes before they joined the others. He settled her next to him and wrapped his arms around her, offering his body as a windbreak.

"Why do you think the Cataclysm is alive?"

She leaned closer to him. "All spells are alive while they're being created. Because this one was interrupted midstream, it held onto its sentience. The more I know about it, the surer I am that one of the original group sabotaged its making."

"By accident?"

She tilted her head and looked at him. "Ha! Not a chance. Given what I know now, I suspect one of the Vampires caught wind the spell was really crafted to obliterate their Vampire power—whether it turned them into Shifters or not. He reacted and sabotaged the casting with sex."

"How'd he find out?"

"How else?" Ketha made a bitter face. "One of the Shifters was in love with him and did what lovers have always done."

"She told him, huh?" Viktor digested the new information. "Did the book clue you in on that?"

She shook her head cradled against his shoulder. "No. My wolf."

"Any chance of meeting your bond animal?" Viktor held his breath. Now that the words were out, he understood how much he wanted to know all sides of the woman in his arms.

"If we get through this in one piece, of course. Assuming my

Shifter magic isn't perverted somehow—and doesn't disappear entirely."

"Then we have to make certain we win."

He pressed his mouth into a hard line to keep from cursing Vampires from here to the Antarctic Circle. Fucking bastards. As usual, if there was a mess, they were smack dab in the center of it. "If we manage to defeat the Cataclysm, is there any chance every-thing else will go back to how it was before that group in Siberia mucked around in things?"

"Yeah, it's possible, but not likely. Magic will change, but I don't know what that will look like. Normally, I wouldn't be so quick to run headlong into trying to kill off the Cataclysm, but we don't have a choice. Not really." She raked a hand through her tangled hair. "This whole thing stinks. It's nearly been the death of Earth, and it still might be."

She pressed against him a moment longer and then got to her feet. "Let's join the others and sort this out. The other Vampire in my vision, not Jorge, but the blond. What do you know about him?"

"Not much." Viktor creased his forehead, thinking. "He's one of the old ones, but Raph didn't make him. He's a rogue, keeps to himself. Rumor has it he was here when Raphael showed up, and had been here for a long time. You might ask one of the other men. I didn't pay much attention to my Vampire indoctrination. Do you want me to hunt him down?"

"Not yet. Let's gather everyone together and kick this around. It's one thing for me to strategize in a vacuum, but I'd be worse than a fool not to throw my plan on the table and let everyone poke holes in it. Once we have a direction, we can decide on Mr. No-Name."

"Oh, he has a name." Viktor stood and wrapped his arm around Ketha again. "It's Raziel."

Ketha sucked in a startled-sounding breath. "This could get very interesting. Raziel is another Archangel, just like Raphael."

Viktor started to protest it couldn't possibly mean anything beyond pure coincidence, but Ketha shot a pointed look his way. "Don't be so certain, and yes, I was in your mind. I admit Raphael scarcely evokes love, joy, laughter, or healing. But Raziel recovers what's lost. Come on. Let's launch this before I lose my nerve."

He followed her over the crest and toward where the Shifters had gathered, along with the three Vampires. Respect for Ketha burned bright in his chest. She'd admitted she was scared, but she was forging ahead anyway. He'd have sold his soul—if he had one left—to spare her what was almost upon them, but things didn't work that way.

14

GATHERING OF UNLIKELY ALLIES

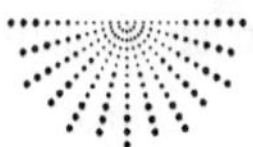

Ketha raised a hand in greeting as she approached her sisters congregated around an impromptu hearth. The smell of cooked fish made her mouth water. The ones she'd devoured earlier hadn't been nearly enough, given her half-starved state. Juan, Recco, and Daide sat off to one side, eating their fish raw.

Rowana smiled broadly and patted the ground next to her, but Ketha shook her head. "It's cold out here. Maybe we could move inside one of the caves. Not one of the condor ones, so we don't disturb them, but somewhere out of the wind." Ketha shouldered her pack and gazed expectantly at the assembled group of Shifters and Vampires.

"I'd be all for that." Zoe got to her feet and wrapped her arms around herself. "These robes are warm, but they don't cut the wind much." Frowning, she peered at debris churned up by the brisk breeze.

"No shit." Aura stood too. "I used to think the weather was bad in Wyoming, but at least we had summer there. I'll bring the rest of the fish we cooked."

Seeing nods from most of the Shifters and a thumbs-up from Viktor, Ketha walked briskly toward the nearest cliff, intent on

187

finding which cave might be the most commodious for sixteen people.

"Second one from the far right should work," Viktor called from behind her. "I explored all of them the first time I was here. That one's large enough and dry. Even the ones without streams and pools tend toward damp places."

Ketha angled right, not questioning his judgment. Viktor was a gem, and it was hard not to follow her heart where he was concerned, but it was a diversion. She focused her mind on Raphael—and Jorge who held what was left of the Master Vampire's essence. The specter of dealing with him in any capacity made her blood run cold, but she didn't see any choice.

For some reason she couldn't fathom he was locked into the spell to break the Cataclysm. Maybe he was the negative energy the spell would need to ground itself. She felt out of her depth and longed for her mentors, but she may as well wish for the moon on a platter for all the good it did her.

Those first few years in Ushuaia, she'd yearned for her cozy lab and all its state-of-the-art equipment, but that hadn't done much good, either.

She glanced at indentations in the cliff and picked the second one, ducking low to crawl inside. Because the opening was small and didn't let much light into the cave, she kindled her mage light, keeping its output low to conserve magic. Ketha felt warmer immediately. Getting out of the wind was a relief. She made her way to the edge of a sandy floor and removed her pack, balancing it against a wall while she withdrew the spell book and her notes from earlier. By the time she was ready, everyone had seated themselves in a rough circle. Several mage lights bobbed near the Shifters.

"We can get by with a single light," she said. "I'll keep mine lit because I need to read."

"What happens next?" Rowana asked. "You were quite close-mouthed regarding details when we used telepathy."

Ketha clutched the book against her chest and faced the group. "That's true enough. I had no idea if anyone could intercept my mind speech, so it felt prudent to err on the side of caution."

"Anyone like whom?" Karin asked.

"I didn't think anyone but us held that type of magic," Zoe added.

Ketha shrugged. "The Cataclysm might be far more sentient than we realize. I taught Viktor telepathic speech. It wasn't difficult, only took a single suggestion. If he could master it, other Vamps likely could as well." She stopped to take a breath. "Doesn't matter. We're together now, so I can speak freely without worrying someone is tapping into my telepathy."

"Can you now?" Zoe sent a pointed look at the four Vampires.

"We need them," Ketha said. "My vision inferred it will take all of us and half a dozen Vampires to cast this working. When I consulted my spell book, it seconded that impression."

"Where are the other two Vampires?" Aura asked.

Ketha held up a hand. "How about if I tell this in order, and you hold your questions until I'm done?"

Hearing a chorus of yesses, Ketha dove in. "Vamps and Shifters combining their power started this, and that's what it will take to end it. Make no mistake, the Cataclysm will fight back. The reason everything is dead or dying is because the Cataclysm has been sucking the life force out of everything it can. That and energy from the original spell gone bad are how it maintains itself."

"That's a dead-end street for the Cataclysm," Viktor spoke up. "What the hell does it do once nothing is left to feed on?"

"Almost doesn't matter," Rowana said flatly. "We won't be here to see it implode—unless we manage to defeat it."

"So far, this doesn't make sense," Recco said. "What Ketha described is a parasite, and they weaken their host, but don't kill it."

"Were you a doctor?" Karin asked.

"Yes, but for animals."

"Focus, people." Ketha made come-along motions with the hand not holding onto her book. "Maybe I'm wrong about the Cataclysm's modus operandi, but I'm not wrong about needing to work together to annihilate it." She withdrew her worksheets from the book and laid it next to her feet, keeping hold of the pages covered with her notes.

"The way I have this figured out, our spell will unfold in layers. Each layer requires two Shifters and one Vampire."

"Can the same Vampire do double duty?" Juan asked.

"If you're asking if a Vamp can be part of more than one layer, it would be difficult, since each group will need to hold their casting in place for the next group to build on."

Ketha waited, but no one asked anything further. Fifteen pairs of eyes focused on her. She swallowed around a dry throat and went on. "Six spell layers mirror the six layers of the Cataclysm."

"How do you know how the Cataclysm is put together?" Rowana asked.

"Like I told Aura, this would go faster if you held questions until the end," Ketha replied. "I know because when I asked the spell book to assist me, that was part of the information I gleaned from it."

She took another breath before going on. "It's possible we could do this in five layers by combining the first two. The book wasn't terribly clear about that part, but basically we'll be working from the outer portion of the Cataclysm inward. By the time we get to the core where we do our serious immolation, we'll all be in mortal danger.

"This is potentially a suicide mission," Ketha went on. "If the Cataclysm is stronger than we are, it will swallow us whole. Suck us into its core where we'll either burn or suffocate."

"You make it sound like a black hole," Daide said.

"I don't know much about them," Ketha replied, "but if you're referring to an impossibly strong gravitational pull, then yes.

Magic will be the only thing holding us separate from the Cataclysm while we focus power to destroy its center. The reason we're doing this in layers is we have to open a passageway to access the thing's core. Individually, or even in pairs, we don't possess magic strong enough to do that in one fell swoop, so we'll open it a section at a time. Each team's job will be to hold their portion open so the following team can reach through it and unravel the next part."

"A whole lot could go wrong," Rowana observed.

"True enough," Ketha answered her. "We don't have to do this. But you need to know what you're getting into if you agree."

"I thought you needed all twelve of us," Zoe said.

"Yes. Either we all concur in taking what is a significant chance, or none of us move forward."

"Have you cast a tarot spread?" one of the younger Shifters asked. "To check the timing of our effort and such?"

Ketha shook her head. "My cards are back in our old grotto. They weren't one of the things I rescued from there, but feel free to take a peek with your own deck."

"What do we do about the two missing Vampires?" Aura asked.

"I'll take care of that," Viktor said.

"Take care of it as in find two more?" she pressed.

"It's not quite that straightforward," Ketha spoke up. "One of the other two that I saw in my vision is apparently an old rogue Vampire named Raziel, who hails from before the Cataclysm."

"Mmph. Not sounding very promising," Rowana muttered.

"Oh, it gets worse," Ketha assured her. "Raphael is dead—"

"They already know," Viktor cut in. "They were there when I told the other Vampires back by the bramble bush."

Cheers rose from the Shifters, but Ketha waved them to silence. "Yeah, I thought him being out of the way was great too, except the Vamp who killed him drank from him, and apparently that means Raphael's essence is now part of his killer."

"Huh?" Aura focused her green-eyed gaze on the four

Vampires and shoved blonde curls out of her face. "Why would one of you be that irresponsible?"

Juan shrugged, looking uncomfortable. "Power is a funny thing. I'm sure Jorge was so wrapped up in bloodlust, he figured he could control the old fucker. Add to it that we've been chronically starved for years. All that blood was likely too much to resist."

"Raziel?" Rowana sputtered. "And Raphael. What the hell is this? A convocation of Archangels?"

"Shit! Aw, shit!" Aura staggered to her feet, her face drained of color. Ketha ran to her and gripped her arm. "Are you ill?"

Laughter with a hysterical edge burst from the other Shifter. "I wish it were that simple," she said once she got herself under control.

"You're talking in riddles, dearie." Karin joined them, poking and prodding to make certain Aura didn't have something physically amiss.

"Stop that!" Aura pulled away from Karin's ministrations. "You're a doctor. Ketha is a seer. What am I?"

"A historian who studies prophecies," Ketha replied automatically. Understanding slammed home, along with an eerie, creeping sensation that made her skin crawl. "Is there some prophecy that deals with Archangels?"

Aura rolled her eyes. "I can't believe you asked that."

Ketha bristled. "Instead of telling me how stupid I am, could you answer my question?"

"Of course, there are prophecies that deal with Archangels. Thousands of them. The question you should have asked is if there's one with Raphael and Raziel—and us."

Ketha battled defensiveness. It had no place here, but she was having a hell of a hard time moving beyond it. "Look. I'm not thinking this particular Raphael has jack shit to do with the Archangel. They just happen to have the same name. He's something like centuries old, which means he came from the old country. It was a common enough name back in the fifteen and sixteen hundreds."

Aura narrowed her eyes. "There's a prophecy that includes Shifters and has to do with the end of days." She paused for effect, but Aura always did have a dramatic flair. "Those same two Archangels are part of it." She leveled her gaze at Ketha. "You can chalk it up to coincidence, but we need every single scrap of advantage we can scare up here."

"I'd like to hear the prophecy." Viktor spoke slowly. "There might be some element of it I can use to convince Raziel to sign on with our side. There was never any love lost betwixt him and Raphael, and I figure his enmity will transfer to Jorge."

"Go on." Ketha let go of Aura. "I'm sorry. I know I can be prickly. I want to hear too."

Aura flashed a grim smile her way. "We can all be prime bitches. Goes with the territory. Okay. Here's that prophecy—and a smidge of background. Raziel is the keeper of secrets and the finder of what's been lost. He has surprisingly loose lips for someone who's supposed to keep his mouth shut, though. There's always been friction between him and Raphael, mostly because he knows all Raphael's secrets and has kicked the door open a time too often. In any event, they've lived in separate places for eons. The prophecy is when they come back together, Shifters will be fighting for their very existence. We will be forced to choose sides, one Archangel or the other. Nothing in the prophecy offers clues as to our proper choice."

"Go on," Ketha urged, drawn in by truth pinging off her power.

Aura looked away. "It's pretty simple. If we choose correctly, we get to live. If we bet on the wrong horse, we'll be swept away forever."

"I wonder if some of that is metaphor," Ketha murmured.

"What do you mean?" Aura asked. "All prophecy is metaphor to some extent."

Ketha nodded, thinking. "If we break the Cataclysm,

Vampirism might disappear—or be incorporated with our magic. Does *swept away forever* mean a significant alteration in our magic, or that we die?"

"Could be both," Karin mumbled. "Not to be a harbinger of doom or anything."

"What do you think?" Ketha turned to Viktor and the other Vampires.

"Hard to say," Viktor answered. "Raphael was mad, insane. He covered it well most of the time, but when he was anxious—or angry—it leaked out around the edges. You saw some of it in his single-minded drive to capture you after you escaped."

"Not quite my take on him," Daide cut in. "He was paranoid and power hungry, but from the reading I did, all the older Vamps were a whole lot like him. They were all like mini-generals with their own fiefdoms. Except for here because Raphael wouldn't let anyone else gain the slightest toehold."

Viktor turned a sidelong glance his way. "You've got one over on me in the knowledge department. I never wanted to learn anything about my new calling."

Daide shrugged, looking uncomfortable. "Knowledge is power, not that it helped me or Recco much. We're stuck here same as you." He focused his next words on Ketha. "What did you mean about Vamps turning into Shifters?"

She turned her hands palms up. "It's one of several possible outcomes—if we survive."

"Better than being a Vampire," Recco growled.

"No kidding," Juan seconded and grinned. "Do we get to pick our animals?"

"Doesn't work that way," Aura informed him. "They pick you."

Ketha focused on Aura again. "Most prophecies have conclusions."

"Not this one. It's one of seven unfinished prophecies. My mentor believed they were left that way on purpose because their stories have yet to unfold."

Ketha wondered what the other six were and then understood her mind was wandering. Maybe gathering most of them in position for the casting was accomplishment enough for today.

"We need a few pieces yet before we take on the Cataclysm." Ketha let her gaze travel around the group.

"We'll cast several tarot spreads," one of the younger Shifters volunteered. "To hone in on the most auspicious time to move forward."

"I'll do my best to locate Raziel," Viktor said.

"While you're at it, maybe you can see if Jorge survived feasting on Raph's blood," Juan muttered.

"You're joking, right?" Viktor raked his hands through his hair. "Jorge may well be Raphael's puppet, but there's no way Raph would've killed his next chance at hanging around."

"Oh, yeah. Huh. I wasn't thinking," Juan replied and then added, "Would you like me to come with you?"

"I can move faster alone. Less chance of discovery. I bet all the Vamps are in an uproar."

"Do you think they'll come back this way?" Ketha's stomach twisted into a hard, painful knot.

"Don't know why they would." Zoe broke in. "I didn't follow the first group of Shifters up the hill right away. When it looked as if those four Vamps were about to break and run, I erased their memories of anything they'd heard and seen in the last hour." She dusted her palms together.

Ketha could've hugged her. "Quick thinking on your part. Thanks."

"Don't mention it." Zoe looked pleased with herself. "Everyone else was knee-deep in either fightin' or arguin'. Least I could do."

"I'm going to get moving," Viktor said, and flowed to his feet before heading for the cave's entrance.

"We need to go with him," her wolf spoke up.

Ketha agreed. She tucked her worksheets into the book and

dropped it into her backpack. "Wait for me." She strode across the cave.

Viktor crossed his arms over his chest. "Not a good idea. I can't shield you from discovery, and you don't move fast enough."

"I can do a fair job shielding myself. Half an army of Vamps marched right by me three times—or maybe it was four." She avoided his second point about her being much slower than he was.

"Why don't you stay here and rest so your magic recharges?" He quirked a brow her way.

She ground her teeth together, struggling to craft a reasonable reply. "If Aura's prophecy is afoot, I'll feel the magic. I want to know if it's one of the elements we have to take into consideration." She paused, gathering her thoughts. "I believed we had to work together. If her prophecy is correct, we'll all be working together except for Raphael. He'll be odd man out, and we'll have to deploy our power to overcome him as well as the Cataclysm. The last group made a fatal mistake ten years ago in Siberia. Whoever was leading the charge assumed they were all on the same side, when they weren't."

She inhaled raggedly. It made sense, but left them short of manpower for the plan she'd laid out. Not much she could do but throw herself on the goddess's mercy. Surely Gaia wanted the Cataclysm gone. It was choking the very essence out of Her creations.

Viktor apparently wasn't convinced since he blocked the cave's entrance with his body. "It's almost full dark. Vampire strength will be at its zenith—"

"Either we go together, or I'll follow you." Ketha drew herself up tall, shoulders squared. "We're wasting time."

A muscle twitched beneath one eye, and he snapped his jaws together. "Fine. You want to come? Douse that light, and you have to keep up. I won't use my full speed, but I won't wait for you, either. With Raphael gone and Jorge an unknown quantity,

Vampires will be on the rampage tonight. Nothing will be off-limits. Still want to ride along?"

A shudder tracked down her spine. The smartest thing would be for her to remain here in the relative safety of the mesa and caves, but she had to know if the prophecy had them in its clutches. Viktor didn't have the magic to sort that out. She did.

"Yes. I don't exactly want to, but I don't have a choice."

He ducked through the cave's entrance and took off across the mesa without a backward glance. If she'd thought he was bluffing, his actions quashed that hope. Ketha killed her mage light and ran lightly after him, deploying magic to keep from twisting an ankle.

Viktor might not have bought into the whole Vampire mystique, but his physical ability was far superior to hers, at least in her human form, and now wasn't the time to shift. Ketha moved faster, determined not to hold them back.

15

PROPHECY

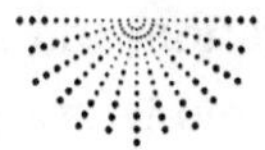

DESPITE HIS WORDS to the contrary, Viktor would've waited for Ketha at the top of the ridge, but he didn't have to. She was making far better time than he'd anticipated, given that she was traveling in the dark. He'd been harsh on purpose to discourage her. He'd sensed her fear and ambivalence and tried to capitalize on it by giving her a good, hard push to stay put.

She hadn't taken the bait, though, and he was proud of her courage on the one hand, but worried sick about her on the other.

"What are you waiting for?" She chugged up next to him, surrounding him with her wonderful wildflower scent. She smelled like the world before the Cataclysm choked the life out of it.

"I wasn't waiting." He kept his voice gruff. Everything he'd said about how dangerous it was to be out and about tonight was true. Softening his demeanor might make her less vigilant, and he needed her to be at the very top of her game.

"Get behind me and keep your hands on my waist," he instructed. "Better yet, grab handfuls of my jacket. We'll be descending fast. Enough of this rock is loose, we need to stay together."

Ketha didn't argue. She fell in behind him, and he felt the tug as she wound her hands into ragged llama pelts that had once been a thick, warm coat.

"Ready," she said. Grim determination lay beneath that one word.

Viktor dialed in his precise Vampire vision. It was like looking through night vision goggles, and the slope turned greenish, but every rock, boulder, indentation, and dicey patch was outlined in bas-relief. He started at a moderate pace, but when she didn't stumble, he moved faster.

They reached the bottom quickly. She untangled her hands from his jacket and followed him as he loped down the trail. At least she wasn't chiding him for being heavy-handed with her. Meant she fully understood what they were up against. She hesitated briefly at the turnoff to the cells. He wanted to say something soothing, like she'd never see the inside of them again, but he didn't want to lie to her.

If she was captured tonight, the Vampires would either kill her or imprison her, but, this time, they'd leave her shackled so she couldn't leverage magic to free herself. They'd post a guard too.

He shrugged and ran faster. No matter what his Vampire kinsmen did, he could free Ketha. Unless they killed her on the spot. Savage protectiveness raked through him. He considered escorting her back to the mesa and leaving her with Juan, Recco, and Daide to make certain she remained there.

"Big mistake," blasted into his mind.

A wry grin split his lips. *"Helping yourself to my thoughts again?"*

"Of course. You didn't want to bring me. I need to stay on top of things."

"It wasn't that I didn't want you with me. I need you to be safe." Viktor grappled with the mind speech mechanism. Using it was far from second nature.

"You can't keep me safe." Her words came slowly, one at a time. *"Hell, I can't even keep any of my Shifters safe. I have an integral role to*

play in what unfolds over the next few days. I'm prepared to sacrifice myself, if it means ending the Cataclysm."

He stopped so precipitously, she pitched into his back. "Oomph. Why—?"

Spinning in place, he crushed her against him and buried his hands in her thick hair. He wanted to say so many things, tell her how important she was to him and how he'd take on the Cataclysm single-handed if it meant she could live. He tried to infuse the depth of his emotion into his touch. Because he couldn't resist her full lips, he fastened his mouth over hers in a quick, hard kiss. She clung to him, kissing him back.

Before he forgot why they'd left the mesa, Viktor released her. Speed was their friend tonight. Survival was everything. He ached to make love with Ketha, bind her to him, make her his for now and always, but they were out here for a reason—and sex wasn't part of the equation.

Beyond that, it was a huge unknown. Sex had dealt a death blow to that ten-years-ago spell in Siberia. Who the hell knew what impact sex between a Shifter and a Vampire would have now? If their current effort came to naught, he'd be damned if it would be his fault.

He ran toward the city, his long strides eating up the trail. When he reached the bottom, he drew into the shadows of a crumbling building.

Ketha joined him, her breath streaming white in the cold night air. "Should we take the tunnels?" she asked, her voice barely above a whisper.

"It's why I stopped. They might be safer for you, but it will take us longer to locate Raziel."

"I thought you all had underground lairs." She focused her golden eyes on him.

"Before the Cataclysm, yeah. The sun's not much of a problem anymore, and as you already saw, what's left of it has very little effect on us."

"Wasn't Raziel here before the Cataclysm?"

Viktor nodded. "So was Raphael. He abandoned his cellar in favor of fancy digs on the upper floors of what was once an upscale condo."

She closed her teeth over her lower lip. "I should shut up. I know less than nothing about how Vampires operate. I'll cloak myself so no one can sense me—including you. I'll be right behind you, though."

He wasn't certain he liked not having constant feedback regarding where she was, but she couldn't very well walk openly by his side. "Do it," he muttered. Viktor smothered astonishment. One minute, her warm glow pulsed. The next, it vanished. He couldn't see or sense her but was certain if he extended a hand, he could touch her.

Warm laughter bloomed in his mind. *"Even if you touched me, your brain wouldn't process it as me. It would tell you that you'd run up against a building or a tree or whatever object you just passed. Let's get moving. This spell is a real energy hog."*

Worry filled him. *"How long can you maintain it?"*

"Long enough to do what we need to, but I'll require rest once we return to the mesa."

Viktor turned and picked the fastest route leading into the center of the city. He planned to ask a few key questions that might make his search easier, assuming he crossed paths with other Vamps. It was night, so running into someone was a decent bet. He hadn't laid eyes on Raziel for years. For all he knew, Raphael's paranoia had gotten the better of him, and he'd killed the other Vampire and hidden his remains.

Viktor wended his way around the piles of bones littering Ushuaia's streets, passing the odd Vampire. He hailed one or two, but they ignored him and kept moving, which seemed unusual.

"Dude!" Someone ran at him from a side street and punched his arm. "Where have you been?"

Viktor twisted to face the other Vampire. "Not much of anywhere. What's shaking, Glenn?"

He made a rude snorting noise. "Can't believe Raph let Jorge get the better of him. Jorge of all people." Glenn lowered his voice to a stage whisper. "That pathetic piece of dung. If I'd known what a weak suck Raphael was, I'd have killed him myself years ago."

"Any idea where Jorge is?" Viktor kept his tone casual.

"Yup. One of the humans was misguided enough to pick today to make a run for something he needed. Jorge nabbed him and drained him, trying to make his first minion."

"Yeah? Did it work?"

"Hell no. When the guy wouldn't feed from him, Jorge began bashing him against a concrete wall. Jesus. What an unholy mess. For all I know, he's still there, beating the guy's lifeless body against that wall."

Breath hissed through Viktor's teeth. "Shit! Raphael always was unhinged."

"Yeah well, it's worse now that he's having to wade through whatever Jorge has left for brains." Glenn shook his head. "Gotta run, man. Lying low till this blows over."

"Hey!" Viktor called after him. "Any idea where Raziel is?"

Glenn screeched to a halt and spun to face Viktor. He narrowed his eyes to slits. "Why?" The single word oozed suspicion.

Viktor did his best to exude innocent curiosity. "He's the only one here who was older than Raph. I thought maybe he could settle things down."

"Mmph. Didn't even consider that. My memories of him are that he was even nuttier than Raphael."

"Mine too, now that you mention it. Have you seen him around?"

"Not for years, dude. See ya." Glenn melted into the night.

"He might know more than he told you," Ketha spoke up.

Viktor had come to the same conclusion. *"Good job shielding yourself."*

"Thanks. We should follow that Vamp you talked with."

"Maybe. Glenn is dumb enough to lead us right to Raziel, but we may be reading him wrong, and he might not have any idea where he is."

Viktor considered the logistics of shadowing the other Vamp, but Glenn would sense he was being tracked. It was a survival instinct. Better to give him a decent head start before following his trail. Meantime, it wouldn't hurt to keep right on hunting. He started toward the building he, Raphael, and several other Vamps called home.

"You decided not to follow Glenn," Ketha observed.

"We can't. Not immediately. He'd sense me behind him. Now if I had your ability to cloak my presence... But I don't. We'll see what we can find in Raph's home."

Viktor covered the remaining quarter mile and trotted up deep-veined green marble steps and into the building. Another Vamp emerged from the stairwell and raised a hand in greeting. "May as well go up and join the party."

"What party?"

"Bunch of us are clearing what we want out of Raph's old digs before Jorge craps all over them." The Vampire snorted laughter, fangs extending over his lower lip.

Viktor pointed at the Vamp's empty arms. "Didn't find anything you liked?"

"Meh. Antique shit never did much for me."

"Speaking of antiques"—Viktor held a casual posture—"have you seen Raziel lately?"

"What is it with that fellow?"

"What do you mean?" Viktor trotted closer.

"Jorge wanted to know where he was too. Before he lost it with that human. Did you hear about—?"

Viktor rounded one hand into a dismissive motion. "Yup. Ran into Glenn. Damn. Sounds like a new low, even for us."

The other Vampire shook his head, leaned close, and lowered his voice. "No shit. Blood and gore don't bother me, but it will be a long time before I walk past that intersection again. Easier to avoid it."

"Raziel?" Viktor persisted.

"I haven't seen him in weeks, but last I knew he had an underground lair north of town. If he knows Jorge's looking for him, I'd bet my last peso he's on the move."

"Thanks." Viktor trotted toward the staircase leading down.

"What are we doing?" Ketha asked. *"I thought we were going to Raphael's apartment."*

"We're going to mine so we can regroup and you can conserve your magic."

He led the way into the sub-basement and opened the door to his room. The only one who'd ever visited him here was Raphael. Viktor wasn't worried about Jorge barging in. The other Vamp was sunk into blood-fury, something that happened to Vampires who lost control after feeding. It would take him a while to recover. Or not. Raphael's energy driving things added many unknowns to Viktor's calculations, making accurate predictions damn near impossible.

The door shut behind him, and Ketha shimmered into visibility. Her gaze moved around his room. "Nice," she said. "Has a homey feel I never would've associated with one of you." Color stained her cheeks. "That didn't come out right. What I meant is, it's a nice room. I can picture you here."

He felt flustered but shoved it aside. He also ignored wanting to draw her into an embrace and lay her on his bed. It only felt safe here. It wasn't really.

"We can't stay long. There wasn't much point in joining the looting fest upstairs."

"Has enough time elapsed we could follow wherever Glenn went?"

"Probably, but maybe we'd be better served to look for Raziel in the tunnel system where it extends north of the city."

"All I heard was underground lair, not necessarily tunnels," Ketha said. She raked her hands through her unbound hair, and it resettled in waves framing her face. "It's like looking for a needle in a haystack, and we don't have that kind of time."

"I'm up for suggestions." Viktor wrapped his arms around her.

"You won't like the one I'm kicking around."

"Try me." He leaned back enough to see her face.

"I can track Raziel with magic."

"How? You've never met him."

Ketha winced. "This is the part you won't like. I can cast a seeking spell linked to the prophecy and follow its magic with my mirror, but I can't do it while I'm cloaked. When I deploy that level of power, someone may hone right in on me—if they're paying attention."

"No." The word burst from him like a shell shot from a cannon. "Besides, you're not even certain this particular Raziel has anything to do with the prophecy Aura outlined. He couldn't possibly be an Archangel any more than Raphael is."

Her mouth twisted into a grim expression that turned her beauty harsh and foreboding. "We'd find that part out damned fast. I can do that from here. Vampires are sensitive to expended magic, so let's hope the curiosity seekers at the free-for-all upstairs are totally immersed in rooting through Raphael's treasures."

She pulled a mirror from her pocket and blew on its surface, chanting low in Gaelic, the same language she'd used back on *Arkady*. He began to protest that he hadn't given her a go-ahead for her plan but bit back the words. She didn't work for him, didn't require his approval for her actions. If she could cast magic that hastened their search, he'd be a fool to tell her not to try.

He moved to where he could look over her shoulder at the mirror in her hand. Oblong, it was about eight inches tall and seven across in a tarnished brass frame. Clouds covered its surface. Ketha tapped on the glass, and the timbre of her chant altered, becoming lower, more guttural. It might have been his imagination, but something warm and shimmery enveloped her and the parts of him that leaned against her back.

The clouds parted from the middle outward, revealing a gravel track and a circle of stunted cypress trees. Viktor recognized the place. He watched Raziel creep from within the circle of trees, stopping at its edge. The old Vampire glanced over his shoulder as if he feared someone was following him. Viktor leaned closer, and the mirror cleared still more, almost as if attuned to his need to view additional details.

Raziel twisted, facing Viktor squarely, and drew his upper lip back, displaying long, yellowed fangs. His eyes were deep-blue whirling pools. Sentient thought had deserted those eyes long ago.

Maintaining her chant, Ketha turned and looked at Viktor, silently seeking confirmation that the fair-haired man in her glass was whom they sought.

Viktor nodded. "That's him, and I know where he is."

Ketha fell silent. She waved a hand over the glass, and clouds boiled out of nowhere obscuring Raziel and the cypress grove. Resignation pinched the skin around her eyes, and she slipped her scrying tool back inside her robe.

"When you said he was mad, I assumed he'd be like Raphael. Crazy but functional. There's something primitive and flawed about the Vampire we saw in my glass."

"And something ancient. Is he part of the prophecy? Or were you able to tell?"

She scrubbed her hands down her cheeks, distorting her features. "Yeah. He's part of it. And we need him, but I haven't got clue one how to talk with him, let alone bend him to our cause. Raphael is wrapped up in this too, never mind the slight inconvenience he's in a different body now. And that he was likely never an Archangel to begin with. Goddess be damned. What I wouldn't give for a wiser head than mine."

Viktor wrapped his arms around her from behind. "We can figure this out as we go. I know where Raziel is, but Vamps move fast. Even crazy ones."

"You're right. Let's go. All we can do is see if he'll even talk with us." She belted her robe tighter around her and moved out of his embrace. "One second and I'll be ready." She vanished in a flash of white light, but the door opening was a dead giveaway of her location.

Viktor followed her, shutting the door behind them. *"We'll take the tunnels. They're a faster route to our current objective."*

"I'll stay right behind you. Just like before."

He ran down tunnels and side tunnels until he hit the northernmost terminus of the underground warren. Stepping aside, he motioned Ketha up the ladder. Not being able to see her was odd, but he'd become more accustomed to the energy seeping from her. It was subtle, not something he expected another Vampire would recognize, at least not immediately. Raphael might have, but being forced to absorb the world through Jorge's filtering would probably mute his shrewdness.

Viktor pushed the manhole cover Ketha had shoved aside back into place and loped toward the cypress grove. It was close. Less than half a mile distant. He didn't expect Raziel would still be there, but they'd be able to track him. Viktor flared his nostrils, seeking to scent the other Vamp, but he didn't smell anything beyond rotting vegetation and a rodent population living in the decaying leaves. It was past midnight. They'd killed half the night and had nothing to show for it.

Shifter magic flashed from behind him, lighting the night in vivid blue-white. Viktor spun on the balls of his feet. Ketha, a visible Ketha, hissed and spat, clawing at Raziel who'd jumped on her back like a monkey. The Vampire was trying to sink his fangs into her neck, but every time he got close, she took a swipe at his eyes with her fingernails.

The world slowed until Viktor felt like he watched time-lapse photography. He hurtled onto the other Vampire, pulling him off Ketha. The two rolled on the ground, grappling with one another as they punched and raked open flesh with their nails. Raziel got his hands around Viktor's throat and closed them like a vise. Viktor pulled hard but couldn't dislodge them. Twisting savagely—while he still had air to fight back—he sank his fangs into Raziel's wrist.

Cursing in an unfamiliar Slavic language, Raziel let go, cradling the gash on his wrist where bone showed through.

Jolts of white light streaked with violet flew from Ketha's upraised hands right into Raziel's back. He tumbled off Viktor and lay panting in the dirt.

"Get up," Ketha urged Viktor. "What I did won't hold him long."

Viktor spat blood and scrambled to his feet. The inside of his lips puckered and burned from Raziel's blood. "What the fuck are you?" he screeched, kicking the downed Vampire in the ribs with a booted foot.

"That's an odd question. What do you mean?" Ketha never moved her gaze—or the power still pouring from her—away from Raziel.

"He's no Vampire. His blood is wrong. Really wrong." Viktor swiped the back of his hand across his mouth and spat again, wishing for water to rinse the horrible taste away.

"Answer me!" Viktor bellowed.

Raziel rolled to a sit and bared his fangs but made no move to rise. His midnight-blue eyes weren't even close to human. Dark, whirling pools, they held green-gold centers. "I'm your future," he snarled in accented English. "I've been waiting for the Shifter for a long time."

"If that's true," Ketha said. "Why'd you try to kill me?"

"It's a future I want no part of."

16

PROPHECY BE DAMNED

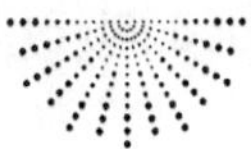

"Why not?" Ketha demanded. This was becoming stranger and stranger. A Vampire had seen through her invisibility illusion as if it weren't there, but Viktor just confirmed the creature on the ground wasn't exactly a Vampire. She stared at his fangs. What manner of being besides Vamps had them? And then she stared harder.

"Damn! They're illusion." She focused a beam of power at the protruding canine teeth, and they disappeared.

"Stop that." Raziel sounded aggrieved. "Do you want to get me killed before you've wrung me dry? Only reason the other ones leave me alone is they're convinced I'm one of them." The fangs returned.

Ketha sent an exploratory beam of seeking magic in Raziel's direction to figure out what he was, but it bounced back hard, cuffing her. "Fine." She snarled, wishing her wolf was in ascendency so she'd have fangs of her own. "You can divert my magic, and it doesn't cost you anything. Hell, you don't even have to be on your feet to deflect my spell."

"Would defeat taste sweeter if I were standing?" Brilliant light flared around him. When it cleared, he was indeed upright but keeping distance between them.

"Yes. No. Goddamn you anyway." A frustrated growl rumbled from her throat.

"Let's backtrack." Viktor had moved to her side, facing the Vampire who wasn't one. "Raziel, or whatever your real name is, which part of the future are you trying to derail? Seems to me the Cataclysm's done a damn good job of fucking things from here to infinity."

Raziel looked from one to the other of them, his eyes a changing collage of color. Long moments dripped past before he shook his head. "I'm tired. I could disappear from this spot, but I can't escape the Cataclysm any more than you can, which means you'd track me down eventually. It was bad enough staying in the shadows so Raphael wouldn't set his minions on me—"

"You didn't answer Viktor." Ketha spoke over him. "You have a role to play in defeating the Cataclysm. I've seen it in my glass. If we're successful, it means we'll at least have a future." She pushed her tongue against her teeth, thinking. "What do you know that I don't?"

"Probably nothing, *Shifter*."

The way he said Shifter sounded like a curse, and she zeroed in on it. "You don't like Shifters, but that can't be what this is about."

"Observant of you. Not overly fond of Vampires, either. Or any of the other host of magical creatures like Faeries, Mages, Furies, Griffons… Eh, Dragons weren't so bad. At least they kept their nests clean and didn't kill for sport, but it's a moot point. They had the decency to die out before your meddling broke the world."

Ketha bristled. "I had nothing to do with that. Neither did Viktor."

"*Ja.*" Raziel's Slavic accent became more pronounced. "But it was your kin. And now we have Vampires who can't predictably drain and resurrect new recruits and Shifters who have a hell of a time shifting." He spat onto the ground next to him. "You deserve death. All of you. Your actions fashioned asymmetrical synergy. The Cataclysm was exactly what you deserved. Unfortunately, the rest of us got stuck with it too."

Anger threaded from her belly outward. Ketha welcomed its energy and rounded on him, stalking close.

"Ketha. Stay back," Viktor warned.

"I'm not worried. He took his shot and missed." She folded her arms beneath her breasts.

"Save your breath, Shifter." The air around Raziel took on a shimmery quality.

Ketha barked a few words in Gaelic, doing her damnedest to hold Raziel in place. Now that she had the feel of him, she could find him easily, but it was a ridiculous waste of both magic and time to have to locate him—again. Not when he stood front and center right now.

His energy tugged and jerked against her efforts.

"Stop that." She made her voice sharp with command. "Hear me out. I can't force you to join us or be a part of my casting. If you don't come willingly, your negativity will ruin the spell, and we'll all be risking our necks for nothing."

Her words must have registered because what had felt like an anchor chain dragging her under snapped free. "Thank you." She inclined her head.

"Never could resist a supplicant." He tossed his head, making his long, fair hair dance around him.

Ketha tried to see into his mind. Not surprisingly, it remained closed to her. Because she couldn't locate an angle to leverage, she went on a truth-gathering mission. Maybe if she understood more, she'd be able to convince him to help.

"I'm guessing you really are Raziel. How'd you end up here on Earth?" she asked.

His mouth twisted crookedly. "Wrong place. Wrong time.

Once I understood what was happening, I pulled out every trick at my disposal to return to my rightful place, but the Cataclysm threw me back. After the third time, I realized I was stuck."

"But you were here for years before the Cataclysm," Viktor pointed out. "According to Raphael, you were here when he relocated from Buenos Aires."

"Your point?" Raziel looked askance at Viktor.

"Not sure I had one," Viktor muttered. "What the hell were you doing in Ushuaia of all places that took years to accomplish?"

"Time is different for me than you, and that's the best answer you'll get." Raziel shifted his unsettling eyes, pale-ocean blue this time, on Ketha. "I'll be taking my leave." He turned his hands palms up. "You'll hunt me down again and find me far more easily now that you've had a taste of what I feel like. I'll give you the slip, and the game will begin anew. Not a bad way to amuse ourselves as we wait for Armageddon."

The anger that had kindled earlier erupted. "This is not a game," Ketha shouted. "I get it that you've spent the last ten years —or maybe longer than that—feeling misused and sorry for yourself. I also get it that your tolerance for anything that's not purely human runs pretty thin."

Ketha balled her hands into fists. "While we're on that topic—"

"Which one would that be? You're skipping around."

"Humans." She spat out the word. "If they're such pets of yours, why didn't you do more to help them? Only reason any of them are left in Ushuaia is because we"—she tapped her chest—"helped them. The Shifters you profess to despise did everything in our power to keep humans safe from Vampires and see they had the ability to grow food."

"They'd be better off if you'd ignored them." Raziel looked away. "At least then they'd be dead."

"That's not your decision." Viktor moved closer to him. "If I remember biblical myths correctly, even God said He wasn't going to engage in mass destruction of humankind after Sodom and Gomorrah."

"You hit the nail squarely on its head when you called it myth." Raziel sneered, displaying his fangs.

"This is scarcely the time or place to argue theology," Ketha muttered. "I have no idea what happened to you. Maybe you had a falling out with God or some of the other Archangels. For all I know, you were banished here and working on finding a way around your punishment when Shifters and Vamps broke the world."

She waved her hands in front of her. "None of that matters. Pull your head out of your ass and stop feeling sorry for yourself. We need your help. I've located a spell that should either complete or reverse the one interrupted ten years ago. If I'm right, the Cataclysm will implode, nature can begin to recover, and we won't lose the possibility of life on Earth."

"And if you're wrong?" Raziel raised one blond brow.

"We'll die, sucked into the Cataclysm's vortex." Ketha swallowed sudden desolation. "We're all going to die, anyway. This merely hastens things."

Raziel took a step toward her. Ketha held her ground and latched her gaze onto his. Viktor closed on them protectively, his eyes never leaving the other man.

"I know the spell," Raziel said flatly. "You'll never finish it. Raphael will storm your fortress and blow it to hell. Doesn't matter he's in a different body. That won't slow him down at all. Something similar happened ten years ago. One of the Vampires found out the truth, was furious he'd been duped, and sabotaged the casting. Didn't hurt he got himself a piece of tail as a consolation prize."

Ketha opened her mouth, but Raziel held up a hand. "I'm not finished. I'm also familiar with the prophecy that includes Shifters, Vampires, and Archangels. It's the fourth unfinished prophecy." His nostrils flared. "Raphael—my kinsman, not the

Vampire—has a role to play, which means that particular divination isn't about to happen. If I can't get out, he can't get in."

Ketha dropped her hands to her sides. "If we know Raphael—the Vampire, Raphael—is a threat, we can watch out for him. Beyond that, aren't all prophecies metaphor? Maybe it didn't mean another Archangel had to be here at all." Her words sounded thin, pathetic, like she was grasping at straws, which she was. They wouldn't have any magic to spare—to quash Raphael or anyone else who interrupted them mid-spell.

She glanced at Viktor. He drew his brows together. "We need to get back to the others, with or without him." He jerked a thumb in Raziel's direction.

Ketha agreed. Every instinct she had said time was running out. She had one last argument in her arsenal and threw down the gauntlet. "If I'm right, and you were banished here at the ass end of South America, you could redeem yourself by helping us."

Raziel hooted laughter. He bent double, slapping his knees before straightening. "That's rich. You think God will extend an olive branch for saving abominations?"

Ketha drew herself tall and pushed her fury aside. Pounding the sanctimonious bastard in front of her to a pulp would be wonderful. She could almost feel bones crunching beneath her fists, but she was bigger than revenge. "Older deities than the one you report to revered Shifters." She kept her tone even and didn't mention that no one respected Vampires.

"Expand your horizons," she suggested silkily. "Regardless of what happens to Vampires—and I hope their power disappears along with the Cataclysm—you will have played a key role in saving Earth and restoring nature."

Ketha had said enough. Sometimes knowing when to shut up was as important as the words that came before. She hooked an arm through Viktor's, waiting.

Raziel looked from one of them to the other and curled a corner of his mouth derisively. "Raphael's blood must've been weak when he made you," he told Viktor. "No self-respecting Vamp would ever trust a Shifter. Never mind holding one in any kind of regard."

"Stop right there." Viktor's tone was even, deadly. "Leave Ketha out of your judgments about me."

"His spirit fought being turned." She jumped in, defending Viktor. "Your words are a diversion. What'll it be, Archangel? Choose now." She infused compulsion into her words.

Light flashed, blinding her. She shut her eyes, shielding them with an upraised hand. When she opened them, Raziel was gone.

"Goddamn it!" She punched a fist into her other hand.

"I wonder what other unexpected things live here." Viktor drew his forehead into a mass of thoughtful creases. "Is it true that the Cataclysm impacted your ability to shift?"

Frustration filled her—hot, viscous, uncomfortable—at the reminder her other half was almost lost to her. "Yes. It's far harder than it once was because it blows through buckets of magic when none of us have had any to spare. Sorry." She blew out a breath. "I'm discouraged—and furious with that bastard. There are good reasons Shifters have steered clear of organized religions."

Viktor snorted. "Beyond them hanging and burning you right along with Witches and Druids?"

"Yeah, that too." She raked her hands through her hair. "He never did disclose why he ended up here."

"No. He didn't, which probably means your theory hit close to the mark. Why is it harder to shift?"

"Lots of reasons. Scant food combined with poisoned air and water have impacted our magic. Shifting under normal conditions uses a lot of magic, but shifting now requires ten times the amount. We've conserved our power for more essential things. Problem is when you remain in one form for a long time, the other one fades and becomes harder to access, requiring still more magic."

"This is fascinating. Say more about it." He wrapped his arms around her. "You must be cold. It's well below freezing tonight."

"I will be once I'm not so angry." She leaned into him, craving his solid presence. "Not much more to say. The animals have a place they exist when they're not with us."

"Where is that?" he cut in.

Ketha chewed her lower lip and hunted for a quick explanation of a complex topic. "Kind of like a parallel universe. I've seen it in dreams, but we can't live there, only the animals can do that. Sometimes I feel my wolf within me, but more and more it's absent, and I know it's running free in its special world. I'm happy for it then because it gets a break from the hell our lives have turned into."

"Why an 'it,' and not a him or her?"

"The animals are genderless. Don't ask why or how. That's how it's always been."

Viktor drew back so he could look at her. "Thanks for the primer on being a Shifter, even if it made me sad for you—and your wolf."

"No point in being sad. Besides, my wolf would spit on pity from any quarter." They had to get moving, and she considered their options. "Let's return to the mesa."

"Don't you want to take another shot at Raziel?"

Ketha grimaced. "Yeah. I'd love to pound that slime-wad into bloody bits, but there's nothing more to say. I did my best, and it wasn't good enough. Not much point wasting time tracking him for a rematch. Can you think of any other Vamps who might be willing to join us?"

"I've been tossing that around. Come on. Let's get out of the wind and map out Plan B. What's your preference? Tunnels or the cypress grove?"

"Which place are we least likely to run into Vampires?"

"It's a toss-up. I never found other Vamps in the tunnels until Raphael sicced them on you."

"Let's try the grove. Cypress trees are ancient, and Shifters draw power from the natural world." She fell into step next to him and didn't duck from beneath his arm when he draped it around her shoulders. Raziel's refusal made her uncomfortable, shook her faith in the integrity of what she'd seen in her glass.

"I feel your mind churning." Viktor led her beneath a canopy of gnarled branches. The ground within the ring of living wood was dry and sandy. Wind howled around the tight circle, but very little leached through. He hunkered in the lee of an enormous trunk and drew her down next to him.

"Maybe this isn't such a good idea," she mumbled.

"What isn't? Raziel? Finding Vamps who might not knife us in the back?"

Ketha scrubbed the heels of her hands down her face. "Any of it." She took a deep breath, hoping for a calm, rational outlook, but it eluded her. "I've never had a vision where one of the key elements told me to go fuck myself. I'm not sure what it means. Or how to proceed."

Viktor folded one of her hands between his, and she laced her fingers into his solid grip. "People in your visions have played changing roles," he reminded her. "Raphael acted quite differently in three separate trances."

"Yeah." She nodded. "That's true, but there's not a doubt in my mind he'll show up for the finale. Raziel refused a direct request for assistance." She paused, gathering her thoughts. "He *knew* about my vision. He also knew about the prophecy, even though he said it didn't apply here—and he still refused."

"Are you interpreting that as a bad omen?"

Viktor's ability to think clearly and articulate her fears warmed her, filling her with gratitude for his unflappable presence. "I guess so."

He tightened his hands around hers. "Sailors are nothing if not superstitious. Something as simple as a wandering albatross in the wrong place turns into a portent of doom."

She glanced at him. "What did you do when things like that happened on your ships?"

He rolled his eyes. "Made damn sure the crew didn't upset the passengers. Wasn't hard. Most of the world's elite wouldn't recognize a superstition if the Grim Reaper showed up with robes and a sickle to escort them to Hell."

Ketha chuckled, grateful for a respite from thoughts that tumbled in weary circles. "I suppose the question is whether we move forward. I was encouraged by how I saw the mesa, and then you knew where it was."

"And we all ended up there without too much effort," Viktor reminded her. "What do you want to do about adding other Vampires to the group?"

"Wish I had an answer."

"What do your instincts tell you?" he pressed.

She pressed her lips together. "To leave well enough alone. Unless maybe you know a few Vamps who are sure bets."

"The only sure bet for Vampires is their attraction to blood and death." He hurried on before she could say anything. "I knew Juan before the Cataclysm, and we got lucky with Recco and Daide. Maybe. They're saying the right things, but I don't know them well enough to trust them. Sure, I could approach some others—like the women, who've kept a very low profile. Maybe a few would surprise me and agree. But you didn't see any female Vamps in your vision."

"What aren't you saying?" Ketha shifted position to look at him, not letting go of his hand.

"One of the big problems for Vampires is the strength of"—he frowned, maybe hunting for words—"competing priorities. We can begin with the best of intentions, but if bloodlust gains the upper hand, it will win every time. You and the other Shifters will be vulnerable while you're immersed in the magic to defeat the Cataclysm..." His words faded.

"Mmph," she mumbled. "Plan B looks a whole lot like Plan A. While you were talking, I was thinking."

"What'd you come up with?"

"I'm certain Jorge will make an appearance, probably at the least auspicious moment. It's possible the casting will exert a pull over Raziel too, and he'll end up in the thick of things. Normally, I'd like a strategy with fewer maybes peppering it, but that's not going to happen."

The fine hairs on the back of her neck prickled uncomfortably. She placed a hand over his mouth and breathed, *"Ssht,"* into his mind. Vamps were on the move. A whole horde of them from the feel of things. What the fuck were they doing all the way out here?

Viktor scrambled to his feet. *"Stay here. I'll take care of this."*

"Hold up." She stood too. *"You reek of Shifter. Let me fix it."*

Ketha sprinkled power in an arc around him, instructing it to eradicate any trace of her or her sisters. Once that was done, she said, *"Go,"* and swathed herself in invisibility. It might not have fooled Raziel, but these were Vampires, not Archangels. She'd be safe enough.

She hoped.

"Viktor!" A voice boomed. "What are you doing north of the city? Find anything warm-blooded to share?"

"You wish. I could ask you the same thing."

"We're hunting," another voice called out with a cheerful note that set Ketha's teeth on edge.

"Humans," someone clarified.

Ketha cringed. Had Shifter magic protecting the enclaves failed? With all of them on the mesa, that was certainly possible. It felt like a different world up there, and perhaps it obliterated the protections they'd placed to keep humans safe from harm.

"Find any?" Viktor's tone was jovial, conversational.

"Not yet," the first voice boomed. "But we're hot on their tracks."

"Sounds promising," Viktor replied. "Mind if I join you?"

"I'd suspect something was wrong if you hadn't asked." First voice again. "Be a shame to kill you, but I'll rule this shithole better than Raph. He was a pansy. Far too trusting. My motto is kill first, ask questions later."

"Good to know." Viktor sounded amused. "Let's get cracking. Dawn's not far off."

The sound of booted feet moving away shook the earth beneath her. Christ! How many were there? Must be half the Vamps in *Ciudad de Huesos*. Ketha snaked a shielded beam of power outward, gathering information. She counted forty-seven. Mostly post-Cataclysm Vamps, but a few old ones too. The energy from one was cloudy, dual-natured. Must be Jorge, who'd killed Raphael and then fallen from grace and drunk from him. Ketha memorized the feel of him, so she'd recognize it if he stormed the mesa.

It's not if, but when, she reminded herself grimly.

She thought about how Viktor described bloodlust. He hadn't said in so many words that it had been his undoing when Raphael turned him, but it had most certainly driven Jorge to feed from his erstwhile master.

She waited through several minutes until it was as safe as it was going to get to leave the grove. Should she follow the band of Vampires? No one suspected Viktor of treason—yet, but that could change fast. Ketha sent a quick prayer asking Gaia to watch over him and took off after the retreating Vampires.

They weren't certain of the location of any of the groups of humans, or the Vamps would have been feasting rather than running through the countryside. *Hot on their tracks* hadn't been much more than idle boasting. She took stock of where she was and altered her course until she was close to the nearest enclave. A quick infusion of power ensured the folk living there would remain invisible to Vampires.

Her magical well was running low. Wisdom dictated she make a run for the mesa where she could rest and eat, but she didn't want to abandon Viktor. A hasty scan confirmed Vamps weren't anywhere near. It also confirmed they had no idea where the humans were, and she breathed a little easier.

Because it didn't feel like too big a risk, she used her mind voice. *"Viktor?"*

Minutes dribbled past, turning into a quarter hour. Her fears for him escalated. Hadn't Jorge said murder was the new normal in Vampire-land? She backtracked, intent on finding the unmistakable trail the Vamps had left. She'd be worthless if she ran her power down to bedrock again, so she did what she could to conserve it.

"Mesa. Now," flared in her mind and she skidded to a stop.

"Viktor?"

"Who else?"

"Where were you earlier? I tried to reach you."

He didn't answer. Did he mean he was back at the mesa and she should join him? Or was he chivvying her back there to keep her safe?

The wind escalated; its howling mirrored desolation scouring her heart. She altered course again and plodded toward the other edge of Ushuaia, staying well hidden in bone-choked backstreets. She'd been a fool to think she could waltz into a den of Vampires and do anything other than get herself killed.

Maybe Viktor would be waiting for her on the mountain track, but every instinct she had screamed he was in deep trouble. And there wasn't a damned thing she could do to intervene.

I'm overreacting.

Am I?

Ketha put a lid on her mental dialogue. It wasn't helping, and she needed all her concentration to make it back to the mesa. If Viktor was in trouble, the others waiting for her in the caves were his best bet for help.

17

SUCKER FOR LOST CAUSES

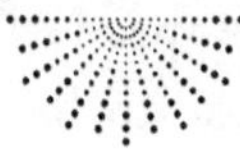

SHOCK ROILED through Viktor when he emerged from the tangle of cypress limbs and laid eyes on Jorge. The man's blue-gray eyes gleamed with a fey light, and his long, dark hair was matted with what had to be blood. Apparently, he hadn't bothered to rinse himself off after his feeding frenzy over Raphael's headless corpse. Or his battering match with the dead human he'd tried to turn. The stench of rancid blood twisted Viktor's stomach into a hard, painful knot. Fresh blood was one thing, but the rust-colored streaks clinging to Jorge in thick, clotted patches gave off a nauseating odor.

Jokes flew fast and furious about finding humans and fresh blood. Viktor forced teasing remarks right back, his mind recoiling with disgust.

Finally, Jorge took off at a shambling trot with forty-plus Vampires fanned out behind him. Viktor fell in and scanned the group. Who could he trust to talk with? Something was desperately wrong. Vampires might be monsters, but they were scarcely pigs to roll in their own shit. And Jorge was moving at about a tenth of normal Vampire speed.

Was some kind of internal battle going on, where Raphael was duking it out for control and Jorge fighting back? That would certainly drain Jorge's energy.

Someone closed from his side. Viktor tilted his head and saw Glenn. The Vamp sent a pointed look skittering Viktor's way out of his clear, green eyes and made the smallest of motions with one hand.

Viktor understood. He dropped back a few feet, still moving forward but not at the same speed as the rest of the pack. Glenn paced him, mouth very close to his ear. "You should've stayed back in those trees, dude. No love lost between me and Raph, but Jorge's got some major screws loose."

"Say more."

"He's nuts. Blood-fury nuts, and it's not going away."

"Why are all of you following him?" Viktor glanced sidelong at Glenn.

"Abe tried to leave. He was subtle enough about it, but Jorge noticed and called him back. Abe was an idiot and trotted right up next to him. Next thing we knew, Jorge swung that saber he bragged about using to kill Raph, and Abe's head bounced into the dirt."

"He wasn't kidding when he spouted off that jewel about killing first and asking questions later."

"No." Glenn bit off the word. "And now you're as fucked as the rest of us. Jorge knows you're part of this pack. He'll figure it out quick enough if you desert."

"Maybe Raph will get the upper hand back. He's got to be in there somewhere."

"Pah. That old fucker wasn't much better. Just as crazy, but he covered it well."

Viktor trotted next to Glenn, shuffling through possibilities and discarding them. Ketha's voice flashed through his mind, but he ignored it, not wanting to risk Glenn picking up on her presence. "There's way more of us than him," he muttered at last.

"So? Raph kept the upper hand. Bastard didn't even have to try very hard."

"That was because he wasn't all that unreasonable," Viktor shot back. "You should catch up with the rest of them. Sooner or later, someone will notice we fell behind."

"What are you going to do?"

"Better if you don't know," Viktor replied and turned left down an alley leading to an entrance to the underground burrows riddling Ushuaia's hills. Glenn might rat him out, but he didn't think so. The other Vampire had seemed genuinely disgusted—and distressed—by Jorge's transformation. Given that Vampires rarely expressed much of anything in the emotional spectrum, Glenn's reaction had been all the more significant.

Christ! The world was turning into an even worse mess than it had been. If Ketha's spell didn't prevail, dying a few months ahead of time wasn't the worst consequence. Living in a world where a lunatic's paranoid whims dictated outcomes would be far worse.

He moved a manhole cover aside, bounded down the ladder, and ran hard as soon as his feet connected with the dirt passageway. He didn't fear for his own life. Regardless of how he'd felt about Raphael, the Master Vamp had been tolerant of him, and Viktor was certain he wouldn't stand by while Jorge raised the saber against him.

Ketha.

She'd be the only bad part about dying. He'd finally found a woman he could love. A woman he wanted to spend eternity with. Was she about to be ripped away from him because none of them had a future?

He hoped she'd done the smart thing and beelined it for the mesa. He couldn't shield his presence. If he'd remained within the cypress grove, his emanations would've alerted the other Vamps. They might not have noticed Ketha swathed in her invisibility illusion, but it was better not to have taken that chance. At least he'd bought her time to flee.

He came to the last leg of the tunnel, the one ending in the ladder that would spit him out not far from the trail up the mountainside. He'd grabbed the metal side rail when a muffled grunt froze him in place. Though he listened intently, swiveling his head this way and that to maximize his range, he didn't hear anything else.

Silence reigned, but it held an ominous aspect. Was someone following him? Someone doing his damnedest to remain hidden? If so, it ruled out Jorge. Subtlety was probably beyond him at this point.

Viktor remained motionless for long moments. He sent out feelers, but the tunnels had so many twists and turns, they masked whomever might be behind him. What should he do? If he left the tunnels and headed uphill on the trail, he'd eventually reveal his destination.

Until he could rule out being followed, he'd be goddamned if he'd put the Shifters at risk. Never mind Juan and Recco and Daide. If Ketha had been smart, she was almost back at the mesa by now, but there was a good chance she was out and about, combing Ushuaia's streets hunting for him.

Viktor let go of the ladder and turned, taking care to be absolutely silent. He wouldn't have to backtrack far. Once he passed a ninety-degree bend in the passageway, the next half mile was a straight shot. He'd be able to determine if someone had tracked him, and who that someone was. He reached the corner and slowed, using the earthen wall to shield his body as he peered down the passage.

Vampire essence bounced back at him.

"Son of a fucking bitch. I know you're there, Glenn. Game's up."

White-blond dreads came into view as the other Vamp emerged from one of the many ladder wells dotting the corridor. Light on his feet, he sped to where Viktor stood. Defiance flashed from his eyes.

"Figured you'd catch me when I tripped over that hole in the ground and made some noise. If you expect me to apologize," he growled, "don't. I'm not going to. I took my chances. Wherever it is you're headed, I'm coming. Let's get moving before someone tracks us. So far so good."

So far so good indeed.

Where to begin?

"You may not want to throw your lot in with me." Viktor started for the place where he'd been when Glenn's bumbling had alerted him he wasn't alone.

"I don't give a fuck if you're planning a swan dive into the ocean. It's better than whatever Jorge has up his sleeve."

"I wouldn't be so sure of that." Viktor swarmed up the ladder with Glenn behind him. He ran for the last street that hugged the hillside and stopped near the same crumbling concrete bunker where he'd waited for Ketha earlier that night.

Glenn ground to a halt and sent a calculating glance Viktor's way.

Viktor readied himself. If the other Vamp bolted once he heard about the collusion with Shifters to defeat the Cataclysm, his life would be forfeit. Viktor couldn't chance him spilling any of the story—to anyone.

He turned and let his gaze bore into Glenn's. "I'm not much safer than Jorge at this point. If I tell you what I'm up to—and you don't like what you hear and don't want to be a part of it—I'll kill you. I'm far more lethal than Jorge because I haven't lost my mind. Choose, but be quick about it."

Desolation pinched the corners of Glenn's green eyes into pinwheels. "What we've been living, it's not any kind of life." He held his hands in front of him. "I was a violinist before the Cataclysm trapped me. Four of us—me, my pianist, my cellist, and my harp player—were here on a concert tour."

Viktor generally steered clear of life-before-the-Cataclysm

conversations, but he needed to know more about Glenn, so he asked, "What happened to them?"

"The piano player and cellist died in the first wave of riots to hit the city after the Cataclysm." Glenn looked away. "The harp player was also my wife."

Viktor waited, but Glenn didn't offer anything further. "What happened to her?"

Glenn shrugged uncomfortably. "Raph turned her too, except it totally changed her. She joined up with the other female Vamps. Didn't want anything to do with me. I don't know. She wasn't the same person. This will sound melodramatic, but her eyes looked dead. Vampires forfeit their souls, but with her, it was far more apparent."

"Maybe that's only because you knew her so well and noticed the difference."

Glenn shrugged again. "Maybe so."

Viktor glanced at a sky edging toward dawn. It was still black, but in another hour or two, it wouldn't be. He had to get moving. Before launching into a discussion with Glenn, one that might well end in the other Vamp's death, he raised his mind voice, hoping Ketha would hear him. *Mesa. Now.*

Her response came immediately. *"Viktor?"*

"Who else?"

"Where were you earlier? I tried to reach you."

He didn't answer. He'd told her enough to get her moving toward safety, and he didn't want to divert his attention from Glenn. Viktor turned toward the other Vampire and said without preamble, "The Shifters have a spell that might break the Cataclysm's hold on *Ciudad de Huesos*. They need our help to pull it off. It's dangerous. Far from a sure thing. It might kill us all, but if it works, it's possible we won't be Vampires anymore."

"What would we be?"

"Not sure. We might turn into Shifters, or we might go back to being humans."

Hope glimmered in Glenn's eyes, painful in its intensity. "I'm in. Let's get moving. You can tell me more on the way." After a brief hesitation, he held out a hand.

Viktor shook it. The small retreat to what had once been "normal" warmed him. Vampires rarely touched. It wasn't part of their culture. He understood at a bone-deep level how desperately Glenn wanted not to be a Vampire anymore. Being dead would be an improvement—if it didn't spell the loss of Ketha right along with it.

He led the way onto the mountain track, filling Glenn in on what he knew. The things they had tacked down, and the long list of things likely to pose problems—including Jorge. He searched for fresh traces of Ketha's energy as he moved uphill, but didn't find it, which meant she was somewhere behind them.

Viktor halted at the turnoff to the cells. *"Ketha!"*

"Yes!" Joy boiled into his mind along with the one word. *"Where are you?"*

"Close to the cells."

"Be there in ten minutes. Maybe less."

Relief weakened his knees, and he sagged against a boulder partially blocking the track.

"What?" Glenn demanded. "Why are we stopping?"

"To wait for Ketha. Remember, I told you she was with me in that cypress grove."

"Yeah, I got that part, but what took her so long?"

Viktor eyed the other Vampire. "She was probably looking for me."

Glenn shook his dreads over his shoulders. "Sorry, dude. None of my business. Maybe if this gig of yours works, I'll get my wife back."

He sounded so hopeful—and so broken—Viktor didn't know what to say. He was still wrestling with variations that didn't come out like condolences when the sound of Ketha's boots pounding up the trail reached him.

"Wait here," he told Glenn, and raced downhill.

She wasn't as close as he'd thought, but he ran until he could wrap her into his arms and sweep her off her feet tight against him. She wound her arms around him, hanging on as if she'd been certain she'd never see him again.

"Damn me, but you're a welcome sight," she said. "I was afraid something hideous—"

"Hush." He loped uphill, carrying her. "None of it matters except we're together. Glenn is at the cells. I didn't ask for his help, but he followed me when I slipped away from Jorge's gang. We need more Vamps, and he's willing."

"You took a huge chance. How much did you tell him? Are you sure—?"

He stared down at her, bewildered by her lack of faith in his judgment. "Yes. I wasn't at first, but I am now."

"That's good enough for me." She offered him half a smile. "Sorry. Didn't mean to hurt your feelings. It's been a long night."

Viktor reached Glenn and set Ketha back on her feet. She held out a hand. Glenn shook it without any hesitation. That, more than anything, convinced Viktor the other Vamp was on board and they could trust him.

"You never did tell me exactly where we're headed," Glenn said.

"Not much longer until you find out," Viktor replied.

Ketha walked in front, setting the pace then Glenn with Viktor in the rear. He was content to keep Ketha within sight. The swing of her hips ignited desire that seeped through him like warm honey. Her dark hair shimmered, its red and gold strands glowing in his amped-up night vision. Apparently, she'd been as worried about something untoward happening to him as he'd been about her. Evidence of her caring touched his soul, the soul he was supposed to have lost once he was turned.

Ketha stopped shy of the enormous bramble bush. She'd slowed before reaching it, and Viktor knew how worn out she must be. He scooped her into his arms. "Get some rest, love. I'll carry you over the hard part."

She nestled against him. "Thanks. Magic's nearly gone again, and I have a feeling I'll need it soon."

"What the hell?" Glenn stared up the near-vertical mountainside, craning his neck. "What's at the top that's worth the struggle? It's so far up, I can't even see it with my augmented vision."

"It's not as hard as it looks," Viktor said, following it with, "I'm not sure how it happened, but there's a plateau up there that escaped the worst of the Cataclysm's ravages. It has clean water, underground rivers with fish, and shelter."

"You're joking. That's impossible. I was a physics professor before I quit teaching at the university to play music."

"And I was a microbiologist. You'll see for yourself soon." Ketha raised her head from Viktor's shoulder long enough to smile encouragingly.

Glenn was still muttering about black holes and vortices when Viktor started uphill, Ketha clasped tightly against him. Energy pounded him in waves as the air came alive with something other than the three of them.

Ketha stiffened in his arms, twisting her head from side to side. "Damn it! What is that? Not one of you? Certainly not another Shifter…"

"Doesn't leave many choices, now does it?" Viktor muttered. Unless some other manner of being chose to storm the Cataclysm, which was impossible, the odd energy had to belong to Raziel. The Archangel wasn't bothering to cloak his essence since they'd blown his cover.

Vibrant light flashed on the slope above him. When it cleared, Raziel balanced on a rocky outcrop, long, fair hair shrouding him to his waist. "Top of the morning to you." He mock bowed.

"Raziel?" Glenn chugged next to Viktor and Ketha and directed his next words to them. "What's he doing here? I didn't know Vampires could control the visible light spectrum."

"You might ask me. I'm right here." Raziel stared down at them for long moments before he started uphill, leaping over obstacles as he moved in a vertical line that defied gravity.

"He's, um, not one of us." Viktor aimed his words at Glenn.

"No shit. I figured that part out, but he sure put on a good show all those years."

Viktor slogged after Raziel, feeling slow and clumsy by comparison. "Why are you here?" he called to the Archangel.

"Maybe I'm a sucker for lost causes."

"Define lost cause," Ketha said.

Raziel shrugged. The motion made light cascade around his fast-moving form. "You never know," he replied. "Could be yours. Might be mine. Hard to say about these things until they're over. I fought the good fight, resisting your plea for aid, but this is where I'm supposed to be. Who knows? Maybe it's one of many reasons I was sent here all those years ago. To bear witness to how the world ends."

"Not sure I trust your sudden change of heart," Ketha muttered.

"If I were you, I wouldn't, either. Beyond that," Raziel went on, "didn't it strike you as odd when you found my garden? The one up there." He glanced toward the top of the ridge.

"You made that?" Viktor battled incredulity that the Archangel commanded enough power to stave off the Cataclysm.

"Who else? It wasn't so much a matter of making as of protecting it from the Cataclysm's ravages." Raziel leapt away from them, moving upward with the grace of a mountain goat.

"There's your explanation," Ketha said to Glenn.

The Vampire shook his head. "Not sure it's any easier to swallow than knowing there's decent water and fish up there. It's like an arcane rebirth of the Garden of Eden myth."

Raziel waited for them, straddling the ridgeline. He took one look at Ketha and extended an index finger. Light flashed, illuminating her forehead.

Viktor set her on her feet and stepped between her and Raziel within the space of two heartbeats. "What did you do to her?" he snarled.

"Restored her magic. Go ahead. Ask her." Raziel skinned his lips back from his teeth, displaying false fangs. "Look, *Vampire*. I already told you I'm fighting on your team. Do. Not. Anger. Me. It's not a good idea."

"No, you look, you sorry sack of sanctimonious shit—" Viktor began.

"It's all right," Ketha cried. "I have no idea how he did it, but I'm back to a hundred percent. Neat trick on his part, since I was sucking fumes on the way up here."

"Apologies are welcome any time, as are thanks." Raziel spread his mouth in an approximation of a smile, faux fangs extended.

"There you are!" Aura pelted toward them at full speed. "Hurry. You have to hurry."

Ketha moved from behind Viktor. "Why? What's happened?"

"We cast the tarot. Did it half a dozen times to make sure, and the only time to do this is at daybreak." She glanced skyward. "I'm guessing we have about half an hour, max." Aura stared at Raziel and Glenn. "I recognize that one." She pointed at Raziel. "Who are you?" She focused her moss-green gaze on Glenn.

"Another Vampire," Ketha said, her tone curt.

"Goddess's tits. I have magic. I know what he is. Why's he here? He wasn't in your vision."

"I'll help any way I can if it'll defeat the Cataclysm," Glenn spoke up. "Just tell me what to do."

Aura sent daggers his way out of slitted eyes. "I'll hold you to that, Vamp. If you give me the slightest reason to doubt you, I'll kill you myself."

"Got it." Glenn didn't sound nearly as cordial, and Viktor didn't blame him.

"Ketha. Come on." Aura latched a hand around her arm and tugged. "You need to parcel out assignments. Rowana tried to pry your worksheets out of your spell book, but the bastard burned her hand."

Ketha ran lightly after Aura. "Of course, it did. I'm surprised any of you would tackle another Shifter's book. They're spelled against anyone but their owner and specific blood kin."

"We knew that, but you weren't back. Dawn was coming, and we were desperate."

Viktor motioned to Glenn and then loped after the women. Raziel struck Viktor as someone who didn't need an invitation. The Archangel punched him in the arm as he flashed past. "Right about something for once, *Vampire*."

"For fuck sake, stay out of my head and stop calling me that. You make it sound like a curse."

Raziel skidded to a halt and spun to face him and Glenn. "It is a curse. You know as much. If you play your parts and play them well, you'll be divested of it soon enough."

Viktor hoped to hell the Archangel had some kind of divine pipeline and knew what he was talking about. He ducked low to enter the same cave where he'd left everyone. Ketha was dividing them into groups and issuing instructions.

"We get one shot at this," she cautioned, her voice solemn. "If we fuck it up, we're all dead."

"You weren't joking about that part," Glenn muttered next to Viktor's ear.

Viktor glanced his way. "I never joke, mate. About much of anything."

18

BATTLE CRY

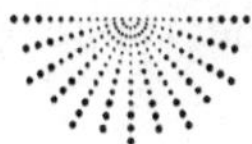

KETHA OPTED for five groups since she only had five Vampires. Raziel was an unknown quantity. He'd been in her vision, but she'd been convinced he was a Vamp. Her spell book hadn't mentioned anything about an Archangel making a cameo appearance. Besides, she had a hunch he'd ignore instructions coming from her. Being one group short would make the front end of the spell clunky and awkward, but she didn't have any other choice.

Thank the goddess, Raziel had restored her magic. Had the Archangel known what she'd need? Ketha suspected the answer was yes, but now wasn't the time to dissect her hunch.

She focused her mage light on the dirt at her feet and sketched the Cataclysm's layers as she understood them. Once she was done, she motioned everyone close, pointing to her diagram as she talked. "We'll attack the outer two layers in tandem. Rowana, Moira, Zoe, and Juan will work together."

"Why not four Shifters," the woman who'd offered to cast tarot spreads asked. "I thought you said two of us for each layer. This is two layers, so…"

"I'm having one of you float between the first and second groups, offering magic as it's needed. Are you volunteering?"

"Um. Yes. I guess so." Her voice shook, but she stood straight.

Ketha went to her and wrapped an arm around her shoulders. "Tessa. You do understand we only have a few months left here, right? If we do nothing, we're all just as dead as we'll be if things go paws up on us today."

"I get that." Tessa rubbed a hand across her forehead, dark eyes pinched with sorrow. Coal-black hair was braided in tight rows, the severe style making her appear even younger and more vulnerable.

"Good." Ketha returned to her schematic. Even though she tended to think of five of the Shifters as youngsters, they'd been in their early twenties when they'd flown to Ushuaia with Ketha, Rowana, and the others. Plenty old enough to have come into their full power, but not old enough to have had much of a life before the Cataclysm screwed them.

Her mind was wandering, no doubt as an antidote to the crippling sense of responsibility that left her with a breathless, choking sensation. She cleared her throat. "Group two will be comprised of..."

It only took a few minutes to divvy up who'd be doing what. "Remember." She let her gaze settle briefly on each of them. "Your job is not only to create an opening in your layer, but to keep it that way so the team who comes after you has space to work. It will become progressively harder—and require more magic—the deeper we get into the Cataclysm. It will fight back. Guard your minds. Even better, ward them if you have any power to spare."

"It's time." Tessa jerked her chin toward the cave's entrance. Night's blackness was yielding to a pallid gray.

Raziel trotted in front of Ketha. "You failed to assign me."

She furled her brows. "I figured you wouldn't accept my direction. Add your power where it's needed most." She bit her lower lip. "Will Raphael—er, Jorge—show up?"

Fierce light flared from the depths of Raziel's blue eyes. "This much magic concentrated in one place will be impossible to ignore—even for a Vampire."

"You wanted an assignment?" She curled her lips back from her teeth. Even thinking about what remained of the Master Vamp made her ill. "Make sure Jorge doesn't interfere. No one else will have enough power left over to deal with him."

"Easier said than done." Raziel bowed low. "Better get moving, or you'll lose the advantage of an auspicious juxtaposition of the sun, date, and time. I know you can't see the sun, but trust me, it's still up there."

Ketha headed outside with Viktor right behind her. "Thanks for being my partner," she murmured.

"Wouldn't have it any other way." His deep voice rumbled near her ear. "Even if you'd tried to split us up, I'd have traded with one of the other Vamps."

Aura joined them, looking pale but determined. "We have the innermost layer. It will be the hardest."

"And the most dangerous." Ketha narrowed her eyes. "If you want to swap places with one of our sisters—"

"Stop right there. If we fail, we'll be first to be swept into the Cataclysm, but everyone else will end up there too. For once being on the front lines isn't any riskier. Too bad the prophecy isn't in play."

"I thought it was unfinished," Viktor cut in. "Doesn't that mean you don't know how it ends?"

"Of course." Aura stared him down. "But another Archangel would almost have to skew things in our favor, and the odds of one showing up are nil." She hesitated a beat. "Prophecies are allegory, though, so this might be a version of the one I recognized— even absent the real Raphael."

A sheepish look crossed Aura's face. "Sorry. I wish I could pin things down better than that."

Ketha didn't agree about Archangels conferring advantages, but she kept her mouth shut. From what she knew about Raziel, she wasn't at all sure two of him would do anything beyond muddy the waters. Especially if the Archangel Raphael was as high-handed, conflicted, and bitter as Raziel appeared to be. Besides, the prophecy suggested they had to pick one.

We did. Raziel.

She sent a prayer winging skyward, hoping to hell they'd done enough, that the prophecy would play itself out in their favor.

The Shifters who cast the tarot had determined the most auspicious spot for their spell was on the far side of the mesa. As the sky lightened, the first group gathered, forming a ragged line with Juan at its center. Condors emerged from their nesting caves, cawing and shrieking before some of the birds—no doubt the ones with younglings—retreated inside. Others took flight, filling the air with outraged squawks. Long, black feathers fluttered down.

Ketha didn't blame them for their fury. They'd likely hidden out here since the Cataclysm, raising generations of condors in the absence of human interference. Scant days had passed since Viktor discovered the place, and the birds' survival was already threatened.

She focused her attention on the four Shifters and Juan. The women's magic surrounded the Vampire. He was there to potentiate Shifter power, strengthen it with his very different brand of supernatural ability.

"This is going to happen fast, isn't it?" Viktor spoke near her ear.

Ketha nodded, never taking her gaze from the tableau unfolding before her. "Everything magical happens fast, but it won't seem that way. It might feel like several lifetimes elapse before we're done. Assuming this doesn't blow up in our faces before we get anywhere near the finish line."

She ran lightly to the second group—two Shifters and Recco—and motioned them into position a short distance from Rowana, Moire, and Zoe, who were chanting furiously, power flashing from their fingertips. Tessa paced between the first two groups, looking tense. Ketha made sure the third and fourth groups were ready before sprinting back to Viktor and Aura.

The air developed an electric quality, and the stench of ozone made her nose prickle unpleasantly. Raziel stood off to one side, his hands lowered. Though the Archangel was still as death, Ketha wasn't fooled. He'd compromised the part of him that hated supernatural beings like herself. This was one task that would have been easy to avoid, yet he'd attacked it head-on.

She offered him points, no matter what drove him.

"Look." Viktor pointed toward the first two groups. Blue-white light arced from the Shifters' fingers before shading to silver.

Ketha blew out a tightly held breath. Soon, very soon, she'd know if they had a prayer of this working. Would the Shifters have enough power to sever the strands holding the Cataclysm together? She focused her third eye, shutting off the mesa spread around her.

The Cataclysm formed in her psychic vision. A roiling mass of angry red, sickly yellow, and vomit-colored brown. Tentacles shot out from it in all directions. Some augured into the sea far below, which explained why it was poison and dead. Others reached toward *Ciudad de Huesos*, holding it in a death grip. The sight was so unsettling, it took all her fortitude not to turn tail and run.

A circular hole developed in one side of the Cataclysm, growing until their adversary reacted. Tentacles surged upward, splaying against the opening to keep it from getting bigger. A shower of blood-hued sparks danced away from the tentacles and headed right for the magical lines streaming from the three Shifters.

"Ward yourselves," Ketha cried and raced forward intent on helping Rowana's group. Magic spewed from her as she directed maximum damage at the tentacles. Still immersed in the world viewed through her third eye, the Shifters and Vamps appeared gray and insubstantial.

"I've got this one, Shifter." Raziel swerved in front of her, surrounded by a nimbus of light that looked gold to her third eye. Thunderbolts of molten metal—gold mingled with silver—headed straight for the Cataclysm. The tentacles drew back, black smoke billowing from them, and the blood-colored sparks disappeared.

Ketha shook her head to bring the world back into focus. "We have to move fast," she screamed, using magic to project her voice. "Second group. Go now."

Viktor ran to her and gripped her arm. "We'll never be able to hold our position long enough to get magic where we need it to destroy that thing."

"Yes, we will. You have to believe in what we're doing because there's no going back. It knows we're out for blood."

"I do believe in us, but there are too many teams. Too much time for that thing to come up with ways to even the score. If everyone joins forces, we can move fast, blast our way inside."

"I agree," Aura cried. "Let's get this done before that thing derails us."

Almost as if the Cataclysm had glommed onto Viktor's suggestion that it retaliate, the sky darkened. Ribbons of fire rained down, mixed with silver dollar-sized dark-brown bugs. Shrieks rose as Shifters and Vamps batted at places their clothing and hair caught fire.

"Goddamn it to hell," Viktor roared and smothered flames on one side of her robe with his hands. Bugs congregated on his fingers. They looked like three-inch-long beetles with hard carapaces, but they were too round and had sharp little beaks. He shook his hands hard, but they clung like limpets.

Ketha plucked one off him. Its legs flapped uselessly, working to find purchase. Yellowish liquid spirted from its hind end, carrying the acrid stench of poison. There were thousands of the little shits, and more dropped from the skies by the minute.

Killing them individually was impossible. Ketha inscribed a sloppy pentacle in the dirt with the toe of her boot and dropped the beetle inside it.

The thing scuttled to the edges of her spell line. When it discovered it couldn't cross it, it reared back on its shell edge and made a sound like razor blades scraping glass. "Do not let them bite you," Ketha shouted.

"How do I avoid it?" Viktor picked them off, crushing them beneath his boots, but more fell from the sky.

"Let me help." Aura threw her magic wide open, strengthening Ketha's pentacle until it glowed white-hot.

Ketha was too focused on integrating Aura's power with her own to answer Viktor's question. She focused a global destruction spell on the beetle she'd trapped on the ground in front of her.

Her spell kindled, and the creature burst into sulfur-smelling fumes. That one might be dead, but Ketha was far from done. She reached through its destruction, sending ruin to each of its kin. "Die," she exhorted. "*Faigh bás.*" She repeated the Gaelic curse three times in unison with Aura.

One by one, the bugs exploded and caught fire. A noxious smell, reminiscent of carrion rotting in the sun, rose around them. Ketha lowered her hands, breathing hard.

"We did good, sister." Aura beamed and hugged her hard before letting go.

"We did, but shit!" Ketha rubbed a grimy hand down her face. "Much more of that, and we won't have anything left for the Cataclysm."

"Which is exactly where it wants you." Raziel materialized out of nowhere. "Nice work, by the way." He rubbed his hands together. "Love it. It's like the plagues all over again."

"Except we're hardly in Egypt," Viktor muttered and held up his hands. "No bites. Guess they didn't care for Vampire blood."

"Good thing. Did you smell the poison?" Ketha asked.

"Of course I did." Viktor shut his mouth with a *clack.*

Ketha looked upward. The sky was still coated in menacing gray-black clouds, but the fiery ribbons had disappeared. "I don't get it. Was the fire attached to the bugs?"

"Me." Raziel tapped his chest. "I killed the streamers." He gestured at the growing group of Shifters and Vamps a few yards away at the edge of the mesa. "The fourth group is almost done. Time for you three to strut your stuff. Be fast, not elegant, and we might have a chance."

A blood-curdling yell froze her in place. Ketha pivoted to see Jorge hurtling toward them with a band of half a dozen Vamps strung out behind him. "Noooo," she screeched.

"We can take him." Aura raised her hands, light crackling from her fingertips.

"Save your magic. This is my war." Viktor bolted toward Jorge, shrieking his fury in German. The two Vampires crashed into one another, and Viktor drove the other Vamp to the ground.

"We did not need this," Raziel snarled, stopping between each word for emphasis.

Ketha ignored Viktor's exhortation to save her magic. She gestured for Aura to follow and raced to where he rolled in the dirt, grappling with Jorge. The Vampire legion caught up, fury blazing from them. One headed right for her, but Aura stopped him with a blast of magic to his heart. It wouldn't kill him. Only beheading could do that, but it did knock him out, and he crumpled to the ground. At least it halted forward motion for the other five who circled around their fallen companion, snarling and muttering. Fangs extended, their rotten sulfur smell mingled with the dying beetles into a noxious mélange.

Beheading.

Where was the saber Viktor had mentioned? Iron was far from Ketha's friend, but she'd do what she had to. Time was running out. The group holding the hole in the Cataclysm would run out of magic, and then they'd all be screwed.

The Cataclysm would win on a technicality.

"We need that blade," Aura shrieked. "I saw it. Where'd it go?"

Raziel ran between Ketha and the Vampires and scooped it up. Shouting in a language she'd never heard before, he cut a broad swathe with the blade. Heads rolled. Two of the Vamps took off with speeds only a Vampire could manage and dove headfirst off the mesa's edge. The other three fell as blood geysered from their headless necks. A metallic reek joined the other nauseating smells.

"Cowards! You'd better keep running," Aura yelled after their retreating backs.

When Ketha looked at Viktor, he was straddling Jorge with his hands around the other Vampire's throat. "You don't want to kill me," the Jorge thing said, except Raphael's Slavic-accented voice emerged from its throat.

"Oh, but you're wrong. I've imagined you dead for years. If I hadn't been such a coward, I'd have ended you long since."

"You don't mean that. Why, you were one of my chosen," Raphael crooned, his words hypnotic. They reminded Ketha of a snake immobilizing its victim.

She ran to Raziel and grabbed the saber. The iron burned her hands, but she carted it to Viktor. "You or me?" she panted. "Who kills that abomination?"

"I do." Viktor let go of Jorge/Raphael's neck, snapped up the saber with Vampire speed, and crushed the blade through the other Vampire's neck. Blood and air bubbled through his windpipe, and then red-black blood sprayed from two severed carotids and four broken jugulars.

"No time to rest on your laurels, children," Raziel exhorted and dragged Viktor to his feet. Blood sheeted off him, dripping onto the mesa, but his green eyes shone with victory.

"Run," Raziel screamed. "Or the Cataclysm will find a way to repair the damage the others have generated."

A quick scan told Ketha her power was waning, but she might have enough. Maybe. A jolt of energy buffeted her. Aura yelped.

"What the fuck was that? It felt like a cattle prod up my ass, but I feel rejuvenated."

"Raziel making sure we have enough juice to finish this." Ketha ran hard for the group of Vamps and Shifters enveloped in layers of spells. All of them were panting. Lines of strain carved deep into their faces.

Ketha and Aura flanked Viktor. The other Shifters and Vamps parted to let them through. Once they were at the leading edge of the spell, Ketha raised her arms and began to chant. Aura did the same. Neither Shifter held back. Destruction flashed from the ends of Ketha's fingers. Her flesh was raw from handling the blade, and the abraded places burned as if someone had immersed her hands in lighter fluid and tossed a match atop them.

She wasn't conscious of switching to her psychic vision, but the Cataclysm—a churning, tempestuous Cataclysm—took shape not a foot in front of her. Heat from the thing made her hands hurt so much she screamed, but she kept magic flowing.

"You cannot win, Shifter," pounded into her head from all sides. Along with the words came an inexorable pull toward the pulsing, roiling mass ahead.

Ketha diverted power into wards, but it didn't help. She felt herself slipping forward. Viktor hooked an arm around her and his other around Aura, dragging them back a few inches. Even with him hanging on, holding her ground wasn't easy. Ketha had to add more and more power to her warding before her footing stabilized.

The voice that had begun by telling her she couldn't win kept up a steady patter about how nice and warm and restful it would be inside the Cataclysm. *"Let go,"* it suggested, its voice—sometimes a seductive male, sometimes a maternal female—silkily hypnotic. When it got around to, *"You'll like me once you get to know me,"* she rebelled.

"Shut up!" she screeched. "Just shut up."

"Glad I'm not the only one," Aura yelled from Viktor's other side.

"Finish this!" Viktor shook both of them. "Drain me dry if it'll help. I can't do a fucking thing on my own. I'm not the one with magic."

Ketha was breathing hard, and she heard Aura's gasping pants through the Cataclysm's perennial roar. *"On my count of three,"* she told Aura and hoped the Cataclysm hadn't heard. The thing was impossibly strong.

Ketha wound her magic in with Viktor's and felt Aura do the same. Anchored in Vampire energy, the women loosed destruction right into the heart of the Cataclysm. If this didn't work, they were done. She and Aura wouldn't have enough magic for another try.

Tears streaked her cheeks, and bone-deep hopelessness churned through her. How could they, puny magical beings, ever dream they could conquer something as potent as the Cataclysm?

Anguish surrounded her, its strands like sticky, ominous spiders' webs. She recognized the Cataclysm's hand in her despair. Anger boiled from her guts.

Ketha squared her shoulders, latching onto her fury like a lifeline. "We can destroy you because we're who made you in the first place," she cried as another blast of destruction rolled through her, targeted right at the heart of the Cataclysm.

Booming crashed around her so loud it ruptured her eardrums. Pain battered her. Fluid ran down the sides of her face, but she was too busy shaping spells to brush it aside. Forked black lightning joined the thunder. The ground they stood on rolled in the throes of the mother of all earthquakes.

The booming intensified until she felt consciousness slipping. Worse, the spell still flowing through her, anchored to Viktor and the earth, was ripped away, siphoned into the Cataclysm. Once that happened, the world went black.

Despair ate at her, a strong acid that made the ache in her hands and ears pale by comparison.

They'd lost.

If they weren't dead yet, surely the Cataclysm would claim them soon, just like it had claimed her spell. Viktor still had an arm around her. Presumably his other arm circled Aura, holding her safe from the Cataclysm's maw.

The earth bucked harder, but the incessant drag toward the Cataclysm stopped precipitously, as if someone had cut a cord. Still holding onto her, Viktor staggered backward, his balance destroyed by the shuddering earth. Ketha fell to her knees with Viktor and Aura beside her.

Rocks cascaded from somewhere, but it was dark, so she couldn't see them until they crashed down. Viktor threw his body on top of hers. She tried to wriggle from beneath him, tried to tell him to save himself if he could, but she was too tapped out to manage words. Her last thought before darkness took her was how much she loved him. It didn't matter if he was a Vampire and she was a Shifter. She saw through to his essence, and it was everything she'd ever longed for in a man.

Epiphanies. Always too little and too late.

Her mind voice might have gotten the last word, but even it was too tired to follow the barbed observation with a longer lecture.

19

WHEN MAGIC ISN'T ENOUGH

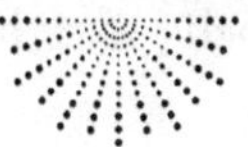

VIKTOR SAW the Cataclysm fold in on itself right before the world went black. At least the hideous pull, the one that came within a hairsbreadth of dragging all three of them into the maelstrom, had ended abruptly. So abruptly, it threw him backward. He staggered and then gave up on remaining upright. They were probably safer close to the ground, anyway.

A house-sized boulder plummeted from somewhere—probably the nearest cliff face. He dragged Ketha and Aura out of its path and threw his body over both women, but Aura wriggled free and placed her mouth near his ear. "Protect Ketha. She's in far worse shape than me since she carried the brunt of our magic."

"Stay close," he warned. The Shifter looked gray-green in his augmented Vampire vision.

"Nah. I'm making a run for the caves. I might not make it, but it's better than being flattened by something like that." She played her mage light over the massive boulder only a few inches from them. "Thanks to Ketha, I have some magic left."

More rocks crashed down. Aura rolled to her knees, clearly fighting for balance.

"Wait." Viktor snaked out a hand and touched her leg.

249

"What?" Aura tried to rise but fell on her ass, the pitching, heaving ground too much for her.

"Were we successful?" Viktor glanced at the churning blackness where the Cataclysm had been.

"I have no idea. I don't know what was supposed to happen afterward, but none of this looks particularly auspicious to me. Shit! No sky. No world. Maybe we killed everything along with the Cataclysm. Powerful spells like the one we loosed are unpredictable."

"Has your bond animal had anything to say?"

Aura shook her head. "It's a mountain lion, and it's been quiet for months now. It's like a part of me died."

Viktor didn't know what to say. The Shifter sounded so desolate, he was sorry he'd brought it up.

The ground quieted, and Aura shot to her feet, running hard while the getting was good. Viktor didn't hesitate. It was as good an opportunity as he'd seen to move Ketha to safety. Even if their spell had worked and whatever made him a Vampire was on its way out—or changing him into a Shifter—he hoped to hell his supernatural strength and speed were up to one last task.

He sprang to his feet, snatched up an unconscious Ketha, and sprinted for the cave with water and fish on the mesa's distant edge. The cliff face wasn't quite as high, nor as rock studded there, which might mean less chance of a falling boulder blocking the cave's entrance and trapping them inside.

At least so far, his superior physical ability was holding up. He scanned the mesa as he ran, looking for other Vamps and Shifters, but didn't see anyone. He heard the disconsolate squawking of condors long before he bent to enter their cave. Viktor stopped at the entrance and took one last look at the mesa. The ground wasn't pitching and rolling anymore, but that might only mean a small break in the action. Earthquakes normally came in waves. The sky remained an unremitting black. The ocean pounded against rocks in the distance, crashing far more aggressively than usual.

Was Aura right? Had they killed Earth along with the Cataclysm? He wished he knew more about supernatural phenomena. Depending on how tightly the Cataclysm had integrated itself with Earth's warp and weft, he supposed it was possible.

The ground he stood on trembled. Might be aftershocks, or the forerunner of an even deeper quake that could collapse the whole damned mountain. He toyed with trying to leave the mesa, but the expanse of steep, exposed hillside between there and the trail was a huge deterrent. His chances of making it through earthquakes and rockfall, carrying Ketha weren't good. Besides, the trail could be blocked by boulders.

He might be strong and fast, but he was scarcely invincible.

The cave was their best bet. He ducked inside. Condors dive-bombed him, pecking with their sharp beaks. Viktor didn't blame them. The sound and fury bombarding the mesa had to have riled them, and they had chicks to protect. He focused a hypnotic, soothing spell their way, drawing on one of the few magics Vamps possessed. It was useful for quieting prey—or luring them to their deaths.

The birds fluttered to the ground, no fight left in them. A shudder racked Viktor as evidence that Vampire power hadn't deserted him reverberated in his guts. If he was still a Vamp, surely that meant they'd failed.

Ketha stirred in his arms, moaning softly. He carried her deeper into the cave system, past nests of young condors until he found an unoccupied side cavern with a sandy floor. Moving well past the entrance, he sank to the ground, still cradling Ketha close.

"You're safe, love." He kissed her forehead.

She opened her eyes, squeezed them shut, and opened them again. "Where are we? I can't see anything."

"One of the condor caves. I can see, but it's my augmented

vision." He stopped shy of connecting the dots. She could do that on her own.

A wavery, violet mage light formed near her, and she cupped the side of his face in one hand. "What happened after I passed out?"

"Do you remember when the suction from the Cataclysm stopped?"

She nodded. "It's almost the last thing I do remember. An earthquake rolled through. Really bad one. Everything went black, and we ended up on the ground—" Her eyes widened, and she struggled in his arms. "Aura. What happened to her?"

"She's safe. At least I think she is. She made a run for the caves on the other side of the plateau."

Ketha sagged against him. "Thank the goddess. Everyone else?"

"I don't know. I didn't pass anyone on my way here, and I did look." Viktor knew he should let her rest, but she was the one with the book, the one with knowledge—and hopefully answers. "Your spell. Did it work?"

She closed her teeth over her lower lip. "Doesn't seem like it. A black sky can't be a good sign. Did it lighten at all?"

Viktor shook his head and shifted her in his arms so that he cradled her head in one hand. "I love you, Ketha. If we're teetering at the end of everything, I didn't want to die without telling you how much you mean to me. You taught me to believe in myself again. Gave me courage to stand up to Raphael. Something I should've done a long time ago."

Her golden eyes sheened with softness. "My last thoughts out on the mesa were about you."

"I hope they were good ones." He smiled.

Instead of answering, she wrapped both arms around him and closed her mouth over his. Warmth and caring flowed from her, and he kissed her back, sinking his tongue inside her mouth and drawing her as close as they could get. She tasted sweet, and her wildflower and Antarctic beech scent eddied around him.

She nipped his lower lip, and he nipped back, sucking a droplet of blood off her full mouth. The taste of her blood ran hot in his veins like fine, aged whiskey. He wanted more of her blood, but his cock raged, demanding attention. Thick and burning with desire, its need outplayed his thirst for blood.

Ketha broke away from his questing tongue and tugged the sash of her robe until the garment fell open. He pushed the sides apart, and the sight of her body seared him. Perfect globes of breasts tipped by peaked golden nipples rode high on a sculpted rib cage. A narrow waist gave way to flared hips, and dark curls nested between her long, well-muscled legs.

His bloodlust receded, replaced by a far more familiar heat, and he buried his face in her breasts, laving her nipples and moving from breast to breast. She moaned and arched into his touch. The movement against his cock was excruciatingly erotic. Without letting go of the nipple in his mouth, he repositioned their bodies so she lay on dry sand, and he knelt above her.

Ketha wrapped a hand around the hardness jutting from between his legs, and a low, guttural growl rose from him. He wanted the woman splayed before him with a ferocity that defied reason. They should be outside hunting for the others. The last of their time before Earth vanished into the solar system should be spent doing their damnedest to find some kind of antidote to whatever they'd loosed, but he didn't care. Nothing shy of a tsunami could've dragged him from Ketha's side.

Her fingers dug at the lacings holding his trousers in place. He pivoted to give her better access and moved his mouth lower until it hovered above the enticing mysteries between her legs. She bucked her hips, and he fastened his mouth over her nub while trailing a hand between her legs, seeking her core.

Scorching heat surrounded his cock as she took him into her mouth. He hadn't orgasmed in forever. Vampire blood fests had been his substitute for human release, but they'd never come close to filling the empty places within him with anything beyond sick resignation.

Her nub swelled in his mouth, and he forgot about everything but pleasuring the woman in his arms. Nothing mattered but her, and he teased her with his tongue, rolling it around her sensitive places and plunging into her with his fingers. Concentrating on her made it possible not to come himself as she licked and sucked the length of his shaft.

He felt the shift as her muscles tightened around him in rhythmic release. She worked him harder, faster as she came. Once her spasms quieted, he pulled away from her mouth and fingers and moved until he knelt between her legs. Words felt beyond him as he seated himself at her entrance, hoping she'd welcome him into her body.

Any doubts he'd had fled as she wrapped her legs around his waist and drew him inside, inch by inch, until he was fully encased in the wonder of her slick center. The heat of her was enticing, alluring, impossible to resist. He balanced on his arms so he could drink in the sight of her body spread beneath his. He wanted the lush moments to last as long as possible, wanted to savor the feelings streaming through him. He'd been taught congress with Shifters was forbidden, but what could that matter, now? Any damage to their world had been done long since, ten years ago in Siberia.

"Viktor." Her magic rose around him, intensifying her heady scent.

"Yes, love?"

"Just that. I love you. I want you. When you're inside my body, there are no differences between us. We're only a man and a woman saying with our bodies what our hearts already know."

"That's beautiful, but not as beautiful as you are." Bending, he brushed his lips over hers, and she tightened her body around his shaft.

Detaching her mouth from his, she murmured, "Make love to me."

"I've never wanted anything quite so much."

She smiled, and desire raced through him, igniting every cell with determination to claim the woman beneath him as his—and his alone.

"I already am," she said, having clearly been inside his mind, but it didn't matter. He had no secrets, not from her.

"Good, because I fear you're stuck with me for however much longer the world lasts."

A smile began in her eyes and made its way to her mouth, slow, languid, filled with needing him. Evidence of her caring smote him to his heart, and longing for her spilled over, cracking his reserved places wide open.

"You never know." Her voice was soft, barely there. "We couldn't save the world with magic. Maybe we can save it with love."

It was an enticing thought. Because he was too far gone to do anything else, he ran with it.

He unwound her arms from where they gripped him and pinned them above her head with one hand. Withdrawing slowly, he teased her entrance before delving her depths again. She moved with him, thrusting and withdrawing until the margins where he stopped and she began blurred, and they became one being careening toward ecstasy.

It might have been a trick of her magic, but he felt her arousal alongside his own. Sensed her body surrounding his cock but also knew how his cock felt inside her. His heart hammered, and his balls tightened. An orgasm spooled deep in his belly, but he rode herd on it until her climax blasted into his mind. Her body heaved beneath his, breasts splotched with evidence of her passion.

Viktor drove into her, letting go of all his boundaries. Semen juddered from him in white-hot gouts that bound him to Ketha, and she to him. He'd never seen sex as a spiritual joining, yet coming inside her united them as surely as if a minister had pronounced wedding vows.

He let go of her wrists and gathered her close, kissing her lips, her forehead, her cheeks as their breathing slowed.

"We should try to find everyone," he said at last. "I've been feeling guilty. Like I checked out on our companions."

Ketha nodded solemnly. "I feel the same, but making love was important in ways I can't explain." After a final nuzzle, she rolled to a sit and set her robe to rights.

He tucked himself back inside his pants, grappling with his laces with fingers that wouldn't cooperate. Flowing to his feet, he held out a hand to help her to stand. "What do you mean?"

"Shifters rely on instincts. We're attuned to the natural world, so we've learned to listen to it. Not that I haven't fantasized what you'd feel like in my arms, but what we just did felt preordained somehow. Like it had to happen exactly when it did."

He grinned crookedly. "I felt the same thing but chalked it up to being overcome by your considerable charms."

She crooked a finger his way. "Keep the schmaltz coming."

"It's not *schmaltz*," he protested. "You're the most amazing woman I've ever known."

"You're pretty incredible yourself. Shall we?" She started toward the portal leading to the main cave system, mage light bobbing next to her.

Viktor hurried after her. "I want to try to locate Juan and the others. Glenn particularly. He was a last-minute add-on and probably ended up with a much fuller plate than he anticipated."

Ketha was well ahead of him, but the condors didn't squawk even once to protest her incursion into their nesting ground. Her muffled shriek brought him at a run past birds that barely glanced his way.

Daylight streamed through the cave's entrance. Hope jabbed him hard, and he ducked his head to step outside. Ketha stood in bright sunlight, looking up at a blue sky studded with white, fluffy clouds.

She raised her arms above her head and spun in place.

Viktor wrapped an arm around her waist, hugging her. "I'm guessing this means it worked. Your incantation worked."

A broad smile lightened her features, accentuating her exotic beauty. "*Our* incantation. It appears so. Look." She pointed at the spot where they'd squared off against the Cataclysm. Shifters and Vampires milled around the edge of the mesa, thrusting fingers, hands, and arms at the sky and downward, presumably at the ocean.

"Come on." He laced his fingers with hers and started across the mesa. Boulders that hadn't been there before dotted the broad expanse. Otherwise, it looked much as it had the day he'd discovered it.

Juan loped toward them; when he got there, he wrapped his arms around both of them. "Damn, it's good to see you! I was sure you two got sucked into the Cataclysm. Aura said no, but the rest of us assumed she passed out when the earthquakes rolled through and missed something—"

Aura reached them next and shoved Viktor aside to latch onto Ketha. "There you are. I told everyone you weren't dead, but no one believed me." Tears ran down her face. "I don't know if I'm more relieved to see you whole and hearty or that now everyone will stop telling me I'm nuts."

"It doesn't matter, sweetie." Ketha moved her hands to Aura's shoulders. "You were amazing back there. I couldn't have asked for a stronger, more capable partner."

"You too." Aura's cheeks turned bright red at the compliment.

"Come on." Juan beckoned. "Everyone's accounted for except Raziel."

"You won't find him." Ketha sounded certain.

"Why not?" Juan glanced her way as they walked toward the rest of the group.

"He redeemed himself by his actions today. I bet his master finally allowed him to return home."

"Do you mean God?" Viktor asked.

Ketha shrugged. "There are a whole lot of gods—and goddesses as well. Raziel serves one of them. It's not who I'd have chosen, but I can't fault him for following his heart."

They reached the others in a flurry of high fives and greetings. "Look!" Rowana pointed downward from the mesa's edge. "The ocean's not perfect yet, but that hideous red color is receding. Parts of the water are blue, and the sky is right again. Finally."

She shook long, matted silver hair over her shoulders. Her face was streaked with dirt, blood, and soot, but an inner knowledge shone through as she skewered Ketha and Viktor with her intense, dark gaze.

"What?" Ketha asked, standing straight under the other Shifter's frank appraisal.

"It was you two. Or more likely, you two in conjunction with everything we did earlier. Some magics are additive like that."

"Rowana." Ketha's tone was sharp. "You're babbling."

The other Shifter shrugged. "Probably. It's been a big day. Blew through way too much magic for an old woman. You and Viktor made love. I recognize the luminance streaming from you, and all this wonder"—she spread her arms wide—"might be linked to that. Maybe. My guess is you went to ground in one of the caves, decided nothing much else mattered since the world was ending, and you thumbed your noses at the ancient prohibition against Shifters and Vampires having sex."

"I'm happy for you"—Aura bent close to Ketha—"but you and Viktor weren't part of the prophecy, so I disagree with Rowana. We broke the Cataclysm, but it took its sweet time receding."

"Not an unfinished prophecy anymore?" Viktor asked.

Aura shook her head. "I need to write everything down. It's how those who walked before me did things, and I have no idea if I'm the only Shifter left who deals in prophecies."

Glenn capered forward, grinning like a loon. "My fangs are gone. I can't make them drop anymore. If I'm going to turn Shifter, it hasn't happened yet, but I say bring it on." He caught Viktor from the side and hugged him. "Thanks, dude. I'm going to go find Bridget."

Viktor grinned, delighted by the other man's joy. "Your wife?"

"Who else?" Glenn raced away, but at human, not Vampire, speed.

"It's going to take time for things to normalize," Ketha warned. "We have good water here, and a food source and shelter."

"Maybe we should stay on the mesa for at least a week," Aura murmured.

"No reason not to." Rowana smiled. "It's not as if we have anything to go back to down there."

"Maybe not right now," Viktor said, "but we can rebuild. All the infrastructure is still there. We'll have to figure out who has specific skills and deploy them accordingly. The humans will help —once they understand Vampires won't be hunting them anymore."

"Oh-oh." Juan punched him lightly. "I worked with you for too many years not to recognize that tone." He cupped his hands around his mouth. "Anyone who's afraid of hard work"—Juan swung in a circle broadcasting his voice—"leave now. Don't just leave. Run. Viktor's a total slave driver."

"Thanks, mate." Viktor punched back, but Juan feinted out of the way.

"Do you suppose what we did freed the rest of the world too?" Daide asked.

Ketha drew her dark brows together, thinking. "I don't know, but maybe my sisters and I can figure that out. My magic is growing stronger, and my wolf is howling from the sidelines exactly like it used to."

"It's a plan." Rowana clasped her hands together. "My eagle is back too. Now, if it's all the same to everyone, I'm going to retire to the cavern where we plotted everything out and sleep until I'm not tired anymore."

A chorus of, "Great idea," bloomed around Viktor, and people padded off in groups of twos and threes, heading for the caves.

"Get good rest. You earned it." Ketha patted Rowana's shoulder and then walked to the mesa's edge.

Viktor joined her and looked at the ocean that was indeed shading to blue. "Not right away," he said, "but once Ushuaia is functioning like a city again, how would you feel about sailing away from here?"

She turned to face him, her expression serious. "On *Arkady*?"

He nodded. "She's a sound ship, and it would give us a way to see if any of the rest of the world is even still out there."

Ketha spread her hands in front of her and tilted her chin to meet his gaze. "Your powers may well change. What if the animal that bonds with you isn't fond of water?"

Understanding hit him hard. As much as he'd hated being a Vampire, turning into a Shifter could create problems of its own. "We'll cross that bridge when—and if—it happens. I can't imagine an animal that didn't like water wanting to join its essence to mine."

"You're probably right."

"Is it important for me to become like you?" He articulated what he was certain had to be in her heart.

She hesitated for long moments before her golden gaze turned soft, liquid. "No. I fell in love with you when you were a Vampire. You'll still be you no matter what happens."

For the first time since he was small, he felt the quick, hot bite of tears, and he vowed to be worthy of the woman standing before him. He folded her hands in his. "Ketha. Darling."

"You're my darling too. Magic will never vanish from the world. We'll embrace it, no matter what form it takes. The best part is you'll be by my side." She smiled, looking young and care-free and happy.

"It's a deal." Bending his head, he nuzzled her neck, drinking her in.

"What's next?" she asked.

"How about this? We'll collect your backpack and spell book. Then we can make ourselves a temporary home in the spot where we made love."

"Perfect. I like it. Except the pack and book can wait. Rowana's there, and she needs her rest." Ketha untangled her hands from his and threaded an arm around his waist.

Together, they started across the plateau.

"It's a whole new world out there," he said.

"And I can't think of anyone I'd rather share it with," she replied, leaning into him. "I can't quite believe we defeated the Cataclysm."

"Me, either. That will take a while to sink in."

"We'll have time. All we need."

He threaded an arm around her waist. "Tell me about being a Shifter. Just in case…"

"Nothing I'd like better." She bent and entered the cave where they'd been earlier. "Back in the beginnings of the world, powerful shamans wished to become even stronger. They summoned a trance state and found the border of the special world where our animals dwell, but they couldn't break through. Not at first. They cast stronger and stronger spells until the barrier crumbled. The animals were angry and tried to drive them away, but the shamans humbled themselves—"

"I thought you said you couldn't go to the animals' world," Victor broke in.

"We can't. Not anymore, but that came from the agreement between us and our animals. I haven't gotten to that part yet." She hip-butted him and moved ahead into the secluded spot where they'd lain while the fortunes of the world changed.

Viktor wrapped her in his arms. She felt perfect. Right. "Go on," he urged. "I won't interrupt again."

She snuggled into his embrace. "Years passed before the animals agreed to share their power. It's how the first Shifters came to be..."

He drew her down onto the sand, never letting go, fascinated by the tale and her melodious voice. Before she was done, something stirred deep within him. He tried to focus on it, hoping against hope it was an animal knocking at the gates, but the harder he tried, the faster the faint presence skittered away.

Ketha broke off her recitation and moved back enough to look at him. "You can't force it." Her voice was soft, and she cupped the side of his face in her hand.

Her mouth was impossible to resist, so he closed his over it. Years of long-denied emotion streamed through him, but he welcomed the sensation sluicing from his head to his feet. Ketha kissed him back so fiercely, she tumbled him onto his back.

Viktor sank his hands into her thick hair, reveling in its silky strands. She could finish the First Shifter tale later. Thanks to today, they had time.

For everything.

BOLD NEW WORLD

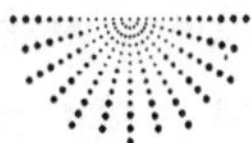

Two-and-a-half Weeks Later

Ketha stretched her body one paw at a time, and then arched her back. She'd been running through the forests north of Ushuaia in wolf form, catching and eating rodents until her stomach was distended. It felt damned good to let the animal side of her nature roam free.

She and Viktor had come down from the mesa three days before, and this was the first break they'd taken. Their initial task had been stopping by all the human enclaves and reassuring them it was safe to emerge from hiding—finally. Many of the humans had been skeptical, but Viktor's reassurance about no longer being a Vampire quelled the worst of their fears.

Beyond that, simply clearing out a place they could live temporarily had been back-breaking work since earthquakes spawned by the Cataclysm's departure had flattened still more buildings. They finally gave up on the wreckage that used to be Viktor's room and ended up in her old quarters next to the Shifters' last hideout. They'd considered *Arkady*, but both of them wanted to be closer to the center of town to assist with whatever needed doing.

Viktor had been shocked by what remained of his sub-basement room. He'd thought it was bombproof, but huge chunks of mortar had punched through the ceiling. The building had creaked and groaned while they tried to clear hundred-pound hunks of material out of the way. Viktor finally dragged her into the tunnels, muttering about not wanting to be there when the whole mess collapsed on their heads.

Her wolf dropped back onto its haunches, lifted its muzzle, and howled. Answering animal cries—some from Shifters, some not—rang from several sides.

The wolf's joy was contagious, and deep affection for her bondmate filled Ketha. *"I missed you."*

"I never went anywhere," the wolf replied.

"I know, but I missed us being like this. Running and hunting in your body, not mine. You don't have to answer this, but did the animals have a fallback position?"

"What do you mean?"

"Something you would have done if the world truly ended?"

The wolf didn't answer for so long, she figured she'd probed into an area the bond animals considered private, reserved for themselves. They loped along, stopping to sniff here and there and enjoying the scents of prey on the wind. Ketha had almost forgotten her question when the wolf began talking.

"We waited too long."

Ketha mulled it over. *"What do you mean?"*

"Early on after the Cataclysm, we—the animals—talked about leaving and resurrecting the barrier around our world. It wasn't affected by the Cataclysm. We could have retreated to what we were before the shamans breached our border."

"Why didn't you?"

"We needed to agree, and we couldn't. Many of us—me included—didn't feel right abandoning our bondmates. It was an all or none decision because once we resurrected our border, no one would have been

able to leave our world. We would have lost all access to our bonded ones."

If she'd been in her human form, holding back tears would have been a struggle. *"Thank you."*

"No need for thanks. Our bond is for a lifetime. Only a selfish coward opts to save his own hide. Anyway, by the time things got truly bad, none of us had enough magic left to do much of anything but hang on by our claws or talons."

"I was truly blessed when you entered my dreams."

"How could I have resisted?" the wolf countered. *"You were such a bright, precocious little girl. So sure of yourself and overflowing with your gift."*

"And you were everything noble about bond animals. It would have been far more difficult living out the years of the Cataclysm without you—even if we didn't access the shift magic very often toward the tail end of things."

"My powers were fading, but I still made you stronger." The wolf stated it as fact.

As always, the wolf's observations were spot-on. *"You did indeed, dear heart. Without you and the other bond animals, we probably wouldn't have defeated the Cataclysm."*

The wolf whuffled low in its throat, pleased she'd acknowledged its importance.

The cries of a raven on the hunt made her smile, and Ketha glanced skyward. Viktor's bird had taken two weeks to make its presence known. Before that, it had flirted with him, moving close and drawing away. Ketha had watched the process with interest. She had no idea how bonding would happen for someone who didn't dream their animal as a child and get to know it that way, solidifying the bond once puberty hit.

It had been damned hard not to intervene, try to hurry the process, but the bond was a deeply individual thing. Nothing she could have done would have made the slightest difference, and Viktor's raven might have resented her interference.

The bird spread its wings and plummeted downward, landing right in front of her. *"The hunt was good,"* it informed her wolf. *"How was yours?"*

"Excellent." The wolf punctuated the word with a tail swish.

"How are things going?" Ketha aimed her mind voice at Viktor.

"Better than good." Enthusiasm underscored his words. *"I'm entranced. Enthralled. I love being a Shifter almost as much as I love you."*

"Ready to be human again?"

Light flared around the raven, so Ketha called shift magic too. They'd left their clothes in the gnarled cypress grove, and it wasn't far. The day was brisk, but the cold wouldn't kill them.

Viktor wrapped his arms around her. "Your wolf is beautiful. One of these days, I want to run my fingers through your pelt."

Ketha tipped her head back and laughed. "Sounds kind of smutty."

Viktor grinned. "When I was a boy growing up in the Black Forest, a wolf used to show up from time to time at our cabin. My father always put food out—usually bones or other meat waste—for it. I loved to watch it slink close, grab the food, and make a run for the woods. One day, I had an idea, and I followed it."

"It must have known you were back there," Ketha said.

"Probably so, but at the time, I convinced myself I was a great tracker." He tightened his hold on her. "The wolf turned out to be a mother with pups. I followed her to her den. I never saw her young, but I heard them. They were absolutely silent until their mother was close, but then they yipped and squealed."

"They knew food was close."

"Probably so, but it was the oddest thing. The wolf ducked into her den to drop the food, but then she returned and stood staring at where I'd hidden myself. She didn't attack me. Didn't raise one hackle. Just leveled these lovely amber eyes my way."

"What'd you do?" Ketha asked.

"I told her she was the most beautiful creature I'd ever laid eyes on and that I'd make sure to put out extra food for her now that I knew about the pups." He slanted his gaze away for a moment. "I felt kind of silly, talking to her like that. She stood there like a sentinel until I turned and threaded my way back through the forest toward home."

"You've always had a good heart." Ketha leaned into Viktor, loving the feel of his nakedness against her body. "We need to get moving. You're shielding me with your body, but you must be freezing."

He dropped his hands onto her shoulders. "Shift for me, Ketha." Longing burned in the depths of his emerald eyes. "When you asked if I was ready to be human again, I was hoping you'd stay a wolf long enough for me to get to know that side of you better."

Ketha understood. She'd nurtured dreams of his raven perched on her shoulder where she could smooth its feathers and lose herself in its avian presence. She opened a channel to her magic and let the transformation take her. It felt right in a way not much had since the Cataclysm started sucking life out of the world. The wolf's pelt was welcome; so were its study pads. When she blinked to clear the visual transition from her human eyes to her wolf ones, Viktor was squatting on his haunches with his arms open.

She walked into those arms, and he dug his fingers into her thick, double coat, petting and smoothing her fur. "You are so lovely," he murmured.

"Thank you," her wolf spoke up. *"I like your bird too. I've known it for a long time, and it chose well."*

"That's a high compliment," Ketha said.

Viktor nodded solemnly. "Thank you. I hope its confidence in me is justified, and I love it that we're dual-natured. I had no idea I'd have a clear sense of myself while in shifted form."

"Yes. We are always two, no matter which body we occupy," Ketha murmured.

She stood still for several long moments while he ran his

hands over her wolf's body, almost as if worshipping it. She nuzzled the hollow of his shoulder and licked his chin.

"*Are you sure you're not cold?*" Ketha asked.

"I'm freezing, but it's worth every minute." Viktor straightened. "Thank you for indulging me. I'm ready to find our pile of clothing."

Ketha took off at a trot with him striding by her side. When they came within sight of the cypress grove, she shifted back and covered the last few yards with her bare feet crunching over sticks and rocks.

"Ouch." She made a face.

Viktor snorted. "Yeah. Human bodies are damn fragile." He pushed a welter of branches aside and motioned her inside, out of the wind.

She made a dive for her clothes and dressed hurriedly, layering tattered garments beneath her warm cloak. Viktor slid into his clothing too, topping off everything with his threadbare llama jacket.

"We should stop by the ship. I have lots of warm clothing there."

"Maybe I could alter some things to fit me?" Ketha quirked a brow.

"There are garments that would work for you too. We provided polar gear for our passengers. It was part of the service."

"Good to know. We'll raid *Arkady's* closets soon."

He sat on the ground and rested his back against a twisted tree bole, patting the ground next to him. Ketha settled so she was leaning against him, and he draped an arm around her. "Thanks for not insisting on leaving right away. I'm selfish enough to want another few minutes with you."

"Me too, but I feel guilty. There's years of work left back in town, and we're not going to stay that long."

"We'll stay long enough to see Ushuaia well on its way to supporting everyone who wishes to remain there." He narrowed his eyes. "What happens to the Vamps who haven't turned into Shifters?"

Ketha closed her teeth over her lower lip. "I wish I knew. The number is growing smaller. How many are left without bond animals?"

"Twenty, I think. They're all pre-Cataclysm Vamps."

She thought about it. "Did any of the older ones become Shifters?"

Viktor cocked his head to one side. "Now that you mention it, a couple dozen have."

"Okay. So that's not it. I was thinking maybe something about the earlier iteration of Vampire didn't lend itself to becoming a Shifter, but that doesn't make sense. The group in Siberia designed their spell to alter the original type of Vampire."

"Do you suppose they're still there?" Viktor asked.

"Who?"

"That group in Siberia?"

Ketha shrugged. "I have no idea, but if they are and I ever find the Shifters responsible for the Cataclysm, I'll see they're dragged before our council—if we even still have one—and censured."

He placed his hands on both sides of her face and smoothed his thumbs over her mouth. "Uh-uh. Way too far ahead of the game. We take this one step at a time. It will take years to sail around the world and figure out what's left. Back to the unbonded Vamps. Do you believe they'll find animals eventually?"

Ketha turned the question inward and asked her wolf, *What do you think?*

The reason they're not paired with an animal is because they're not open to the bond. We never force our way in.

She nodded. It made sense. "Did you hear that?" she asked Viktor.

"I did. Many of those old Vampires—or ex-Vampires—are hundreds of years old. They liked being Vamps. They're probably in mourning rather than looking forward."

"Maybe so. How's Juan taking to his mountain lion?"

Viktor angled his head and nuzzled her neck. "Like a duck to water. All the Vamps I knew well enough to do more than flip them off are delighted. Maybe we all had closet fantasies of having an animal sidekick as children. It's funny."

"What is?"

He twisted a corner of his mouth into a wry grin. "When I knew I'd become a Shifter because I felt an animal lurking, I assumed I'd be a wolf like you."

Ketha cocked her head to one side. "Were you disappointed?"

"That's the funny part. Quite the opposite. When my raven finally showed up front and center in my mind's eye, it was love at first sight." He kissed the tip of her nose. "Kind of like it was with you. From the moment I saw you, something changed in me. From the moment I met my bond animal, I understood it was the only one for me."

"And you welcomed it with your heart, mind, and soul." She stroked copper hair back from his face.

"Exactly. It was like a lock and key finding each other. Or puzzle pieces clicking into place and showing me the way to be whole." Color rose from the neck of his jacket, staining his tanned skin. "I'm babbling."

"Babble away." She kissed him once, quick and hard, and then got to her feet.

Viktor scrambled upright. "You're right. Much as I'd love to hold the world at bay, we should get moving. I love you, Ketha."

"Love you too. You're such a beautiful man. I thought maybe when the Vampire enchantment faded, some of that gorgeousness would dwindle, but it hasn't."

He walked by her side, and they left the protected grove. Wind hit them full in the face as soon as they turned south toward town, so she set a good pace.

"Would that have mattered?" he asked.

She glanced at him. "What?"

"If I'd turned into an ordinary sod." He grinned rakishly, making him so stunning she had a hard time looking away. A near stumble over a pile of tree roots redirected her gaze.

"I like to think I'm not that shallow," she mumbled. "Your eye candy looks are a plus, but I fell in love with your soul. For chrissakes, you were a Vampire when I met you—Shifters' sworn enemies—and I still couldn't reel in my longing."

"Did you try?" The corners of his mouth twitched as though he was trying not to laugh.

"Not very hard. Don't get me wrong. I love it that you've joined the Shifter ranks, but it wouldn't have mattered if you were still a Vamp. We'd have figured things out."

He laced his fingers with hers. "That we would. And that was the right answer, by the way. Where do you want to go first when we get back?"

She thought about it. "Let's stop by my old room and see if any of the Shifters are about. Bet they'll have a project list cooking."

Viktor laughed. "Juan accused me of being a taskmaster, but I swear Rowana must have been a drill sergeant in a previous life."

Ketha laughed too. "She did a stint in the Marines. You should ask her about it sometime."

She squeezed Viktor's hand. With him by her side and her wolf within, her world was damn near perfect. What lay beyond Ushuaia and the Beagle Channel might be a shambles, but they'd figure it out as they needed to. The worst was behind them.

It had to be.

21

INTO THE UNKNOWN

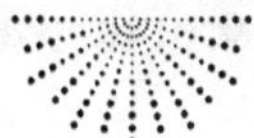

Two months later

Ketha navigated *Arkady's* steep steps to the quarterdeck wearing oversized men's clothing left over from the ship's previous crew. The mud-colored parka was warm and functional. So were the black insulated bibs and green Pac boots. She'd been grateful for the selection of cold weather clothing aboard the vessel. The crew's clothing was a definite step up from outdoor duds meant for the ship's passengers, which was why she'd opted for items that didn't fit as well but were far better constructed.

They'd fixed a lot of what was wrong in Ushuaia, but things like raw materials to sew clothing had been in short supply. The city wasn't totally resurrected, but it had a functioning water system, sewer system, and electricity. Delighted to be free from the Vampire scourge, humans emerged from hiding and worked like demons, helping set the city to rights.

Juan had been right about Viktor being a dogged worker. He'd gone without sleep many nights as he worked out how to restore *Ciudad de Huesos* to a habitable place. The piles of bones had been moved and incinerated, the streets swept clean. Minus the stacks of skeletons, the city's grim nickname had fallen out of use.

273

She and the Shifters—including the newly bonded ones—had helped with magic, but also with their brains and muscles. Though they'd tried, they hadn't been able to determine if the Cataclysm still wreaked havoc elsewhere on the globe. Satellites and cell towers appeared to be a thing of the past. No Internet. No landlines. No radio or any type of broadcast. Once they'd repaired the power plants to produce electricity, they'd tried every avenue to communicate with the rest of the world.

Nothing worked.

Her eleven sisters were aboard *Arkady* with her and Viktor. Juan, Recco, and Daide had joined them as well. Good thing, because a ship as substantial as *Arkady* needed crew. Even with sixteen of them, they were shy manpower.

Glenn had reunited with Bridget, and the two of them had hooked up with others in Ushuaia and were playing music every chance they got. All in all, the world was shading back to normal. At least at the southern end of South America.

Arkady's fuel tanks were full, courtesy of storage chambers in the dry dock, but taking her into blue water was still an unknown. She'd asked Viktor, and he'd said full tanks meant a thousand tons of diesel. Enough to travel from where they were to the Arctic, with fuel left over. They also had desalinization equipment aboard, capable of producing fifteen to twenty tons of freshwater a day.

Footsteps clattered down metal risers leading from the deck immediately above. Viktor trotted toward her, a broad smile on his face. He was wrapped in a thick down parka, but its hood was back, and his tawny hair streamed behind him, tossed by the salt spray.

He inhaled noisily. "Love that smell. It was one of the worst things about the Cataclysm. The ocean didn't smell right anymore." He wound an arm around her and kissed her forehead.

"Worse than being a Vampire?" She angled her head so she could look at him.

He made a face. "No. That was worse. I didn't realize how much I hated it until…" His voice petered out.

"Until what?"

Viktor shrugged. "It was complicated. If I'd owned my anger and resentment, I'd have had to do something about it. I was getting closer, though. The night I left you aboard *Arkady*, I headed straight to Raphael's. I made certain he had the saber before we left his quarters because I planned to kill him. Jorge stole my thunder, though."

"Yeah, and we know how well that turned out." Ketha leaned into him. "We can put all that behind us. No more Vampires. Shifter magic is back in spades, but we can't grow complacent. Something evil will show up to balance our power, and we need to be ready for it."

"We will be."

He looked so fierce and so protective, happiness beat a path through her. "On a far more pleasant note, how are things going with your brand-new bondmate?"

A broad grin split his chiseled features. "Someone somewhere must have known I've always loved birds, but my raven is amazing. It's perceptive, and it fulfilled one of my earliest wishes."

"Flight?" She quirked a brow.

He nodded. "Yup. I always wanted to leave Earth behind. I used to pilot small aircraft, but this is a thousand times better."

Ketha grinned back. "I'm glad. I kept my mouth shut, but your bonding process had more than a few rough edges in the beginning."

"I noticed. Why was that?"

"Lots of reasons. Shifters usually dream their animals as children and have years to get to know them. Part of you may have wanted a bond animal, but another part was reticent. Understandable since you were forced into being a Vampire."

She narrowed her eyes. "I couldn't do much. No one can assist another's bond."

"What you did was perfect, encouraging me to embrace my fate, no matter how it played out. Once I stopped trying to control every last nuance, the raven popped into my head, told me to get rid of my clothes, and there we were, flying above the mesa." Wonder spilled from him, scattering Shifter magic.

Ketha laughed. "I remember. I was working on cooking a passel of fish for dinner when this enormous raven landed right next to me and pecked me with its beak."

"You didn't shoo it away," he pointed out.

"Only because I figured it was hungry," she countered.

"'Fess up." He smoothed her windblown hair out of her eyes. "You knew it was me."

"I may have." She winked. "I'll never tell."

"In a more serious vein, how are the other women doing? Everyone's animals are hale and hearty from what I can tell."

Ketha chewed on her lip. "The younger ones are bouncing back faster from all the years we didn't have enough of anything. Rowana and Karin were around fifty to my thirty-five when we first came to Ushuaia. If they hadn't been Shifters, they might not have survived."

"Will they be all right?" Concern shone from the depths of Viktor's green eyes, and she loved him for his kindheartedness.

"I think so. We all will be, given a bit more time." She switched topics. "You seem happy. Really happy. You're well-bonded, but it feels deeper than that."

"I am happy. We've only been at sea for a day, but this is my home. Having you—and my bondmate—to share it with makes it all the better."

"Aw, bet you say that to all the girls. And ravens."

"Nope. Only to you." He smiled shyly. "I've never had a wife before. It was generous of that human to marry us. He knew what I'd been but didn't hold it against me."

"We're even. I've never had a husband, either." She liked the sound of the word as it rolled off her tongue, so she repeated it. "Husband."

"There's an echo in here." He kissed her lightly, and she tasted salt spray on his lips.

"Speaking of the Reverend Moore, I'm grateful enough humans remained to rebuild the town."

"I had no idea there were so many left," Viktor replied. "You guys did a great job hiding them."

Ketha laughed. "They hid bunches of their numbers from us too. Wily lot, humans. Guess they weren't certain we wouldn't turn against them if it came to an out-and-out confrontation with the Vampires. And they certainly never revealed their youngsters. I had no idea they were still producing children."

"Captain. You're needed on the bridge." Juan's voice blared over the loudspeaker system.

"They're singing my song." Viktor hooked an arm through hers. "Care to join me?"

"Sure." She moved ahead of him and mounted the stairs to the next deck up. The bridge was one deck beyond. "In the absence of satellites," she called over a shoulder, "how are we navigating?"

"The old-fashioned way. Every sailor has a sextant, and I'm no exception. The electronics that paint the bottom so we don't pitch up on underwater rocks are still quite functional. Plus, I know these waters. I've sailed from Ushuaia to Antarctica and the Falklands hundreds of times."

She topped out on the sixth deck and pulled open the door leading into the glassed-in bridge. Juan stood behind a large mahogany wheel.

"What's up?" Viktor asked.

Juan pointed at clouds bubbling on the horizon. "Weather's coming in. Which way do you want to head?"

"Now that's what I miss satellites for," Viktor told Ketha and strode to Juan's side. "What do you think?" he asked his navigator.

"It's a crapshoot. We could angle across the Scotia Sea for the

Falklands and South Georgia, or we could cross the Drake for the Palmer Peninsula. Both places have deserted whaling stations and research outposts—and probably stores of diesel to power *Arkady*. Not that we'll need to refuel anytime soon..."

Ketha listened as the men discussed the pros and cons of their options. She'd figured they'd head north, mostly because she wanted to go home, but Viktor had convinced her they were better off staying close to a place he was familiar with—and gradually increasing their range. It made sense, so she'd agreed. Besides, they couldn't sail to Wyoming. And none of them had any idea what they'd find in San Francisco or Seattle or any of the other port cities on the west coast of the United States.

Viktor was wise to counsel expanding their range slowly. If the Cataclysm still reigned in other places, it would be out for revenge and hell-bent on their destruction. She ground her teeth together, hoping they'd never have to duplicate the battle that had nearly been the end of them.

"Ketha." Viktor's voice broke into her thoughts.

She walked to where he stood behind the wheel. "Uh-huh?"

"I'm taking over here for a little bit. It'll be dinnertime soon. Feel like getting some chow online for everyone?"

"Sure. I'll rustle up a couple of the other women. Good thing the galley was well stocked."

Juan tossed his head back and laughed. "Doubly good that shit in cans never goes bad."

"Don't forget the dried food," she shot back, thinking about rice and noodles and flour and sugar in fifty-gallon drums. "Shit! If the humans had gotten wind of all the food you had stored on *Arkady*, they'd have broken into that dry dock and robbed you blind."

"They'd have tried," Viktor countered. "The galley was locked. They'd have had a hell of a time getting into it. Now, you Shifters would've been a different matter, but you never suspected it existed."

"How come you didn't eat any of it?" Ketha asked, thinking wistfully that she and her sisters would have been delighted to stumble across such a rich trove of edibles.

"Viktor and I kicked it around," Juan said. He'd moved across the bridge to a large, flat table spread with maps. "But we never could get past the spoilage aspect. Fifty-gallon drums are huge. And most of the cans are at least two gallon-sized. If we'd opened one, we'd never have come close to eating all of it before it rotted."

"Yeah and I hated the other Vampires enough, offering to share never occurred to me," Viktor muttered.

"Cheap ass," Juan retorted.

"No. Just particular about whom I break bread with." Viktor turned to Ketha. "This was a research ship," he reminded her. "Sixty plus passengers and another twenty-five crew. That many folks eat a lot." He sent one of his million-watt smiles her way. "Dinner, love?"

"On my way."

Ketha let herself out into the interior corridor and across the hall to the cabin she shared with Viktor. They'd sat in this same space the first time he brought her to *Arkady* when the ship was in dry dock.

"We did good," her wolf spoke up. Ever since the death of the Cataclysm, it had developed a decidedly chatty side, and Ketha welcomed its nearly constant presence. Clearly, it had missed her as much as she missed it.

"Which particular thing?" she inquired.

"All of it. Maybe later, we could shift and run around the ship."

"As soon as I'm done with dinner."

"I like Viktor—and his bird," the wolf went on. *"I've known that bird ever since..."*

The wolf recited a tale it had told her half a dozen times since Viktor's bondmate emerged from the parallel universe and claimed him. The animals were inveterate storytellers, and she loved listening to the wolf's yarns, no matter how many times it repeated them.

She shucked her parka, hanging it on a hook, and took in the tidy cabin. The scent of lovemaking hung in the air, and she breathed it in hungrily. Viktor was endlessly inventive and an incredible lover.

Yup. And now he's hungry for something beyond my body, she reminded herself and trotted into the corridor, pulling the door shut behind her. Living on the ship would take some getting used to. Everything she needed was here, but on a compact scale.

Midway down the stairs, she ran into Rowana, Zoe, and Aura heading up. "We saw a flock of wandering albatrosses," Rowana announced. "My eagle was fascinated."

"We figured if we were higher, we'd get a better look," Aura said.

"They were amazin'," Zoe chimed in. "Just the fact that they survived somewhere gives me hope."

"I need a volunteer to help with dinner." Ketha glanced from one to the other. "If you gals are busy, I can rustle up someone else."

"I'll help." Aura trotted back down the risers.

Ketha scooted by the other two women and joined her. "It makes my heart glad the Cataclysm didn't kill everything."

"Mine too." Aura stopped outside the swinging doors to the dining room and galley beyond and turned to face Ketha. "We have a lot to be thankful for."

"That we do." Ketha waited, sensing Aura had more to say.

The other woman licked her lips. Color rose to her cheeks. "I'm done feeling sorry for myself," she said. "For that first little bit of time when everything was a struggle and my mountain lion didn't return as quickly as Rowana's bird or your wolf, I really sank into a funk." She tilted her chin at a defiant angle. "I'm done with that. Getting my cat back made a world of difference. I was afraid it had deserted me."

Ketha hugged her. "I've had Viktor to distract me, but you could have talked with me. I'd have been happy to listen."

Aura waved a dismissive hand. "Aw, sweetie. Thanks. You were so happy it oozed out of your pores. Last thing I wanted to do was bother you with anything. After the hell we lived through, we deserve every single good thing that comes our way. It all worked out. Once I stopped fussing, my cat jumped in with all four paws."

"Was it ready to explore a new life with you?"

Aura grinned. "Hell, yeah. More than ready. Eager."

"That's the spirit." Ketha pushed the door open. "My wolf wants to run around the ship after dinner. Maybe your cat can join us."

"It's yowling. I'm taking that as a yes." Aura rolled her expressive green eyes.

"Excellent. Meanwhile, let's see if we can figure out where things are."

Aura winked. "I peeked in here a little bit ago. Come on. I'll show you."

Ketha followed her friend into the stainless-steel galley. Hope for the future ran strong in her. She had the best man in the world and was ready for adventure—however it unfolded. If they had to take on the Cataclysm again, so be it. They'd beat it once. They could do it again.

Somehow.

Last time they'd leveraged Vampire energy. This time they wouldn't have that to work with. They wouldn't have Raziel, either.

If it comes down to it, we'll figure something out. We have to.

Whistling a cheery folk tune to bolster her spirits, Ketha stood close as Aura opened cupboards, drawers, and food storage bins. "I never knew you had the soul of a chef," she told Aura.

"Oh, I'm full of surprises. And this is the best kitchen I've seen since we left Wyoming."

Ketha laughed. "How about the only kitchen."

Aura chuckled. "That too." She rubbed her hands together. "How does fettucine alfredo with canned green beans and canned peaches sound?"

"Divine. I can open cans with the best of them." Ketha laughed along with her friend.

"Excellent. I found a greenhouse room with planter boxes full of dirt and grow lights beyond the galley." Aura extended an arm to point.

"Are there seeds?" Enthusiasm filled Ketha. If they could grow simple things like lettuce and spinach, it would make their shipboard meals far more interesting.

"Didn't find any, but we could ask Viktor or Juan."

"Sounds like a plan." Ketha pulled a large can opener off a board studded with hooks and utensils, and the two women began assembling what they'd need to make dinner.

You've reached the end of *Deceived, Bitter Harvest, Book One*. Please leave a review for it. Doesn't have to be fancy. A sentence or two will do it, and reviews make such a huge difference. Thanks in advance!

If you're still in a reading mood, a sample from *Twisted* is tacked onto the end of this book.

ABOUT THE AUTHOR

Ann Gimpel is a USA Today bestselling author. A lifelong aficionado of the unusual, she began writing speculative fiction a few years ago. Since then her short fiction has appeared in several webzines and anthologies. Her longer books run the gamut from urban fantasy to paranormal romance. Once upon a time, she nurtured clients. Now she nurtures dark, gritty fantasy stories that push hard against reality. When she's not writing, she's in the backcountry getting down and dirty with her camera. She's published over fifty books to date, with several more planned for 2018 and beyond. A husband, grown children, grandchildren, and wolf hybrids round out her family.

Keep up with her at www.anngimpel.com or http://anngimpel.blogspot.com

If you enjoyed what you read, get in line for special offers and pre-release special reads. Sign up for Ann's newsletter on her website or her blog.

TWISTED: BOOK DESCRIPTION

The sea is the only life Juan's ever known—not counting the decade he spent as a Vampire. Those years gave him a healthy aversion for anything supernatural, but he's a shifter now. It's way better than being one of the undead, but he still doesn't trust magic. Paired up with Aura to teach him, he falls and falls hard, but she spurns his advances.

A history professor before the cataclysm, Aura deals in prophecies for her shifter pack. Juan is one hell of an attractive package, but he left a string of broken hearts during his years as chief navigator on cruise ships. She'd be an idiot to sign on for a fling. She has enough problems without adding a broken heart to them.

What began as an exploratory mission to see if anything is left of the world turns sour fast. A Vampire attack, a possessed priest, and a gateway to Hell mean fallout from the spell gone bad that pinned them in South America is far from gone. Retreat is tempting, but nowhere is safe. Surrounded by hardship, they sail on.

Evil is leaching in from somewhere, and they have to find the breach.

286

TWISTED, CHAPTER ONE: THAT'S IMPOSSIBLE

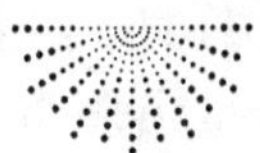

AURA MACKENZIE ROLLED her shoulders to get the kinks out of her back. She hadn't had much space to roam in Ushuaia, but *Arkady*, a sturdy Russian research vessel that had once ferried tourists back and forth to the Antarctic Peninsula, was smaller by far than any other place she'd spent much time.

She'd retreated to her cabin to shower now that the vessel wasn't pitching and rolling quite so much. The journey south from Ushuaia had grown rough once they left the Beagle Channel and turned southeast. If it hadn't been for a healthy dose of magic, she'd have been horribly seasick right along with several of the dozen female Shifters aboard. As it was, she'd been queasy the entire time.

Four men traveled with them. Men who'd once been Vampires but were now Shifters, courtesy of a powerful spell that had nearly killed them all. Viktor and Juan had worked together for years, and this was their ship. Pre-Vampire, Recco and Daide had been veterinarians in Ushuaia, and both men had a hell of a time with the transition from animal healer to animal killer. For whatever reason—maybe some leftover Vampire juju—the seasickness gene had bypassed the men, and she was jealous.

Until about two months ago, they'd all been trapped in Ushuaia, and she still couldn't quite believe their gambit to escape had paid off. The wicked enchantment holding them prisoner lasted ten years, and she'd been certain they'd all die in the remote location at the tip of South America. Between increasingly toxic water and a lack of food, their fate didn't require her skill with prophecies to predict.

Yet they'd broken free. Whether it was permanent, or a momentary respite remained to be seen.

Back home in Wyoming, she'd been a historian, one who'd enjoyed her comfy academic position at a university where the hardest thing she had to do was deal with unruly graduate students. A cat Shifter, she was bonded to a mountain lion, and it missed Wyoming's mountains and the forests where they'd roamed. She did too. Ushuaia had mountains, but they were nothing like the Rockies that towered above her erstwhile home.

She rolled her eyes. It would be a long time before she saw Wyoming again. And a strong possibility existed she never would. The plan was to explore the Southern Ocean in gradually widening arcs to see if the Cataclysm—the wickedness that had held them prisoner—was wreaking havoc elsewhere.

Or if their counter spell had wiped it out for good.

One thing was certain. If the Cataclysm lived anywhere, it would be out for blood. The evil was sentient, and it knew good and well who was responsible for its destruction around Ushuaia. A shiver tracked down Aura's spine.

"Yeah," she muttered half aloud. "Not much point pining for home. Maybe I'd do well to assign that label to wherever I am." The thought pleased her, and she chuckled. It was an improvement over the fear that gripped her whenever she thought about the Cataclysm. She'd survived those years in Ushuaia by leveraging denial and cunning, useful traits she'd do well to keep front and center.

"Get moving," her cat urged. *"Don't you want off this boat?"*

"You bet," she told her bond animal.

Aura tucked her blonde hair under a thick, wool cap and grabbed a pair of gloves. That done, she slipped into a waterproof jacket and popped out of her quarters. Bundled to the gills in warm clothing, she was already sweating, but they'd pulled into a sheltered bay, and Viktor had announced over the boat's PA system that anyone who wanted to could go ashore.

Ketha, a wolf Shifter and Aura's closest friend, rattled down a nearby staircase buried in her own pile of winter gear. Her long, dark hair with its red and gold streaks was covered by her parka hood, and her golden eyes shone with excitement.

"Great!" Ketha beamed at Aura. "Anyone else want to go?" She cupped a hand around her mouth and addressed the empty corridor.

"Me!" Rowana shuffled into the passage. Strands of silver hair had resisted her efforts to cover everything with her hood, and her brown eyes sported dark circles beneath them. "Sheesh. I've never had to wear so many clothes. My eagle wanted to fly, but I didn't figure it would be any warmer than me outside this ship. They're not usually cold weather birds."

Ketha shot an indulgent smile Rowana's way. "You're overprotecting your bondmate. Eagles live in Alaska."

Rowana puffed out her chest. "Next to the Chilkoot River because it runs *warm* all year, which means a ready supply of salmon. I wouldn't presume to tell you how to take care of your wolf—"

"Fine." Ketha waved the other woman to silence. "I apologize."

"Where exactly are we?" Aura cut in. All of them were edgy from the rough transit of the Scotia Sea. It had taken six days, and according to Viktor and Juan that was three days longer than what they considered normal.

"A deserted whaling station on South Georgia Island called Grytviken," Ketha replied.

Aura sent a speculative glance at her friend and sister Shifter. "I'm going to bet you read up on it."

Ketha shook her head. "Nope. My secret weapon is Viktor. He adores this part of the world and regales me with stories."

Rowana snorted, her eyes sparking with mirth and her usual good humor apparently restored. "And here I thought all you did was paw at each other."

"Oh we do plenty of that too." Ketha grinned.

"Don't leave without me," Karin called, slamming her door behind her. She was their doctor. Once plump, her face showed the ravages of the hell they'd lived through, but her shrewd copper eyes didn't miss much. Today, her snow-white hair was covered by a wool cap and a hood. "Good news! I found a stock of Phenergan in the infirmary."

"What's that?" Aura asked.

"Seasickness medication. Means I won't have to use as much magic once we get underway again."

"Don't those things have expiration dates?" Rowana asked.

Karin made a noise between a grunt and a snort. "Yes, but they mean nothing. The pharmaceutical industry wants to make sure you keep spending money, so they slap 'use by' dates on everything."

"Good to know," Rowana murmured.

Aura tossed her shoulders back and tried to forget how miserable she'd been. "Maybe I won't need anything next time."

Karin shrugged. "We'll see."

"Come on, women. Let's go." Ketha headed down the corridor toward a door that led to one of the outside decks and a gangway. "Viktor told me two of the rafts are still seaworthy."

"What happened to the other ones?" Rowana asked.

"They're rubber. They rotted."

Aura's cat made a low, hissing noise inside her and said, *We can swim to shore. Let's do that.*

"Maybe you could," Aura countered. "I'd drown wearing all these clothes. They'd drag me right to the bottom."

"What was that all about?" Ketha asked and latched the door open.

Cold air blasted through. It felt bracing after the warmth of the ship. "Just my cat weighing in. Not sure it liked the idea of a partially rotten raft."

Ketha trotted the length of the ship to where a long, metal staircase led down to water level. "This one isn't rotten, silly." She ran lightly down the swaying stairs.

Aura followed, but she held onto the handrails. When she reached the bottom, she gazed across an expanse of water at falling down buildings and the hulls of wrecked ships partially submerged near shore. Ketha had identified it as a deserted whaling station, and it certainly looked the part.

Viktor stood in a large, black raft with pontoons curving around every side. He helped Ketha aboard and then Aura. She sat on one of the pontoons while the two other women got in.

A large-bore rifle was propped next to Viktor. "What's that for?" Aura tipped her chin at it.

"Never know what we might run up against," he replied. "It's what I used to guard against polar bear attacks in the Arctic."

"What are you expecting?" Rowana asked. "There aren't any polar bears here."

"I'm not expecting anything, but I like to be prepared."

"Thanks for taking care of us." Ketha glanced fondly at her husband.

"Welcome. No one else wanted to go?" Victor furled his tawny brows. Tall and broad-shouldered, he still held the ungodly beauty common to Vampires. Aura guessed he'd always looked like that with brown-gold hair and eyes the shade of uncut emeralds. Unlike them, his hood was tossed back and his hair blew every which way in a stout breeze.

Ketha shrugged. "Guess not. I put out the call in the corridor."

"Seasickness can be a real bitch," Karin spoke up. "Between all the magic I ran through some of you and not having the stomach to eat anything for a few days, my bet is everyone else is sleeping."

"I wanted to make sure we weren't waiting for anyone." Viktor pulled a starter cord, and the raft's engine roared to life. They hit the wake dead center as they motored toward shore.

"Do you suppose we'll find anyone here?" Ketha eyed Viktor. "I meant to ask you before I got all duded up to spend time outside."

"I have no idea. The far end of this cove"—he pointed—"has barrack buildings that were built by the Brits after the Falklands War. They're substantial, like everything British. Big enough to house maybe five hundred men. As I recall, they were reasonably self-sufficient with solar powered desalination machinery and solar electricity generators."

"What about in the winter?" Rowana asked. "When there isn't any sun?"

"No one lived here in the winter," Viktor countered. "The war only lasted a couple of months, and it's been over since 1982. As I recall, Argentina didn't exactly roll over and agree to British sovereignty, hence the barracks to house enough men to discourage further hostilities."

"Winter," Rowana prodded.

"Yeah, winter." Viktor smothered a snort. "Thanks for the redirect. There used to be a skeleton force in the barracks and people to man the post office and museum during tourist season. That was about it. They all went home to the Falklands around April, so I'd be surprised if we found anyone here. Anyone alive, that is."

Aura chewed her lower lip. "Mmph. Let's see. The eclipse was in late November, which is the Antarctic summer, so the Cataclysm hit this part of the world when there were likely to be folk here."

"True enough," Viktor said. "We can hope for something beyond corpses, but it's not likely."

Karin frowned. "Maybe I should have brought the medical bag I cobbled together from supplies in the ship's infirmary."

"Nah." Ketha shook her head. "If we find anyone and they're in that bad a shape, we'll haul them into the raft and—"

"Maybe." Karin broke in. "The Cataclysm created isolated pockets of humanity. Whatever viruses and bacteria incubated where we were, we all developed the same immunity to them. That is not true about the place where we're about to step out of this raft. Our Shifter magic will help, but it's not a guarantee we're protected from everything."

"But I never had any problems," Viktor protested. "And I've spent months on South Georgia Island. Hell, I spent three weeks here once when a bad series of storms blew through and it wasn't safe to leave."

"That was before the Cataclysm," Karin said and turned to Ketha. "Feel like providing a microbiology lecture about mutation and natural selection?"

"Not right now," Ketha replied, "but I'd be happy to do something like that later once we're all back aboard *Arkady*.

Viktor swung the craft around so it's stern end hit the beach. "I'll get out," he told the women, "and drag the raft ashore. Perch on the pontoon about where I am and time the waves. Wait until the tide is moving out before you jump down."

"Before anyone goes anywhere," Karin said, "exercise reasonable caution. Don't touch anything. Don't collect anything to bring back to the ship."

"Don't drink the water and don't breathe the air," Rowana muttered.

The lyrics from Tom Lehrer's song, *Pollution*, struck Aura as humorous, and she laughed.

"I wasn't trying to be funny," Rowana looked askance at her.

"I know," Aura said, "but I was thinking about the life we left behind. What you said reminded me of another aspect of it: music."

Ketha followed Viktor's direction and jumped off the pontoon, wading through the surf to shore. Aura and the other women followed her. All of them wore knee-high Wellington rubber boots. The ship's mud room had been stocked with them and their waterproof jackets and bibs.

"Where to?" Aura asked Viktor once he'd tied off the raft's anchor rope to some handy rocks.

"We should be methodical as long as we're here," he replied. "Maybe we'll walk down to the barracks, check them out, and then make our way back this way." His mouth twisted into a sad expression. "There used to be fur seals here. Lots of them. They'd block the road and bark at you, but I'm sure they're all dead. They lived on fish and krill."

"That way?" Aura pointed.

At Viktor's nod, she set out along a rutted dirt road that hugged the shoreline. The ocean was only a few feet away, so close it must have washed over the road from time to time. She skirted an enormous hole. The track was wide enough, someone must have built it to accommodate vehicles. She passed a couple of crumbling buildings on her left. Rotting carcasses that had probably been seals and seabirds dotted the track, and she stepped over and around piles of them. Mostly bleached bones, they reminded her of Ushuaia's streets before they'd cleaned them up.

Caught up in the simple joy of movement, something she hadn't been able to indulge in on the ship, she breathed the chill salt air, drawing it deep into her lungs. The air in Ushuaia had become progressively more toxic, so she appreciated being able to breathe without assuming each breath brought her one step closer to her grave. She saw rows of tan buildings long before she reached them. From long habit, she sent her Shifter senses ranging wide. If anything was alive out there, she wanted to know about it before she got too close.

"Watch it!" Her cat was close to the surface, and a snarling hiss punctuated its words.

Aura ground to a halt. She'd pulled well ahead of everyone else with her long-legged stride. Viktor and Ketha strolled with their arms wrapped around each other as lovers often did, and Karen and Rowana brought up the rear, chatting.

"Watch what?" she asked her bond animal.

"I caught a whiff of wrongness. Check for yourself."

"What is it?" Ketha pulled up next to her. "Why'd you stop?"

"My cat thinks something's not right."

Viktor slipped the rifle off his shoulder in a fast, fluid motion that spoke to his familiarity with it.

Aura shut her eyes, urging her senses to preternatural sharpness. Something unpleasant and eerily familiar zapped her. She curled her hands into fists and looked again. She had to be wrong.

Before she was through dissecting what she sensed lay beyond, perhaps in the barracks a couple hundred yards away, Ketha muttered, "Shit! It isn't possible."

Aura opened her eyes and gripped the other Shifter's arm. "You picked up on Vampire emanations, right?"

Ketha nodded, her eyes wide with disbelief. "How can that be?"

"How can what be, dearie?" Rowana asked. She and Karin had finally caught up with them.

"I have no idea how," Aura gritted out the words, "but Vampires are here."

Karin narrowed her eyes to slits. "Don't be ridiculous. They all died with the Cataclysm."

"Or not." Rowana twisted her face into a grimace.

"Check for yourself," Ketha told the other two women.

Aura scrubbed the heels of her hands down her face, urging rational thought, and then she scanned the place that felt menacing one more time. "It's not quite right for Vampire, at least not the Ushuaia variety," she muttered.

"Not exactly," Ketha agreed. "But there are at least two of whatever they are, and their emanations are closer to Vamp than anything else."

"The question of the hour," Viktor said, "is whether we move forward or retreat. That's a group decision."

Aura thought about it, and when she spoke her words came hard. "We left Ushuaia to figure out what was left in the rest of the world. If we turn tail and run the first time we encounter anything, we may as well have never set sail."

Viktor grinned wryly. "Spoken like a true explorer. Shackleton would have been proud of you."

"I remember him," Aura muttered. "If this is Grytviken, isn't he buried here?"

"He is, indeed," Viktor said. "His grave is on the far side of the post office, but only because his wife told the ship with his remains to bring him back here. I guess he was quite the philanderer, and she wasn't interested in footing the expense of bringing him home."

"Interesting," Aura said, "but we're stalling. My vote is to see what the hell feels like Vampire."

"Mine too," Rowana said.

"I'm in," Karin said. "If we could survive Armageddon against the Cataclysm, how hard could this be?"

Viktor cocked his head to one side. "Depends. If they're Vamps, only beheading with iron will do them in."

"Maybe they'll be friendly." Ketha screwed her face into what might have been a hopeful expression, except it looked more like a grimace.

"Friendly and Vampire in the same sentence is an oxymoron," Viktor said in a flat, dead tone. "It appears we're all game, so all of you get behind me and stay close. Deploy your magic. It's still far more finely honed than mine." He shouldered the rifle. "If I have to, I'll use this. It should at least slow them down."

"Do we have any way to communicate with the ship?" Ketha asked.

Viktor slapped his forehead with an open palm. "Crap. It hasn't been that long since I've ferried Zodiac rafts ashore. Hang on." Reaching inside his insulated parka, he withdrew a two-way radio and depressed the push-to-talk switch.

"Juan. Come in."

The radio crackled. "Juan here."

"Possible Vampire sighting. Secure *Arkady* and come now."

"Aw Jesus! Really?" Juan's words held a strangled note. "I'll drop the other decent raft into the water and bring Recco and Daide with me. Where are you?"

"By the barracks. Don't waste your time stopping in the town."

"Roger that. Be there in half an hour. Maybe less."

"The iron saber is in the equipment locker. Bring it along and make damn sure it doesn't puncture the raft."

Juan chuckled. "Aye, aye, Captain. Your faith in me is touching."

Viktor rolled his eyes. "By the time you get here, we'll either be dead or turned or breaking bread with the bastards."

More static. "You're sure it's Vamps and they're alive?" Incredulity underscored Juan's question.

"Affirmative on the alive part. See you soon."

"Roger that. Over and out."

The radio sputtered to silence. Viktor clicked it off and dropped it back inside his parka. "Let's get moving."

"Don't you want to wait for Juan and them?" Aura asked.

He shook his head. "No. They'll bring the Zodiac to the beach down there." Viktor pointed at the barracks. "Vamps have ears like lynxes. They'll hear an engine that close even over the roar of the surf. We need to be near enough to do some good once they figure out we're here."

Aura was still trying to make sense of how the demise of the Cataclysm could turn Vampires into Shifters in Ushuaia and leave them untouched a few hundred miles away. Maybe it had something to do with Karin's mutation theory.

"Guess we're about to find out," she muttered.

"What was that?" Ketha asked.

"Nothing. I'm with Viktor. Let's get this show on the road."